From the award-winning author of *The Mercury Visions of Louis Daguerre* and *The Beautiful Miscellaneous* comes a sweeping historical novel set amid the skyscrapers of 1890s Chicago and the far-flung islands of the South Pacific.

With critical praise lavished on his first two novels, Dominic Smith has become a celebrated and deeply revered storyteller. *Bright and Distant Shores* offers a stunning exploration of late nineteenth-century America and the tribal Pacific.

In the waning years of the nineteenth century there was a hunger for tribal artifacts, spawning collecting voyages from museums and collectors around the globe. In 1897, one such collector, a Chicago insurance magnate, sponsors an expedition into the South Seas to commemorate the completion of his company's new skyscraper—the world's tallest building. The ship is to bring back an array of Melanesian weaponry and handicrafts, but also several natives related by blood.

Caught up in this scheme are two orphans—Owen Graves, an itinerant trader from Chicago's South Side who has recently proposed to the girl he must leave behind, and Argus Niu, a mission houseboy in the New Hebrides who longs to be reunited with his sister. At the cusp of the twentieth century, the expedition forces a collision course between the tribal and the civilized, between two young men plagued by their respective and haunting pasts.

An epic and ambitious story that brings to mind E. L. Doctorow, with echoes of Melville and Robert Louis Stevenson, *Bright and Distant Shores* is a wondrous achievement.

Also by Dominic Smith

The Beautiful Miscellaneous
The Mercury Visions of Louis Daguerre

BRIGHT
AND
DISTANT SHORES

A NOVEL

DOMINIC SMITH

WASHINGTON SQUARE PRESS
New York London Toronto Sydney New Delhi

WASHINGTON SQUARE PRESS
A Division of Simon & Schuster, Inc.
1230 Avenue of the Americas
New York, NY 10020

The map on pages vi–vii is printed with permission from Allen & Unwin Book Publishers.

First Washington Square Press trade paperback edition September 2011

WASHINGTON SQUARE PRESS and colophon are registered trademarks of Simon & Schuster, Inc.

For information about special discounts for bulk purchases, please contact Simon & Schuster Special Sales at 1-866-506-1949 or business@simonandschuster.com.

The Simon & Schuster Speakers Bureau can bring authors to your live event. For more information or to book an event contact the Simon & Schuster Speakers Bureau at 1-866-248-3049 or visit our website at www.simonspeakers.com.

Designed by Jacquelynne Hudson

Manufactured in the United States of America

10 9 8 7 6 5 4 3 2 1

Library of Congress Cataloging-in-Publication Data

Smith, Dominic.
   Bright and distant shores / Dominic Smith.—1st Washington Square Press
   trade pbk. ed.
   p. cm.
Washington Square Press fiction original trade—T.p. verso.
   1. Chicago (Ill.)—Fiction. 2. South Pacific Ocean—Fiction. 3. Oceania—Fiction. I.
Title. II. Title: Bright and distant shores.
PS3619.M5815B75 2011
813'.6—dc22   2011002995

ISBN 978-1-4391-9886-5
ISBN 978-1-4391-9888-9 (ebook)

For the original clan, with love and gratitude—
Fran, Lanny, Tamara, Nicole, and Natasha.

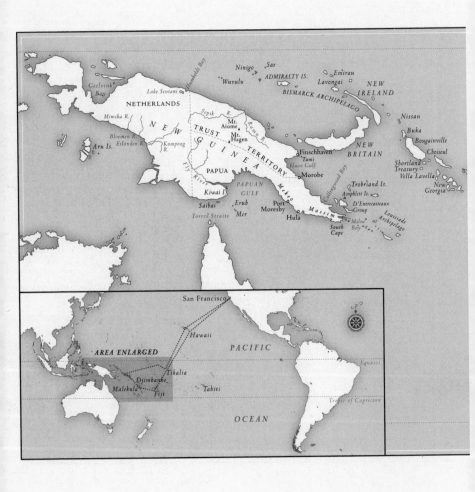

Ninigo · · Sae
Wuvulu · · ADMIRALTY IS. · Emirau
Lavongai
NEW
IRELAND

BISMARCK ARCHIPELAGO

Geelvink
Bay
Humboldt Bay
Lake Sentani

NETHERLANDS

Mimika R.

N E W

Sepik   R.
Ramu R.
Mt.
Aiome
Mt.
Hagen

Bloemen R.
Eilanden R.

G U I N E A

Aru Is.

Kompong
R.

T R U S T

T E R R I T O R Y

PAPUA

Fly River

PAPUAN
GULF

Kiwai I.

Saibai

Erub
Mer

Port
Moresby

Hula

Torres Straits

Mekeo

Massim

South
Cape

Milne
Bay

Nissan
Buka
Bougainville
Choiseul

NEW
BRITAIN

Shortland
Treasury
Vella Lavella

New
Georgia

Finschhaven
Tami
Huon Gulf
Morobe

Collingwood Bay

Trobriand Is.

Amphlett Is.

D'Entrecasteaux
Group

Louisiade
Archipelago

San Francisco

Hawaii

PACIFIC

AREA ENLARGED

Djimbanko
Tikalia

Malekula
Fiji

Tahiti

Equator

Tropic of Capricorn

OCEAN

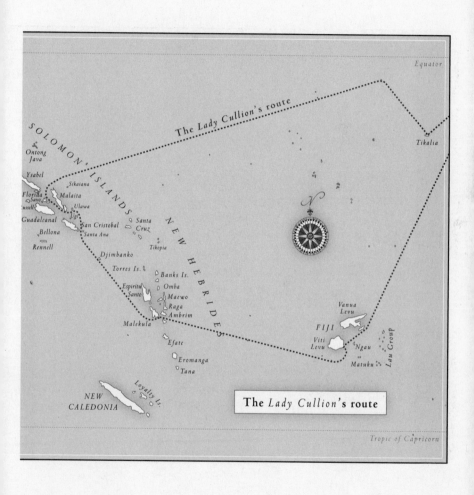

The *Lady Cullion*'s route

Equator

The *Lady Cullion*'s route

Tikalia

SOLOMON ISLANDS

Ontong
Java

Ysabel

Sikaiana

Florida   Malaita
Savo
ussell   Ulawa
Guadalcanal   San Cristobal   Santa
Bellona   Santa Ana   Cruz
Rennell   Tikopia

NEW HEBRIDES

Djimbanko

Torres Is.

Banks Is.
Espiritu   Omba
Santo   Maewo
Raga
Ambrim

Vanua
Levu

Malekula   FIJI
Viti
Levu   Ngau   Lau Group
Efate   Matuku
Eromanga
Tana

NEW
CALEDONIA   Loyalty Is.

The *Lady Cullion*'s route

Tropic of Capricorn

BRIGHT
AND
DISTANT SHORES

Prologue

Summer 1897

They were showing the savages on the rooftop—that was the word at the curbstone. The brickwork canyon of La Salle Street ebbed with clerks and stenographers, messenger boys astride their Monarch bicycles, wheat brokers up from the pit at the Board of Trade. Typists in gingham dresses stood behind mullioned windows, gazing down at the tidal crowd. Insurance men huddled together in islands of billycock hats and brown woolen suits, their necks craned, wetted handkerchiefs at the nape. The swelter hung in the air like a stench. All summer long the signal station had issued warnings and proclamations. Water-carriers at construction sites fainted from heatstroke and were carried off on stretchers. Coal and lumberyard workers could be seen at noon, shirtless, wading into the oceanic blue of Lake Michigan. People spread rugs on their stoops to eat supper in the open air, watching, with something that approached religious awe, the horse-drawn ice wagons pull along the streets.

Despite the heat wave, the Chicago First Equitable was opening on schedule. Destined to be the world's tallest skyscraper for a little over a year, it jutted above the noonday tumult, twenty-eight stories of Bessemer steel, terracotta, and glass. For months, welders and riveters had worked by night to meet the deadline, tethered to the steel frame by lengths of hemp rope, laboring in the haloes of sodium lamps. Laden barges hauled along the roily dark of the Chicago River. They came from a bridgeworks on the Mississippi, pulling loads of rivet-punched girders and spandrel beams. By late spring the glaziers and carpenters had taken over, finishing out, thirty men to a floor. The clock tower was calibrated and set in motion, each hand as broad as a man. In the final stages the *Tribune* reported a death a week: pipefitters down the elevator shaft, electricians over the brink. But, as the glass-paneled walls began to hang from the girded floors like drawn curtains, not bearing weight so much as channeling light, the newspapermen turned their ink to the soaring itself. They stopped writing about the insurance company's grandfathered building permit, the backroom deals that trumped the city's height limit, and instead wrote about the effects of altitude on business acumen, about the hawks and falcons that roosted above the high cornices and gargoyles. By mid-morning, they wrote, with the sun up over Michigan Avenue and the shadows shortening inside the Loop, the juggernaut is nothing but a wall of lake-hued light.

Owen Graves stood among the crowd waiting to enter the mahogany cool of the building's lobby. The company would conduct tours by hydraulic elevator but only VIPs—insurance executives and their wives, journalists, councilmen—were invited for the topside exhibition. Owen was one of the rooftop invitees and he stood a few feet from the bloodred mayoral ribbon, staring down at the elegant shoes of his fellow skyscraper travelers, squinting through the brassy aura of a noonday hangover. He was wearing a pair of stovepipe boots, scuffed at the toe and split along one seam. Perhaps there had been a mistake. Ever since returning from a Pacific trading voyage two years earlier, he had been dodging the letters of his creditors so that he'd opened the company envelope with dread. Arriving as it had by private messenger, he'd thought it was surely a summons for failure to pay. But the elegant lettering inexplicably requested his presence at the opening and suggested he would have a private meeting with the company president at the conclusion of the event.

The city teemed at his back. A concession wagon made a slow orbit through the welter of derby hats and bicycles, selling tripe to famished telegraph boys. Herdics and hansoms rode up to the human wall and fell back, their passengers alighting in the side streets and alleyways. The wind was scorched with smoking lard as it whipped through the financial canyon and he could smell the dredge of the cess-filled river. Owen Graves did not like crowds. There was no happier place for him than on the foredeck of a sloop or clipper, alone and keeping watch in the spectral hours before dawn at sea. He missed the ocean and the rituals of sailing. He raised his eyes — tender as peeled fruit — to see a clutch of policemen escort the mayor and company president toward the building entrance. A wave of applause lapped through the crowd, echoing off the windowpanes and masonry, punctuated here and there with a stadium whistle and an alley whoop. The recently elected Carter Harrison, Jr., edged forward in a bowler and double-breasted, his epic mustache riding above a grin. Hale Gray, insurance magnate and company president, trotted at his side, doffing his hat to the ladies. Bearded in the manner of frontier explorers, Hale brought to Owen's mind an Irish wolfhound — there was something woolly and quietly menacing about him.

The mayor and company president floated pithy speeches about progress and the insurability of the common man. Above the foot shuffling and the iron-rail whinny of the cable cars, Hale said, "Chicago is a city of country people with values that bear those origins." The man beside Owen — a cheerless, onion-breathed fellow who'd been sent by God to avenge insobriety — tugged at his own shirtsleeves and said, "I'm dying out here in this oven. Could they show a fella some mercy?" The rest of the speech was clipped by the wind before the great clock sounded — a C-pitched freighter calling through a high fog. The mayor turned to the ribbon with purpose. The outsized scissors sliced through in one motion and a collective sigh, then cheering, passed through the multitude. Chicago was now ahead of New York by two floors. Two doormen opened the hand-carved doors and the official party, wives first, stepped inside. The lobby gave out a breath of cool, sanctified air and Owen felt the draft on his face as he moved forward: the first reprieve in the halting crush of daylight.

The lobby warrened away into alcoves and cloistered nooks, a tobacconist, a barbershop, a telegraph office, each in a recess of cherrywood paneling and rubbed bronze. A stained glass dome lit from above the bust of Hale Gray's grandfather. Elisha Edmond Gray, merchant underwriter, had amassed a fortune on the calculus of loss and yield. Life insurance has never had its Plato or Aristotle, Hale was saying now in a pulpit voice, there were no poetics or treatises, just the burial clubs of Rome and a fraternity of prudent Britons. Practical men with shipping charts on their walls, actuarial tables mounted like maps of the Atlantic. Owen was aware of his frayed collar and his nicotined fingers as he sidled toward the grillwork of the elevators. The operators stood at attention: dough-faced pallbearers in brass buttons and epaulets. Somebody mentioned a cocktail table waiting roof-side and Owen brightened. He filed into one of the waiting cars, its interior hushed with velvet. The operator fashioned a congenial smile for his passengers—a few executives and their wives, and Owen, backed into a corner—before closing the doors and setting to his controls. A lever was moved into place before the car rocked then began to rise. Owen felt his stomach drop away as they lurched skyward. One of the ladies rested a nervous hand against the crushed velvet siding, steadying herself. Easy now, the husband admonished, as if to a skittish mare, and Owen wondered if he was speaking to his wife or the elevator itself.

Hale Gray was the tour guide and he marshaled the group from floor to floor. In the document repository—a wooden metropolis of floor-to-ceiling filing cabinets—Owen imagined thousands of policies neatly filed, men's lives tallied and reduced to a few pages between cardstock. Next, they moved into the adjacent typing pool, where Hale gestured to the rows of desks, each with a Remington No. 2 museumed in a cone of lamplight. For several minutes, he sermonized on the benevolence of the company's stance toward its employees. His army of policy clerks and typ-ists would enjoy free lunches in the cafeteria, subsidized visits to the doctor's suite, affordable haircuts in the lobby barbershop. There was no reason to leave the building during business hours. Turning solemn, Hale said, "Think of this skyscraper as contrib-uting to the elevation of the species."

Every time Owen thought the tour was winding down, that a gimlet was within reach, Hale took up a new thread of tedium about the building—the system of pneumatic tubes that carried policies between floors, the mail chutes that ran parallel to the elevator shafts, the uplifting array of evening classes available in the second-floor library: actuarial science, sewing, first aid, En-glish, citizenship. Owen drifted from the pack when they passed a washroom. His stomach was a little squiffy from the elevator ride and he needed to splash some cold water on his face. The white-tiled bathroom was cavernous, broken up by a long line of urinals. He washed his face in the sink, drank from his cupped hands, regarded his hangdog expression in the mirror. What did these people want with him, these insurance men and their spaniel-faced wives? Even in the washroom there was a kind of order that threatened to suffocate—the hand towels were stacked in a neat tower, each embossed with the company logo of a lion with one paw on a globe, and a white-faced clock hung above the urinals, the red second hand a needling reminder of time's stri-dent passage. Was this to prevent a clerk's watery rumination? A workingman couldn't be fooled; he knew when he was being hemmed in. It might not be the stockyards, Owen thought, but it was still long hours hunched at mindless labor. A clerk might take his free lunch at noon, his evening class in English verbs, even get his shoes spit-shined in the lobby, but he'd emerge from the glass tower in the falling dark each day with a secret kind of malice toward the benevolence up on the twenty-eighth floor.

When Owen came out the party was waiting for him by the elevators. The attendants stood at attention, waiting to load.

Hale laced his fingers across his stomach and launched onto the balls of his feet—"And now the rooftop beckons. We're all mountain climbers today, even you, Mrs. Carmody."

An elderly woman looked over the rims of her glasses and tapped her cane good-naturedly. "Will it be any cooler up there in the clouds?" she asked.

"Could be breezy, so hold on to your hat," Hale said, ushering people into the elevators.

The iron railing of the observation platform kept the VIPs a dozen feet from the abyss. Cocktails poised, hats fastened, they stepped onto the deck and edged toward it. Owen was now in front and he placed one hand on the metal guardrail while the other held the sacrament of gin over ice. La Salle Street dropped away, a river of hats, flecked cloth, upturned faces. "Give them a wave," said Hale. Owen set his glass on a table and raised both hands, crossing them above his head in a nautical look-here-now. The mob hollered in response. Errand boys tossed their hats in the air, tooted their bicycle horns. The other VIPs joined Owen and there was a full minute of waving down into the pit as a photographer flashbulbed beside them.

When the euphoria subsided, Owen picked up a pair of opera glasses and took in the panorama—the ziggurat skyline with its middling towers and sunless mercantile valleys, the lake a sapphire backdrop to the east. The streets, glimpsed through the endless procession of flat roofs, dizzied with placards and advertisements—miniature lettering for Brown's Iron Bitters and Roxwell's Corned Beef Hash. Over on State he could make out the Masonic Temple, Chicago's now-eclipsed high point, and the Reliance, with its wide bays of glass and Gothic tracery. His father had once demolished buildings in that vicinity though he couldn't remember the exact blocks. The El cut a narrow path between office façades, between walls of red-pressed brick, and Owen saw the dotted faces of passengers at the windowpanes as it flashed into a narrow gap of open space. The cross-hatching of streets and avenues stretched for miles, bordered on one side by the shoreline, but continuing south and west through a scrim of smoke and soot, the grid thinning into tenements and vacant lots and cemeteries, out farther to the Livestock Emporium and stockyards, before it all faded into a distant patchwork of dun-brown farms. The Midwest of the country was just beyond, the great plains furrowed and sown. This bucolic reminder continued closer in, on the flat rooftops of nearby buildings—chickens, a running dog, a boxed flower bed. A custodian's perch topped a ten-story office building, a leaning tin shack with a man standing shadowed in the crude doorway. Laundry flapped from a line and a scrubwoman was beating a Persian rug into dusty submission.

"The great mongrel city," Hale said, sipping his neat whiskey. He looked off at the clouds scudding in from Canada, at the ships hauling timber from Michigan pineries, before turning abruptly and raising his glass. "We've outstripped the Masons and the church steeple and of course the easterners are clambering after us. But no matter. This is our moment. To the dream of a fully insured populace. To them, down in the hole." Everyone drank and Hale tilted his glass as if to anoint the laborers and shopgirls with a single drop. "Now," he said, stepping away from the edge, "I believe it's time for lunch and a little demonstration. Ladies, we will enjoy the buffet together but then I'm afraid it will be gentlemen only for a few minutes. Forgive me on this account."

They moved to the alcove by the clock tower, to a canvas tent filled with chairs and banquet tables. Bow-tied waiters, flushed in their dinner jackets, tended the reception. Slices of salmon and mackerel were stacked on ice; crescents of fruit and sandwich triangles were arranged on trays. Owen moved among the tables, a chip of ice cooling his tongue. As long as he didn't linger in one spot there was little chance of conversation. Itinerant trader, orphaned son of a housewrecker, what did he have to discuss with Mrs. Carmody, widow and baroness, who kept a lockbox of jewels in the basement of the First National? Precisely nothing, he thought, retreating to the cocktail table.

Hale guided the women from the tent, inviting them to take another spell at the observation deck. When he returned he asked the men to be seated while a pedestal was set up in the rear. A man in coveralls, sitting on a high stool, tinkered with a contraption that burned a small lamp bulb. The mayor whispered the word *Vitascope* and the tent flaps were shut. The scent of warming mackerel and body heat on wool. Darkness except for a shiv of daylight along the tent's ground-seam. The projector hummed through its gears and a grainy, silver-blue light threw itself against the canvas siding. At first the images were dark and jumbled—a wedge of pristine beach, a flickering of date palms, a settlement of thatched treehouses—before the view crystallized on a band of tattooed savages dancing in a circle. A ragged line of bare-chested women clapped sticks together. A silent montage spilled across the canvas—canoe races, black men with kinked hair paddling through the waves, a masked figure rampaging through a village with a club, a pig roasting in a coral hearth, an old woman asleep on the sand. The audience sat rigid, cocktail glasses and cigars poised. An insurance broker held an asparagus tip inches from his mouth. Owen leaned forward in his seat. A jittered sequence tracked a naked girl coming out of the ocean with a fish writhing in her hands. She smiled and took off running in the sand and a few of the insurance underlings whistled before Hale placed a finger to his lips. A young boy on a clifftop blew into a conch shell. Villagers sat in the dirt, feasting on what Owen guessed was taro and pork. Somewhere in Melanesia, he suspected. The last image was of a native hoisting himself up a banyan tree. He sat in the fork of two branches, a betel-nut bag over his shoulder, looking out to sea. After a moment, he took a brownish clump from the bag and put it into his mouth. He chewed slowly, eyes fixed on the horizon, before the image faded and bled away from the screen.

The tent flaps remained closed but Hale lit a kerosene lamp. The nitrate smell of heated filmstock lingered. Hale walked among the men, handing each of them a postcard. On the front was a picture of an idyllic beach where two black natives faced each other with spears and wood-carved shields. Their muscles were tense, their stances martial. The reverse side featured a printed message made to look like handwriting: *Dear Sir, The Chicago First Equitable Insurance Company invites you to see an exotic spectacle on the rooftop of their new landmark downtown building.* Then, below, in smaller font: Life Insurance Delivers Men from the Primitive Rule of Nature. A murmur broke out among the vice presidents as they lit to the idea of sending postcards to thousands of suburban households, out into the third-acre plots where Mr. O'Connor or Haroldson still kept a smokehouse and a potato patch in back and was waiting to be brought in from the frayed edge of his workaday life.

"This is just the beginning, gentlemen," Hale said. "Think of this building as our totem pole. Our chief advertisement up in the clouds. Tourists will flock to the observatory. They'll try to spot their houses and neighborhoods, pointing this way and that. We'll rent them spyglasses and hand out policy pamphlets and lemonade in the elevators." He moved to the tent entrance and drew back one of the canvas flaps, letting the daylight blanch their faces. "And each night when the clock tower stops chiming and the beacon comes alight, they'll remember that we stand for permanence and fair-mindedness. Something beyond the grime and gristle."

Owen pictured the galley slaves in the typing pool, the filing clerks perched on their stepladders like steeplejacks. He stood up from his chair, feeling the pull of a breeze and a tumbler of gin somewhere outside the canvas furnace. Hale Gray let him pass without a word but was soon upon him, an assured hand at his back.

"Mr. Graves, when all these niceties are over, I have a business proposition for you."

Owen's hangover had receded behind an inebriate hum in his chest. Hale was making them another drink and embarking on a voyage of uncommon knowledge, clipping his way through a flotsam of historical totes and trinkets. Something about the deadbeat escapement of Old World clocks and wasn't this preferable, to separate the locking mechanism from the impulse, to let the pendulum swing continuously? Owen had no opinion on the subject of clockworks. Besides, he was taking in the display cases that covered an entire wall of Hale's enormous office. It was a private museum, a thousand artifacts resting on velvet. Japanese woodblock prints, Chinese rhinoceros-horn cups, Malagasy beaten brass, Hopi funerary bonnets and sashes, obsidian knives, canopic jars, scarabs, Pacific Island clubs and tomahawks, a haft imbedded with shark teeth.

Owen's hands ghosted up to the glass. Ever since those boyhood days spent razing houses with his father, his lust for objects had been unceasing; by age ten he'd assembled a scrapyard museum of fixtures and architectural flourishes. Long before he'd ever been to the Field Columbian Museum, he'd felt the libidinal pull of cold, dead things. Now he studied the filigreed edges and native brocade work and felt something like object-lust. It was a desire to look at the carvings and whittlings of people long dead, to witness the lasting sediment of their minds. Owen thought of the policy files some floors below, the wooden towers reamed with paper, or the pneumatic tubes that carried addendums to Hale Gray's desk for signature. It was a different kind of collection—a living museum of riders and annuities, the typewritten odds of a man's decline. Owen heard the president click across the floor with his cane. Even his walk was tightly coiled, a metronome of calculated steps.

Owen turned and received a glass of gin from his gently drunk

host. Hale moved for the east-facing windows and Owen followed. Dusk was hardening over the rooftops. The yellow lights
of schooners stippled the blackening lake. An office worker—
bent in lamplight at his desk—could be seen through the window
of an adjacent building.

"You must be the first one in the city to see sunup," Owen
said. He was aware of their reflections in the windowpane, the
glimmer of Hale Gray looking north toward Canada. The whiskey gave Hale a pawky, speculative air. A few of the westward
windows were open and a draft came up from the street, carrying
the metallic sound of the El grinding into a turn.

"What do you think of my collection, Mr. Graves?"

"Very impressive. Is that a Papuan skull?"

Hale raised slightly onto his toes. "Good eye. See the engravings. But why? Why engrave a geometric pattern on a human
skull?"

"Some kind of ceremony. Funeral rite perhaps. I've heard
them lecture on it at the Field."

"What a lot of tweed and chalk dust they burn through at the
museum these days. Wasn't one of the curators trying to measure
the ears of Chinamen not long ago?"

"I didn't hear that."

"Yes. He wanted to prove a correlation between ear length and
philosophical disposition. It came to him while standing in front
of a portrait of Lao-Tze in a New York museum. Now picture
him chasing Mongols down Clark Street with a tape measure and
all the Oriental merchants running like bandits."

Hale shot out a laugh that took them both by surprise. A
cloud of breathy vapor fogged the glass pane in front of him.
Owen smiled and held a swallow of gin in his mouth, nodding in
afterthought. When would the wolfhound get on with it?

Hale turned his back to the skyline and gestured with his drink
to the sitting area. His tumbler led the way, a steady prow cutting
across the room. A dim and smoky portrait of Elisha Edmond

Gray hung above the mantel—the great man in repose, floating through the woody pall of an English manor. He sat waistcoated by a hearth, hound at his side, slightly ablaze in the cheeks, as if he'd rushed indoors from a pheasant hunt.

Hale sat, looked up at the portrait, nostalgia pursing his lips. "Leadership skips a generation, that's what I've come to believe, Owen."

The sound of his Christian name seemed oddly misplaced, as if a coin had dropped from Hale's pocket onto the hardwood floor.

"Jethro, my son, is back from college in New England and I suppose I should be finding a place for him at the firm. But, to be frank, I have elevator boys who show more shrift. At Harvard he studied natural science and art and dickered about for four years. I hope to have my portrait on that wall someday and for Jethro to be sipping single malt in this very seat. The problem is one of— what?—character and preparation I suppose." Hale crossed his legs and removed a speck of something from his pant leg. "Tell me about your Pacific trading voyage from a few years back. I'm partial to sailing myself."

"Let's see . . . A stint in the South Sea Islands. A circuit of trade, mostly."

"What did you bring back?"

"All sorts of things. We also dropped off a cargo of trepang in Shanghai."

"I'm not familiar."

"Sea cucumber. They cure it and sell it for epicures in the Orient."

"Any mishaps?"

"The ship ran aground and had to be rehulled in Queensland. A seaman ran off and married an Australian girl."

"Too much sun. A tropical fever, perhaps."

"Being at sea for months can turn a man."

"And did you sell your items to the Field Museum when you returned? Not long after they opened their doors after the fair I noticed one lunchtime they had a whole batch of new tribal weapons from the Pacific."

Owen touched the rim of his glass. "I've heard that there's some old rivalry between you and Marshall Field. That you're trying to outdo the museum."

Hale persisted: "Did they pay you well? I heard not. Then again, those were hard times. We're just now rounding the bend."

"I'm sure they thought it was a fair price."

"They say the Pacific is fast running out of artifacts. That you can more easily find good curios at Jamrach's in the East End of London than on Thursday Island. That first cargo load in the Christy Museum was all because of the sandalwooders, God bless them, and now that's done it's slim pickings. Time is of the essence before someone drains the whole bathtub." Hale took out an envelope from his breast pocket and placed it on the low table between them.

Owen noticed there was a bloom of moisture—probably Hale's sweat—trailing one edge.

"I like to make proposals in writing. Consider it an underwriter's old habit. You'll find a list of categories I'm interested in and a sum specified for delivery. A percentage up front plus funding for the voyage, the remainder upon return. There are also a few special conditions, should you decide to enter into the contract. Taking the railway to San Francisco and contracting a ship and crew out west would be the most cost-effective, I believe. The ship should be arranged before you leave, of course. Naturally, have your lawyer look the contract over if you like."

Owen had never spoken to a lawyer, let alone retained one. "I look forward to reading it." He picked up the envelope and placed it inside his jacket.

Hale got to his feet and Owen did likewise. They walked out through the double doors, a paternal hand now on Owen's shoulder. Hale stopped and pressed a brass button on the wall of the landing. "Elevator's on its way up."

"Congratulations again on the magnificent new building. It seemed to go up overnight."

"The glaziers' combine didn't finish my sheet glass on time. Half of it had to come from Canada, some from Mexico. I'm no friend to price fixing and union organizing, let me tell you. A man needs to count on certain things. Are you married, Owen?"

"No, sir. Being in trade makes it hard to settle." In fact, he'd been on the verge of asking Adelaide Cummings to marry him for four years. But he'd been waiting for a more solid livelihood, a chance to make his way before asking for her hand. Adelaide, he knew, was fast losing patience with his delays. And now another voyage.

Hale opened one of the doors and Owen stepped out into the corridor.

"Well, there's no shortage of eager women in this building as of tomorrow. Take one to lunch sometime. City girls with silt still on their hands. Honest and hard-working. You could do worse."

"Thank you for the hospitality today."

"Will you be all right on the elevator? You looked squeamish earlier."

"I think I have the hang of it."

"Good night, then," Hale said, returning to his office.

Owen stood on the landing, aware of the air whistling in the elevator shaft. He took the envelope out of his pocket and broke the seal with his penknife. The typewritten document was thirty pages of minuscule font, separated by headings that indemnified against acts of God, payments to subsequent heirs, delays and failures, et cetera, et cetera. It was hard to tell exactly what the contract proposed. The elevator arrived and the attendant sat slumped on his stool. He gave a cursory nod to Owen and the doors closed. Gone was the ceremony of earlier hours; the pomp had been reduced by the hordes to something shuffling and miffed. Owen was glad for the silence and the light coming from the elevator ceiling. He positioned the contract and traced a finger over the elliptical text. The car swayed downward, stuttering here and there in the windy shaft. The gist of the proposal was buried in the addendum. Jethro Hale Gray to enlist in the voyage as "ship's naturalist," under the direct protection of Owen Graves. An itemized list of desired cargo: shields, canoes, painted masks, tribal weapons, adornments, textiles, et cetera, and there, listed like a handmade artifact or a woven skirt, was the phrase *a number of natives, preferably related by the bonds of blood, for the purposes of exhibition and advertising*. A single dotted line awaited his signature at the bottom of the page.

I

OWEN

1.

Owen's love of objects first began with afternoons spent prospecting in the rubble of his father's trade. Ada, mother and wife, had died in the Great Fire and Owen had only a dim recollection of her—raspberry leaves pressed into a hymnal and braided chestnut hair. Porter Graves kissed his fingertips every morning and touched her daguerreotyped face on the way out the door. *Graves & Son Wrecking & Salvage,* the two of them on the box seat, riding to another falling tenement or warehouse. Porter bellowed through a bullhorn at his crew while Owen, aged about twelve, helped pry wainscoting or de-nail floorboards. Brawny men labored with crowbars and sledges, loosing bricks from the lime mortar, hurling debris down a shaft that had been hewn clear through the center of the building. They plied pickaxes, wrecking adzes, pneumatic guns. When all else failed, a stick of dynamite bored into a wall of solid masonry. The heady cocktail of nitric and sulfuric acids, glycerin mixed with porous clay, all of it blended and wrapped in brown paper like an orphan's Christmas present. Dynamite was Nobel's gift to the wreckers of the world and there was no better moment in Owen's short childhood than standing with his father and the men after the fuse was lit. Dusty silence followed by a sonic clap; runnels of smoke and billowing clouds of falling plaster. The bite of gunpowdered air. And for fifteen minutes the men relaxed, waited for the all-clear from Porter, for it was the boss himself who inspected the aftermath. They rested on crates and haunches, smoked cigarettes, spoke of wives and girlfriends, recalled pints of ale in neighborhood watering holes and mythic accidents in teardowns. A grand piano falling six stories down the shaft and landing on a mason doubled at his work, the crazed arpeggio of splintered wood and warped notes ringing out for twenty city blocks. Or the mechanic who fell into a side chute, tumbling into a skip of broken glass. They spoke to Owen as an equal, a fellow destructionist and rubble-maker, and he could feel their respect for his father as Porter came back from his inspections with the steely demeanor of an artillery specialist, two thumbs in the air.

They salvaged as much as they could: pipes, fixtures, beams, marble and granite, trim, even plate glass wrapped in muslin. The scrap wood was bundled and sold to immigrants for kindling. The granite was recut for tombstones. Secondhand-brick dealers carried off an endless bounty. Owen wasn't allowed within twenty feet of the shaft and he worked the trim and fixtures with a hammer and chisel. And it was here that he made his private discoveries. Every building harbored secrets, tiny embellishments that would never show up on a set of blueprints. Stone-carved figurines above a mantel or hand-painted tilework; gargoyles and stained-glass windows of despairing saints; architraves with messages encoded on them. Hidden chambers and forgotten strong rooms replete with pistols and tinned cherries. Owen began to assemble a salvage museum in the back of his father's scrapyard. He labeled and catalogued his finds, writing down building names and the dates of demolition onto pieces of cardstock, attaching them by string, a thousand toe-cards in a morgue of objects.

At the end of each workday he came away with something new. It could be as small as a Spanish coin or as large as a Gothic window. Porter indulged his son's appetite for collecting, saw it as an adolescent flurry of seriousness that might someday pay dividends. He knew that although a life of junking could be profitable there had to be a passion for the science of destruction. Times were changing. Penalty fees and late clauses, the men demanding better wages. The beginnings of steel-frame, multi-story construction would mean more labor, a hundred men snapping the heads off rivets and boring them out with drift pins. Derricks and steam shovels and power winches—all of it would increase his overhead. Let the boy find some speck of delight in all that razing.

After work they rode home through the Loop and assessed the office buildings with a wrecker's cold regard.

"I could fell that one in thirty days if it came down to it," Porter said, angling his chin up at a new ten-story offering.

"Top to bottom. Sixty-man crew," Owen affirmed. He re-knuckled the reins, making sure his father saw he had a tight grip.

Porter smiled and lit a cigarette, looking off into the store-fronts where clay mannequins modeled the latest tweeds. "You have the eye for it. Just like me. You walk past a building and can't help gauging the brickwork and lintels, figuring the way it might topple."

Owen felt his father's pride like a wool blanket around his shoulders. It was dusk and people were heading to restaurants and theaters in their frocks and tails. The pedestrians eyed the wagon with its ramshackle load and Porter tipped his hat. They ignored him, eyes down on a fastened glove or a pair of tickets. Even then Owen knew that he and his father lived apart from polite society. They ate soup and bread for supper and pork sausages on Sundays. They weren't much for religion but believed in shaping one's destiny through honest work. There was grease under their fingernails, cinders in their hair. Owen could read and add numbers but didn't know how to ride a bicycle. What Owen thought now but did not tell his father was that he never noticed bricks or lintels when he walked by a grand building. He never thought about its demolition and the thousand man-hours it would require to level it. Instead he wondered about the artifacts it might contain, the remainders of other people's lives. What did a man keep in the concealed compartment beneath the floorboards? Whose initials had been engraved in the handle of a forgotten pistol?

The summer of Owen's thirteenth birthday, a collar beam dislodged during one of Porter's post-dynamite inspections. The beam dropped without warning, bringing part of a stone wall and several rafters with it. Helpless, Owen watched from behind a barricade of rubble as a cloud of mortar dust mushroomed then fell away. In the chalky air he could make out his father's prone form, pinned beneath rafters and limestone. Porter's work boots, still attached, faced in opposite directions. The wreckers charged forward and began working the pile, prying beams and plumb-lifting massive sheets of stone, all the while calling to Porter as if he stood a chance. Owen knew his father was dead by the angle of the boots and the depth of the pile. Nonetheless, the foreman led the son away when, an hour later, three men removed the final ceiling joist and picked off the smaller, covering debris. Owen stood at the edge of the demolition site, numb, but also filling with dread. He saw the wreckers doff their helmets and bow their heads. Someone covered the body with a canvas tarpaulin, leaving only the scuffed boots exposed. Owen broke free from the foreman's grip and ran forward but the wreckers held their circle as he tried to take hold of the canvas. The foreman, the oldest of the crew, came up, panting: "You can remember him whole or broken up like he is. It's your choice, but trust me, he wouldn't want you to see what's underneath." Owen looked into the men's faces, their eyes averted, and let the foreman lead him out by the shoulders. He waited on the street until it was near dark and the coroner arrived by carriage to take the shrouded body away. Behind the lighted windows of nearby apartments people were eating supper. Owen heard the men talking as they came out into the falling night, already reliving his father's death, formulating the cause, naming the linchpin joist or beam, inducting Porter Graves into the pantheon of fallen wreckers. Owen paced in the half-light of the street and watched the coroner's wagon disappear from sight. He heard the foreman utter the word *orphaned* to a stranger, an official of some kind, and it was the cold finality of the word that struck him. He withdrew into an alcove, away from the wreckers, and gave himself permission to weep into a grease-smeared handkerchief. A building could be razed or felled and a child could be *orphaned*. Like an old house, life was waiting to topple.

The scrapyard was the only thing Owen inherited and he refused to sell it. By now he had amassed hundreds of items in his salvage museum. He leased the yard to a colleague of his father's and received a small monthly stipend from the rental. The tin shed museum was locked and the entire compound—an acre of coiled metal and building innards—was guarded by a pair of mongrel yard dogs. Everything but the yard had been mortgaged and financed, down to the pneumatic guns. And so at thirteen Owen found himself without relatives and packed off to the South Side Tabernacle Industrial School for Boys, a Catholic lair of moral training and practical instruction that boasted a separate department for crippled orphans. During his six-year stay, he learned to fix small engines, say the Hail Mary, fear the Holy Ghost, fist-fight, masturbate silently and in the dark. He hoarded books from the City Hall library, an excursion that happened once a month. Owen always chose seafaring tales and missionary journals, epics that unfolded in the tropics or the Arctic, in a brig being slowly crushed by pack ice or in a shanty beset by warring cannibals. He preferred books with digestive-smelling pages, odorous proof of their hoary contents; marbled inside jackets and ink-drawn maps, frontispieces that depicted voyage routes with indigo dotted lines. He was so moved by these tales of adventure that he began to prepare for a life of deprivation in equatorial climes or the Arctic Circle. He did not love Jesus enough to be a missionary but free-lance adventurer, bounty hunter, and buccaneer all seemed like possibilities. Attempting to strengthen his constitution, he left his bedside window open in August and February and went out of his way to eat foods he didn't like—cow tongue, liver, sweet potato, tinned trotters, cabbage soup.

By the time he was sixteen, he would sometimes escape into the city—run out into the South Side streets, jump a cable car, and be inside the Loop within fifteen minutes. He felt at home in the avenues and side streets, the alleyways of perpetual shade. Owen moved among the newsboys and bootblacks, the hundreds of children making their living at the curbstone. The bustle of deals and arrivals was everywhere—high-flyers, down-easters, men on the make. Sandbaggers met the country trains, waiting for unwitting couples from Dubuque, showing them parklike estates then producing deeds for marshland and backwater swamp. Farm girls arrived by the platoon, valises in hand, sunhats fastened, rooming on Van Buren and warring for jobs as milliners and secretaries. Chicago was a battlefield of wits. But more than anything the city contained Owen's father—in the awnings and cornices, in the weary admiralty of janitors smoking on their building stoops. The ghosts of demolished buildings lingered, somehow, behind the plate-glass windows of pristine towers.

2.

By the time of the Esquimaux rebellion, Owen was on his own, half a dozen years out of the Tabernacle School and sleeping in the tin shed at the back of the scrapyard. He worked sporadic wrecking jobs but, as his father had predicted, building methods had changed and eroded the profit margin in traditional demolition. More and more, wrecking was done by derrick and power winch instead of adze and sledgehammer. He idled along, scraping by. He took carpentry jobs because he'd always been handy with a hammer and awl, but building kitchen cabinets wasn't nearly as satisfying as dismantling a building from the top down. Many afternoons were killed off at the City Hall library, reading travelogues and the letters of Robert Louis Stevenson in the *Tribune,* South Sea dispatches describing life amid coral reefs and archipelagos. Owen followed preparations for the Columbian Exposition and was determined to attach himself to a voyage. He would gladly spend fifty cents on admission for the chance to approach a whaling skipper or merchant captain. He had no interest in river and lake routes, the commercial steamer lines to Montreal and New York. He wanted open waters, distant latitudes, volcanic shores.

The Esquimaux were brought in for the fair from Labrador, in the fall of 1892, so they could acclimatize before the onslaught of a Chicago summer. Under the watchful gaze of an overseer, fifteen of them raised a native village, an exact replica of their native home down to the skin tents and corral of sledge dogs. Photographers captured them with their fur coats and hooded eyes, whips unspooled midair, pack dogs wheeling. But as the temperatures mounted they grew despondent, then restless. They threw off their skins and furs and huddled in the shade. They exchanged handicrafts and bone harpoons for German lager. On the first day above seventy degrees, a group of them burned down the tent village and ran off into the streets with their dogs. The city police patrolled a wide perimeter. The overseer sent teams of men out into the back territories, the immigrant neighborhoods and meat-packing district, but they were nowhere to be found. For a month there were sightings of huskies, traveling in pairs, loping through Washington Park or along the shoreline of driftwood and squatters' huts.

Indians and South Sea Islanders fared better. By the time the fair opened, they filled the Midway Plaisance with spectacle. The Samoans wrestled, the Javanese worked traditional puppets, and the Quackahl Indians performed a Sun Dance that shocked the gathered crowd. On a float in the main lagoon, two braves were led around by heavy twine attached to slits in their bare backs. As thousands looked on, they moved to a low drumbeat, faces upturned, braided hair quilled with blood. Women fainted. Men reached for snuff pouches, wiped monocles, averted their eyes. Owen watched the gruesome sight with more curiosity than disgust. At the Tabernacle Industrial School for Boys he'd been encouraged to think of the Holy Ghost as divine ether that filled the hearts and minds of good Christians; it animated their beliefs and conduct. Despite the nuns' affirmations, however, he'd always pictured the spirit as vengeful, something furious and consumptive, and this was what he saw in the crazed dance that floated before him—a ghostly ancestor presiding over the punishment of human flesh.

Owen spent his day at the fair struck in a kind of trance. The combination of people and objects was overpowering. He found himself framing his view with cupped hands so that he could see a thing in its singularity. He scrawled notes in his program.

The interiors were split between order and whimsy—weather stations, model farms, livestock, steam engines, the latest phonograph, a Liberty Bell made from oranges, a rooftop fountain of beer. Some exhibits invited the fair-goer to touch a machine or display and he lined up and jostled with the rest of them, probing metal recesses and hatches, fingering a latch-pin, trying to fathom a machine's construction and design. The peculiar beauty of a perfectly placed eyebolt. The simple genius of a fillister groove.

The stock market had crashed five days before the opening, but there was no denying the bravado, the gritty optimism of the speeches. America felt at war, incendiary in her pride. Cream of Wheat, Aunt Jemima, Juicy Fruit—how had the nation ever lived without them? The next century stretched away and here was Chicago, a marshland and frontier fort within living memory, waiting impatiently at the gates.

The Columbian Guard circulated for pickpockets and rabble-rousers, fined those attempting their own photography. Owen rode the movable sidewalk, sat through two revolutions on the Ferris wheel. He moved through the crowd, elbows jutted to keep the drunks at bay. People cheered and shouted and he felt his senses strip away. He stared at the ground, counted his footsteps. At the midway he broke into a jog. He passed the balloon ride, the ostrich farm, and the congress of forty beauties without a second glance. It was his first crowd and he'd had no inkling of its terrors—a thousand men clearing their throats, hawing at their wives, the surge of bustled skirts and preened gloves. He ran past the lagoons and slowed in the wooded croft where folk houses from various nations had been built. Studying the workmanship, the plumb of a wall, relaxed him. He found himself thinking about the most efficient way to tear each one down.

By the time he approached the Anthropological Building it was evening. There were no crowds this far down. Distantly, he heard the report of fireworks and caught a whiff of gunpowder, a smell that inevitably brought him to the image of his father's scuffed boots protruding from a mound of rubble. They were no longer a terrifying vision, the boots, but rather an omen, a testament. What Porter Graves expected from life could be seen in his shoes—toes capped in steel, seams resewn, leather tongues like two ancient pelts. Every day had been a battle. Suppose a man's fate, Owen thought, was carried in the mold and cut of his shoes. Had Porter lashed his bootlaces in a square knot every morning for decades, a safeguard against tripping, just so that he could make it safely to his own scheduled demise?

Owen buttoned his coat and walked along the South Pond, where an ethnographic encampment had been set up. Lank Indians stooped in front of wigwams, made supper over small campfires. A few women thumbed pottery or wove baskets in the outlandish light of an electric lamppost. Farther along there were Apaches in wickiups, Mohawks whittling birch bark canoes. A single family remained from the Esquimaux group—a husband, wife, and child—and they withdrew into the candlelit interior of their tent, wavering shadows on the skin walls.

Owen entered the Anthropological Building and was relieved to find it almost empty. It had the lofty but neglected atmosphere of an old bathhouse—a vaulted ceiling with trussed skylights, but a dank odor permeating the corners. He moved through the South American ethnology section, amid objects of flint, obsidian, mica. In his program he sketched a monkey-tooth necklace. The Pacific Islands and New South Wales shared a section. Here, Owen tried to match his mental images of the Pacific—the black-beach warriors and volcanic atolls of Stevenson's letters—with the objects themselves. Easter Island effigies, poison-tipped spears, mud-daubed shields, war gods etched onto the hull of a canoe. He'd read of the natives burying themselves in the sand at night to get away from mosquitoes and pollywogs and had assumed it was an exaggeration on Stevenson's part. But now he saw a sketch of just such a thing by a ship's naturalist: five

Papuan heads, still attached, protruding from a beachhead under a full moon.

After an hour poring over idols and amulets, he moved toward Psychology, where a few curious fair-goers were having their sight and color sense tested. Attendants in lab coats offered them chilled water and hand towels between tests. A chromoscope claimed to measure hundredths and thousandths of a second. Something called a kymograph plotted blood pressure on smoked paper. He drank a cup of iced water and moved on.

The department of neurology was an alcove of bottled brains. A young woman—*Miss Adelaide Cummings, Department Secretary*, declared a plaque—sat at a small desk with a ledger. The aspic-gray light spilling from the glass jars offset her patrician beauty. But her high, flushed cheekbones and straight, dark hair, the delicate line of her pale neck, all of it seemed to defy the floating cortexes. Owen smiled at her and put his hands behind his back, hoping to affirm that he was no tourist, that his interest in neurology was substantial. The truth was the brains unsettled him, some dulled by wax, others swimming like jellyfish in brackish waters. They had the coloring of diseased livers and it was almost impossible, standing there, to accept this organ as the parliament of human thought and desire. It had to be the most obscene organ in all the body. He fingered the book spines in the small library and picked up Vesalius's *Structure of the Human Body* from 1543. He affected a manner that suggested he'd been trawling the city for it. Miss Cummings failed to notice, however, making a mark on the ledger before her, and he set the book back on its shelf. He shuffled toward a chart that correlated gender and age with the weight and volume of the brain. A stifled female giggle rose from Psychology and Owen thought he detected a vexed sigh on the part of Miss Cummings. He looked away from the chart and met her eyes with a diffident shrug.

"They've been testing reflexes all day over there," she said. "Tipsy girls from Milwaukee come over here after the beer gardens."

Owen liked the way she wagged her pen when she spoke—a slow pendulum swinging over her bony, unwed finger.

"I'm here to answer any questions if you have them," she said.

"That's very kind." Owen planted himself in front of a photograph that featured the brain of a murderer who'd been electrocuted the previous year. "I don't see much difference between his brain and the others," Owen said.

Miss Cummings looked up from her papers. "I think that's part of the point. If you look at the brains of the insane and ours they look remarkably alike."

"And what about male and female?"

"Also the same."

"That would explain why lady bicyclists are terrorizing the city. You're just as savage as we are."

She let out a careful laugh. He gestured to a photograph caption that read *The Brain of an Idiotic Male* to expand on his point. She looked at the caption, then at him, smiling. He felt a flush of confidence, like fingering the edge of a banknote in his pocket. He realized with some heaviness that it had been two years since he'd kissed a woman. Scrounging between wrecking jobs and cabinetry, spending his nights drinking beer with secondhand-brick dealers, he'd removed himself from the company of women. Was he going to bring a woman home to his tin shed emporium? Lay her gently on the straw mattress that floated like a raft in a sea of etched glass and broken cornices?

"Do you have a specialized interest in brains?" he asked, moving closer to the desk.

"Not really. But a few of us take turns sitting here. To help the public."

The word *public* struck him; a girl with a mission.

"Ready with the smelling salts, no doubt," he said.

She looked down, smoothed a hand over the desktop. "I also attend departmental meetings, take minutes and dictation. We're preparing to open a museum after the fair. Marshall Field is going to donate a million dollars." She covered her mouth for a second, as if that amount were the most scandalous thing ever to graze her lips.

Owen edged closer, hands in pockets. "That's what I've heard." It occurred to him that she might know the names of skippers and traders, that perhaps she had typed memoranda and bills of sale for numerous artifacts. For a brief moment he imagined his interest in her was practical. He swallowed. "Have you tried the carbonated soda, Miss Cummings?"

She studied her ledger, breathing. She had tallied the number of visitors to Neurology on the left side of the wide-margined page and Owen could see only ten strokes, two sets of rickety fence posts struck through with blue ink.

"I'm terrified of hiccups," she said plainly, not looking up.

"But you seem so intrepid," Owen said. "An administrator of brains and typer of headhunting memoranda."

"Typist," she said. "Or typewriter. Whichever."

"What did I say?"

"Typer."

"And the Ferris wheel is out of the question? I suppose you're afraid of heights as well."

"I love heights, actually. But I found the wheel rather dull." She shook her head at the ledger, biting her bottom lip, enjoying the look on his face.

"A gondola ride in the lagoon? A walk on the Japanese wooded island?"

"You're persistent and I don't even know your name."

"Owen Graves. I'm sorry if I'm being impossible."

She clasped her hands, elbows at the edge of the desk, looking up now. It was a warding-off stance. But then came: "I'll be off in thirty minutes. I'll meet you out front. I haven't been to the wooded island yet."

Owen nodded, smiled, looked out into the main exhibit. He had taken a half-step out of the brainy enclave when she said,

"The exhibit hall is full of hatchets and tomahawks, Mr. Graves. Professor Putnam would love nothing more than to scalp any man who preyed on his favorite secretary. Good shorthand and dictation are hard to come by. But I'll tell him that your intentions are honorable, shall I?"

Owen was at a loss, staring at a case of reed blowguns. After a pause he managed to say, "Tell the professor that he has nothing to worry about."

They walked north toward the wooded island, past the Indian camps and wigwams, the simulated ruins of Yucatán. A breeze came off the lake and Adelaide pulled a shawl about her shoulders. Paper lanterns swung between burr oaks and a Japanese temple floated through the trees, an apparition of paper and wood. A couple sat kissing in a darkened teahouse and Owen saw Adelaide stare then abruptly look away, as if someone had called her name. He led her by a stony brook, onto the moon bridge that overlooked the village of Japanese carpenters, musicians, and stonemasons. All had retired for the evening—a shifting tableau behind rice-paper walls. There was a moment of quiet, the fair seeming far off, but then they noticed another couple in a thicket. A hatless man in shirtsleeves, a woman pressed into the hollow of a tree. This time there was a flurry of searching hands and boozy whispers.

Owen said, "I had no idea this was such a lair."

"I have a better idea," she said. They left the island by the nearest bridge and headed east. Adelaide walked briskly and Owen wondered if she was angling for the viaduct and the midway. Perhaps a thousand-foot ascent in the captive balloon or a camel ride was more to her taste than the Ferris wheel. She greeted several guards by name, exchanged pleasantries with turnstile attendants and cashiers coming off shift. Owen quickened his step to keep up. He was being led, whisked through a late spring evening by a woman of industrious plaid and whalebone barrettes. They moved between the Bicycle Court and the Woman's Building and were suddenly flanked by scores of women in serge riding skirts and hopsack jerseys. The riders unlocked their bicycles, affixed white helmets, spats, headlamps.

Owen said, "I take back my earlier comment about the savagery of lady cyclists. I would trust these women with my life. That one there is attaching a first aid kit to the handlebars. Fit for an expedition."

Adelaide turned. "They're coming from a lecture at the Woman's Building. It's one of the best halls if you haven't already seen it."

This surprised Owen. He'd assumed the Italianate building was full of exotic draperies and tapestries.

She said, "One of the building's benefactors is Mrs. French-Sheldon."

"Ah," Owen said. He had no idea who that was.

"She led a caravan through eastern Africa, unattended by any of her sex, bartering and trading in the Arab coast bazaars."

"Yes, of course. And what did she come back with?"

"It's all on display in there. Weaponry, brass beads, that sort of thing." Then Adelaide began a summary of the speeches she'd heard inside, from Lady Aberdeen to a Russian princess and Swedish baroness whose names Owen could not hear above the pealing of bicycle bells. Something about leagues and temperance unions affirming the rights of women. Adelaide raised her voice to be heard: "The vote . . . not as a privilege, you understand, but as a right, Mr. Graves."

Her formal tone bothered him and he found himself thinking about the midway, about the Hungarian wine they poured into goblets over there. Adelaide turned north again, walking back along the lagoon, past the Illinois Building. She stopped in front of the Fisheries Building, a baroque arcade of taxidermied fish and living sea dwellers in glass tanks. Despite his interest in seagoing, Owen had avoided the exhibit earlier in the day. With its high-blown façade, its colonnades and flags aflutter, the building seemed to be full of cheap, touristic novelty. To top things off, it was fronted by the North Canal, where a merchant navy of singing gondoliers—South Siders trying to pass for Venetians in their striped shirts and broad felt hats—ferried couples from one concrete shore to the other.

"It's closed but I know one of the night watchmen. Come on," she said, trotting up the stairs, her skirts flaring.

He had no choice but to follow and feign enthusiasm. Adelaide struck up a conversation with a certain night watchman—avuncular, smelling of some exotic supper—who said that they could have thirty minutes but not to touch anything or it would be his hide.

A few sconces lit the way and they passed through trapezoids of light and shadow. The rooms and annexes twisted and burrowed, smelling of fish-bloat and iodine. Owen walked behind Adelaide, watching the way her hair hit her shoulders as she walked, barely noticing the maritime marvels—floating luminous eggs in a wall-side tank, dried fish strung like silvered sheets of paper; specimens of the deep, cured, salted, or stuffed in wooden box frames. A series of nets, traps, and lobster pots was accompanied by odes to Yankee enterprise. They stood beside the articulated skeleton of a sperm whale. She walked around it slowly, touching the alabaster ribs in the underwater gloaming.

"He said not to touch anything," Owen said.

"He won't know the difference. Isn't this something?"

"The whole place is something."

She paused, turned to him, wiped her hands down her skirt, muttered *forgive me,* then carefully lay beneath the suspended skeleton on the floor, looking up into the giant rib cage. She did this with ladylike precision, as if she were reclining on a gurney for a renowned physician, modesty intact. She made it seem like a perfectly natural thing to do on a Sunday evening. Palms down, she closed then opened her eyes, her braided hair coiled beside her head.

Watching her, prostrate on the wooden floor, he said, "Have you been swallowed whole?"

"Like Jonah. You could fit a house in there. Do you want to see the view?"

"I'm terrified of whale stomachs."

She laughed and sat bolt upright. She crouched and came out. "You must think I'm deranged."

Owen extended his hand and she took it as if alighting from a carriage. She straightened her skirts.

"I'm sure you're not the first one to do that."

"I bet not. Shall we see the rest?"

Owen put his hands in his pockets and followed her into the adjacent building. It was even more elaborate than the last, with porticos and loggias, a basilica for fish. They went inside and found themselves in a room of glass tanks. Spandrels of moonlight braced the high windows of the central dome. In the diffuse light Owen could barely read the placards let alone see the inhabitants lurking behind the glass walls. Supposedly there were catfish from muddy western rivers, halibut and cod from the Atlantic, king crabs and lobsters prowling the sandy bottom.

"Come over here," Adelaide said.

She was standing by a large tank, her face pressed to the glass.

"I can barely see a thing," he said.

"Your eyes will adjust. They brought these three by railcar. Can you imagine?"

He stared at the tank. "Still nothing. My father used to tell me stories of them bringing live lobsters by railcar for the downtown oyster houses. I never believed him until he took me there one day and showed me. They were all crawling around in a tank and you could walk up to one and tell them to throw it into a boiling pot." He saw a looming shape inside the tank. Then another.

"You have to come right up to see in this light," she said.

He could see the whites of her eyes.

He hooded his gaze and peered into the watery gloom.

He could hear her breath against the tank wall. His elbow was up against hers and she made no effort to move it. He blinked, squinted, then the gray maw of a shark passed just inches away, teeth serried and hinged, eyes inscrutable and white. The animal hit the tank with a thud and Owen jolted back, his hands raised in front of his face. A view of flared gills flashed by as the shark recoiled and turned. Adelaide had a hand on her breastbone, awed, stifling a panicky laugh. She had to steady herself against the wall. They stood three feet from the tank and watched the sharks for ten minutes, neither of them talking. The sharks' marbled gray flanks were flecked with white and a dozen tiny parasites clung to the sandpapered skins, dangled and swayed like wilted flowers of the deep. Every now and then there would be a thud against the glass—were they blind or trying to escape?—and Adelaide grabbed his arm each time, anchoring them in place. Of all the foreign and exotic encounters at the fair, these creatures seemed the most far-flung to Owen. Barely of the planet, Darwinian relics, as unlikely and apocalyptic as some sightless, mud-dwelling griffin. How did he and Adelaide appear through those cold, lightless eyes? Was there something in there looking back, by turns curious and appalled?

When they left the Fisheries Building it was almost nine. Owen offered to buy Adelaide a late dinner but she declined. He insisted on buying her a cherry-flavored soda and listened to her hiccup all along the Grand Basin, past the orb-bearing goddess of the Republic. The belching was retribution for the terror of the sharks, he told her. He walked her back to the Anthropological Building where Professor Putnam's assistant, Franz Boas, was waiting to escort her home on the streetcar. They stood outside for a moment.

"When are you on brain watch again?" he asked.

"It changes every day. It might be the psychology experiments tomorrow."

"But always the same building?"

She nodded, tightened her shawl.

"You can tell Putnam and Boas that there is no need for the tomahawks. You're in one piece."

"For now," she said, turning, dashing up the stairs. He added the word *now* to his mental catalogue of the day. It lay wedged between the sight of her prostrate beneath the whale skeleton and the otherworldly stare of the sharks. More than amulets and bamboo tinderboxes it was these moments that would stay with him, something in the way they hovered just beyond the grasp of plain reckoning—like apartments glimpsed from the El at night. The strange orbit of other lives. He walked back through the fairgrounds and bought a hamburger at the first place he could find. He sat on a bench in front of a bandstand, not far from where he'd witnessed the bloody Sun Dance, and ate with abandon, like an invalid back from the brink. He was sure his two-year slump was about to end.

They fell into a steady rhythm of afternoon walks and early suppers, working around her schedule at the fair. Over meals in which Adelaide described her charity work—teaching immigrants to read at Hull House, taking an elderly neighbor to church each Sunday—Owen marveled at the way she ate soup, bowl tilted carefully away, spoon idled and de-dripped at the ceramic curb before making its ascent to her lips. He could watch her do this for hours. The long, pale line of her neck was something he thought about on the streetcar or crossing the street. She was so remarkably decent and kind and her refinement came off as care—even grace—rather than privilege. Owen felt himself pulled by the promise of future shared meals, by the thought of loosening her braided hair so that it spilled—smelling of rosehips—over her delicate collarbone. He had to remind himself of his seagoing ambitions, of the need for a livelihood and the tin shed squalor in which he lived. Forcing himself to be practical, he asked her for voyage leads. She told him about the men who showed up at the ethnographic exhibit with bones and artifacts in burlap sacks. Word that a Chicago museum was forming had traveled far and wide. They came from all over: German copra traders, New England clipper mates, brig captains. They'd forged careers in the South Seas, hauling sulfur, felling teak, ferrying sugarcane recruits, but most of that had given way to wool and transport. They traded with the islanders for ethnographica as they went. A fathom of calico, a sack of glass beads, a steel-bladed knife, each of these could buy fine native weapons or artifacts. Owen listened and took notes, mesmerized as much by Adelaide's mouth as by the words spilling from it.

In search of a hiring captain, Owen frequented the barrelhouse saloons in Little Cheyenne, the levee district. Some of his father's men had come here on weekend benders—the *grand tour* they called it—spending their way from saloon to dance hall to brothel. They hocked wedding bands and fob watches at pawnshops and posed for midnight portraits with street waifs in tintype galleries; they ate oysters from the shell and bought virility potions at voodoo apothecaries. One Saturday morning Owen found Otto Bisky, a crapulous German clipper captain, breakfasting on eggs, sausages, and beer in a saloon eatery. He supported his head with one hand, holding a stump of bratwurst at bay with a fork in the other. A folded newspaper lay beside his plate. His face was sun-ravaged, his lips blistered, his complexion ruddy. Each time he took a swig of beer or bite of wurst his face turned increasingly sour, as if he were eating a lemon by the rind. Owen sat two bar stools down and ordered a shot of whiskey. He wanted to get the German's attention but Bisky failed to take his eyes off his newspaper or his eggs. Eventually, Owen asked him about the list of names he was tracing with a finger in a column of newsprint—*Argo, Nemesis, Peregrine, Industry, Aramac.* Beneath a heading of *Shipping Intelligence,* the names appeared under the banner *Wrecks and Casualties.* Bisky thereby began a bleary-eyed lament for all the ships he'd ever captained in the Pacific and the

Atlantic, and their fates. He detailed each ship's peculiarities, the way she acted in a squall or the way she took in wind and water in high swells or smelled like baleen in her lower reaches, before giving the exact nature of her demise. Scuttled, hogged-up, reefed, run aground, he gave each word a throaty, Germanic inflection. He discussed the quirks of his current ship, the *Paramount*, which was being repaired and due to set sail in the morning, eventually making for the South Seas. Then Bisky began a diatribe about the wretched state of the Chicago River and its bridge-opening schedule, the humid weather, the many hazards of falling asleep in a brothel. It was during a brief pause that Owen asked him outright for a job.

Bisky turned on his stool, sized Owen up while tonguing a morsel of food, pushed some air between his lips, and finally said, "You look more idler than able-bodied. Can you cook for two dozen men hungry enough to slit your throat if they miss a meal?"

The vision of preparing countless fishy meals at sea hovered before him. "What about ship's carpenter?" he asked. "I have experience and my own tools." He knew from his years in the library stacks that a ship's carpenter made general repairs and kept the masts in good condition. That seemed easy enough.

Bisky said, "Do you have a bevel gauge?"

Sensing this was a trap, Owen said of course and waited for the captain's reaction.

Bisky drained his mug of beer, folded the newspaper, and said, "We leave tomorrow at dawn."

This was not exactly what Owen had in mind, but he shook Bisky's calloused hand, received the details of the dock, and went out into the street. On his way back to the wrecking yard, he stopped in a hardware store and bought a bevel gauge. The salesman said it was the perfect tool for replicating pieces that weren't square. Owen arrived home and penned a letter to Adelaide in his finest Tabernacle cursive.

He tried to be brief but something poured out of him in the kerosene lamplight, his collected spoils spread before him, everything ordered and arranged, none of it seen by another person since his father's death. What was the point of all these objects? A private rummage; his solitary childhood labeled, filed, boxed. He wrote of his mother's daguerreotype, his father's death, his desire to find his place in the world. She was the loveliest person he'd ever known and he prayed for her forgiveness. The word *pray* felt like a falsehood—he hadn't communed with God in years—but within a month he was doing just that. Bunked down in the idlers' deckhouse of Bisky's clipper, his hands smelling eternally of tar and brine, he floated prayers out to the white stars, to the ocean mounting against the groaning ballast, even to the Holy Ghost. He prayed for land, for a steak medium rare, for the sight of Adelaide tilting her soup bowl in the wan light of a café.

Somehow, while he was at sea learning the petulant ways of the old clipper from stem to stern, Adelaide had forgiven him. He was gone a little under a year and the exchange of letters—three on each side—took on a life of its own. Entreaties and dispatches from San Francisco, Hawaii, and Sydney, all by commissioned mail steamer, each of his letters blotted with sealing wax stolen from Bisky's cabin. Whenever he got the chance, Owen fled the fusty nooks and fetid warrens below deck, the fishy brume in the cookroom, and climbed onto the foredeck to pen what he saw: the bruised green in the troughs between swells, the seabirds riding high on the trades without so much as a wing flap, the iron blue of the sky before a storm. He did not mention the debauchery that went on in the forecastle, the flagons of grog, the fistfights in the spiritroom, the pornographic reminiscences in cabins and bunkrooms. Owen drank with the seamen, spoke of women as sport when required, but used his station as carpenter to live on the periphery. He reported directly to the captain and shared quarters with the other idlers—the bosun, the sailmaker, and the cook. Because he did not have to stand watch like the ordinary and able-bodied seamen, he found time to read, write letters, and try his hand at trade whenever they anchored.

Adelaide began her letters a little stonily, describing the move to the new museum without much flair or affection. She kept to the facts—meals, weather, appointments, errands, books read in the buzzing light of the cable car. But by the time she responded to Owen's second letter, in which he reiterated his sincerest apology and stated his desire to be with her upon his return, she was warmed through. Not only because of those simple declarations—underlined with Indian ink—but because his letter was full of exotica and anthropological sightings from island ports: baskets made from sedge, a jew's harp made from bamboo, native boys surfing waves on rough-planked boards, women's girdles stripped from bark, the sight of missionaries from the Society of the Divine Word playing cricket beside a volcanic beach. She was won over by such details and showed parts of his letters to colleagues at the Field Columbian Museum. They asked her to write and express the museum's interest in buying certain objects upon his return. Owen kept this to himself and used his wages, such as they were, to buy calico and tobacco for trading in the islands. He made a deal with the cook and kept his tribal artifacts in flour sacks in the messroom larder.

By the time he received her third letter he was a few months from being home. While the stationery smelled of jasmine, the letter spoke of hard times. Eighteen ninety-four saw striking mobs in the railroad yards, runs on wildcat banks, the homeless sleeping in City Hall and precinct police stations. Adelaide continued to volunteer at Hull House, prepared meals and taught immigrant children how to read, sat on the porch alongside Jane Addams, the great social reformer herself. After a long day of service they listened to street orphans singing Slavic hymns. With the distance and perspective that came from nearly a year at sea—so many nights in the brimming stomach of the brig—Owen suspected that at least part of Adelaide's interest in him was sociological. On her father's side she came from New England brahmins, men with high-bridged noses, honorary degrees, and a blue-blooded zeal for philanthropy. Adelaide had come west to strike out on her own, type memoranda and take dictation at the museum by day, improve the lot of the poor in her off hours, petition for women's rights, but all the while receiving a monthly stipend from Boston that was wired to the downtown post office.

Perhaps, Owen thought, he was one of her causes. The orphaned son of a housewrecker, partially raised and educated by South Side nuns, a little unrepentant and raw in his scuffed blucher boots, he fit the profile for Adelaide's wider mission. But surely the parents back east did not condone a romantic alliance with someone of Owen's prospects and parentage. And yet Adelaide's letters unfurled suggestions for future plans—going to worker concerts in the park where men in coveralls would eat pork sandwiches while listening to Brahms, standing amid the dotted brushwork of the Impressionists at the Art Institute, attending one of the Friday lectures or poetry readings at the Chevron Tea Room on Michigan Avenue. It was clear to Owen that she wanted to refine him, to bear him up. And though he preferred the subterranean charm of a poolroom to a lofted lunchroom, a pitcher of stout to a carafe of burgundy, a midnight platter of ribs in Little Cheyenne to a midday bowl of chowder in some downtown clam house, he was willing to go partway along with her vision. She was a missionary of the plainspoken and practical kind, moved to service not so much by God but by some inherited belief in humanism and the common plight of all. It wasn't the Bible that had been read aloud during her childhood, but the musings of Whitman, Thoreau, Emerson. Owen would go to the lectures and concerts, attend the Christmas pageants at the houses for the poor, but he'd also keep a racetrack form guide in his back pocket or a ticket stub for a curio museum where a bearded lady farted and belched on demand. The truth was, he trusted Chicago's armpit more than her jeweled fingers.

But it was also true that he'd grown smitten with Adelaide at sea. His recollections of her had become almost devotional in their tone—she sat reading a chapbook in the half-light of a cable car, her chest rising between stanzas. He was always at the other end of the cable car, in those daydreams, coming toward her. When she looked up at him her whole face came alive, as if he'd brought her happily back from the brink of a desolate poem.

His homecoming. Adelaide in a bustled skirt and shawl, fighting the bluster of March to meet him at the train station. They kissed on the mouth, briefly, and it was she who leaned in first. Owen felt a surge of affection, and lust, but also a mild sense of dread. He was clearly in her benevolent sights and it wasn't long before the afternoons and evenings of ballroom dancing and civic-minded pastimes grew heavy with expectation. Sometimes he had to shake himself free for a few hours and drink himself into a stupor in a dramhouse where patrons spat and ashed their cigarettes on the floor. Whereas the seamen's lewdness and excess had made him more upright at sea, Adelaide's noble intentions drove him to gin. He slept off hangovers in the tin-wire shambles of the wrecking shed and showed up clean-shaven and breath-minted the next day, ready for another round of self-improvement.

And yet there was no denying Adelaide's allure, her implacable friendliness and lightness of spirit. Owen was happiest in her company and even amid the din of a taproom she was the object of his thoughts. The way she chatted with strangers, doled out bus fares and petted strays like an urban St. Francis, thought nothing of removing her shoes to walk in the frigid waters at the lake edge or tuck a napkin into her neckline to eat pork ribs for a lark. She was buoyant, high-minded, affectionate. She kissed Owen with increasing pluck, allowed his hands to run the fences of her undergarments, but it was clear that an invisible line had been drawn and only a marriage proposal would suffice to cross it.

The prospect of marriage unsettled Owen but not because he couldn't imagine happily spending his days with Adelaide. It was a question of means, of what he might bring to such an arrangement. It was also a matter of doubt. What if Adelaide's affections were conditioned on some act of conversion, on Owen joining some gilded society or humanitarian circle? He wanted to be sure she loved the wrecker's son and the orphan and not some phantom of her moral imagination. On one of their afternoon walks he asked her why her affections for him ran so deep. She spoke freely, as if he'd asked the simplest of questions. "I admire you greatly, for one thing. You know how to do so much in the world. I like your broad smile and shoulders and that schoolboy curiosity . . . and I've never seen hands like that. They're so . . . capable."

He held up his calloused hands. "They could be in a window display."

She took one of his big hands and held it. "The men I knew in Boston were timid, with soft hands and no opinions. But don't get a big head. Being fearless is fine, but recklessness isn't a trait I admire."

"I'll keep that in mind." He stopped to kiss her, pulling his scarf up to protect them from the gusting wind.

Owen placed all his hopes for future respectability—and therefore marriage—in the sale of his artifacts. On the voyage, he'd managed to assemble over a hundred items, from Melanesian masks, daggers, and spears to Polynesian baskets and clay bowls. His eye for signature details, indelible marks of an object's maker, led to the possession of carved figurine war gods and ornately trimmed dance shields. He hauled the items in a wagon to the rear of the Field Columbian Museum and several of the curators came out for the appraisal. Owen could tell they were delighted and surprised by his bounty, but they were also stone-facing their reactions to keep the prices down. The artifacts were arranged on the loading dock by region, Owen referring to detailed notes in his journal. The curators studied each item while describing, in great detail, the financial strain of founding a new museum. "We've bought thousands of artifacts from the fair and now it's a question of remaining funds. We'll have to consult the board and come back with a figure for the whole lot." The phrase *whole lot* did not do justice to Owen's months of careful acquisition and he could already sense that they were out to scam him. When the handwritten figure came on museum letterhead, it was ten times less than Owen had expected. It was enough to float him for a few months, but not enough to secure a mortgage or rent an apartment without worry. He accepted the offer and a month later he saw some of his artifacts in one of the museum's velvet-lined cases. They'd been given pride of place in the main gallery.

Within a year, Owen stopped talking to Adelaide about moving to an apartment. He had spent his sea wages and the money he'd received from the Field Columbian Museum. "They paid me like it was native bric-a-brac," he told Adelaide bitterly. She wasn't sure that he'd been swindled but she sympathized nonetheless. Soon he was back to occasional wrecking jobs and renting out half the salvage yard to an ironworker. The economy was still bad and he occasionally borrowed money from pawnbrokers and loan sharks. Adelaide never asked him about his finances, never once came to the yard, because to do so would be to stare into the gravel pit of his working-class roots. She remained determined and hopeful, told stories of her father's financial generosity as a way of lighting the trail that might lead the way forward.

3.

In the grip of a second hangover, Owen left the First Equitable and took to the streets with Hale Gray's contract in hand. The crowds had thinned out but groups of revelers still choked the doorways of taverns and restaurants. He headed down La Salle and across to the shoreline where the darkened lake was dotted faintly with navigation lights. The long walk into the South Side was just what he needed to clear his head. He bought some fried potatoes from a vendor and ate them as he walked along, a greasy thumbprint becoming his unofficial seal on the first page of the contract. Under a streetlamp he stopped to study the list of tribal artifacts, considering where each item could be acquired, but soon he returned to the signature page with its dollar amount and the phrase *a number of natives*. The money was enough to buy a modest house in a good neighborhood, perhaps with a small mortgage. He wondered how much had been apportioned to the artifacts and how much to the islanders. Was *a number* as little as *two*? He felt himself calculating, justifying. He had a complicated moral aversion to bringing back natives for an insurance spectacle, but he also had a simple aversion to continued poverty.

It could be done ethically, he supposed, walking again. He would vouchsafe the welfare of the natives, find a few that genuinely wanted to travel abroad, ensure their safe return passage. But even as he made these mental commitments he felt Adelaide's disapproval like a shroud around his own thoughts. As someone who'd never done without, whose livelihood had never been in doubt, could she fully comprehend the proposition? He found himself striding out, making assertions. His own misgivings would make him careful and he'd strike a balance between self-interest and morality. He told himself this all the way home, falling into bed amid the spoils and curios. He was twenty-nine years old. Not since the Great Fire of 1871 had the Graves family owned a house.

The next evening he invited Adelaide to dinner. The restaurant was darkly paneled and sconce-lit, held a kind of religious light. There were ferns in copper pots and leather booths with the patina of worn luggage. The waiters were old men in butterfly collars and bow ties, shouldering between white linen tablecloths, a vintage bottle of wine cradled in the crook of an arm or a cellar-cured steak held aloft, smoking and spitting on a china plate. Tableside, they glumly boasted about the provenance of their meat, of the iced railcars that carried their porterhouses as far as New York and San Francisco. With grim, judicial faces, the waiters gave the impression that there were other, more pressing obligations than taking orders and delivering meals, that each misguided entrée selection was not only a personal insult but a blow to civilization. They looked to the male diners for compliance, upgrading the good lady's dalliance in fowl to something the restaurant could stand behind.

Owen and Adelaide sat in a booth, reading menus the size of broadsheets in the flicker of a wall sconce. The ornate woodwork of the booth, the church light of the dining room, reminded Owen of going to confession at the Tabernacle School, of distant afternoons sunk in penance. Telling Adelaide that he was going to sea again felt like a confession, a cardinal sin. He found it hard to look at her and stared off at his fellow diners or at the oil paintings on the walls—bucolic scenes of livestock in paddocks at dawn, steam rising from the hides of brindled cows, but also breaching ships in a gale, their prows pitching through heaving swells. Only people who'd never gone to sea would find the drama of a squall romantic, something to hang on the wall like clouds and seaside picnics. To Owen the tossing ships depicted the very real threat of oblivion, not only from the unfathomable deep but the countless diseases that could fester in the planking of a clipper—scurvy, flux, rheums, fevers. He was glad that their booth's painting was a still life of glossed pears and corpulent grapes. He looked at Adelaide over the top of his menu. She was wearing a pale organdy dress trimmed in ribbons and lace and an heirloom necklace. It was a far cry from her usual industrious clothing, the museum plaids and streamlined cottons, the tight sleeves and necklines, and it worried him. She had removed her gloves and her ringless white fingers drummed gently on the back of the menu.

"They make it so difficult," she said.

"Choose carefully. The waiters are constables and jailors."

Her eyes softened. "I think I'm going to have the Iowa pork chop. What about you?"

"The Angus steak. Aged a thousand years in a cave."

"I like it here. It reminds me of Boston."

They set their menus facedown on the table and, on cue, the waiter came with his hands clasped behind his back, listening now with his head cocked, gravely agreeing with their course of action. He lingered for a moment, eyes tracing the arabesques of the rug. "And the wine, sir?"

It had slipped Owen's mind completely and he was forced to ask the waiter for his recommendation, which wasn't so much a recommendation as a statement of fact: "I'll bring you the 1865 Beaune Grèves Vigne de l'Enfant Jésus. A perfect match." Owen didn't speak French but remembered enough from his Tabernacle days to realize the wine name contained a reference to the infant Jesus. Wasn't 1865 the year that Lincoln had died, the body touring the country by train just as the grapes were budding on the vines in France? The wine sounded both pricey and inauspicious.

The waiter smiled for the first time, perhaps at Owen's

expense, and turned to Adelaide, taking her menu. It was in the waiter's patronizing smile that Owen saw the unraveling of the evening. Adelaide was expecting a marriage proposal, had dressed for it, was wearing an antique locket that no doubt had been passed down the maternal line. The waiter sensed the imminent occasion and had aged his wine selection on its account. Had Owen seen the profile of a wink when the waiter uttered *a perfect match* and turned to Adelaide? As the waiter hobbled away, Owen saw visions of a mythic bottle of wine being pulled from a bed of straw in the cellar. He saw the old man bringing the bottle up like a relic from a tomb, smug with the knowledge that he was making Owen pay through the nose for his moment of posterity. Owen had twice caught the bastard looking at his weary shoes under the cover of the linen tablecloth.

Adelaide put her hands in her lap and spoke of her day at the museum. She had paper cuts on her fingers from so much cataloguing. She spread her fingertips as proof. Owen took her hand spontaneously, then remembered his mission and set it gently on the tablecloth. Then she spoke of a museum in New York that was bringing in some Inuit to study and he felt his heart drop into his stomach.

"You remember Boas, my old boss? He's the one behind it. A terrible thing to bring natives here. Remember what happened to the Esquimaux at the fair?"

Owen looked down at the table, nodding, unable to speak. Did she know about the voyage, about the contract to bring back savages? Thankfully, the wine came and the waiter proffered the label. Owen nodded and watched the man remove the cork and pour an inch of amber into a glass. He pretended to sniff the rim but couldn't get past the taste of iron in his mouth. He sipped the burgundy, let it sit dutifully on his tongue, then swallowed with deliberation. The waiter said, "Hints of chalk and lime, an overlay of caramel," and Owen found himself nodding mutely. The glasses were filled and the wine bottle was wrapped in a napkin and placed on the far side of the table. Owen would let Adelaide finish a glass and eat her pork chop before launching into his plans.

But by the time she had eaten her pork chop and baked potato she had finished two glasses of wine and was flushed in the face. The delicate recesses behind her earlobes were blotched red.

"Do you taste the caramel overlay?" he asked.

"I do, as a matter of fact. Why do you always have to poke fun at anything refined?" she said flatly.

He felt obliged to answer in earnest. "I suppose I've never been comfortable with privilege. Places like this."

She wiped her mouth with the edge of her napkin, her head slightly bent. There was good breeding in that demure, polite gesture. He remembered his father drinking soup from the bowl and using a crust of bread to shovel-end a pond of beans from his plate.

"Adelaide—"

"Mr. Graves."

"Miss Cummings."

"I'm a little tipsy."

"I have something to tell you."

"Good, because I have something to tell you as well."

They both breathed, sipped their wine. Finally, he said, "Ladies first."

"Very well then." She smoothed her palms on the tablecloth and placed her knife and fork at six o'clock on her plate. "George Dorsey, one of the curators at the museum—"

"I know Dorsey. His work anyway."

"He plays poker with a few businessmen, likes to keep in with potential donors and benefactors. Anyway, he had an interesting chat with Hale Gray the other day. You know, the insurance man."

Owen felt the muscles in his neck go taut. "I've heard of him."

One of the ancient waiters was singing "Happy Birthday" in a far-off corner—Christ, was it in Italian?—his voice low and providential. A champagne cork popped and hit the tin ceiling. Adelaide lifted her chin, waiting. She had the same warm skepticism as that day amid the bottled brains at the fair, sitting like a bookkeeper with her open ledger, warding him off but also inviting him in. How surprised and delighted he'd been that night when she lay on the floor beneath the whalebone skeleton and pondered Jonah's fate. He'd fallen in love in that single, enigmatic moment, but had never quite figured her out. She was complicated, practical, elevated, homespun, recited Whitman in taffeta but also read comics barefoot on a divan, took her tea with lump sugar but loved to drink in the oaken shade of a German beer garden. She gave directions to tourists with infinite care and precision but also blasted her bicycle horn at wayward pedestrians.

He said, "I'm going so that I can be in a position to ask for your hand. Hale Gray is paying handsomely."

"So I hear."

"It will be less than a year."

She folded her arms.

"Six months or so. I promise."

She picked up her water glass and took a long, slow sip. The gas in the wall sconce hissed and she glanced up at it, slightly bothered. "It's been four years. My father thinks I've made you up."

"And I'm still living in a tin shed on the South Side. I need this voyage to make my mark." He wanted to talk about the objects he would bring back but was worried it would prompt a discussion about the natives. He couldn't be sure she knew about the savages. Perhaps the mention of the Inuit had been a coincidence. Yes, he thought, that was possible.

She looked at the backs of her hands and waited a long time before speaking. "If we were engaged while you were at sea . . .

well, I suppose then the whole thing would seem very different to me."

There was nothing to be said after that. It was a declaration, definitive as a ship's bronze bell. He waited for the check and paid it with large bills, straight from the dwindling stash he kept in an old powder keg. They went outside and walked into the balmy evening, the streetlamps pearling through the lake fog. It was uncomfortable to breathe and they walked heavy and silent. They headed in the direction of the La Salle Street cable car stop and at the corner of Adams he saw the skyscraper, reared up and electri-fied, its clock face like a second moon in the ether of night. Every floor was alight—Hale believed the building itself was the com-pany's best advertisement—and the windows were alive with the glints of work lamps. There was no denying the building's power, like a bishop presiding over a stone canyon. Owen stopped and craned but Adelaide refused to do likewise, as if the building was partly to blame. At the streetcar stop they waited. Owen would escort her home to the flat she shared with a curator's sister. Then he would jump a car and spend the remainder of the night in the dun-and-ale splendor of a levee district tavern. Then Adelaide said, "I'd like to see where you live," with a simple tone of entitle-ment. There was no question mark attached or rising intonation. He said nothing but bit his bottom lip and nodded almost imper-ceptibly, resigned.

They arrived at the yard after a long walk from the cable car. It was a neighborhood that Adelaide did not know and he watched her feign casualness as she took in the leaning tenements full of raucous arguments and carousing in six languages, gypsy women smoking penny cigarettes on sagging wooden stoops, old Russian men betting on dominoes while dogs growled and barked and were kicked, the smell of charcoal and sawdust and dank laundry, the sidewalk petering out into a goat track of cedar blocks and mud. Although she worked among these people at Hull House, Owen knew she had never been on their native turf; she listened to their quaint singing and folklore and taught them to read *Tribune* English, utilitarian verbs and nouns, but had never actually seen their kitchens and bedrooms, the beds made from apple crates and tables sawn from railway ties. A few of the rabble-rousers called to Owen and he bade them good night. A chorus of wolf whistles and a heated *Someone's lucky tonight* followed them down to the yard.

He opened the chain-link gate and led Adelaide past the hulking piles of scrap metal, the copper pipes and iron bars waiting to be smelted. Inside the tin shed he lit a few spirit lamps and their shadows loomed as they moved among the workbenches. Here were decades of salvage from the rubble of teardowns, arranged and organized by function, windows of every mullion and design, ornate doorknobs, lintels engraved with the first initials of dead wives or secret lovers, glasshouse and conservatory panels, greened copper turrets, doorjambs with bored-out compartments for pistols, balcony railings and orchestra-pit podiums, box seats from condemned theaters. On a lone table under a window were the artifacts from the Pacific that he'd not sold to the museum. A few shell adzes and stone hammers that were sentimental to him, suggesting that the natives of Melanesia might also be adept at wrecking and dismantling. They stood by a wall of tools, the bradawls and gimlets taking on a sinister, surgical bearing in the lamplight. Adelaide surveyed the chaos of objects, the endless rows of fixtures, the subsections of brick and mortar so numerous that a fortress lay in pieces. "Where do you sleep?" she said lightly, continuing the theme of inveterate explorer of the ghetto.

Owen, with nothing to lose by now, pointed to the bed he'd made from king posts and metal trusses, a leadlight window standing in for a headboard, the calash of an old carriage acting as canopy. It looked to him now—imagined through her eyes—like a Chinese junk, something forged and welded from scrap, as whimsical as a parade float.

He said, "It's ridiculous, I know."

"I love it," she said, walking toward it. "Bring the lamp over."

He followed her with the light, thrusting her shadow against the wall. She stood at the banister that doubled as the end of the bed frame. He waited for her to say something but she didn't. Finally, he said, "I don't have a ring," and saw her shoulders go loose. Without turning around, she said, "Be quiet and lie down with me." He watched her pull the barrette out of her hair and knew, in that moment, the engagement was sealed. He came forward with the lamp.

II

ARGUS

4.

Argus Niu found the Reverend Mister's body on the veran-dah just before breakfast. The preacher had gone outside to plumb the nuances of Sunday's sermon in the dawning light, smoke his pipe, sip his first cup of Darjeeling, while Argus fixed eggs and soda-scones to his liking. The fleet Scotsman—a Pres-byterian missionary in his twentieth year in Melanesia—reclined now in a wicker chair, head back, pale blue eyes startled and fixed on the thatching overhead. The tea had spilled down his shirt-front, creating a narrow strip of steaming celluloid. He clutched the handwritten sermon in one hand, fingers knuckled white. Argus set down the breakfast tray, called out *Sir* and *Reverend Mister,* shook the preacher by the shoulders. The old man did not respond. He knew his employer was dead but felt compelled to put two fingers on one of the missionary's copper-haired wrists. He had learned this trick from the doctor who came out from Port Moresby once a year to give the Reverend Mister his wine and spirits permit. The wrist did not throb. But it was still warm and Argus wished he knew how to blow resurrection into a man's mouth. He put his hand in front of his employer's nose and felt for breath. Nothing. The schoolteacher who knew first aid had recently eloped with a Sepik River woman, forcing the Reverend Mister to teach the *Catechism of Christian Truth* himself. It made him angry to be pulled away from writing his phrasebooks and tending his garden of celery and artichokes.

Argus had seen dead men before but not since his father's funeral off the Bismarck Archipelago six years earlier. At home the custom was to bury the dead under their stilt houses or, if they lived in a pile house on the lagoon, to bury it near the ancestral gardens. But first they were put on display with their best possessions surrounding them—dogs' teeth, obsidian-tipped arrows, yams, traded shell armlets—and propped against the house ladder. Then the body was wrapped in coconut leaves and sheaths from the nibung palm. A fire was lit. People mourned. The body was buried. The finger bones and skull were placed into an earthenware pot in the rafters of the house. The spirit of the dead lingered and presided over the household; it punished infidelity, reckless debts, bad housekeeping. Argus had not seen a funeral ceremony on his adopted island of Nimburea but had heard that the ritual was to leave the dead in trees or weigh them down with stones and toss them from canoes. That seemed crude and ill-omened. How was a Presbyterian minister supposed to be buried? Who would give the Sunday sermon? He looked off the verandah and saw some of the night fishermen dragging their canoes onto the beach. It wouldn't be long before parents and pupils from the school would come looking for Reverend Underwood. Punctuality was a close neighbor to cleanliness.

Argus would tell them the reverend had taken ill and send a message to the head mission and wait for instructions. Keep the timber house locked. Shutter the windows. The preacher would have wanted that. Some of the locals—the heathen militia, the reverend called them—might show up with spears and clubs and begin looting. Raid the linens and crockery and tinned peaches, throwing him aside or clubbing him in the head and back. Argus could see it all very clearly. He was an outsider here, a houseboy and a Christian convert who knew how to bake bread, speak a butler's English, sing hymns, recite psalms. They tolerated him but only because he did not talk to their women and worked for the big holy man who handed out tobacco after church on Sundays. He was eighteen years old and uninitiated on any island. To the locals he was something between a man and a boy. Like words for *bear, snow,* and *ice,* he was something they had no use for.

Argus placed the teacup on the side table, wrenched the unfinished sermon from the stony hand, and hefted the Scotsman off the wicker chair. He began dragging him inside, hooking his hands under the preacher's armpits and walking backward, taking small steps. The dead weight of the man's torso and head was awful; two hundred pounds of hoop iron in a gunnysack of clothes. The long, hairy arms, which had once flailed during a sermon—*Who among ye hath felt the fury and sublime in ye very human core?*—scraped across the floor. His ears, viewed from above, were cave-like, tufted and pink from too much sun; they resembled things that shouldn't be seen in the naked light, like a mother-in-law bathing in the ocean or a cassowary's jaundiced hide. The clergyman's mouth was open, the whitening lips slightly parted. He wouldn't speak anymore, no longer say, *Modesty and temperance, Argus, these will vouchsafe virtue.*

Argus made it into the sitting room and hoisted the monster into the captain's chair. He propped the head up with a pillow and placed the steamer blanket over his lap. This was where the Reverend Mister spent his evenings with a glass of claret and the ornamental Bible, mulling over the pestilence and plague of the Old Testament, worrying the gilt pages with his thumb. A digestive biscuit before bed then his arsenal of evening remedies—boric acid for his carbuncled feet, sulfonal for insomnia, ginger essence for his overwrought stomach, each of them brought by Argus on a lacquered tray. Then prayers on calloused knees, the dimming away of earthly pretensions in the stammer of private worship. Each night, Argus retreated to his small room and quietly pulled out his woven leaf mat from under the iron cot. The Reverend Mister would have suffered apoplexy if he ever caught his house-boy sleeping on the floor.

Now the master was something lifted from the miry pages of Genesis, a husk-skinned ancient, ascended from ribs or clay, surely a hundred and twenty years old. Argus combed the preacher's gray-red hair, applied some brilliantine, perched his spectacles onto the bridge of the nose. He began to assemble favored objects—the leather-bound Bible, the quill and ink he used for calligraphy, his Oxford cricket bat, the amber-tipped pipe, the nickel shaving dish, the hand mirror, the daguerreotype of his sisters rambling on a heath in Sunday whites. But just as he placed these items on the side table, beneath the brass spirit lamp, Argus realized this was not the right resting place for the preacher. It was the workroom at the back of the house where he had been happiest.

This time he kept the dead man in the captain's chair, worked a rug under each of the legs, tilted the chair slightly back, then slid the entire rig toward the rear of the house. He bore the Reverend Mister down the sparse hallway—*be wary of adornment, the seedbed for idolatry*—steamer blanket over legs, spectacled eyes vacant and heavenward, a rheumy passenger being taken deckside for a spot of fresh air and sun. He settled the chair in a sheet of early sunlight, right beside the inked letterpress. By noontime he would need to shutter the louvered windows, be vigilant against the musk and rot of death, but for now he would let whatever remained of Underwood's spirit tarry a while in the brightening room. There were two separate book projects spread out—a *Melanesian Phrasebook of Pidgin English* and *A Presbyterian Missionary's Compendium of Practical Advice*. When Argus wasn't cooking and cleaning he assisted with these projects, sometimes acting as translator or letterpress operator. He had learned to ink the metal letters, to know the measure of each of the printer's marks, the tiny horizons hemmed in by *em* and *en*. He carried reams of paper up from the dock when they arrived from the Brothers of Biblical Charity. Now he stood over the pages, tracing a finger across lines of text in the phrasebook:

My wife is always vomiting: *All-time all-time mary belong me he-throw-out*

All the white men are having a big celebration: *Alltogether master he-make-im big-fellow Chris'mas*

Then he moved to the compendium:

For candlesticks that fare well in the tropics I recommend Haddock's Belmont Sperm, a first-rate diminisher of darkness. In the way of lamps go with a "Hitchcock" or an "Empress" lamp and a "Hurricane Lantern."

Pack along a shotgun, No. 12 bore, for the pigeons and to deter heathens after too much kava. No. 2 shot is the ticket for pigeon-shooting and may be purchased in Sydney or Auckland. Be sure to oil and clean your weapon often. Bring a rag as cloth is a rarity.

This reminded Argus to fetch the shotgun and set it beside his master. The preacher, who told stories of grouse hunting in the Scottish Highlands, had been fond of setting out at dusk on a pigeon shoot, gun cocked over one shoulder, cooing into the woods, a few naked village boys trailing behind him with reed spears and bark shields. Argus went along and received instruction in handling a weapon; how to let the tang and bore extend from the shoulder, from the eye itself. He set out all the objects on the worktable and this is how the presbyters would find their fellow—rigidly reclined, objects of work, grooming, and study about his person. Argus would tell the church elders that he died as he lived, simply and without fuss, passing silently before breakfast. He remembered some coughing now, heard over the flames of the stove, but he would omit that from the account. They would not bury him under the house, but take his body away in a pine box. Maybe his bones would go back to a churchyard in Scotland where everyone had red hair. If only the Presbyterians had a bishop and a big mission like the Anglicans, who trained the new recruits on Norfolk Island, taught them Mota and how to conduct themselves among the natives before sending them out to the islands and atolls. Meanwhile, the Presbyterians were losing their hold on the islands. If the Reverend Mister had been an Anglican, the bishop might have come on a steamer to fetch the body himself.

Five days later the house was turning rank. He couldn't wait any longer. Wild pigs had begun grunting and snuffling under the stilts and piers. They smelled it. Several times he had to ward off visitors and well-wishers, telling them that the minister was bedridden with influenza. They asked which spirit he had angered and left manioc and bowls of coconut milk. Tomorrow was Sunday. If the reverend didn't show up for his sermon there would be a gathering on the verandah. They wanted their tobacco as much as their Gospel According to Mark. They would demand to see him. Argus had dispatched a typewritten letter to the main mission—*On the occasion of the death of Reverend Mister Underwood*. Canoe teams had relayed the sealed envelope across the islands. A blackbirding schooner was recruiting in the islands and expected in the bay that afternoon. If the black-clad presbyters weren't on it, if a new missionary didn't get rowed ashore, then Argus planned to go aboard. He had no desire to go sugarcaning in Queensland, but he could catch a ride to the outer islands as the men recruited kanakas. He had enough of his monthly wages to buy himself a passage. The schooners didn't go out as far as Poumeta but he could come within a day's canoe ride. It had been six years since he'd seen his family.

Then there was the matter of the minister's cat; surely that was a favored object. No one on the island had seen a cat prior to the Reverend Mister returning from a trip to Brisbane with the ginger tabby. He had carried it in a small crate and the dogs and children came running to take a look. The village elders warned that the unsightly beast would curse the yam harvest or doom the annual canoe race. They recommended that the minister and Argus never sneeze in its presence for fear of the cat's sorcery. Fresh off the pitching steamer, the cat was skinny, dazed, terrified. The minister had found it skulking around a dilapidated wharf and couldn't bear to leave it behind. Within a few months the animal—now named Mr. Nibbles—had become a fat housecat, living on tinned milk and morsels of fish, preening itself in every room. The minister loved nothing more than to sit in his captain's chair at night, the ginger tabby in his lap, the cat nuzzling the edge of the King James or chewing on his pinky finger. Argus had to witness the cat's transformation from savvy derelict to kept sloth. The cat was guilty of avarice, a serious sin, and was frequently out of sorts. Argus had to feed it and change its sandbox, for the animal remained housebound. The minister feared any number of ugly fates outside the timber walls of the mission house—attack by dogs, drowning at the hands of unruly children, being plundered by a wild pig. The locals found it amusing that an animal lived in a house and dubbed him the Reverend Mister Nibbles. They suggested that just as a sow could be blinded to prevent it from wandering too far, the cat could be rendered sightless to keep it close to the mission verandah. Argus did not translate this piece of advice for the preacher and kept the cat out of plain sight for fear of an assassination attempt.

Now the ginger tabby slunk into the workroom, hindquarters in the air, tail quivering, rubbing its dander against the cold, dead feet of its benefactor. Argus remembered stories of Egypt from his daily lessons and wondered if the cat shouldn't be buried along with his employer. Was it slaves or cats that were buried with the pharaohs? He couldn't quite remember. Maybe it was both. The body smelled now like pestilence itself—*head belong em he-stink finish*—a fact the cat didn't seem to mind; Mr. Nibbles chewed on a yellow-gray finger, perched in his owner's lap as if nothing out of the ordinary had occurred. Argus shooed the cat away and finished washing the reverend's face with soap. Maybe he would let the cat into the wild after all. The beast would either recover its natural instincts or perish within hours.

But when it came time to release the cat, Argus was unable to follow through with his plan. The recruiting schooner had anchored in the bay and there was no sight of a delegation from the synod. Teenage boys had gathered on the black beach to be bartered over. Fathers negotiated over their sons, allowing them to go to the cane fields in exchange for guns and knives, sticks of tobacco, beads, fathoms of cloth. Argus opened the back door of the mission house but the cat offered an indifferent gaze to the acacia fronds that swayed in the foreground, then it retreated to the sitting room. In the room where Argus slept, he packed his belongings, borrowing the minister's portmanteau and some of his clothing. He wanted to arrive home looking distinguished—starched cotton shirt, silk cravat, Panama straw hat, khaki trousers, alpaca coat, perhaps the Reverend Mister's ironwood cane at his side. He would return home a Christian gentleman. The dead no longer needed their possessions, especially if they had reached the bounty of heaven.

After dark, with all the cane boys boarded, Argus locked the rank-smelling mission house and placed the key—the minister had been a big believer in the sanctity of English-made padlocks—under the doormat, just as he had postscripted in his letter to the synod. He made his way down to the mission rowboat, his portmanteau in hand and the howling cat, encased in a leather satchel, under one arm. Although the reverend had done much to wean Argus from his supernatural belief in sorcery and witchcraft, he continued to believe that the cat was capable of great harm. He suspected that the dreams of cats were filled with carnivorous sport and vengeful taunts against the humans who cared for them. They remembered empty milk bowls and intemperate nudges of the foot. If dreamers left their bodies, as Melanesians suspected, then the cat would surely chase him across the archipelago to repay its abandonment. He rowed out through the coral reef, the waves drenching the gunwale and further angering the cat. He approached the schooner and sidled up to its hull. One of the seamen on watch called out, a lamp hoisted: "Tell the recruiter we av another un." Some ropes and a ladder were lowered. Argus passed up his portmanteau but retained Mr. Nibbles at his side. By the time Argus stood on deck there was a small party of squinting seamen gathered in the lantern light.

"Christ on high, we got a real showboat here," one of the men said. "Never seen a pickaninny in a cravat before."

Another said, "E'll get that pretty little hat knocked awf in the cane fields, but."

Argus looked out from under the hat's brim, trying to make out the faces before him. The cat mewed warily from the leather satchel.

A man in a flannel jacket, evidently the recruiter, came forward and said, "You-fellow work-em sugar place?"

Argus straightened his cravat against his celluloid collar, stroked the cat's protruding head, and said: "I'd like to buy a passage to the western islands, out by the Bismarck Archipelago, or as far as you'll take me. I'll pay extra to keep the cat with me. And can you bring the rowboat up on the davits? I'll need a way to get about once I'm there." He put his hand in his pocket but thought better of showing his shillings and pounds. He would negotiate a fair price, just as the reverend had taught him.

Ten seconds of silence as they took in the sight of the bush dandy speaking the Queen's English. Finally, a voice said, "Don't he speak like a book? Say something else. Say us a joke or a limerick. Dressed like a fuckin duke, he is. Go on, little blackie, speak."

5.

Argus shared the second mate's cabin, a nook that smelled of wood bloat and lime powder. The schooner drifted toward New Ireland, canting a wake through a procession of lowland atolls. There were tiny beaches rimmed with green underwood and bights of coral. They stopped at the larger islands, the ones with wide bays or cloud-capped volcanoes. The recruiter told the coxswain where to anchor and a party rowed ashore with guns and glass beads. At each place it was the same ritual: the boys and young men assembling on the shore, the settling of *goodbye payment,* the fathers paddling their sons out to the ship. A flotilla of canoes with burning husk torches surrounded the ship as it weighed anchor. The new recruits were signed on, handed a stick of tobacco and a blanket, and sent down the hatchway below deck. By the time the schooner reached the Solomons, there were sixty boys aboard.

The kanakas slept in the bunkroom and whenever they saw Argus on deck with the petulant cat they called him *gnat-gnat* or *trouser mary*. Argus sat up on the bulkhead with his Kipling and Dickens, watching the ship hands clew up the square sails or lean against the halyards in beleaguered silence. He sketched the broken backbone of islands, the sun paling away the distances into faint blues and greens. He worked a sketchpad with a cut of charcoal; the Reverend Mister had taught him about the unbending laws of perspective and vanishing points, about the imagined zenith floating beyond any scene like heaven itself. Argus drew the shadows of clouds passing over receding tidal flats, the darkened bulwarks of sea turtles rising to the surface, the seabirds pinned to the updrafts. He had a surge of memory about being at sea with his father, an outrigger pounding through the surf, spindrift wetting his face, the beat of slit-gongs and his father chanting to a drowned uncle from the stern. He'd been woken without warning, tranced half sleeping down to the black shore where the boats bobbed against the narrow ribbon of daybreak. He was being taken along on a trading voyage, auditioned for manhood and betrothal. He would someday need to sponsor his own voyage and return with enough shell armlets to win a girl he had never seen but whose name he had known since the age of three. But when the outriggers stopped to fish in the shallows, he dropped a net and spear over the side and was made to dive in after it. After that, his paddle was taken away and his father did not speak to him for the rest of the voyage.

Now he watched the islands pass, the basalt cliffs and mangrove swamps, trying to remember the contours of Poumeta, its reefs and stony beachhead. There were the tiny surrounding islands where porpoise teeth were strung between trees and the bones of enemies lay bleaching in the sun. The pile houses were clustered by clan around the lagoon, canoes tethered beneath. He remembered following the women on the beach after his failure at sea; he'd been given back to his mother. He trailed behind her as she bent with a hoop net, flinging his reed spear at the silver clouds of minnows in the tidal pools. He lacked dexterity and accuracy and it wasn't until his mother taught him how to harvest fish by suffusing shallow pools with poisonous leaves, waiting for the stupefied fish to rise to the surface, that he caught anything. From then on he waited in the shade of a fern tree, watching the fish float up one by one, a dozen silver ghosts making the transit. He'd wondered if they possessed a vapor in their chests, whether they left their bodies during sleep. Had he been marked for religion even then?

He went with the Reverend Mister not only because his father was dead, not only because his mother and her in-laws offered him up like a machete boy for the sugar fields—one less mouth to feed and an ungainly bugger at that—but because he understood the revelation of Christ-the-Son, had understood it on first gleaning. At twelve, Jesus came to him as a half-demon conceived by an ancestral ghost. Sometimes He took the form of a wild pigeon. Why not walk on water? Why not infuse the hard lump in a man's abdomen with righteous fury? And then there was the blunt object of faith, something that could not simply be tutored and schooled but had to be uncovered like a turtle egg in the sand. Reveal the yearning for God, the jewel waiting on the mudsill of the heathen mind.

The Reverend Mister had begun the process of digging, unpeeling, molding. At suppertime, Argus sat straight-backed in starched cotton while the preacher taught him manners, clipping the boy's knuckles with the edge of a butter knife when he dropped his cutlery or let his elbows touch the tabletop. Argus listened to the rumble and drone of English with all its verbs and names until it furrowed in his mind, until the world was cleaved in two. Everything doubled, multiplied; he knew two words, two explanations where there used to be one, understood that yaws and measles were diseases of imperfect men cast down from heaven but also the result of vengeful ancestors, spurned uncles, strangled widows. He knew that a church service was a kind of séance, that the reverend administered the Lord's Supper just as a woman with a dead son could administer a call to guardian spirits. The blood of Christ and the armlet containing a piece of a murdered man's rib. The chalice and the gourd, both raised to the vengeful dead. Not just the holy revelations, either, but the practicalities of daily life. He learned to cook rice and kippers, to soft-boil an egg. He sliced toast into little spears and placed them around the edge of the reverend's china plate.

And somewhere along the way he'd learned to covet things, despite the Reverend Mister's homilies about simplicity and the emptied cup of man. In his portmanteau there were books and drawings, a watch that ran slow, shirts and ties, a spare pair of trousers and flannels, clean socks, a gun rag with money coiled inside, a gilt-edged Bible, a set of cutlery and a silver serviette ring. He remembered his boyhood on Poumeta and how the children played with bark, raffia, and reeds, keeping them only as long as the game itself, improvising dams and sailboats on the muddy river. They watched their fathers return from their epic trading voyages to the island of Tikalia, hundreds of miles to the east, armlets and dogteeth gathered in the bows of the outriggers. They rushed to the beach to cheer for the bounty. But for Argus it was playacting. He had never understood the thrill of the bracelets that connected them to the distant island. They were frequently tarnished and chipped. His father recited the provenance of each strand of shells, naming the hands through which it had passed. Meanwhile, the children kept twigs and leaves for half a day, never once amassed a bowery of fish spines or gold-flecked stones. They watched the women wash each other's hair, bathe in mallow-scented pools, and argued in the shadows over who was the tallest, oldest, or fastest. They watched the adult affairs of the village with a dedicated lack of interest. The dull litanies to the dead, the stupid haggling over pigs and brides. They were allowed to stay out until dark and were beaten only if they damaged property. The water pots and limed jugs, the shell and tooth empire, so many things were hallowed and beyond reach back then. He leaned against the schooner bulkhead, wending his way home after six years, his new life revealed in the props he carried, in the leather suitcase that belonged to a dead priest.

6.

Argus came upon Poumeta just before dark, the rowboat winking through the dusk. The *Lady Duncan* had taken him within five miles of the island, the coral reefs preventing closer passage. The seamen had lowered the rowboat from the starboard davits, the maudlin cat whining from the stern, the kanakas on deck to wave and snigger. Argus leaned into the oar strokes, into the familiar slap and draw. He had often rowed the Reverend Mister out to visiting ships or to satellite islands to interrupt séances. He could scarcely remember paddling a canoe anymore and the motion of the oars, of traveling with his back to the approaching destination, felt entirely natural. He rounded the first of the islets, coming upon the coral skirt that fanned out from the main island. A shipwrecked brig lay hogged up on the reef, its mizzenmast slanting through the falling light. He hadn't heard news of the island in several years and he wondered how long the ship had been there.

He tried to make out the estuary and the mouth of the lagoon that led to the village. He looked for signs of hearth fires, for slats of light coming through the walls of the pile houses. But he could only make out a campfire on shore, just east of the river. Perhaps there was a feast, a cousin having his ears pierced or a celebration for a returned voyage. He turned a course for the beach, keeping the cat's reproaches and the slapping of the oars downwind. The waves nudged the boat into the reef channel and he used one oar to steer the boat onto the beach. He took off his shoes and socks, jumped into the knee-high water, and dragged the boat up. The fire surged beyond the mangroves, between his landing and the village itself. He tied the cat by its collar to the iron bowring with a piece of twine. If his cousins heard a cat in the darkening thicket during a call to ancestral spirits, they might just send a bamboo spear into the undergrowth for good measure. He stashed his portmanteau in the bushes, buttoned his alpaca coat, and set off in the direction of the firelight.

Within fifty yards he heard men's voices. He crouched amid the banyans and edged forward, staying low, the voices dying away then rising again through the thicket. It was English— gruff, bawdy, sibilant, the spitting doggerel of British seamen. In a bowl of firelight the men gathered, twenty or so, torn weskits over bare chests and beards grown in, reclined against a ship's salvage—barrels of rum, crates of tinned food, an ash-smeared divan, powder kegs, crates of ammunition, a canvas sail laid out like a carpet. They passed gourds and green bottles and cigars back and forth. A suckling runt was turning over a spit and yams were baking in the coals. A dozen tents were pitched in the shadowy background, spread among planks and scantling. The taffrail had been removed from the ship and was set up like a tavern bar in a grove of trees. The men were armed with weapons of every description—rifles, old muskets, flintlocks and carbines but also bamboo spears, iron tomahawks, stone daggers. They sang in the firelight, gunmetal glinting, the bower filling with bawdy limericks and hoary ballads.

Argus leaned against a tree trunk and saw that some of the men had adorned themselves in the style of natives, ochre and vermilion lines beneath their eyes, patches of turmeric-yellow cloth over buckskin boots, shell armlets and dogtooth necklaces over torn sailcloth shirts. There were gunnysacks cinched up with kinked human hair. A black and mushroomed ear hung around a deckhand's neck. A line of smoked and shrunken Melanesian heads, eyes hollowed, mouths stricken, lay spiked on wooden stakes. On the filthy divan two Poumetan girls slumped, their eyes closed, naked except for their grass skirts. A sailor sat between them, arms slung around their necks, a breast cupped in each filthy hand. Argus felt the wind go out of him. He thought of the Reverend Mister's pigeon rifle and wished now he'd brought it. He thought of his sisters and mother and was up and running low toward the village.

He came up behind the lagoon where the folds of red clay fingered out to the ramparts and houses. The boggy trail was still there, weaving a narrow path between the broken reeds and rushes, and his feet pounded the mud as he ran. He could smell the reeking desolation long before he saw the burnt-out village. The carcasses of gutted dogs and maimed human bodies floated in the brackish water. A few houses remained, ramshackle and stripped bare on their pilings. He climbed up the stepladder to one and found a rummage of wool blankets and straw bedding. The floor slats had been pried up for kindling; clay pots and earthenware jugs lay in shards. Defecation was heaped in the corners. It was the aftermath of biblical tribes, the marauding Amalekites or Hittites, Old Testament infidels.

Argus continued on to the men's longhouse on the other side of the lagoon, his mouth open, eyes stinging, the blackened smell scorching his throat. The tambaran, hewn from teak and sandalwood, was the place of men's business. It had been decorated with an armory of engraved weapons, famed knives and murderous spears, but also the finger bones of warriors from a previous century, from a thousand moons prior; in the rafters the cauterized hearts of mortal enemies hung like roosting bats. Now it was piled with the bodies of village children. They had come up here in terror, he could see, for only an apocalypse could drive them up into the taboo dwelling, ominous on its leaning stilts, high above the swamps and coral gardens. They lay slender-armed and ball-fisted, faces stricken, huddled behind a useless armada of ornamental shields.

Argus staggered into the bush, fell to his hands and knees.

He cried out once, with his face buried in his hat. Turning on his back, he looked up into the canopy, the moonless dark pinned above a clearing. He tried to gather his thoughts but his mind felt stripped. He was aware of the coarse volcanic dirt against his fingertips and his unblinking eyes and the taste of ash in his mouth. Did the Christian soul wait behind the bludgeoned senses like a camphor flame behind mottled glass? He tried to think of something distant, concrete, and particular—the knife and fork and serviette ring in his portmanteau, the reverend's pigeon rifle, the memory of his mother teaching him to catch fish with poisonous leaves—but these grappling half-thoughts were run through with the dead children's faces. He lay breathing, staring up, formless. He whispered the begats—*Rehoboam begat Abijah, Abijah begat Asa, Asa begat Jehoshaphat*—not as prayer but to still his heaving breath.

There was a sister who'd moved away—Malini. It came to him like an awakening. She had married into a village up on the caldera. The Kuk were shy and untrusting; they had been driven into marginal lands by the warring Poumetan fishermen. They came down off the volcano only to trade several times a year, swapping sago, hardwood, and betel nut for barramundi and snapper, for twists of Louisiana trade tobacco pilfered from missionaries. He had not seen Malini since before he was ten, since the time of the child's republic, when they stayed out until dark and held reed-spear battles in the swamps, since before her head was shaved for the wedding and she'd had to cover her face when the timid Kuk father-in-law came to fetch her. Argus remembered them walking single file up the hill, a cloak over her face to avoid the taboo of seeing her husband's father's face.

Argus would walk through the night to find her. First, he would retrieve his shoes and portmanteau, drag the boat up, and tie the cat in the woods until morning. He stood and fumbled through the dark, listening to the break of surf to make his way.

7.

Argus reached the outskirts of the bush settlement in the dawning light, the raucous birds teeming overhead. He stumbled forward with his portmanteau, sleepless, blundering through the vines and fledged leaves, the hardwoods strangled in fig. His feet and hands were blistered, his throat raked with thirst. He shambled out into a clearing with his ivory shirt oranged by clay, the alpaca coat strewn about his shoulders. From above him came the piping sound of roused voices and he remembered that the Kuk lived in treehouses. He craned his neck to see shadows flitting between rope walkways. The houses were carved into the bowls of trees, timbered and thatched, wound taut with sennit and rattan. The tree-dwellers called above him, chittering back and forth, house to house, until four of them emerged from the woods. The Kuk were shorter than the coastal folk and their faces were caught up with their mountainous isolation, their features narrowed and scornful, their eyes myopic from lack of visible horizon. They had matted pompadours and the septa of their noses were pierced through with crescents of pearl shell; they wore rope belts and penis gourds and carried rifles and iron tomahawks. In the days of Argus's childhood they were known for their blowguns and arrows fletched with bowerbird plumes. The guns had no doubt been traded up from Poumeta, come ashore from trading voyages, swapped for canarium nut and virgin brides.

As they approached warily, Argus put his hands in front of him and looked at the ground, signaling submission. The warriors sidled up crabwise, guns poised. One of them slowly removed Argus's straw hat, exposing the brilliantine worn to dull wax. They stared, spat in the dirt, considered his ravaged church clothes. Was he a black missionary flung out? A deranged Malay halfblood wandering alone on the caldera? A vengeful ancestor, a ghostly bastard from the smoky lagoons? He could see it in their whited eyes. Argus pointed to his left wrist, where a tribal scar ridged against the surface—a shark tooth singed into the flesh, its jagged contours like the head of a delta where the veins met and divided. It was not an initiation scar but a brand of clan affinity. The Poumeta were known for catching reef sharks in rattan nooses then clubbing them in the shallows. Shark teeth were among their most prized objects. One of the warriors recognized the mark and said, "Poumeta fella?"

The Kuk hadn't known a word of pidgin when Argus lived in the village.

"Malini," Argus said. "Sisa Malini."

They ignored him and began touching his ragged clothes, prodding his trouser legs with the muzzles of their rifles. The Poumeta and the bushmen were no longer sworn enemies but had become reluctant traders of goods and brides. Nonetheless, they remained suspicious of each other's coy houses and livelihood and weapons. They shared a dim but collective memory of the days of their forefathers, when villages were raided and burned, when kidnapped girls were taken into men's clubhouses to be shackled and whored. Argus looked into their walled eyes, repeating his sister's name. There was something between them he could not name, a need for atonement from generations ago. A few of the women and children began emerging cautiously from the trees, edging forward, clumping sago from coconut bowls, infants nursing and slung on hips. Malini approached slowly, blinking in the early sun, her hair dreadlocked and braided with flowers. It was clear she was embarrassed by having to lay claim to the vagrant who'd wandered up the caldera in stolen clothes. He studied her feet, avoiding the tenacity of her naked breasts. The reverend had taught him the tenets of Calvinist modesty like a string of phrasal verbs and now he couldn't help but look away, slightly appalled but also annoyed by his own prudishness. She spoke softly to the four warriors and they took a few steps back, their weapons dropping to one side. She was a foot taller than the men, Argus noticed, clearly a Poumetan pureblood among the tree-dwelling pygmies.

She led him to a fire pit and they sat cross-legged. The villagers gathered and circled at a distance of twenty feet. She spoke their childhood language, quietly at first and in the clipped style offered to vexing children. But then she warmed and brightened. He hadn't spoken Poumetan for six years and it came in a halting rush, his mouth now slackened by English. He mispronounced *forest* and *volcano* while recounting his overnight ordeal, his sister's eyes skipping a beat on each botched word. Despite her own years of absence, she spoke their native tongue perfectly. He'd spoken Poumetan in his mind every day for years, a locked room where not even the Reverend Mister could find him, but now it was a hash of half-words and ideas without names. He looked at his hands and tried to puzzle it out. The lack of distinction between *he* and *she* and *it,* the merged pronouns, the occasional and odd formality of *thou art my brother* and *I am thou sister,* something he heard now through the marching rhythms of Shakespeare, plucked from so many nights of *Macbeth* and *Hamlet* read aloud from the captain's chair. But wasn't there also affection in those elevated greetings, a sense of absolute kinship? Everything was stated roundside, drifts of words that died away, weakened into implication and repetition, again *thou art my brother* and *I am thou sister,* like a renewal of vows. He tried to tell her about the village and the dead children in the longhouse but she said: "Do you remember the time our father took us to harvest honey?"

"No."

"Don't tell lies."

"The wild bees living on a cliff face?"

"Us girls at the bottom fanning a green fire to send up smoke. The bees were supposed to fall asleep."

He said, "I still don't like the taste of honey. I like white sugar now."

"You came down with a dozen stingers in your arms and belly."

"And you and our mother pulled them out one by one."

She nodded once, drew a series of lines in the dirt with a twig. He watched her thin, bony fingers and wondered if she had ever held a pencil.

She said, "They came from the ship, crawling across the coral with the swimming rats. We tried to help our cousins but then the sickness came and the fish were gone. People are dying in the trees from fevers and measles. We put them all up in one tree like a bigfella hospital. We give them blankets and water and wait for them to die with the devilment."

He looked off at a lone treehouse that was set apart and saw some of the fevered propped against branches and limbs, their skin sallow, eyes flatly regarding the siblings between walls of clay and reed. The yam and taro gardens smoldered in the background, swidden mounds and swales of smoking earth. He was brought rainwater and fried bananas and he listened to the story of the shipwreck. The bearded barbarians floated into the village on barrels and deck boards and were taken in. It wasn't until they salvaged the ship that the weapons were brought ashore. They were given the beach to make camp and began organizing a rescue mission; a team of whaleboats rigged up with sails was going to make for New Ireland. But then the rum madness began and the pox and the fever. The bush villagers watched from the edges of the forest, deciding what to do, while the Poumetan elders hid the women and children in the mangrove swamps. The seamen began fighting with each other, voices pounding through the gun-smoke, and then something took up in their midst, a mangled fear of dying on the black beach or the native bloodthirst of English-men far from home. They promptly razed the village, raped the women and girls in the fronds and thickets, severed men's arms, and bottled the shaman's head in a glass jar as a testament. The men of the village fought to the last spear and bone-handled knife, fired what bullets they had, until everything went quiet and still. She was ashamed to say that some of the Kuk had stolen from the beach while the battle was going on, that instead of fighting for the fishermen they retreated into the forest with woolen blankets and tinned beef. And now a third of the Kuk were dying. Men woke in the middle of the night, their lips blue and trembling with plague and the reprimands of dead uncles. There had been so many bodies that they tossed them into the volcanic pit, amid the belching sulfur plumes. Argus listened and watched her scratch the dirt.

"My husband is in that tree," Malini said, pointing with her chin.

"And your children?"

Without looking up she whispered the Poumetan word *mar-lok*: barren.

"What will you do?"

She let out a sigh that ended in resigned laughter. "Learn to become a good widow. Carve wooden bowls all day like a leper. Wear breast bands and cut my hair. Hide from my mother-in-law. A terrible woman."

Argus laughed, too.

She said, "Did you find a Christian wife?"

"Not yet."

"Because you wear filthy rags. You look like you stole another bird's feathers."

"I need to wash them."

"Burn them and put a lime gourd on your penis."

She said it matter-of-factly but they both blushed and looked off into the undergrowth.

"Little brother . . ."

"Sister."

"What will happen now?"

"I don't know, but I am going to pray to Jesus Christ and Mother Mary."

"Are they dead or living?"

"Both."

The villagers looked on. Someone brought them some pepper leaf and they chewed it, sitting through long silences. Argus couldn't stop thinking about the two girls on the beached divan, about the dead children in the clubhouse. He wanted to do more than pray. He wanted the fortitude of Celtic saints, the fury of crusading moguls, the bloodlust of headhunters in the Papuan highlands, anything except the timid watchfulness burrowed inside him. His desire to think and pray, to float clouds of possibility in his mind, felt like a weakness. Could something be done in God's name? He looked at the warriors and imagined them in battle. There were a dozen guns in plain sight, a stash of tomahawks and spears and slingstones. They were lean, short, broad-shouldered, godless, but he would tell them it was better to die fighting than to die of fever and cholera and shitting blackwater up in a tree. He would tell them that the last two women of Poumeta were being kept prisoner, raped by barking Englishmen, and that once they died the bloodline would vanish. No more coastal brides. He would stand in front of them and bring the Reverend Mister back from the dead, lean and call as if from the pulpit, evoke the catechism of fire and the blood of the lamb. He would speak of blinding vengeance, wound for wound, burning for burning, the Exodus code that righted all things for the Israelites. Never mind they'd think the Israelites were a fabled tribe on the Papuan mainland, out beyond the Sepik River. For three hundred Sundays Argus had watched the Reverend Mister fill with the demon-breath of his sermons, down a shot of whiskey after breakfast, mumble *shitfire* to himself when he thought the boy couldn't hear, then march up the hill to the tin roofed church in his Inverness cape. The shoulders carried the message, the voice pitched like a zither in the rafters, and then came the offertory of pigs and breadfruit, an outpouring not just for tobacco but for protection from the wrath above. Six years of sitting in the front pew, lighting votaries and waiting patiently for the singing of hymns, he knew every sermonic rhythm cold. He got to his feet and took a step forward. The village circle moved in, sensing he was about to speak. The sick and dying looked down from their tree-line parapets as he made the sign of the cross, which to the Kuk seemed like an anointment before death.

8.

They came down from the caldera in the predawn fog, swift and quiet, their faces daubed with ash and vermilion, blackened pig grease in the hollows of their collarbones, a motley infantry in dog-fur pelts, bearing cutting rasps and rifles, makeshift weapons hewn from barrel staves and boar tusks. Their hair was oiled and clayed; they wore hornbill beaks as talismans against defeat and cowardice. Argus strode in front with a pin-fire revolver and a dagger, dressed in fresh flannels, leading them in the holy war against the shipwrecked and the damned. He could imagine the Kuk on horseback, mounted on sorrels with their flanks ribbed white, sabers and lances held aloft, something lifted from a rectory oil painting, a medieval battlescape and field of dying souls. Instead of an eastern foe it was a band of western drunkards and infidels waiting to be slain, barnacles on the hull of the British Empire. This was *comeuppance*—what a strange English word—not just for the death of his family but for a century's blood in the name of sandalwood and indigo. Did the Doctrine of the Elect extend to the haggard circles of the heathen wronged? Could a clansman kill in God's name without ever kneeling in prayer? Argus looked out from under his hat brim, willing himself forward. There was no turning back. Twenty women, his sister included, trailed behind with provisions, sharpened rocks, jugs of water, his scuffed portmanteau carried like a stone tablet. He had roused them with nothing but fire speak, intoning the dead reverend, trembling in his alpaca coat. He knew he wasn't much of a warrior—he'd never been in a fistfight but had a decent aim

from so many twilight pigeon hunts. The Kuk didn't look into
each other's eyes the whole way down the volcano.

At the outskirts of the encampment they waited in the
trees amid the screaming parrots and throbbing tree frogs. The
Englishmen slept in weskits and native adornments, their faces
and hands smeared with guano to ward off pollywogs and gall
nippers. A fire pit smoldered with fish bones and an iron stewpot.
The Poumetan girls were still tied to the divan with lengths of
rattan, their grass skirts gone and their wrists welted and swollen.
Argus could see Mr. Nibbles under the tattooed arm of a midshipman, the cat peering out, the only wakeful thing among them.
They had found the rowboat. He whispered to his comrades to
take up position in the trees and ten of them climbed tropical
chestnuts with blowguns and single-barrels. He told the women
to place the rocks in piles and retreat to the hillside. They cocked
their rifles and waited for the sailors to waken; killing a man in
his sleep would bring a thousand-year curse. Argus counted
the Englishmen's guns, hatchets, and knives, tallied the boxes of
ammunition. No doubt they had expected to be at sea for up to
a year and it showed in their armaments. The element of surprise
was all the natives had but then he saw another option lurking in
the pandanus and underbrush.

He told the warriors to wait for him and took off running
into the woods, weaving between the bracken ferns, back into the
marshy hollows of his childhood. The volcanic soil turned to mud
and soon it was a bog hemmed in by overgrowth, orchids and air
plants perched above a riot of vines and leaves. He began collecting
seeds and shoots, plucking plants that he knew by name and color
and texture. Sometimes the poison announced itself in the iridescent vein-work of a leaf or a fiery berry or the foamy sap that bled
from the severed ends, but mostly it was invisible and scentless, a
plant venom that tasted no worse than burnt sugarcane. He carried the poisonous salad back to the warriors, who had expected
him not to return. He dipped the shredded plants and seeds into

a water jug and squeezed them over a piece of curved bark. The tincture was blue-green and a hundred times more potent than anything used on fish. He carried it forward in the makeshift bark bowl like an offering. They watched him from the shadows, eyes dilated, skeptical, resting rifle butts against their greased shoulders, one man with his jadeite axe at the ready.

Argus rolled up his pants and went barefoot into the clearing, walking on the sides of his feet. The sailors slept on pieces of canvas, in tent doorways, on salvaged hammocks slung between trees. He looked at each ruddy face and huddled body in succession, not only to catch any sign of waking but to mark them off as dead. He thought of Scottish Highlanders with claymore swords keening the air, the ancestors of the Reverend Mister bearing down on English mongrels as bearded and barbarous as Vikings. The ground was strewn with shell casings and pig bristle and he had to step over several broken bottles. Beside the fire pit was a water barrel and he poured half the tincture into it and then the other half into the pot of charring stew. The girls on the divan were only a few feet away and he quietly threw a seedpod, making contact with one girl's ankle. She stirred, looked up, did not speak. He removed his hat so she could better see his face. He raised a finger to his lips then remembered this meant nothing to a Poumetan. He pointed to the water and the food, shaking his head vigorously, arms crossed at the forearms. The glazed and wounded look in her eyes affirmed nothing. Argus flashed her his tribal scar, turned, and headed for the trees where gun muzzles and spear points trained out of the foliage, providing cover. Mr. Nibbles squirmed from the arms of a murderer and began mewing just as Argus got to the edge of the clearing. One man stirred in a hammock, letting his mite-bitten and filthy feet dangle from the sides. Another man adjusted the slouch hat that was covering his face. The cat called out in hunger or recognition and a tree-dweller inhaled behind his blowgun and aimed at it. The cat quieted just as Argus walked free of the clearing and retreated into the woods.

After some time the Englishmen began stirring, stretching in the early light, hands on paunches and privates, dipping tin cups into the water barrel or scraping the caked stew out of the pot with stubby fingers. The girls were offered water and Argus was relieved when they refused. Not everyone imbibed the poison but within minutes a dozen sailors were racked with pain, bent and writhing on the ground. A couple more followed suit, retching on all fours then staggering off to shit in a bamboo thicket. Someone yelled *poisoned!* at the top of his lungs and this gave rise to bedlam, sailors reaching for their rifles and firing rounds into the air and the trees, someone hurling a shoe at a shipmate yammering obscenities from a hammock. Before long, men were wandering in circles like almshouse inmates, braying and wailing, limp at the knees, hands batting at their own heads. The men still standing spun and reeled with their shotguns, firing at will, while Argus and his fellow ambushers held cover in the dappled light of the woods.

A demented sailor lurched for the native girls, a tomahawk raised, and Argus uncoiled his little pinfire revolver, some keepsake no doubt bartered from a British sloop, and shot the man in the back of the head. The bullet felled the sailor, the hatchet still raised in one hand. He buckled, bowed, fell back into the fire-pit embers. Without Argus's say-so, the snipers opened fire, unleashing arrows and blow darts and buckshot. They burst screaming into the encampment, wielding crude truncheons and clubs at the stricken and shooting the able-bodied where they stood. Several dazed and wounded Britons ran for the black beach and the clansmen gave chase like swineherds, bringing the sailors down with barbed spears and iron bludgeons at the water's edge. A wrack of sea foam crimsoned with blood and Argus thought of the shark kills from his youth, the sound of gnashing teeth as the argonauts were noosed into shore, the villagers whooping as the giant fish drowned on air.

Argus came forward to cut the girls free of the divan. Bodies lay everywhere, darkening the sandy dirt, the air thickening with the smell of human offal and excrement. He took up a knife and cut the rattan from the girls' wrists and ankles. Their lips were parched white and they could not speak. Their throats were bruised raw. He placed his alpaca coat over their trembling bodies and called to the women in the brush, who came into the clearing with water and taro cakes. Malini tended them, murmuring softly in Poumetan, dipping a finger into her water jug and running it over their lips. The warriors came back from the beach sated and out of breath. A few of them had been injured and they walked around the encampment and put the few living Englishmen out of their misery. Argus saw Mr. Nibbles's prone body lying in the bushes. Somehow he'd been caught up in the crossfire. Argus was relieved that he wasn't the direct cause of the cat's death and pitied the man who'd blown the stray dart or wielded the errant club.

They burned the bodies on the black beach, lighting a funeral pyre with thatch torches, the bodies piled three deep. Watch and trouser pockets, what was left of the marooned sailors' clothes, had been picked over, fobs taken, engraved teaspoons and locket photographs laid out on the sand for later dispersal, each warrior with a kill to his name laying claim to the specifics. Argus claimed a good pair of boots, size 11, from a dead man's feet. The flames bristled, billowed foul smoke, flared with bursts of cotton and hair. The warriors watched the cremation, grimly satisfied, while the village women retreated to the shelter of the forest to care for the Poumetan girls. A few of the Kuk punted out in canoes to the reefed ship, their strokes ungainly, and set the whole thing ablaze. It went up like a tinderbox. The forecastle plumed yellow then orange and the mizzenmast candled with flame. Shreds of sail-cloth flapped and came away from the mastheads in delicate, fiery tendrils, sending a spray of cinders downwind. The planking and hull went up next, the timbers splintering and the hobnails popping under pressure, debris hissing into the sea. The brig broke then fell apart, toppling into the shallows above the reef, her bell clanging mournfully on the coral reef. The men returned to shore and took their torches to the village, burning what was left of the pile houses and leveling the men's longhouse to smoking stumps. They sang and called while they worked and it became clear to Argus that they intended to rebuild the village as their own. No longer pushed up the caldera where the sun had to be mined through the canopy, they would learn to fish and hollow out tree trunks for canoes.

When the commotion died down, Argus went in search of his rowboat and found it dragged into the woods. In the morning, after the victory feast, he would begin rowing, pulling himself between islands, looking for work in a mission school or house. Perhaps he would return to the Presbyterian island of Nimburea to see if a new preacher had arrived. He still had a complete set of clean clothes in his portmanteau and he would camp wherever the locals allowed him, reading Exodus and *David Copperfield* by candlelight. He saw his sister coming down the beach with her woven bag over her shoulder. He could tell from her determined step, from the way she swung her arms and held her head, that she was going to abandon her dying husband and avoid the penance of widowhood. There was no waiting until the morning. They would have to leave while the pile houses still burned.

III

BY RAIL AND BY SEA

9.

Owen and Adelaide were saying goodbye at the train station when Jethro Gray and his farewell party arrived with a caravan of luggage. Hale Gray and his wife, an entourage of cousins, aunts, uncles, and grandparents, all of them dressed as if for the races, fanned out behind a grumbling porter as he parted the crowds with a cart of kidskin valises. Jethro trailed behind, hands in pockets, walking under a straw kady with a red club stripe.

"That must be the heir," said Adelaide, forcing a smile.

"God help us," Owen said, glancing over.

They fell in behind the procession and made for the outbound platform. The air brimmed with steam whistles and the smell of burning coal. Passengers and well-wishers milled, waited, held hands, kissed, sang anthems, waved kerchiefs like tiny white flags. Owen and Adelaide walked toward the Union Pacific's *Enterprise*, a predominantly immigrant train that would change to Central Pacific rails in Utah, carrying hundreds of Europeans westward on wooden benches, toward the promise of California. Up ahead, Owen saw the Gray party stop beside a Pullman sleeper car that had been appended to the dining compartment at the rear of the train. The sleeper was funereal in its splendor, something lifted from a statuary yard—a chassis like greened copper, punched through with rivets, the sash windows opaline with the midday light. From what Owen could ascertain, there were a dozen first-class sleeper passengers and they gave each other curt nods as the porters, harried as coolies in a plantation field, scrambled to load their suitcases, tennis rackets, and fishing poles into the baggage car. Hale Gray, smoking a meerschaum pipe in a fawn-colored peacoat, a train schedule rolled in one fist, turned on his heels and made eye contact with Owen. Jethro stood next to him, thin, tall, fingers idling beneath his raglan sleeves, following his father's gaze.

"Ah, Mr. Graves, we were wondering when we might see you," said Hale, letting the pipe shank rest on his lower lip. He swiveled thumb and forefinger to point the pipe at his offsider. "Jethro here is champing at the bit to get moving. A few of us took the liberty of adding a Pullman and a dining car to the back of the old iron horse. Hope that suits."

Owen looked down at the porter clambering through a doorway with a giant trunk.

Hale said, "Jethro's packed along a few cameras and books."

"So I see. This is Adelaide Cummings." A brief pause. "My fiancée."

Hale leaned into a shallow bow but looked a little surprised. "Delighted."

"Very pleased to meet you," said Adelaide.

Jethro pursed his lips in a polite smile, wiped his hands down his shirtfront. "Pleased to meet you both. I've saved you a seat and a berth, Mr. Graves. I have some maps I'd like us to look at together. I sent away to the National Geographic Society." The son was bread-faced, ash blond, high in the forehead and pink in the cheeks, had a small, nervous mouth that seemed uneasy about the excursions of the tongue. He licked his lips between sentences—a country parson on the brink of his first sermon.

"Please, call me Owen. That's very kind of you but I'll be riding second class." He shot his gaze from son to father, tightened his hold on Adelaide's elbow.

"Up with the Polacks and the chickens, Mr. Graves?" said Hale, amused, letting his words ride a plume of pipe smoke. "How noble."

"I'll feel right at home," said Owen.

Hale said, "I give you until Nebraska before you come back here for the feather pillows. One time I slept all the way through the Middle West. Woke up in the Black Hills of Wyoming and was promptly handed a glass of rye on ice. Luxury is good for the economy, Mr. Graves."

"Well, once we're on the ship we'll be living like sardines. Might as well get used to it. If you take a water closet and turn it on its side—that's about the parameters of a seaman's berth."

Jethro worried the space beneath his cuffs with his nail-bitten fingers.

The conductor bellowed *all aboard,* walking down the platform, and the passengers began taking to the footboards. Mother and son said goodbye and Jethro was passed through a receiving line of stout uncles and their teary wives. Owen guessed the heir was less than five years younger than himself, but he could pass for a gangly adolescent.

Hale leaned close to Owen, his breath smoky with tobacco and single malt. "Hope you have the list. And remember, no double-dealing. Nothing off this voyage can go to the chalk burners at the Field Museum. We have an understanding on that front and you'll find it stipulated on page twenty-two of the contract." He offered his hand and they shook. "Don't let the scarecrow fall overboard or get murdered by a savage. He's the only son I have and I intend to see him rise to the occasion."

"I'll do my best," Owen said.

Hale turned to the familial sobbing and farewells. "Enough tears! Let the boy board the train!"

Owen took Adelaide by the arm and said *I'll see you aboard* as he passed Jethro. Let him wonder whether he meant aboard the train or aboard the ship in San Francisco. They made their way toward the engine, catching sight of the mail and baggage compartments, the reefer-holed boxcar said to be carrying fruit and supplies, up along the immigrant cars that were clad in peeling timbers. Faces and hands pressed against the smoky windowpanes of the second-class cars. Goodbyes in a dozen languages. Owen threw his duffel bag over his shoulder and kissed Adelaide on the mouth.

Adelaide toed the platform with one shoe, blinking back tears. "Eat plenty of limes and keep off the island women."

"Will do."

"My parents will come for the wedding. A year from now in the spring. Do you think you'll remember?"

"I have a feeling you'll remind me once or twice. We'll write as before?"

She said, "I've already written the first letter in my head."

He felt her arms through his coat, an insistence at his rib cage. The steam whistle blew shrill and loud and they kissed again. He turned for the footboard just as the train rocked and began. He jumped into the carriage, leaned out the doorway, arms folded, watching Adelaide diminish in the farewelling bustle. This had been their pact: no warship waves or hand-blown kisses and no trotting alongside the moving locomotive. They wanted to downplay the goodbye, reduce its status and therefore the coming absence. She adjusted her hatpins, elbows reared, looking slightly put out by the mob scene. People hurried and funneled around her, ladies in satins, velvets, chintzes, furs, hats topped with ostrich feathers, giving her a wide berth, creating a traffic island where she stood in her pale gray frock and simple felt hat. It was a Sunday afternoon in August and she was on her way to teach unmarried Bohemian girls how to sew.

The *Enterprise* rattled through the shoreline switchyards, jolted and clanged through a hundred strands of interconnecting trackage, the brakemen watching for drifters and hobos, surveying every standpipe, signal box, roundhouse, and water tank for a potential ambush. *No free rides* was company policy and the conductor was docked for unticketed passengers. A trio of newsboys moved through the cars for an hour, selling the afternoon papers, gum, lollipops, cigarettes, cigars, bricks of soap, alighting at a station on the thinning cusp of the city. The train gained momentum then sped out of the urban rim, out from the hundred-acre skirt of stockyard, slaughterhouse, and foundry, where the gray-stone and redbrick factories gave way to cattle sheds and cedar barns. The smells turned to alfalfa and the heady ammonia of fertilizer and dung. To keep the air circulating most of the windows had been opened in second class and an occasional up-slant of dust or a flurry of concession tickets and leaves was drawn inside. Blasts of coal smoke and the shudder of the boiler rushed in from outside. Owen sat with his feet on his duffel bag, slumped on a bench beside a sleeping Dutch girl, her head bouncing against his arm. The parents sat opposite, a mustached father peering over horn-rims at a homeland newspaper, a bonneted mother knitting and occasionally looking over to ask in halting English if the girl's head was getting too heavy. Owen assured her all was fine and stared out at a field of high and tasseled corn.

The press of human bodies and the low wooden ceiling of the carriage reminded him of quarters below deck. Up above the seats were crude couchettes, plank-board bunks cantilevered from the wall and suspended with iron rods. A few passengers, mostly women and children, lay in these tiers with brought-along bedding and straw pillows they'd purchased from a trackside vendor for a dime. Feet, arms, fingers, every now and then a child's drowsy face, appeared over the bed railing. Two teenage sisters played a game of cribbage and gossiped at the end of the carriage, leaning into the aisle from their bunks, two griffins holding forth above the door to the convenience. At the other end of the car was a rusting anthracite stove that was mercifully unlit, but come suppertime Owen supposed there would be a steady stream of improvised dinners, skillets, and frypans emerging from underfoot. His plan was to buy his meals from the immigrants who'd brought along hampers and pails of food. The train would stop briefly for the second-classers to purchase dinner, but for a few coins he was told he could obtain enough bread, hash, onions, sausage, and eggs to see him through the night.

Just before nightfall some of the wooden blinds were lowered but Owen kept his open, watching the Iowa farms pass by, the split-rail fences and grain silos, the plain houses coming alight in the growing, hemispheric darkness. A New York Irishman was passing around a bottle of bourbon and Owen took a swig, avoiding the clucking stares of the Dutch couple across the way. The girl was still asleep on his shoulder. He drank from the bottle slowly, careful not to wake her, then handed it back into the aisle. Some Germans started up with a fiddle and there was a bout of singing. Owen bought some pork sausage and cold rice from a woman selling food from a tin pail. He felt himself drift toward sleep, his reflection framed in the window, the blackened prairie unbroken by farmhouse lights. He pulled the blind shut and leaned against his coat as a makeshift pillow.

Somewhere in Nebraska, not yet midnight, Owen was jolted awake by Jethro, lank and stooped, shaking him by the shoulders.

"It took me half an hour to make it back here. Crossing between cars is a feat of courage, let me tell you," Jethro said. He was still wearing his punter's hat.

Owen could see that Jethro was drunk, pink-cheeked. Someone hollered *keep it down* from an overhead couchette.

"What are you doing?" Owen sat up.

The Dutchman gave him a brimstone stare, his head angled against the shutter.

Owen stood and the daughter immediately stretched horizontal across the bench. He led Jethro to the back of the carriage. They stood, rocking, by the door that opened out to the groaning coupler head.

Jethro said, "I nearly got into a wrangle in the Chinese car. I stepped on somebody. Entirely an accident. Scuffle avoided, however. Good thing I was runner-up in the varsity boxing championship. Welterweight, in case you're wondering what class."

"What are you doing here?"

"I'm deep in a winning streak." He drummed his fingers in his trouser pockets and jounced on his feet.

"What are you talking about?"

"Poker in the first-class lounge. I'm up fifty dollars."

"Jesus, you woke me for that?"

Jethro took his hands from his pockets and raised them over his head, touching the ceiling, breathing to a silent count, as if he'd crossed a dozen cars for some calisthenics. "Between games and needed a stretch. Clears the head. Would you mind coming along to watch?"

"I don't think so."

Shoulders squared, conspiratorial, he said, "One of the players—I saw something under the table . . ."

"Legs?"

"The banker's son has lost nine hands in a row." Jethro glanced down the corridor of hanging limbs and shifting bodies, suddenly appalled. "I think he has a pistol attached to his ankle."

Owen waited for more information but when none came said, "And?"

"Well, I suspect having someone else on the home team might be the way to go."

Owen let his eyelids close for a second. "This isn't a regatta."

An old lady, trying to sleep nearby, let out a mortal sigh.

"Please," Jethro whispered. "The steward is staying up just for the game. The banker's kid is paying him hand over fist to keep the food and anti-fogmatics flowing."

Owen turned away, unable to look at him. "Aw, Jesus, I feel sick in my guts. I don't even know where you've come from. Have you ever been on a boat?"

"I rowed as well as boxed in Cambridge."

"I may be ill."

Jethro placed a collegial hand on Owen's shoulder. "Just sit in a chair and watch."

"I'd rather jump off this train than watch two rich boys gamble their fathers' money away."

Jethro gave his trouser pleats a tug. Nothing jangled and Owen guessed that he didn't bother carrying change. Copper and nickel were beneath him.

"If I come down there I intend to get dealt into the game. Understand?"

"Whatever you want."

Owen opened the door and stepped out onto the bridgeway where the metallic bawl hit him in the chest—the undercarriage grinding along the steel rails, the concussive tamping of the air brakes, the boiler and smokebox rasping from behind, unseen, barreling them through moonless Nebraska. Below his feet, Owen could see a spindrift of hot sparks against the chip-stone ballast and he thought briefly of wreckers soldering, of the tin and lead patchwork that his father sometimes did to prevent a truss from falling on his men. Churning machines always reminded him of his father. The smell of scorched oil. A life spent tied to the turning wheel.

They passed in and out of the immigrant cars without talking, stepped through the tunnel of human limbs and wool blankets. Between each car was a five-second slat of rushing dark and steel, Owen in front, Jethro off-balance, clutching his straw hat with one hand. They passed through the stately dining car and arrived at the Pullman sleeper and lounge with their hair wild, jackets disheveled, dustings of soot on the lapels. The sleeping compartments were drawn behind velvet curtains and they gingerly made for the far end of the carriage. Four men sat at a table in the lounge area. It was hard to believe this was the same train, that this tube of mahogany and velvet was being wrenched through the Midwest by the same blackened boiler. It was a drawing room in miniature—heavy drapes, ornate mirrors, plush carpets, wicker chairs, a barrel ceiling with carved moldings. The movement of the train seemed inconsequential, a distant, clicking pleasantry. The sour-looking steward, a tray in one hand, stood by the double doors that were open at the absolute rear of the car and train. A trackside balcony hung over the flashing rails and he stared down at them, perhaps contemplating his life in the diminishing ties.

"Scotch, please," Jethro said to the steward. The middle-aged man moved slowly to the liquor cabinet.

"Would you make that two?" Owen added.

Jethro said, "Ah, gentlemen, this is Owen Graves. Head trader for my voyage. He'd like to join us, if that meets with no objections."

They nodded, turned their drinks.

"Twenty-dollar buy-in," said the youngest and Owen knew right away he was the banker's son. He sat in his shirtsleeves, collar open, face freckled and burning. His ginger sideburns drew attention to his pointed jaw.

Owen took out a twenty-dollar bill and threw it on the table. A barrel-chested man in a Stetson changed it out and handed him small banknotes. The steward approached with their drinks and they moved a few paces away from the table to meet him. Jethro gave Owen some brief, whispered details of the men: Clarence Milford, rancher from Abilene, wealthy by dumb luck, has a tell like a Fourth of July parade, watch the fingers on the Texas A&M class ring; Arty Bloomberg, department store baron, sore at losing but with a decent bluff; Winthrop Kronen, undertaker and owner of a funeral parlor consortium, has been trying all night to sell the Texas kingpin a plot to call his own; Wilson McCarthy, heir to a banking empire, and at some point take a look and confirm that's an ankle holster under the table. They returned with their drinks, sat between Clarence and Arty. Clarence was talking about some recent dental work he'd had done.

"An eight-dollar filling seems about the going rate to me, gents. But this bonesetter in Chicago had me down for fifteen apiece and now I have a mouthful of mercury and metal. Feels heavy when I talk." He hinged his jaw open to give them better vantage of his molars.

The mortician had a shock of perfect black hair, small and neat teeth, a tiepin of gold crossed shovels. He leaned forward on his elbows. "Earthly reminders are everywhere, Clarence."

"Oh, digger, please!" said Clarence.

"Teeth and bones."

"I'm not drunk enough for this vaquero. It's like the day of the dead at that end of the table."

The undertaker shrugged, bit his bottom lip, settled back in his chair. He drew up his cigar from the side like a smoking sword from a scabbard.

Arty fingered his dwindling stack of bills, morose, touching the presidential portraits with the tip of his pinky. His burgundy tie was so tight it jutted from his neck near to a right angle.

"Shall we begin again?" Jethro asked with too much glee.

"We've been waiting half the night," said the banker's son, letting his ice clink in his glass.

Clarence said, "Seems we took a spell. Any longer and Winthrop was going to sell me a mausoleum, bury me like a goddamn emperor. Let's proceed. Feels like midnight. Second shift. The dentist had me on the ether and I felt nothing but the blood being drained from my billfold. Let's see, now, for the sake of the newcomer . . . stud horse poker with a five-dollar bring-in. No limit. No variations. That sound congenial to you, Owen Graves?"

"Yes, sir." It was a lackluster game, he knew, but at least there was no limit. It relied on patience more than skill at bluffing, with all but one card showing.

Clarence dealt them each a facedown followed by a faceup. Wilson had the lowest upcard—a four—and placed his bring-in five dollars in the center of the table. He passed on betting more.

The undertaker, a mouthful of smoke, said, "Consider the peace of mind that comes with prudent action. A burden lifted from the grieving."

"Shut your crumb-hole, Winthrop. You're making me grum," said Clarence, puckering.

They each called and Clarence burned a card and set it to his left. He dealt them each another card faceup, Owen now with a queen and ten visible. He surveyed the open cards and raised to ten dollars. Jethro called with his king and ten showing. Arty—six and nine visible—folded with a flourish, his cards spinning across the table. The banker's kid cornered up his hole card and raised twenty more dollars. He was showing a jack in addition to his four. The undertaker gently moved his cards toward the muck pile. Another round of faceups and it wasn't long before Clarence, who had a seven, a nine, and a jack showing, began twitching with his class ring. He had nothing in the hole but intended to take it all the way to the river. Owen folded when he saw the flush cards he needed in Jethro's hand. The game moved briskly to a showdown between Jethro and Wilson. Jethro turned an ace over, making two high pairs, and Wilson lost with numbers and a pair of jacks. Jethro collected the pot and stacked the bills in front of him. Owen took the liberty of dropping his matches and looked under the table. Sure enough, snug against Wilson's left shin was a holster with a pearl-handled pistol in it.

Apart from a three-hand winning streak on the part of Arty, and a few wins to Owen, Jethro dominated the game. Owen watched him handle his cards, his face anxious no matter what he had before him. He licked his lips, gritted his teeth, leaned forward in his seat, touched his brow with a kerchief, raised his arms winglike at his side. He was impossible to read. Meanwhile, Wilson seethed and burned, twice went to his valise for more banknotes. He played as if sheer rage could break his losing streak. Arty drank himself silent then fell asleep in his chair. The undertaker stayed sober as a tin whistle. Somewhere in the proceedings the steward had been sent to bed and they marauded the Troy-like fortress of the liquor cabinet. For two hours they drank straight from the bottle. The mound of cash in front of Jethro was obscene—close to five hundred dollars. The night thinned out and they hit the shallows of dawn somewhere in view of the Rockies, a blue rim paling up behind the peaks. Clarence blustered into song about lonesome boundary riders and loyal dogs and got up from the table. He swaggered in the direction of the mountain view, all those cliffs and evergreen ridges off the end of the balcony rail. Winthrop was still talking, addressing the Texan's back as he lumbered away. He was needle-voiced, obdurate. Now he was saying, "The price of marble goes up and what do people do? They choose granite for the loved one. I say lock in the pink marble at today's prices."

"You're all gum, digger. Shut the hell up and come out here," Clarence called.

Winthrop got up and Owen followed him. Jethro and Wilson played on. The sun was cresting in a valley like some dim candle at the end of a hallway. Clarence threw out a hand at the wake of backlit sagebrush but said nothing. They were drunk, bottomed out, awed.

"Where do you think we are?" Owen asked.

"This is the American West," said Clarence. "Owen Graves, tell the mortician not to say anything just now."

"I think he heard you," Owen said.

The undertaker shrugged and smiled at himself. Back at the table there was a sliding chair and a brandished weapon. The moment, now that it was here, seemed inevitable. Like an eyebolt swung into place. Wilson scarlet and wordless with ire and Jethro with his hands limply in front of his chest. Neither of them looked sure of what to do next. The gun demanded some attention and a sort of escalation, so Wilson obliged with: "He's been cheating me all night. This is against all probability. Thirty-five hands in a row."

Jethro shook his head and turned to the men on the balcony.

The undertaker took a somber step forward but, for once, had nothing to say.

Owen said, "Put the gun away. He's no cheat."

But Wilson blinked hard and squinted down at the short barrel, his thumb squeezed pink.

Clarence said, "This is all disappointing me a great deal." He loosened his shoulders and reached inside his coat jacket and pulled out a Schofield revolver, its chestnut handle bent like the nape of a horse's neck, the blued iron somehow serene in the first glint of dawn. "Kid, this thing will wake the wives, not to mention poor Arty Bloomberg."

Arty continued to sleep with his head on his chest.

Clarence said, "How about putting your handgun on the table? The lawmen out this way will fry you up like a skirt steak. Be reasonable. Don't get shot before breakfast."

They all looked at Clarence's unequivocal weapon, almost a foot long, still-stocked in the air as if it were resting on a fence post. Owen could see the inner lining of Clarence's coat and made out a tailored gun pocket stitched out with canvas. It ran the length of his ribs. Wilson turned his head slowly and looked over his cocked shoulder. The rails clacked and Arty gently snored. A curtain was drawn back farther down the car and somebody's wife emerged from a sleeping nook, hair tousled, barefoot in her nightgown, tiptoeing to the washroom. She did not look back at the lounge but it was enough for Wilson to come to his senses. He placed his pistol on the table and rubbed his eyes with both thumbs. Jethro bundled up his banknotes and began jamming them into his pockets. Clarence moved to the table and picked up the firearm. "I prefer something with barrel. A dueling pistol but with caliber to say you mean it." He removed the bullets and handed the weapon back to Wilson. "You lost badly but there was no cheating at that table. I can guarantee you that. You ride the rest of the way to California with the immigrants or I'll tell the conductor what you just did. He'll have some marshals or other kinds of lawmen meet the train." The banker's son unfurled his shirtsleeves, buttoned his cuffs, but would not look Clarence in the face. They watched him walk away.

After a moment, Clarence said, "I could eat a substantial breakfast after that ballyhoo. You almost had a casket order there, Winnie."

"I believe I could have had several," said Winthrop, lightened.

Clarence said, "What time does the dining car open? I believe Jethro is buying us some eggs and bacon. Maybe some biscuits."

Jethro wiped his hands down his trousers and grinned. His neck was raked with sweat.

Owen touched Jethro's arm and said to the others, "We'll be along in a little bit."

Clarence and Winthrop woke Arty and walked him groggily to breakfast, recounting what he'd slept through. Owen stepped out onto the balcony and Jethro followed him. They stood a while without talking. The landscape was warming through with browns and grays, the low ledges of caprock and gypsum still choked with shadow. A herd of antelope fed in a low meadow and Owen counted them to over a hundred. Jethro grabbed the balcony rail and turned his back to the panorama. He had a rosette of dollar bills protruding from his coat pocket, corners up like a pressed handkerchief.

"I need a better view," said Owen.

There was a set of grab irons that ran parallel and to the left of the balcony. Owen raised his left foot and planted it on the first rung. He hoisted himself over and pulled his right foot in behind. Jethro watched him climb up to the roof of the car.

Owen pivoted his torso and sat on the edge, his feet dangling above the doorway as if wetting his feet poolside. "Are you coming up?" he called down. He didn't like the grin on Jethro's face and all those pockets full of small denominations. It bothered him. He couldn't be sure the kid hadn't cheated and if that were the case—if he was a card counter or another form of unrepentant cheat—then he'd be murdered at sea and Owen would be denied his voyage payment. Owen would be doing both of them a favor by flushing him out now.

Jethro looked up, puzzled, pretended he hadn't heard. He even went so far as to raise a cupped hand to one ear.

Owen beckoned with one arm.

Jethro blew some air between his lips and took his hands slowly off the rail. He stepped toward the grab irons and took hold of the third rung. Climbing up, his two feet steadied on each rung before the next step. He pressed his face close to the train, refusing to acknowledge the churning ground below. Owen offered him a hand when he got to the top and Jethro grabbed hold of the wrist. He hefted himself level and sat down awkwardly. For a full minute he breathed, adjusted his trousers, kicked out his legs. When the commotion subsided, Owen pointed off to a stand of ponderosa pines and wildflowers. Jethro nodded appreciatively and turned to see the train bend into a curve.

"I need to know . . ." Owen said.

"What?" yelled Jethro.

"Did you cheat?"

Jethro lifted one side of his mouth, incredulous. He surveyed the flitting landscape with a kind of skepticism. Finally he yelled back, "I've never cheated at anything in my life."

Owen cupped his hands around his mouth and leaned close. "The probability is off. So many winning hands in a row."

"They don't fool around when it comes to parlor games at Harvard. I played every night of the week. Freshmen to senior. Also twenty-one. Or *vingt-et-un* as we called it in the dorms."

Owen stared at him blankly. "Just the same, don't be winning like that when we're at sea. You're liable to end up with your throat slit."

Jethro touched his throat without meaning to. "I should lose on purpose?"

"Just to vary things."

They sat for a moment while Jethro let this revelation sink in with some heavy nodding. There was a roaring sound coming up behind them. Owen turned his head and saw the white face of a mountain bearing down the line. The middle cars were pressing into the full black of a tunnel, two feet of clearance above the train's roofline. He could feel the wind shearing out of the mountainside as the train smashed into the darkness. He took hold of Jethro's elbow and pitched off the back, a dozen feet down onto the balcony. Jethro landed in a crumpled heap, gripping one ankle. His boating hat came off and blew, end over end, onto the tracks. They watched it for a second as it righted and pinwheeled for an open meadow, its red club stripe wobbling through the sagebrush. Owen felt his eardrums flinch at the colossal wall of noise before the world shuttered to black.

10.

Argus and Malini rowed south for days across the sun-glazed straits of the Bismarck Archipelago, coming ashore at night to sleep on windblown skerries and coral atolls, huddled on nameless islands, flying foxes wheeling above their heads. They ate rats, skinks, lizards, sandpipers, crabs, whatever they could catch with their hands. Argus flinted driftwood fires and harvested rainwater from pandanus leaves. He fashioned a hat for his sister from woven reeds. It never once touched her head and she used it to gather minnows at the shoreline. Her years among the Kuk, days spent in the deep shade of strangler figs, had made her quieter, more introspective. They went hours without talking, lulled by the groan of the oarlocks and the lapping of the water. Malini thought Argus looked weak in the hot sun and whenever they landed he searched for places to sit in the dappled shade. He didn't act like a coastal boy. He kept saying in English that he was trying to collect his thoughts, and when he translated this into Poumetan for her benefit she stared at him in confusion. She watched his eyes twitch when he said grace at night and wanted to know what he could have to say to anybody before eating a fish the size of his middle finger. When they spoke it was about the missionary jobs they would both have—Argus as a houseboy and Malini as a governess or cook or laundress in a white cotton dress and apron. More than anything, Malini wanted to be around children, preferably girls with good singing voices.

Argus had obtained a compass and a chart from an island trading post but the map was full of inconsistencies and omissions.

Entire islands were missing and the nautical distances were rounded estimates. They strained down the archipelago and when the trades died off Argus pulled into flattened sheets of turquoise, passing through the hulking shadows of mountain islands, the two of them craning their necks to see stunted trees with gnarled crowns staring down from a thousand feet above. Or they saw islands cleaved in two, one side barren from volcanic outpouring and the other side teeming with life. Fields of pumice and blackened lava, cinder cones stippled with liverwort, while the other side, beyond the dominion of ash, was a mutiny of hibiscus and fern.

They steered alongside New Ireland but kept their distance because it was a traditional enemy of Poumeta. Seacoast elders and even their own father had spoken of New Irishmen with two thumbs on each hand, albinos with pink eyes, weekly earthquakes, tumbledown villages set beside boiling sulfur springs. The Lemakot in the north strangled widows and threw them into the cremation pyres of their dead husbands. If they defeated potential invaders the New Irish hanged the vanquished from banyan trees, flensed their windpipes, removed their heads, left their intestines to jerk in the sun. The reverend had confirmed these heathen atrocities. The preacher remembered navigating the New Irish coast in a steamer and the natives lining up to fire their Birmingham trade muskets at the ship, discouraging the good news of Jesus Kris from coming ashore. The New Hanover men weren't much better, the reverend said. They would sell their own children for hoop iron and Winchesters and ate smoked red clay and carried daggers in their big mops of hair. But Argus also remembered hearing stories from a seafaring uncle who spoke of the New Irish with hushed reverence for their artistry and stature, the women lithe and kilted in ocher-dyed leaves and grasses, the men ferocious, athletic, hardworking, stocking their joss houses with cowrie shell money and tortoiseshell ornaments alive with fretwork. Whether they were ungodly brutes or savagely gifted artists with beautiful wives, Argus had no desire to learn for himself.

The southeast trades came up most afternoons, smelling of salt. Argus luffed up into the wind and took shelter in leeward firths and sheltered bays. But if they were between calms and pulling in open waters there was nothing to do but ride it out, tossing over swell and spume, his shoulders and hands burning, his sister sullen and horribly seasick in the stern. The reverend had envied the Anglicans their mission whaleboats, each fitted with a lugsail and jib for windy conditions. The old man joked that it was Calvinist thrift that had given him a sentence of infernal rowing and that he lapped the oar blades through his evening prayers. When Argus lay beside his sister at night, he felt his arms pulse with the day's dip-draw passage and his dreams were all set in motion — sliding, falling, tumbling through water and air.

In the stilled waters between islets, Malini held the map over her head to keep the sun off her face. She waved gnats and flies away with one hand. He had made her wear one of his clean cotton shirts because he couldn't row with her nipples flouncing at him all day long. She kept the grass skirt and sat with her legs apart, her knees calloused and swaying. "We are dying out here," she said with no particular emotion. "The seabirds are waiting to eat our faces."

"Tomorrow, you iron clothes and learn hymns." To use the future tense in Poumetan he had to prefix everything with *tomorrow*.

"I don't want to sing hymns. I want to eat something bigger than a rat."

Argus looked into the sun-bleached distance and a line from the "Song of the Sea" came to him: *The horse and the rider have drowned in the sea.*

It rained all afternoon, a deluge that forced them to look for shelter. Drenched and exhausted, they made for an island of yew and scrub, a copse of coconut palms fringing a beach. Malini hadn't spoken to her brother for several hours and she leapt from the boat the instant it banked on the sand. She was eager to take matters into her own hands. The hunger was embarrassing, her brother a child in filthy rags. She took his leather suitcase box from the prow, took it up into a small clearing, emptied its contents into the wet sand, and proceeded to fill it with green coconuts. She remembered from her coastal days that there was more coconut water when they were unripe and the flesh was easier to pry from the husk. She would bring the coconuts along in the rowboat for the bloodiest stretches of daylight. Standing beneath each tree, she lobbed a heavy rock into the branches and took a step back as a nut landed at her feet. She knew perfectly well how to scale a tree, a custom the forest-dwelling Kuk had bestowed on their women, but out of respect for her brother she settled for the rock. Only Poumetan men were allowed to climb trees. Was he still Poumetan or was he Christian and half white?

Argus dragged the boat up and went to rescue his possessions. He made a display of collecting driftwood into a pile for a fire but knew it was too wet to catch. They would have to find dry leaves somewhere in the bush. He watched Malini lug the portmanteau up and down the beach and, once it was full of coconuts, she began gathering shellfish in the tide pools with the hat he'd made her. When she wasn't glaring back at him, he arranged his books and clothes and spread his alpaca coat in the sand for her to sleep on. The bruised clouds had cleared and the sky was high and blue again. He wrapped the Bible inside a cotton shirt and set it down as her pillow. He opened his roll of damp sketches, blew sand from the broken watch, buffed the cutlery with a hank of gun rag, and arranged his books—*The Jungle Book, David Copperfield, Kidnapped*. According to the Reverend Mister, outside of the Holy Scriptures, these made up the divine trinity and contained all the escapades, morality, and lessons in self-determination that a boy could want.

Argus recited the full and epic subtitle of *Kidnapped*—"*Being Memoirs of the Adventures of David Balfour in the Year 1751: How he was Kidnapped and Cast away, his Sufferings in a Desert Isle; his Journey in the Wild Highlands; his acquaintance with Alan Breck Stewart and other notorious Highland Jacobites; with all that he Suffered at the hands of his Uncle, Ebenezer Balfour of Shaws, falsely so-called: Written by Himself and now set forth by Robert Louis Stevenson.*" It had been a Christmas gift from the Reverend Mister in 1895 and he'd insisted on the full title whenever Argus read a chapter aloud after dinner. The long title not only honored Underwood's fellow Scotsman but acted as an incantation before the offering itself.

Argus flipped through the book to Chapter XIV, wherein David has come ashore a small islet after the shipwreck. Were there survival tips buried in those pages, instructions for setting snares or traps, something that might save Argus from his sister's nagging wrath? What he found was this:

I knew indeed that shell-fish were counted good to eat; and among the rocks of the isle I found a great plenty of limpets, which at first I could scarcely strike from their places, not knowing quickness to be needful. There were, besides, some of the little shells that we call buckies; I think periwinkle is the English name. Of these two I made my whole diet, devouring them cold and raw as I found them; and so hungry was I, that at first they seemed to me delicious. Perhaps they were out of season, or perhaps there was something wrong in the sea about my island. But at least I had no sooner eaten my first meal than I was seized with giddiness and retching, and lay for a long time no better than dead.

Argus had no idea what a *limpet* was. On Poumeta it was women's work to fish the shoreline while the men fished the open sea. It stood to reason, then, that Malini knew more of what to gather in the tide pools. He was in charge of building fires with the reverend's flint stone because it was taboo for a seacoast woman to handle flame. Argus was overcome with a desire to read more Stevenson, or to sketch, to loose himself from the present, but Malini was already striding toward him with the suitcase full of coconuts and shellfish.

"Where is the fire?" she asked.

"I need to gather dry leaves."

Malini produced a handful of twigs and pine needles. Argus dug a small bowl of sand beneath a stick of driftwood and placed them inside. He knapped the flint against a piece of granite, aiming the sparks into the bowl. Nothing caught. It was too damp. After several minutes of exasperation, Malini took up *David Copperfield*, ripped four pages from it, and placed them flat into the bowl of sand. "Now try."

Argus could not speak or look at her. He read a few lines of text upside down and saw that David was walking the road from London to Dover, sleeping at night in fields of hops. "Wait, not those," he said. He removed the frontispiece from each book but the Bible and swapped them with the excerpted Dickens. He flinted against the granite again and the pages blued with flame. Malini threw the shellfish into the kindling fire and walked off without a word.

She returned a while later with tern eggs, wild figs, and a strangled lizard, dragging several dozen pandanus fronds behind her. Argus put the big lizard into the hot coals and they ate in silence when it was cooked. He used his cutlery to cut the lizard into pieces then ate them with his hands because of the look in his sister's eyes. Malini put some driftwood ash into a husk of rainwater and let it settle. She skimmed the top layer off with a shell, poured it onto her food, and handed it to her brother: "Salt." It tasted good with the sweet smoky flavor of the hot figs.

In the fading light, they heard the gulls and terns roosting noisily in the cliff rookeries, the surf breaking on the narrow

reef. With their bellies full, their moods brightened. Malini began
weaving the pandanus leaves and Argus guessed it was to make a
new skirt or a sleeping mat. They drank warm coconut milk and
Argus removed his boots, picked up *Kidnapped* and began reading to himself. He didn't want to read any more about the island
and the shipwreck but turned to the chapter called "I Come into
My Kingdom" wherein Ebenezer admits to wanting to sell David
into slavery in the Carolinas. A book, once read from front to
back and with no skimming, could be taken piecemeal. Unless it
was the Bible, in which case it could be read according to the lesson at hand. It sometimes occurred to Argus that all the parts of
a story existed at once and that people in other places were reading ahead and behind him, the words alive and unraveled across
islands and oceans and continents.

After some time, and without looking up, Malini said, "Are
you praying again? I see your lips move."

"I am reading." In Poumetan he translated *reading* as *thinking
aloud*.

"What happens?"

"I make the words that are on the paper in my mind and
mouth."

"How do they stay on the paper, the words?"

"Ink. Like blood or the stain from a squid or octopus."

"Does it smell?"

He handed her the book and she smelled the leather cover. She
said, "Like pigs sleeping in the sun," and handed it back to him.

"Do you want me to think aloud from one of these stories?"

"Will I understand it?"

"I will make the words into our language."

"Yes, all right," she said, plaiting the fronds.

Argus read from the opening chapters of *Kidnapped*, trans-
lating into Poumetan as he went along. There were immediate
difficulties, concepts and words that had no native equivalent.
Key and *mansion*, the words *muckle* and *laird*. But why not *big*

house for *mansion* and *headman with many gardens* for *laird*? He looked up at his sister, who started to blink very slowly in the firelight. He took out *The Jungle Book*. She was briefly enthralled by the idea of a boy being raised by animals but Argus had to stop to explain at length what a wolf was. "A wild dog with a bat's face," was all he could come up with. Malini considered this a moment, clucked her tongue. "This story is impossible. Everybody knows that dogs don't like children." Argus moved another piece of driftwood into the coals and lay back on the sand. His sister didn't make any move to lie down and he was lulled to sleep by the husking sound of the leaves being woven and pulled taut.

In the morning, the sky was streaked with high clouds and sand blew up the beach. Argus stood, stretched, and saw Malini, still sleeping beside her woven mat of leaves. It was now a giant sheet and she had surely stayed up the whole night working the pandanus. He raked the coals and placed some wood in them to kindle the fire. She stirred and sat up.

Argus gestured to the mat. "What is that for?"

"The boat. If we find a bamboo pole we can use it to catch the wind."

Argus looked at the sand. She had woven a sail after living in the forest for ten years. Had she studied the seacoast fishermen from afar during her girlhood? Did she also know how to thatch a roof? He was disgusted with himself.

Softly, she said, "Will you find the bamboo pole?"

He nodded, put on his boots, and walked off, feeling her eyes on his back. He wanted to eat a piece of toast with blackberry jam, an omelet with capsicum and bacon. He missed the brown-sugared porridge and the tins of peaches. Tramping into a bamboo thicket he searched about for a fallen pole. He wanted a piece of roasted pumpkin and slices of salted tomato on a plate. A bamboo pole, dried and twenty feet long, lay on a hummock of weeds and he pried the smaller branches from it. Back on the beach he carried it like a flagpole, marching proudly. This was for Malini's benefit and she smiled enough to show her teeth when he approached. She rewarded the find with a tern-egg omelet— not exactly bacon and capsicum—boiled in a coconut husk. It was yellow-gray and smelled as bad as it looked. They choked it down and went to rig up the sail. Since the portmanteau was now full of coconuts, Argus had to carry his books and clothes under his arm. He placed them in the lockbox along with the flintstone. They fastened the woven sail to the bamboo pole and bound the mast to the middle bench with a catch of rope. Malini stood holding it square across the wind while Argus tillered in the stern with an oar. The wind came slowly, then all at once.

11.

In San Francisco they had to locate Captain Baz Terrapin, an associate of Captain Bisky, the commander of Owen's first voyage. A wire had been sent from Chicago, and the steam clipper in which Terrapin owned a majority share was now contracted. A crew of twenty-four had signed articles, supplies had been ordered, and the *Lady Cullion* was due to weigh anchor in three days. Owen and Jethro dropped off their luggage at a downtown hotel and set off on foot. Owen had been unable to convince Jethro to trim his luggage and send half of it back to Chicago by rail. He explained that a clipper was light on storage space and that extra baggage meant fewer artifacts for the return trip, but Jethro insisted that his equipment was essential. They passed an outfitters' storefront and Owen persuaded Jethro to purchase some clothes fit for seagoing, something sturdy and utilitarian. The truth was that he feared showing up to Terrapin's rooms with Jethro dressed for Sunday brunch at the clubhouse. The straw kady had been mercifully lost en route but now the raglan sleeves and the blazer were traded for blucher boots, several broadloom cotton shirts, worsted trousers, dungarees, and a serge cap. With his dandy get-up in a brown paper parcel, favoring the heels of his new boots, Jethro walked through Chinatown, tipping his cap at strangers.

They took a cable car into the Potrero District and alighted a dozen blocks from Irish Hill, the neighborhood where Terrapin was said to board. South of the shipyard and Steamboat Point, it was an enclave of workers' cottages and shacks built along serpentine hills in the lee of the Union Iron Works and the Gas & Electric Company. The bay hazed at the foot of the hillside, a muted blue-gray. The mud streets were planked and sawdusted, run through with fissures. Coalsmoke plumed out of the ironworks and the frowzy smells of gas and damp laundry were everywhere. In the murky windows of several bleak storefronts handbills advertised vaudeville and a Saturday hayrope boxing match. Owen asked for directions and made for the Big Brown House, a rooming establishment that took in San Quentin parolees and whose proprietor got them jobs in the rolling mill down the hill. Terrapin leased rooms on the top floor year-round and this was where he moored himself between voyages.

Son of a freed Tasmanian convict, Terrapin had a soft spot for former San Quentin inmates with seafaring ambitions. They worked cheap and hard and were generally loyal. He'd been commanding vessels and hauling Pacific cargo—tea, copra, teak, sulfur, Australian wool more recently—for thirty years and knew the South Sea Islands intimately, having spawned illegitimate children from New Zealand to the New Hebrides. The rumor was that he dodged creditors and ex-wives in San Francisco, running a brisk circuit between the steam beer dumps of Irish Hill and the brothels of the Tenderloin. He now owned two-thirds of the *Lady Cullion* outright and took no more than two passages a year. Trade clippers were practically a thing of the past—even if they had auxiliary boilers—but Terrapin refused to change with the times. He called the Suez Canal the Devil's Ditch and vowed to never command a steamer.

Owen and Jethro stood on the balcony where Baz Terrapin slouched against the railing, big-knuckled and half naked, a white towel around his flaccid middle. He was drinking beer before noon and staring into the mire of his glass. "I prefer bottom-fermented beers, like to taste the yeast and hops . . ." He took a swig from his jug of fizzing ale, still dripping from his daily plunge in the frigid bay. "Constitutional swim is what it is. Testicles like a pair of clams winking shut from the cold. Ah, but the heart expands and pumps . . . gets as big as a Christmas ham. Ticker of a racehorse in here." He tapped at his rib cage, grinned. His enormous girth, coupled with the constellation of scars and moles spread across his torso, reminded Owen of the barnacled hull of an ancient, waterlogged ketch. He hunkered across the balcony, a hand spread against his paunch, thumb tucked into the edge of the wrapped towel. Tattooed on each forearm was a succession of dates—*Nov 21 '82, Mar 2 '84, Jan 14 '89*, and so on—arranged in perfect columns of blue ink. He took up a small telescope from a bench seat and glassed the bay, his mouth forming a Roman arch. "I'd swim out to it just to see the look on the Alcatraz guards' faces. They got Hopi Indians out there just at the moment. Those docile mother-worshippers can't swim neither." He moved the spyglass down toward the mill and the works. "I audition crew members from up here. Spy on the Dutchmen coming out of the sugarhouse or the Scotch toppling out of the countinghouse or mechanical-repair yard. I watch the way a man walks with his mates. Way he holds himself. The Irishmen come knockin 'cause all they wants is to leave their twenty-six skirling kiddies and the pasty fat wife and sail away for a set of Tongan kanookas. If you ever worked in a steel mill you'd understand this sentiment." He swiveled his mass and lowered the spyglass.

Jethro stood in his new dungarees, holding his brown paper parcel, biting and licking his lips.

"This is Jethro Gray, the son of the underwriter, and he'll be coming aboard," Owen said. "He's a man of science, among other things."

Terrapin's face fell a little, a squint working into the sun-cracked ravines around his mouth and eyes. "Ship's surgeon? Not usual on a windjammer like this. These ain't the slavin days and the cook knows some of his medicals and surgery."

"He's no doctor," said Owen.

"What then?"

Jethro turned his serge cap in his hands. "This is my first time at sea. You can put me to use anywhere you like. I plan to take some samples. Plants and animals. I'll be the ship's naturalist."

Terrapin adjusted himself through the towel and considered Jethro Gray from head to foot. "I've taken plenty of virgins offshore, working men and prisoners who paid their dues for theft and manslaughter—won't touch rapists and arsonists, mind you, consider it bad luck on a bark to have that kind—but fuck me blue, this one's a buttercup, ain't he? Look at them fingers and hands and the milky-veined arms. He's like a custard tart."

Jethro said, "I've been studying my maps and have a good sense of direction. Maybe I could be a deckhand when I'm not studying specimens. Sleep in a hammock on the deck. Under the stars."

Owen stared down at his feet, heard the crinkle of Jethro's nervous hands on brown paper.

Terrapin leaned his massive head back and coughed up a phlegmatic laugh. When he'd regained his composure he lifted the jug of steam beer to his lips and let the situation settle on his tongue. "Makes no difference to me whether you're the King of Siam or the son of the money behind this jaunt, any new crewmate starts out before the mast, as a deckhand proper. No special treatment. You'll be scrubbing and tarring on deck, lovelace. You'll sign articles of waivering just like the San Quentin forgers and muggers. Captain Basil Terrapin and unnamed minority silent partner indemnified against all loss of life and limb et-bloody-cetera."

"My father's lawyers—" Jethro began.

"He'll sign and note that he's on my docket. Nothing happens to him without my consent," Owen said.

The captain drained his jug and tightened the cinch in his towel. "Amenable. And what about you, Mr. Graves? What will your assignment be? Heard from Bisky that you was carpenter. I already have a handy carpenter and I got a cook who can also barber and suture a wound shut, as I mentioned prior."

"Like I said in the wire, I'll be the trade master. I'll direct the coxswain where to make landfall and do all the purchasing. Until we get to the islands I'll help as needed."

"You can have the steward's cabin, right next to the first mate's. I've never believed in stewards and the men respect me for it. Lord Buttermilk can bunk down with the apprentices because I'm afraid what might happen to him in the fo'c's'le. This afternoon, I'll be up at the shipyards. The *Cullion* is moored up there, having some sail and hull work taken care of. Any return cargo I should know of?"

Owen hesitated, wondered whether Jethro knew that he was assigned the task of bringing back Pacific Islanders for his father's advertising campaign. "Artifacts mostly. I'll fill you in when we get to the Southern Hemisphere. I'm finalizing the island route. We'll start by heading to the Sandwich Islands. No real trading until after that."

They shook hands and Terrapin showed them to the door, still in his towel.

The *Lady Cullion* was a twenty-five-year-old steam clipper originally built for the tea trade. She was square-rigged, sharply raked in the stem, spanned two hundred feet from gudgeon to bowsprit. At the shipyard she'd had her hull freshly coppered—one of Terrapin's flourishes along with the nymphal figurehead—her masts tarred, and the topgallant sail replaced. Extra ballast of rock and sand had been loaded to keep her at proper trim because she had a tendency to sail high. Despite the repairs the ship looked off-kilter and weary, a sloop-of-war fallen on hard times. Hatch covers were out of plumb, the brass capstans had been lacklustered by salt, the forecastle had the buff of driftwood. Owen and Jethro watched the commotion of the crew loading supplies—crates of tinned meat, dry biscuits, sauerkraut and limes, munitions, sacks of rice and flour, duff, dried apples, kegs of tallow and lamp oil, a dozen wire cages of chickens, a fretful sheep, two sack-bellied sows. Davey Unsworth, boatswain and rehabilitated kidnapper, stood by the gangway in his oilskins and slouch hat, checking off inventory from a clipboard.

Owen and Jethro had brought their belongings down to the dock and the supply loading slowed as the Chinese rickshaw driver unloaded Jethro's convoy of kidskin luggage. Jethro tipped the Chinaman and took stock of his possessions, unfastening each case or bag to reveal butterfly nets, camera obscuras, flower presses, a japanned tin box of watercolors, sheaves of herbarium paper, specimen jars wrapped in newspaper, barometers, glass beakers, bottles of formalin, dissection instruments, magnifying glasses, a Bausch & Lomb microscope, pillboxes, sketchpads and inks, a small library of science, art, and literature. The seamen slowed their hoisting and watched Jethro squat to check the final two objects: a brass camera with a hand crank on the side and a wooden tripod. Owen stood with his hands on his hips, staring down into the gaping bags, flushed in the face.

"Cinématographe," Jethro said, looking up. "It's like Edison's Vitascope but made by the French. They're a little ahead on this count."

"What do you intend to do with it?"

Jethro paused. "Observe."

"What?"

"Birdlife and whatnot. It also doubles as a projector and I brought some practice reels I made in Chicago. They might entertain the men."

Owen leaned down a little so that he would be out of earshot of the bosun. "I'll put it to you plainly. I ordered several crates of trade items. Without those items we'll be returning empty-handed. If storage space is lacking, half of this junk will be going over the side. Do you understand?"

Jethro rummaged for something in a leather bag, refusing Owen the eye contact he wanted. "This journey was my father's idea, but I intend to fulfill my own vision for it. We're all collectors of a kind. You, me, my father. Instead of artifacts I want sketches, glass slides, photographs. A ship's naturalist needs supplies if he's to be of value."

"To who?"

"Whom." Gauging Owen's temper, Jethro added, "I went light on maps and almanacs." He wrapped a muslin cloth around a film canister. "A mounted rare bird or pressed flower—it's just as important as weapons from some lost tribe."

Owen straightened, decided the San Quentin inmates could hear all they wanted. "This isn't an expedition into unknown waters. You're about a hundred years too late for that, sport. Everything's been discovered out there. Did you think you were going to haul up some ancient sea creature and pickle it?"

The men laughed and Jethro began snapping the cases shut.

Owen continued, "And as far as I can tell, you're no botanist or zoologist or naturalist. A dilettante is what your father implied."

Jethro picked up two bags, one in each hand, and sidled toward the gangplank. "Science has always been kind to amateurs with broad interests. Franklin and Bell spring to mind." There was something smug and contemptuous in the looped shoulders and wiry voice, the averted eyes, the way they refused to confront or yield. Owen could tell he'd spent his life walking out of rooms in the middle of arguments.

Owen watched him board the ship and the seamen gathered like a silent, slack-jawed chorus. None of them offered him directions or assistance; they were nervous and uneasy in their demeanor, as if a priest had come aboard. Jethro drifted from bulkhead to stern with his monogrammed luggage, seemingly baffled by how to penetrate the ship's entryways and hatches. The first mate, Mandrake Pym, a veteran sailor with no criminal background, watched Jethro dither. Captain Terrapin reclined on a settee in the poop deck charthouse and looked on with quiet amusement, a hand working the fur of an English terrier sleeping beside him.

"Lovelace, you can store your fidgets in the bosun's store if there's any room. The rest will have to go below. But wait until the provisions and chooks are settled in."

Jethro nodded and set down his bags. "Very well. I'll bring the other bags up and set them right here for now."

Terrapin let his mouth drop open. "No you won't, pikelet. That's the main deck and it's to be kept clear at all times. There's an order to things on a ship. The *Cullion* isn't a venereal old whore with her skirts hitched up. She's a temperamental lady what likes to be wooed into submission. So we keep her clean and orderly. Go 'ave yourself a cup of chamomile tea and come back in an hour." The idle seamen chuckled at this and Terrapin gave them a cauterizing stare. The men returned to hauling supplies and lubricating the capstans while Jethro carried his bags back down the gangplank, his head down.

They weighed anchor in the late afternoon, sails furled and the auxiliary engines steaming them out of the blustery bay. When they passed Alcatraz they edged into the no-go around the island and all of the seamen, Terrapin included, stood cheering at starboard, waving to the inmates in the exercise yard. Jethro was settling into the apprentice berth with his butterfly nets and instruments. Owen stood at the bowsprit, watching seabirds pass in formations over the headlands, a thousand specks in the oyster sky. He stared down into the churning depths beneath the prow— like rippled iron before it all drew in and whitened to foam. The clipper opened out into the wide mouth of the bay, tacked to port, the wind rattling the halyards. The open sea wind hit them abeam, like an iodine breath coming across a mirror. It always smelled like death to Owen and yet he couldn't explain the calm he felt whenever he was aboard. It was more than riding above the fathomless deep, the watery oblivion glassing out in all directions. It was the sense of being beyond reach. Sea life was an outer current of land life; it somehow ran parallel and separate. The weeks between ports were valleys without newspapers, letters, or tele-grams. You worked until your limbs ached, collapsed into a ham-mock each night and swayed into a dreamless state of exhaustion. The days bled together. Meals and weather and the throb of your own thoughts was all that mattered. Sometimes you stood on deck in the faintness before dawn, somewhere between wakeful-ness and sleep, and felt without body or mind as you watched the line between sea and sky grow visible. He grew introspective at sea. Owen wanted to believe that he was making this voyage to secure a windfall that would set him on track, earn him the right to Adelaide's hand in marriage and a shot at a prosperous future, but he also suspected as the ship furrowed into the great plain of the Pacific that he was avoiding the claims of the present.

Captain Baz Terrapin stayed in his cabin most of the way through the Horse Latitudes. The starboard and port watches had been chosen by first and second mate—a coin toss deciding who would get lumbered with Jethro Gray. It was Terrapin's habit not to come onstage until the action was well begun. He'd directed the coxswain to skirt the belt of dry, dead air as they plied for Hawaii, planning to shoot across the weatherless ridge under steam, but the former San Quentin inmate (blackmail) had got drunk and allowed the bark to peter out. The wind, when it came at all, arrived in gentle drifts, seemed to fall vertically from overhead before evaporating. Wanting to ration the coal for later use, Ter-rapin announced to the men that they would flounder a few days and the Sandwich Islands would be delayed.

They had been at sea less than a week but already it felt like a month. Jethro had been assigned the job of scrubbing the chicken shit off the deck every morning, collecting the eggs and carrying them to the cook before breakfast. He was yet to trim a sail, touch a capstan or halyard, because Terrapin insisted that he know the taxonomy of a ship and her lady parts before he was allowed to help govern her motion. This perplexed Owen and Jethro both, since many of the former steelworkers and inmates, for whom this was also a maiden voyage, were already scaling the mastheads and handling the rigging.

Mid-morning they met in Terrapin's cabin. Owen came along with Jethro on the pretext of brushing up on his own maritime knowledge, but mostly he feared leaving the Harvard graduate alone with the hulking, whimsical captain. They sat at a hinged table, the meager light of a spirit lamp burning, a leather-clad nautical encyclopedia spread before them like a pigskin Bible. Terrapin's quarters were a woody, oiled hollow and oddly effeminate—tapestries, plush Turkish cushions, a feather mattress under a filigreed iron frame, Anatolian rugs, wingback chairs of buttoned velvet. A gramophone and several snake plants stood on an end table directly beneath two portholes. An upright piano dominated the port side of the berth and Owen speculated, given its width and the dimensions of the companionway, that the cabin had been unroofed to insert the instrument. Late at night, when the seamen not on watch started to drift up from the spiritroom to retch overboard or sing lewdly under the rush of stars, low-set music could be heard coming from under the planks of the poop deck. It was all nocturnes and vespers and fugues, forlorn and delicate pieces that were hard to reckon with Terrapin's gruff and pustulant form. Some of the men who had sailed with him before said it wasn't unknown to see him come weeping out of his cabin in the middle hours of the night, a carafe of rum in one hand (he switched to spirits at sea) and his little terrier—Nipper—in the other. He would go up to the bridge and check the compass under the binnacle lamp and proceed to recite the names of his illegitimate children, his fingers climbing the ladder of birth dates tattooed on both arms. The incantation of their names made him maudlin and he'd set to rubbing the dog's underbelly the way a lonely seaman might stroke a woman's hair. Davey Unsworth swore that one time the dog panted with carnal delight and slipped out the pink tip of his dingus during this show of affection.

In the stateroom, Terrapin hunched in his minatory way, a plump hand on his belly, reclined in a wingback chair, listening to Jethro pronounce the nautical forms—the ship, sail, spar, and rigging types that were as ancient and venerable as Vedic prayer. Clipper to corsair, brigantine to bark, galley to galiot. The geometry of sailcloth: genoa, spitfire, lateen, mainsail, skysail, spinnaker, topgallant. The truss-and-web conjunctions of spar and rigging, as delicate and precise as lacework. All of it was to be memorized by rote or mnemonic, never mind that half of it didn't apply to the *Lady Cullion*.

"What we're after here is the arrangement of known objects in the sailing universe. Does a physician go into surgery without knowing where to find the spleen and the liver? The anatomy of a ship is tenacious in its obliquarity." Terrapin was pushing against the limits of his own jerry-rigged education and vocabulary, trying to impress upon Jethro Gray that he had also read works of the gilt page. He thought nothing of making up a word in a pinch. "And since we got an Ivy Leaguer aboard he should be top-notch and savvy at book learnin, the bloody Pascal of the ratline." He leaned back, grinning at this neat turn of phrase.

Jethro pressed on dutifully, reading aloud from the maritime Torah, tracing a finger over the feathered script and cross-sectioned hulls. Terrapin asked him to close his eyes and see what he could parrot back.

"These aren't multiplication tables," said Jethro after an hour of muddling. "If you'd let me take the book to my berth I could study it at night."

Terrapin shot up. "The holy book does not leave its tabernacle, mate. The fate of this ship depends on this tome. I'm superstitious deep down, like all seamen. Believe in fiery apocalypse and what-all plague of ruins and frog brains if the lamps ain't lit just so. Now repeat the sail types from the top. Mr. Graves, you can feel free to lend assistance as propitiated."

Owen and Jethro teamed up through another page of taxonomy.

When Terrapin was satisfied he poured them each a nip of rum into a sherry glass and crossed to the gramophone. Before they were released topside, they had to sit through Dame Nellie Melba floating an aria across a sea of static. He delicately placed the needle and arm onto the spinning disc, obsidian-black and lustrous as it wobbled. Melba's soprano seemed to seep out of the joists and caulked walls. They sipped their rum and Terrapin closed his eyes, a hand conducting the space in front of him. "Aw, she makes me cry out of both eyes the way she angelizes that Puccini. She's the Stradivarius of the human whistle."

The captain used the idle Horse Latitudes to train and prepare the remainder of the crew. In the stilled, black air—hours before a sun-driven zephyr rose from the east for fifteen minutes—Terrapin liked to rouse all hands and assemble them on deck. Three-thirty in the morning was his favorite hour for this ritual. It was the transit between debauched drunkenness and the crucifying light of a hangover. He enjoyed the haggard line of men, their mouths caked shut with thirst, eyes gravied with sleep. Nipper trotted at his side or barked at the chickens in the pen. The solitary rooster commenced to crow, mistaking the commotion and lamplight for daybreak.

Jethro lined up in his union suit, fleeced from ankle to wrist, flanked by bare-chested seamen in gymnasium shorts and jockstraps, hands cupping their predawn erections. They laughed at his pajamas, leering at the fireman's flap that buttoned in the back, calling it a buggery hatch. Jethro told them that the great heavyweight boxer John Sullivan, who challenged any man in America to a fight for five hundred dollars, wore just such an outfit into the ring. Owen wiped his eyes and tucked his guernsey into his shorts. He ranked somewhere between an officer and an idler on this voyage and wanted to speak his mind with the captain. He was growing tired of the man's caprices, wanted to remind him that his dock bonus depended on trading success. By that logic, this charade of not steaming through the weatherless latitudes was a colossal waste of time and money. Coal and wood could be bought in Hawaii. But Terrapin left no room for comment, bellying out along the deck in a flowered Samoan sarong. He swore that this was the most comfortable way to sleep in tropical or subtropical climes and wasn't afraid to admit he'd given up on undergarments entirely. He was fond of soft draperies, both on his body and in the velvet grotto of his cabin.

After some joking and banter about last night's dinner giving him the Johnny-trots, Terrapin proceeded to lead the men in calisthenics. This was his own brand of improvised contortion and consisted of various yogic stances coupled with squats, dips, push-ups, and a kind of self-massage designed to push the blood through the extremities. This regimen, just like swimming in frigid ocean waters, was a cure-all and had been known through the ages to diminish winds, catarrhs, and bilious complaints, many of which he had suffered until a swami deckhand inducted him into the shiny halls of perfect health. Given his girth, he was remarkably agile, bowing and stretching into any number of fleshy, cat-like poses. Several of the men, still drunk, fell on the deck as they craned upward, for which they received a kick in the midsection from Terrapin. When they had exercised for twenty minutes, Terrapin inspected them for hygiene and made them each eat a lime as prevention against scurvy, as if it were the eighteenth century all over again. There was no bodily part whose upkeep Terrapin was not concerned with. He considered all the men—their bodies, souls, and dreams—to be under his care and supervision.

"Now, you lot, wash with castile soap. Get inside the crevice of the buttocks and under the flap-trap of ball and tackle. Behind the ears and inside the whirligig of the navel. Christ, if it don't smell like a Dutch cheese cave below decks." He doled out the sacramental limes, coming down the deck, watching them peel and eat them on the spot. "Excellent. Now go back to your bunks and hammocks." Everyone but the seamen of the middle watch was dismissed until first light. By Owen's reckoning the men were subsisting on three hours of interrupted sleep a night and it would only be a matter of time before someone dozed in the high rigging and toppled deckward.

Owen spent the windless days finalizing his trading route and writing a letter to Adelaide. He kept a watchful eye over Jethro and made sure the seamen didn't interfere with the college graduate. Apart from his morning study sessions in the dawning light of Terrapin's cabin, Jethro was assigned various duties that took him into the lower reaches of the bark. He carried coal from the scuttles to the boiler room for future use, ran sailcloth from the bosun's storeroom, helped the cook peel potatoes and onions, stocked the bread room with hardtack. The tin-lined sepulcher of the bread room was the only place that the water and rats could not penetrate. His least favorite task was mopping down the orlop with citric acid. An emergency sick bay below the waveline, the orlop smelled of bilgewater.

When Jethro wasn't cleaning and hauling, he found time to begin collecting specimens. The crew watched with mocking delight as he sent dredge nets over the side and hauled up countless jellyfish, slicing them open to study their gelatinous architecture before bottling them in glass. He scampered about with his net and haversack as they came near some atolls, catching everything from flies with iridescent legs to giant silver moths and paper wasps. The winged insects were pinned to blotting paper, their Latinate names printed neatly below. Jethro consulted *A Naturalist's Guide to the Pacific Islands* by H. R. Whitcomb. With special permission from Terrapin, he was briefly allowed to mount the sacred altar of the poop deck—strictly reserved for officers—to film with his cinématographe a pair of terns roosting on the mizzenmast. He spent several hours with camera, binoculars, and notepad. Owen watched him make his diligent observations and sort his bugs into labeled pillboxes. He supposed it was akin to collecting artifacts but failed to see the value in gathering tentacle, wing, and claw. A dead starfish was nothing like a piece of handicraft. And a yard of jostled filmstrip—birds huddled in migratory fatigue or whatever it was—hardly counted as science. His own interest in objects, from the native to the urban, had always been about the story each one represented, about possessing material proof of something transient. There was something endlessly fascinating about divining the purpose of a lacquered box or the sequence of cuts in a sculpture, plumbing the mind of the man who'd made it.

When Jethro came to dinner in the messroom he moved in a heady cloud of smells—arsenical soap used to prepare bird specimens, mollusk-brine, the residual taint of spending hours in the feculent orlop. The seamen sat as far away as possible and only Owen would endure proximity. The men ate in two shifts because they couldn't all fit in the cramped messroom.

Owen spooned through his gravy-colored soup and dandy-funk—a mixture of powdered biscuit and molasses—and watched Jethro make little islands of hardtack in his soup bowl. With Honolulu two days off and the promise of better winds, Owen had watched him give up on food. He turned to Jethro and said, "We'll be seeing your eye sockets if you don't start eating."

Jethro bit a corner of hardtack, smiled. "Not much of an appetite. So many things to do. My observations are picking up steam. No pun intended."

"Flat chat, are we?" said Terrapin, overhearing. He was standing in the galley waiting for a refill of his pewter coffeepot. He was brought a tray each night and ate dinner alone in the stateroom, serenaded by Dame Nellie Melba or Caruso.

Harvey McCallister, able-bodied crew member and ironworker from Irish Hill, looked at Jethro from the adjacent bench and said to Terrapin, "Must be the private cache he's got bundled in the apprentice quarters. Young Dickey Fentress tells me he hears feasting when he's trying to sleep of a night. And his seachest is locked—and we all know that is not the custom forward of the mast."

The captain turned his head slowly, like a man with a neck injury. His elbows and chin came out a little as he cleared his throat. "Ship's ordinance says no private food pantries in the berths, isn't that right, Mr. Pym?"

The first mate set his cutlery down to give his own answer full attention. "On account of rats and vermin risk. Correct, sir. Also no personal firearms."

Terrapin swiveled in one fluid motion and came out of the galley and into the messroom. He placed a meaty hand on the table where Owen and Jethro sat. "What do you have back there in the berth, Mr. Gray? Niblets? Bikkies? Lollies? Out with it."

Jethro fingered some crumbs off the table and placed them on the tip of his tongue. "Just some of my equipment and books. What you saw come aboard."

Terrapin took a swill of black coffee and held it in his mouth, nodding, wincing but also agreeing with its bitterness. "Righty-o, then. Davey Unsworth, as bosun and witness, would you please accompany me for a berth inspection." He pulled a fob watch from his flannel trousers. "Mark the time in the log as eighteen hundred hours."

At this the other men set down their spoons and knives and began for the door.

Terrapin held up a hand. "I'll bring said bounty into the mess but take your seats. I reckon we might find something besides pinned honeybees."

Owen watched the men light up with Jethro's unfolding humiliation. One man started beating the table with a set of spoons, his teeth flashing. Owen wanted to speak up but he knew this was part of Terrapin's elaborate hazing ritual. Once the captain was satisfied that Jethro belonged to the brotherhood of ship and sea, knew its occult rituals and names, then he would be welcomed into the fold. He might even sup at the captain's table once or twice because, after all, he was in the bloodline that was paying for the whole trek. But for now Jethro had to be brought in from the haughty, feckless wings, used as both a diversion in the oceanic desert and a signpost for future wrongdoers and ordinance wreckers. Owen had known men like these since his days with the demolition crews; he knew them to be rough-mannered but ultimately well-intentioned. He waited for the whole thing to play itself out.

Terrapin and the bosun left the messroom for ten minutes and returned with a muslin sack of contraband. Jethro, resigned to the intrusion, sat back in his chair, nervously touching thumb to fingertip on each hand. The captain brought the sack of goods to the front of the messroom and began emptying the contents onto the hinged galley counter. Hendrik Stuyvesant, the cook, a querulous, wiry counterfeiter who'd skipped his parole, pushed up his shirtsleeves and came forward to enjoy the show, a dripping ladle in one hand. Terrapin put his hand into the sack to produce one item at a time, his face placid and supremely satisfied. Tins of ham, jars of English conserves, Danish shortbreads, ryebread crisps, water crackers, Dutch hard cheese, Belgian chocolate in cylinders of foil, sardines and mussels in flat tins, a box of candied ginger, ropes of licorice, blocks of marzipan, nougat, whiskey-and-cream fudge.

"Merry-fucking-Christmas," said one of the seamen from the back.

Terrapin looked over at Jethro and puckered. "What we have here is fruit from the tree of wealth. I've sworn an oath to make all men equal at sea—even officers cannot ferry out beyond their station. Those who sleep in the bow and us in the stern, we are of separate rank but all one under God's parasol. Yes, that's it. But this, this is something special and foul. Apparently our slop and hard biscuits aren't good enough for Mr. Gray. So, I'm in two minds here." He paused dramatically, thumbs in belt loops, a barrister before the bench. "Either"—he turned to grin at each crewmate—"we toss this cannery treasure overboard since there is no fair way to distribute the spoils." The men heckled and booed at this suggestion. "Or—now wait a minute, gents—we don't attempt to divvy but just say that we eat all of it in the here and now. We pass around the tins of piggy and palaver and let every man take his morsel. Drink it down with a new keg of rum and be done with it. All those in favor say aye." The deafening, affirmative reply brought the other shift of diners down to the messroom and soon there were two dozen bodies crammed in. The second mate and two of his watch were the only ones left on deck.

For the remainder of the evening Terrapin presided over the drunken feast. Crew hands ate crispbreads with blackberry conserves laid over with hard cheese or sardines in the buttery wake of Danish shortbread. They were rummed enough to eat any combination. The cook poached a few dozen eggs and served them over wedges of ham that were skewered with toothpicks. Several times Owen and Jethro attempted to leave but each time they were ordered to stay and drink more rum. Jethro ate and drank cautiously, staying close to home with a handful of cashews and some candied ginger. His face was pale and he looked down at the table.

Owen said, "Didn't they ever haze you in a fraternity out east?"

"I was thrown into the pond and had to kiss the wine steward's hand and call him Your Excellency like something out of *Don Quixote*."

He said it so plainly that Owen couldn't bring himself to laugh. Jethro might as well have been some migratory bird who'd chosen to alight on the ship. He was so completely alien and ill at ease, making no attempt to join the nautical fold; he was like a ruck-faced stepchild standing at the edge of a family portrait.

As they entered the embryonic hours of morning, the food mostly gone, a litter of tin cans and foils strewn about, the talk fell from low to base. The seamen competed to make Jethro blush. Gaddy McKlure, a mechanically minded Scotsman, recounted, with painstaking precision, all of the women and barroom brawls he'd survived. He spoke about bedroom tactics, coital names and threats, the fireman's hold he liked to give his old lady when she stood in the kitchen without knickers to fry bacon, the puncture wound in his leg from a jagged beer bottle. The others listened and made excursions to piss in a slop bucket in the corner. Terrapin, not wanting to be upstaged, delivered a monologue on the opus of his life's lovemaking, from Samoa to Tonga to Tasmania. He offered theory and conjecture about the evolution of conjugal prowess.

"Now, my general theory is that the closer you are to the equator the less the women act out in the vaudeville of sexual coupling. Coital stage fright is what I call it. As an extreme, Esquimaux broods copulate like their savage little lives depended on it. Whereas in the tropics they can't be bothered half the time. You think the Horse Latitudes are bad? Wait until we hit the Doldrums, where the women fornicate like sleepy old mules. Don't know what it is. In the land of penis gourds it's like dogs in heat and it's over before you can say Fanny's ya fuckin aunt. But"—he hitched his pants up by the belt buckle—"some of the highland women are much more demanding. They eat all three courses if you receive my meaning. There's an island off the coast of New Guinea where I swear it's an island of sexual divas. They can drain your lifeblood. Stories of mutineers swimming ashore only to become sex slaves, drunk and dazed all the time on quiffy lady parts. I've double-backed pygmies, lepers, head-hunter's wives, pearl divers, Maoris, bushmen virgins, hermits, and I have to say nothing compares to a little redhead I once had in the Tenderloin." The men cheered at this, as if rallying behind a hometown sports team. "A shopgirl who broke me big racehorse heart. There's nothing this waif wouldn't do for you. Unspeakable things dredged up from the pit of a man's bowels. Nothing could tarnish her. Give her a chocolate éclair and she was yours, from the toenails to the tongue, gents. I can see her now—the pinks of her breasts, the strawberry hilltops of her nipples." He sat back down, caught in the entrails of sexual memory. "But—and here's the turn—when I found out her Christian name was

Delaney . . . well, it played with my mind and I came undone. I had assumed—quite wrongly—that she called herself Delaney as a joke, a simpleton shopgirl lark. Imagined her name to be Rosie or Delilah or Beatrice, for Chrissakes. But once I found out her given name was Delaney, well, gentlemen, I could only ever penetrate her buttocks after that. Stayed in the stern of the brig and things soon died off."

Jethro, unable to take the lewd one-upmanship any longer, stood and shouldered through the crowd. He stopped in front of the captain, hands on hips. He blinked before speaking. "I've had just about enough of this slander and lewd reminiscence. You're not fit to sail a dinghy, let alone a ship of men and rest assured I'll be instructing my father to spread the word with underwriters and investors to blacklist you."

Owen sat with his head in his hands. This was, of course, exactly what Terrapin and the seamen wanted, to goad Jethro into a puny, petulant display of anger.

Terrapin took a deep breath, sucked his lower lip over his jagged bottom teeth, let out a breathy whistle. "Mr. Pym?"

Mandrake Pym was slumped against the wall, his shirtfront covered in sardine oil and biscuit crumbs. A nearby seaman pulled his head up by a plug of hair. "Yes, captain."

"Who's on watch at oh-four-hundred?"

"Starboard watch, sir. My crew."

"Make a note in the log that apprentice deckhand Jethro Gray has volunteered for extra watch duty."

"Yes, sir."

Owen came forward and placed a hand on Jethro's shoulder. "He's drunk," he said to Terrapin. "We've all said some things that weren't well considered."

Terrapin said, "A man should stand behind everything he says, drunk or not. Get him out of here and ready for the watch."

Jethro buttoned his peacoat. "You think that because I come from money I'm a trinket for your amusement. You can have me clean your rotting ship from head to foot and it won't change the fact that someday I'll be running one of the wealthiest insurance companies in the world while you're buying day-old bread on your sea pension."

Terrapin considered this, leaned back, lifted one haunch to give his sphincter the latitude it needed to blow a scorch-hole through his trousers. The men sprayed rum mid-sip with laughter, guffawed, keeled over, groaned with pleasure. Jethro was speechless, his left eyebrow twitching. Owen, appalled but also amused, led Jethro by the elbow out of the messroom.

Moments before Jethro was due to come off the forenoon watch, a deckhand ran up to tell him they had pulled a strange beast from the water. Owen overheard and followed along to inspect the catch. A dozen men, blearing and moaning through the first waves of sobriety, stood over a monstrous form. It was clearly a hoax but no less disturbing for its mangle of body parts: an octopus head, beak upturned, conjoined with the flattened torso of a stingray. A cleaved shark fin had been attached to the spine of the ray and tropical bird feathers gummed to the dorsal wings. Jethro's eyes watered with rage. Owen saw that the monster had been cobbled together from various parts of Jethro's specimen collection, the animals he'd bottled and shellacked in the hold. He'd taken to using the orlop as a repository.

"Who did this?" Jethro asked, his stare fixed on the creature.

The men murmured but made no direct reply.

"I'll ask again. Who did this?"

"We all did," said one of them.

Owen said, "You had no right to interfere with his specimens. The food was all in good fun but this is different. You men are to keep your hands off his work, or you'll be making your own way home. Jesus, this is a circus."

Jethro said, "But *whose* idea was it?" His voice uncoiled across the deck.

Not wanting to be shown a coward in front of his peers, Harvey McCallister stepped forward. He was the same man who'd outed Jethro's culinary stash.

"Do you have any idea what you've done? Those are my specimens you've hacked apart. For what, a joke? To make you look good in front of your dim-witted mates? I've never known such idiocy."

"Be careful what you say just here," said McCallister, tonguing a plug of tobacco into his cheek. He spat a tannic stream into a tin cup.

Jethro looked directly into the Irishman's face. "Perhaps you and I should settle this between ourselves. This needs to go noticed and the captain certainly isn't going to do anything."

"What do you have in mind?" said Harvey, rolling up his cuffs, relaxing into a big hooligan grin.

"Not here. Tomorrow morning. Ten three-minute rounds. Queensberry rules?"

"Whatever you want, mate. Queen-fairy rules or whatever else. I'm a scrapper from the Hill, a hayrope match winner."

"Well, this will be a fair fight with a referee and timed rounds."

"Terrapin will want to be ref." McCallister flexed his shoulders, raised a fist in the air in front of him.

Jethro said, "Fine with me. Shall we put some money on it, just to make it a little more lively?"

Owen said, "Terrapin won't allow gambling on his ship." Jethro was digging his hole deeper by the minute. Varsity welterweight or not, McCallister was built like a lorry horse.

"He'll make an exception for this," said Harvey. "How much?"

"Your entire wages for the rest of the trip. How much is that?"

"Ten dollars a month."

"Done. Let's say sixty dollars, as an estimate. If you lose, the captain will instruct the paymaster to garnish your wages on my behalf."

"And when you lose you'll hand me the same in cash."

Jethro held out his hand and McCallister shook it firmly.

The fight was the final piece of business in the Horse Latitudes and Terrapin, delighted by the announcement of a spectacle, had ordered that the *Cullion* steam her way into Honolulu Bay by the end of the day. Forty miles off the islands they dropped anchor and roped in a makeshift ring behind the foredeck. The single sheep, the pigs and penned chickens, were moved to one side to make more room. The men lowered the sails and lined up to watch. Terrapin dressed in his cabin and emerged at noon, ascending in a sonic cloud of Caruso. He wore a cravat and jacket, hair raked and brilliantined, face freshly shaved and raw in the hard light. Nipper trotted at his side.

The pugilists came from separate ends of the ship, Harvey McCallister bare-chested and jogging from the stern and Jethro up from the shade behind the bowsprit. Owen had volunteered to be Jethro's trainer, largely because he envisioned having to intervene in the event of serious head injury or blood loss. He walked with him now, the rangy boxer in his union suit, his fists wrapped in French flannel. Jethro kept his clad fists under his armpits as if they were something to behold, a pair of dueling pistols still in their velvet-lined case. Harvey came into the light alone, arms and fists clenched. He had refused all offers of trainer or second and had likewise declined a bucket of water and rags for his corner. To accept either was to elevate Jethro above the status of griping bitch.

"You don't have to go through with this," Owen said, hovering at the hemp rope.

Jethro said, "I've fought bigger." He ducked and entered the ring, bringing his hands out into the open air for the first time.

Terrapin gestured for the two men to come into the middle and inspected their hands. In a speechifying, ceremonial manner he welcomed the sailors to the first inaugural bout of the

Lady Cullion Pacific Voyage in the year eighteen hundred and ninety-seven. "In the starboard corner we have Harvey Hallelujah McCallister, weighing twenty stone and some ounces, a steel miller, womanizer, loafer, and scrapper from Irish Hill." The men shouted and cheered. "And in the port corner we have Jethro Jellybones Gray, weighing twelve stone, one for each foot of height, Ivy League graduate, heir to an insurance empire, ship's naturalist, prig, and dandy." The men heckled and swore. A few pieces of dried apple were thrown into the ring. Terrapin, satisfied with the reception, turned to the fighters. His accent broadened as he listed the transgressions of the ring. "Now, listen, you blokes, this will be a clean fight. No holdin, trippin, pushin, spittin, bitin, wrestlin, kickin, head buttin, rabbit punches, kidney blows, or below-the-belt nut and pebble shots." The men laughed at this last little flourish. They were smoking cigarillos and raising tin mugs of rum, a rare privilege during daylight. "We'll 'ave ten three-minute rounds and the timekeeper will announce the sunrise and sunset of each round with the ship's bell." The bell rang for good measure and the crowd looked toward the catheads to see apprentice Dickey Fentress, barely fifteen, grinning with his fob. "If a man goes down then I will inspect the bludgeoned face and head for gravity of injury and determine the victor. Go back to your corners and come out swingin."

The two men touched fists and returned to their corners, Jethro with his looped shoulders and bantling legs, Harvey with his brawny arms held high for the men to admire. The ship's bell rang as if in a squall and Terrapin shot Fentress a stare before the clanging died away.

McCallister came out light on his feet, jabbing and breathing. Jethro stepped toward the center of the ring, tender-footed, a doe picking its way into a clearing. He raised his arms, blinking madly. The Irishman tested the waters by fibbing with his left before striking through with a right cross. Jethro parried and slipped back, the ham-fist whizzing by his right ear. The men were chuffed at this, cheering obscenities and thumping their feet on the planks.

McCallister circled and probed, letting his footwork and jab push Jethro against the ropes. Jethro swayed his torso, fading in and out of striking distance. Owen watched Jethro's spooked eyes stare out between his cocked arms, the fists slightly curled over the top of spindled wrists. Was he going to blink and telegraph before he punched? Harvey let off little grunting noises as he came in again, his body turned, elbows tucked. He aspirated with each headward blow but Jethro pivoted and took nothing more than a grazing on the side of his neck. Jethro startled off the hemp rope and cantered to his left, bringing his guard up, swinging to face his opponent. This kind of dance continued for the rest of the round—McCallister bum-rushing Jethro into a corner, jabbing furiously, while the Harvard welterweight parried and weaved in stumbling circles, still averting anything fatal.

"What the hell are you doing out there?" Owen said between rounds. "Throw a punch at least so they don't think you're a coward."

"Let him chug a little," said Jethro, taking a sip of water.

By the middle of the second round Jethro came up onto the balls of his feet and began punching when the Irishman one-twoed his way forward. His arms shot straight out from the elbow, the loose fists clenching hard mid-flight and the arms stem-stocked at right angles. He came up onto his toes and connected a right on McCallister's chin, sending the Irishman backward. Harvey shook his head and shoulders loose, spat, came in with uppercut-and-hook. Jethro sidled, took a step back, then landed a short jab in Harvey's side, ducking low and coming in at an oblique angle. It was clear that what Jethro lacked in poise during everyday life he had in the ring. The nervous face, the twitches and stammers, were all still there but they were somehow channeled and rarefied in the uncoiling hands and shuffling footwork.

McCallister was yet to connect a punch and it showed in his

face. He came into the third round without water, mouth hinged in thirst and rage. Meanwhile Owen had doused the back of Jethro's neck with wet rags and the fighter had brought a few handfuls of water to his mouth. He looked oddly invigorated. A reluctant seaman told him *fancy footwork* and *nice snappy left*. He came back out looking more relaxed and upright than Owen had ever seen him. Some of the Gray blood—the vinegar of the mercantile risk takers, the profiteering bravado of the men who did not go to sea but floated their countinghouses on the backs of a nameless Atlantic crew—was coursing through his veins now. During one of Harvey's onslaughts Jethro leaned into a full crouch, arms up, then bobbed out of the pen with six punches in as many seconds. Two of them landed on the Irishman's nose and beside his left eye socket. A line of blood appeared at Harvey's temple, a cut right at the edge of the hairline. His face dropped with unspeakable humiliation and fury. He looked at Jethro, hangdog, almost blind with ire. His technique fell away in the pitched yells and stamping of his crewmates. They were calling him every colorful noun and adjective they could think of, interspersing it with practical instruction. He let out an oxen bellow and came forward again, this time his arms swinging wide with barroom haymakers and bolo punches that never had a chance. He collapsed into a clinch and held Jethro's arms down with his biceps, his hands gripping in the back. Owen could see the seaman's face and made out the words: *I'll kill and rape your mother and sisters.*

Terrapin intervened, took a quick look at McCallister's bleeding wound, and sent the two fighters apart again. Rather than being drawn in by this sloppy display of technique and malice, Jethro drifted forward, leading the way with his left held high like a lantern, holding it there as if beckoning a cow in from a darkened field. The raised hand left his rib cage wide open and McCallister took the bait, cutting his way forward with sledging body blows. The Irishman steam-shoveled his way in, fists pounding, head down and chin cocked behind one shoulder for protection.

Jethro slipped back, feigned with a hook, and followed through with a downward right cross. The pickaxe punch was textbook perfect, the weight transfer and pinioned back foot, as if voltage had sprung up through his raised heel and flowed to the knuckles and burrowed fingertips. It walled into McCallister's jawline and sent him to the planks. The din of booing was cut through with raised cheers, for it was clear that the Irishman wasn't getting up anytime soon. Terrapin stood over him and counted aloud to ten. Incredulous, he raised Jethro's thin arm in the air and declared him the winner.

12.

The afternoons blanched white with heat, the rowboat skirting in the wind. The sky-country had as many moods as Malini—leaden, bright, brooding, placid, cheery. Their clothes were veined with salt and worn thin. She had boils on her bum from all the salt water and sitting and had to haunch to one side. When she was thirsty she punctured a green coconut on the oarlock and brought it to her mouth. Argus was sometimes able to catch bonito fish with a bamboo pole and hooked nail. She made him recite the names of long-dead fishermen in their clan because this brought good luck and was the proper thing to do. He braced the sail to windward and, during calms, rowed the boat in his Panama hat. There were days without landfall and they slept huddled under the alpaca coat, drifting off course, pressed into the prow of the rowboat.

Argus sang and preached to pass the seared afternoons. All the hymn songs sounded the same to Malini and she wanted him to quit his bellowing. His voice was good but the rhythm was plodding. When she heard the pent-up and breathy *Aaaameeeen* she knew things were finishing up. But then he would hum into another hymn without pause. Eventually, out of sheer boredom, she joined in the singing but caroled in her own language. She made up lyrics about wedding feasts and babies being born in the middle of the night while he bullroared *God* and *gladsome light*. She imagined what the Kuk were saying about her. Women who ran away were usually adulterers. She missed the straight-stemmed trees and wanted to smoke.

Argus blessed the flock and gave communion from his gun-wale pulpit. He imagined himself a prophet who could say the right things to the godless. He had the power to turn the wretched devout. The Reverend Mister had trained him as a houseboy but also as a catechist, someone who might walk among the unbelieving and reveal the truth of Jesus, riven and bleeding on the cross. He understood the native mind. Maybe the new missionary would let him lead the hymns and light the candles and carry the Book into the pagan villages. Maybe some-day he would be made a deacon and go to Oxford or Sydney and study the scriptures and play cricket in front of Christian ladies in lavender and lace.

He saw Malini watching him preach into the gale. Would she ever know that the world was a watery ball spinning in God's endless black space, that day and night flowed from such spin-ning, that the hurricanes came from yearly orbits around the sun, that the ends of the earth were made of ice and guarded by sav-age white bears and flightless birds? Argus knew all these things and knew there to be continents drifting on the briny ocean like potsherds. By lantern he had seen the world's parts laid out on a map where the scale held three fingers to be a thousand miles and Melanesia was like a trail of breadcrumbs. If they stayed at sea long enough they might come ashore on a distant coast where there were cities of stone and glass and churches as big as moun-tains.

After several weeks of drifting, rowing, and pinch-sailing, the New Hebrides seemed as far away and implausible as America or Africa. Malini's bum boils were living sores and they festered her into putrid silences and full-blown scorn. For three days she refused to get into the boat and lay on the volcanic sand, look-ing skyward and weeping like a new widow. Argus gathered fire-wood and fished the reef and, once they were fed, read silently from the two Davids—Copperfield and Balfour. He watched the clouds dismantle and re-form over the endless waters. According to his map they were several hundred miles north and west of the mission.

Days later, a brigantine of Malay pearl divers anchored in the bay and Argus rowed out to meet the boat. In return for some money they were willing to tow the rowboat behind but the kanakas couldn't come aboard. For the next few days they were tossed and pulled south, scraping the dried flesh from coconuts and sitting in the shade of the dropped sail. When one of them had to defecate they squatted over the stern while the other held the portmanteau as a screen from the leering shipmen. Occasionally one of the Malay divers pulled in the towline and tossed them some fish scraps. The meat was enough to bring Malini briefly from her prostrate position. Her boils throbbed all day long. Argus fed her, wiped her forehead with a cloth, promised there was a doctor who came to the mission. To cheer her up he told her that one time the Reverend Mister had to have his bottom drained with a syringe—sharp and thin as a pine needle—by the freckle-faced Anglican doctor. He had watched the holy man drop his trousers and seen the doctor work the pomegranate moon of his arse where a Tanna-like eruption cratered and glowed. The preacher squealed like a runtling pig. Every night for a month, he told her, he had to sleep with a yam poultice in his feather bed. She smiled at this but did not laugh. When she was done eating she lay back and closed her eyes and was soon twitching into feverish dreams.

The Malays untied them five miles from the mission and Argus hauled toward the shimmering sliver of land, his sister whimpering at his feet. He rowed against the tide and arrived before evening, his shoulders on fire. They pulled onto the beach, the mission church and house in plain view.

"You can stay here and I will find the new reverend who will know about boils and how to use the first aid kit. I saw the Reverend Mister use sticky ointment."

"No," she said. "I am not staying here."

"All right. But I'd like to say a prayer in the church before we go up to the house. I need to give thanks for making it back here."

Malini got to her feet and leaned against his shoulder, limping up the beach. She could feel the poisonous blood draining into her feet as she hobbled along. She saw the building with the white walls and the cross just like the one around her brother's neck. It was raised up like a men's clubhouse, only there were sheets of glass in the walls, clearer than bead glass so that you could look inside and see the long wooden planks for sitting down. But some of the sheets of glass were broken and she was surprised that they let pigs and dogs sleep inside. Argus went ahead and she limped after him. Through the open doorway there was a straw pigsty in one corner and three mottled dogs eating scraps from the floor. A pigeon flapped in the rafters and flew into a rent of sky torn into the thatching. The floor was spattered with guano. Her brother walked slowly up to a platform at the front of the clubhouse and looked around with torment on his face.

The pigs had beveled and grated the corners of the pew ends with their teeth and the dogs had scratched the Norfolk pine floorboards with their claws. Argus did his best to shoo the animals out of the church, waving his arms in the air. They scattered and converged indignantly amid the pews. The building was perched on a hillside and the animals had come in through a hole in the back wall, a place level with the ground. The timber siding had been prized from the church frame for firewood so that the vestry where the Reverend Mister paced before a sermon now gave onto a bamboo thicket. No one from the Presbyterian synod had come; they had abandoned the mission and here was the godless result. He mounted the stairs to the pulpit and rested his hands on the lectern, looking down into the pit of consecrated ruin. The saints and virgins and apostles were all gone from this place. No more offerings of breadfruit to God the Father. It was a pigpen and barnyard, a place where fruit bats roosted instead of the dove of the Holy Ghost. Argus told his sister what had happened, that there was no one here to give them work or write a letter of introduction so that she could look after mission babies or wash cotton clothes. Malini thought of her husband, feverish and dying up in a tree. She had abandoned him to die alone and wondered if she had been cursed for it.

They took the overgrown path down to the mission house, Malini favoring her left side. On the verandah they were greeted by Pomat, the village headman. He was wearing a shark-tooth necklace, ochre penis gourd, and the reverend's tartan slippers. He recognized Argus and asked him where he had found a wife and was she sick. Sisa, Argus told him. They stood on the front steps, the shadows lengthening, Pomat trying to block any view of the interior. There were betel-nut mortars and spears laid out on the mantel and the fireplace was full of arrowroot. Pomat had been a troubled political figure in the village, having killed his brother-in-law in battle then taking the man's widow as a second wife. But he sponsored enormous feasts and kept the shamans plied with kava and tropical chestnuts, so that Argus wondered if he wasn't holding court in the mission house, sleeping with a murdered man's wife in the Reverend Mister's feather bed. Argus asked what had happened to the preacher's body. Pomat knew a smattering of English and some pidgin.

"Church men come for stink body with big wooden box," Pomat said. He picked something from his teeth and inspected his fingernail.

"No more big men?"

Pomat shook his head. "They think fire-hair preacher kilim by village. Poison. Maybe tingting you kilim and go away. Now no more tabak or church sing-sings. My ailan now." The big man smiled at Argus, his head slightly cocked in reckoning. "Sisa from up north way? How old sisa?"

Argus bowed his head slightly. "She sick. The fire-hair preacher had a medicine box."

Pomat looked at him blankly.

Argus said, "Marasin box. Feel mobetta powders."

Pomat leaned in the doorway. "What things live in the mobetta box?"

"Ointment creams. White powders for het I pen."

"Het I pen." He nodded. "Where does it stap?"

"Cook room next to the stove."

Pomat went and retrieved the gray metal box with the red cross on the front. He handed it to Argus and watched as he opened the lid. Argus picked through the bottles and jars, reading the labels for any mention of boils. Nitre for asthma, Dover Powder for chill, Opium Tincture for colic and nerves, Aromatic Chalk Powder and Castor Oil for Diarrhoea, Asperine for rheumatism, a thermometer, a set of needles in a hard case. Finally, wrapped in a roll of gauze bandages, he found a small tub of magnesium sulfate *for the relief of boils and carbuncles*. He held it up to Pomat as well as the case of needles, the bandage, and the Opium Tincture because he remembered now the reverend had taken this after having his bottom lanced. "She has feva. We must leave away or olgeta samting get sik."

Pomat took a step back and put his hand over his mouth. The Reverend Mister had taught them to be afraid of germs and that sneezing and coughing without covering their mouths would lose them a part of their soul. For good measure, Argus grabbed the thermometer, handed the first aid kit back to Pomat, and turned to go.

"Stap," said the headman.

Argus dropped his sister's wrist and turned.

Pomat came forward and handed the first aid kit to Argus. "Waitman gone now. Nogat tobak and nogat marasin."

Argus took the kit. No doubt the headman suspected that typhoid had spread like wood dust in the pews of the church on Sunday mornings despite the inoculation of prayer. The waitman with his box of creams and powders and Holy Ghost was surely to blame. Pomat stood in the reverend's tartan slippers, waving; behind him, trophy skulls lined the fireplace mantel.

Argus said *tenkyu* and backed down the stairs, Malini at his side. Pomat leaned in the doorway and watched them retreat through the thicket toward the beach. After a few hundred feet they came into a clearing fringed with rhododendron and Argus saw a singed wooden frame overgrown with creeper weeds and flowers. The blackened middle rose up like a guillotine. It wasn't until he saw the levered handle and the unhinged block and the metal type still wedged in place that he realized it was the reverend's letterpress. The islanders had carried it from the house, dropped it beside a bog, and tried to burn it. But the press was only lightly charred. The jungle had begun to swallow it whole. Argus stripped back the vines and tried to pry the letters free but they were rusted in place. He removed the entire letterplate and read the reversed font in the dying light.

Natives abhor the general. Speak of the lamb and the dove but not the Ten Commandments without citing itemized punishments and rewards. Further, beware of uttering the future. An Englishman says, "When I get to the village it will be nightfall," while the Melanesian says, "I am there, it is night." The Scotsman says, "it will soon be dark and we will need to eat" while the savage says, "I am hungry and it has become already night." We possess the power of realising the future as present or past; the native does not possess such power. For the Melanesian, everything is unfolding now.

13.

The *Cullion* crossed the equator and slouched into the Doldrums. Jethro, after jabbing his way to victory and passing his oral maritime exam (*If present, is the jiggermast the third or fourth shortest of the masts? Explain the customs between privileged and burdened vessels.*), was now free to clew the sails. But the wind was days away. Terrapin fired up the engines to cross the equator slantwise at the 180th meridian, the International Dateline, at the stroke of midnight. An entire day was erased from the calendar. This accorded Jethro and the other sailors the status of Golden Shellbacks and thereby began a series of maritime rituals — a mock revolt, baptism by bilgewater, a beauty pageant. Teddy Meyers, veteran seahand, won the pageant with his mother's retired silk evening gown and a whalebone corset he'd brought along for just such an occasion. Terrapin closed the equatorial proceedings by bungling some Coleridge: *All in a hot and copper sky . . . Day after day, day after day, we drifted idle as a painted ship upon a painted ocean.*

When the winds did pick up, Jethro and Owen worked their way from jib to mainsail, blistered their hands slackening and tightening hempen lines through the groaning mouths of blocks, cinching halyards around belaying pins. Owen hadn't worked like this in several years and he liked the way the labor strained his lungs, burned his shoulders, benumbed his thoughts. The uptake of air in the topsail as they sped away from the flaccid Doldrums was like the sound of a thoroughbred snorting mid-race. The keening of the wind against the shrouds and the billowed sailcloth on a tack were part of his dreams at night. At dinner he ate his weight in beans and rice before collapsing into his hammock and letting the day's thoughts tick over and empty out into sleep. His dreams were crystalline and sun-drenched: a country house with Adelaide baking bread, a glimpsed orchard, white bedsheets flapping in the yard. He wondered how he could make himself worthy of that future vision, what had he done to deserve such tenderness in his life.

He went to breakfast each morning with a growling pit bull in his stomach and ate whatever gruelish thing the cook-cum-surgeon had prepared. And it was surgery and sawbones more than comestibles that came to mind whenever Hendrik Stuyvesant laid out a platter of bleeding mutton and formless eggs. Owen climbed to the deck and took his assigned position from Terrapin. The captain had become affable now that all the dockside bluster among the men had been settled. All were equalized, he said, by the demands of confined living and the whims of the sea herself.

The men had also been mellowed by their carnal Hawaiian days, the pageant of crossing the line, and close to a week of riding the trades with all sails out. This was when Owen liked it best—hauling up on a starboard tack, the seamen bent at their work, fierce as Maori warriors. The piston-and-crank of their arms flurried in his peripheral vision as the ship cleaved the lip of a colossal swell. For hours at a time between tacks and jibes, Owen and Jethro perched silently up in the rigging, roped to the mizzenmast, trimming the topsails.

To Jethro the work was a revelation. He felt sinew in his back and arms for the first time. He noted the way his bones hummed in a high wind and the salt caked his mouth with a satisfying thirst, the way a dozen men sat in the rigging wordless and sullen like boys sulking up in trees. An occasional whistle or quip emerged from the high rigging. There were rules for whistling. It beckoned the winds and should never be done when under gale. Jethro did his best to observe their customs. The equatorial sunsets were brief and chromatic, the final seam of light gone in a burst.

His shipmates were congenial enough toward him but he floundered for common ground with them. His brief encounters with women had been lackluster and didn't warrant mention. After hearing the grisly details of other men's exploits he couldn't help feeling a lack—he'd never buttered a naked woman's toast or kissed a pretty girl without knowing her name. At Harvard he'd dated country girls from Radcliffe who were well bred but horsey. They were prim in their opinions about his dinner attire and the books on his shelf. The most reckless thing any of them had done was steal sherry from their father's liquor cabinets and ride bareback at the beach. They saw Jethro as a gentle dabbler, an uncertain bet. Despite the fact that he was heir to a mammoth insurance empire, he was pulled in too many directions—science, fine art, poetry, card games, boxing—not so much a Renaissance man as a dilettante, a competent traveler. The Radcliffe girls inevitably left him for firmer ground—future accountants and lawyers, even politicians. But for now this was no matter; tied to the mizzenmast, the clipper trued in a sheet of sunlight, he felt loosed from all worldly expectations. He had reserves and stamina. The South Seas were upon them. The collection of specimens was growing below deck now that the men had stopped interfering. Looking down at his split knuckles he thought, *I may make a contribution to science.* His senses felt sharp, his mind elastic. For several days now, he'd sensed the edges of a poem taking shape somewhere inside him. *The sea brims and I brim* was a definite candidate for first line. The truth was, this acuity and sensory elation had started the very moment he knocked Harvey McCallister to the deck, his temple bruised and bleeding. Terrapin had come out to raise Jethro's arms above his head and he'd felt faintly reborn. Somewhere in all this watery splendor there was a resolute self waiting to be formed.

Introspection was unavoidable at sea. The immense sight lines had a way of turning a man inward. Up in the rigging, Owen watched a progression of coral atolls and saw his life in outline, a lineage of bare rocks that stood for future events—marriage, children, even his own death could be reckoned in the crags that dotted then diminished above the ocean. He saw the other men in the cross-trees, each of them sunk in his own reverie between tacks. Somehow, the sea offered a reprieve from the turning wheel. He could see the workings of his life more clearly, felt a fondness for it that he seldom felt ashore. Time slowed and the days were graspable things, bright objects waiting to be taken up.

He saw Jethro musing in his notebook and wondered what those pages might contain. Was the heir really concerned with science and the common good? It seemed far-fetched that he wanted to benefit mankind through his bird-poaching and mammal-stuffing. Yet Owen couldn't help envying what Jethro knew of the world, at least its scientific fabric and underpinnings. But Jethro also plainly knew about art and literature, tossed off casual references to this philosopher or that poet. Owen felt somehow accused by this body of knowledge. What had he done to improve himself, to prepare for a life with Adelaide? What had he ever accomplished for nonmaterial gain? Perhaps he could learn something from the heir that would raise him in Adelaide's estimation, make him a fuller citizen of the world.

Then again, was philanthropy and worldly concern only for the rich? He thought of Adelaide's efforts with the Bohemian poor; yes, she had an elevated perch from which to dispense charity, but he suspected she'd have volunteered at Hull House even if she were living solely off her secretary's wage. Again it came to him that he was unworthy of her, despite her efforts to bear him up. Every time he thought of bringing savages back so that he could receive his contractual bonus he felt a glimmer of shame. But he wasn't sure if it was his own shame or Adelaide's. Her disapproving regard and folded arms played out in his thoughts. Her wifely recriminations would be something to behold. Surely the whole enterprise could be done ethically . . . One of the tethered seamen started singing and he joined in, their voices seeming to fill the topsails.

Owen shared his trading route with the captain and it was in the New Hebrides, on the island of Malekula, that the collecting voyage would begin in earnest. The *Lady Cullion* resupplied and watered in Fiji. The seamen loaded the bark with a fresh supply of chickens—most of the laying hens had been eaten—in addition to dry goods and wood. For two hours after dawn, Jethro went birding with his wicker creel and 12-gauge shotgun, a pair of Bond's placental forceps looped through the buttonhole of his suspenders in case he shot something he didn't want to touch with his bare hands. Owen sent a wire to Hale Gray to report on their progress and obtained some additional trading goods. He converted some U.S. dollars to English and Australian pounds and French francs. He managed to buy a few tribal clubs from a missionary with a church by the port in Suva. The pink-cheeked Anglican—Reverend Bulstrode—had a collecting kit for tropical butterflies, much to Jethro's delight, and promised he would keep an eye out for artifacts the next time he went upriver. Owen gave him ten pounds and wrote down a shipping address.

As the English minister turned from the dock he said, "And how do you intend to get along in Malekula, Mr. Graves? Nothing but cannibals and Presbyterians is what I hear. They bandage their babies' heads to make the skulls conical, like so many tiny volcanoes. One wonders about such people."

"I agree with you, Reverend; Presbyterians are a strange lot," joked Owen.

The missionary smiled but said nothing. Jethro shuffled nervously at Owen's side, arranging his bird pelts to fill the silence.

Turning for the church, Reverend Bulstrode said, "I hear there's a French trader living on the southern end of the island. I would recommend securing his services, such as they are."

Two days later the ship anchored in a southern Malekula bay. Owen stood by the cathead and watched the anchor line run out, sluicing the water like a smelter's knife through waved lead. Three men stood aloft and furled the mainsail. Terrapin was on deck to oversee the operation and had barely left the charthouse since Fiji. He was said to be in a blue funk. In these latitudes, Owen was told, the captain had a standing obsession about the *Cullion* getting hogged up on a reef or running aground on a sandbar. One night, Owen had overheard one of his lectures to the first and second mate: "You both sail by the book, but it's more than seamanship that gets a bark through these waters. It's instinct, a feeling in the skin. I look for harbingers and omens, the way the buntlines whisper against the sailcloth. From my cabin I know when the ship is stuttering or off-kilter . . . Lying in bed I can feel the tension in sails, whether she's drawing twenty-six feet or less, whether a seaman on the dogwatch is pissing too long off the starboard railing and is therefore drunk . . ."

When the eastern sky seamed with the day's first light, a small landing party rowed ashore in one of the dinghies. The whaleboats, Terrapin said, were reserved for shipwreck or matters of nautical state. Owen and Jethro were accompanied by Giles Blunt, the introverted carpenter, and Dickey Fentress, the woolly-headed cabin boy and apprentice. Giles leaned whistling against the gunwale with a hunting rifle slung over one shoulder while Dickey rowed them toward the beach. Jethro sat in the stern, a finger trailing in the small wake, his nets and collecting creel at his feet. Owen took inventory of his trading stock—a bag of glass beads, six steel knives, three machetes, a dozen mirrors, a ream of paper, bottles of ink, a carton of matches, three looking-glasses, a fathom of calico. The lush mountains drew up from the pale beach and the trading station stood at one end, a ramshackle cottage made of driftwood, a tendril of smoke rising from its chimney. Dickey feathered the oars into the shallows and they dragged the boat up onto the beach.

They approached the cottage and a tall man dressed in filthy dungarees came out holding a revolver and a demitasse of coffee.

Giles slightly lifted the rifle at his side then lowered it at Owen's insistence.

Owen said, "Reverend Bulstrode sent us. We're out here to do some trading."

"I'm sure the priest had some complimentary things to say about me." The Frenchman tucked the revolver into his waistband and blew across his smoking coffee. He gestured with his cup at the anchored bark and the sailors followed his gaze. Captain Terrapin was taking a constitutional morning swim, executing his backstroke rather sloppily while several men rowed a whaleboat beside him and kept the shark watch with pistols.

"I am Bernard Corlette. Would you gentlemen care for some coffee? Camille has just made some." The formality of the invitation seemed out of place with the Frenchman's dirt-smeared clothes. Although his face was aristocratic—a high-bridged nose, mineral blue eyes—it was also sunken. Something about the jawline suggested missing teeth.

Owen introduced the party and accepted the offer. They mounted the makeshift stairs and entered a bare room, the walls chinked with daylight. A figure moved at a woodstove and they saw a native girl, not more than sixteen, tending a coffeepot. She turned, eyes down, and laid out four chipped porcelain cups onto a bamboo table. She wore a flimsy floral blouse and a fringed skirt made of woven grass. For a moment Owen wanted to believe that the girl was the maid and not the wife. But Bernard removed any doubt with: "This is Camille. She is pretty, no?"

"Lovely," said Dickey, swallowing.

Bernard said, "Twenty-five boars. All with tusks. Can you believe it? A fortune. A bloody king's ransom for this girl." He blew her a kiss with his fingers and she shrugged then commenced chopping green bananas.

Jethro could not look at the girl directly. He cupped his coffee in his hands and sipped it. It was bitter and hot. With the grounds left in, it tasted more Turkish than French.

They sat on low stools and took in the room. Owen had expected a space filled with tribal artifacts but it was empty save for a stash of French newspapers, a bed, a storm lantern. Everything was covered in a fine layer of silt. It was not squalor so much as exiled ruin, the one-room abode of a man who'd fled civilization. Bernard took a refill from Camille and touched her buttocks in a way that made them all turn their eyes to the wall or the floorboards.

"How long have you been out here?" Owen asked.

Bernard returned and sat on the floor definitively, as if this answered the question. He downed the shot of coffee with one swift throwback of the head. "Years. I am almost one of them. However, I keep a little pinky finger in the world with my trading. I have a brother in Paris, an astronomer, who sends me *La Gazette*. I read of bunting and taffeta and it makes me laugh aloud."

Owen watched Bernard examine his blackened fingernails and thought of Adelaide and the smell of starched cotton. She was his insurance policy against this sort of existence.

"Who do you trade with?" Owen asked.

"Lately it is the Germans. They are crazy for everything they can get their hands on. Baskets. Penis gourds. I could sell them a toothpick if it had touched tribal lips."

Jethro let his gaze sidle over to Camille, who was now frying the green bananas in a skillet. Her dark hair was long and matted and clumped at the neck. She stood barefoot, shifting from side to side, raising one heel at a time. The bottoms of her feet were pink and calloused. He watched as the glints of firelight from the stove hatch threw her breasts into flickering relief. To change the course of his libidinous thoughts he said, "Are there snakes on this island?"

Bernard formed a peak with his fingers. "Why do you ask?"

"I am the ship's naturalist."

A tandem sigh from Giles and Dickey.

"And you will be wanting to collect snakes?"

"All manner of things."

"Then you will be happy to know that the land snakes are not poisonous. Of course, the sea snakes are another matter. Venomous and difficult to catch." He turned back to Owen, who was clearly the man in charge. "What is it you wish to collect, Mr. Graves?"

"Tools, masks, weapons, that sort of thing. Baskets. Handiwork."

Bernard crossed his arms, lightly flushed from the coffee. "And naturally you will desire the rambaramp."

Owen paused. He'd never heard of such a thing and wondered if it weren't some kind of canoe.

"For the sake of your men's edification: this is an effigy, sometimes life-sized, for a man of rank. They smoke and dry the body and cut off the head. They make a kind of statue with tree ferns, wood, and compost, perhaps some resin and cobwebs, then cap the whole thing off with the skull and occasionally use the dried facial skin of the dead man. It is a marvelous sight. Also terrible."

The Frenchman delighted in the details as if he were recounting the ingredients of a renowned bouillabaisse.

"Ingenious, no? Quite a ritual. It takes a year for the entire process to be completed."

"Can such a thing be obtained?" Owen said.

"Anything can be obtained, but naturally it is a question of means. The village down here only has one left and I doubt they would part with it. What are you intending to trade?"

Owen repositioned himself on the stool and emptied his coffee cup. He was conscious of his shipmates watching him. "In the rowboat we have glass beads, knives, matches. We also have some calico. That sort of thing."

Bernard touched his left earlobe and grinned sarcastically. "Perhaps you think it is 1797."

Jethro couldn't help feeling smug; Owen had said just such a thing to him before departure, something about wanting to make new discoveries a hundred years too late.

"I'm not following," said Owen, bristling.

"Have you been voyaging in the South Seas before?"

"Yes, a few years back."

"Well, things have changed. The savages do not want matches and mirrors and little glass marbles anymore. They want guns, cash, pigs, tobacco. I have done my best to keep guns off this island because I do not wish to be shot in my sleep. Last year the German New Guinea Company bought some land on Matty Island in the Bismarck region and set up a trading station. The trader was dead within weeks. My suggestion is that you make a list of things you would like and I will quote a total fee and bring the goods out to your ship. Payment terms will be in francs, naturally."

"We'd prefer to do our own trading," Owen said.

Jethro added: "And I'd like to collect some specimens."

Bernard drummed his fingernails on the dirt floor. "Do you imagine you will walk into one of the villages and ask to see the cannibal forks?"

Jethro said, "We will happily pay you as our guide. And we have some chickens and pigs on board the ship which perhaps can be used for trading purposes."

Owen turned quickly to Jethro but did not look him in the face. "The livestock is not ours to trade."

Jethro looked at the stove. "Not yours, at any rate, but bought with company finances."

"Yes, in order to feed the men fresh meat. Or do you intend to incite a mutiny so that you can bag some lizards?"

Dickey bit his bottom lip to stifle his laughter.

Bernard scratched the underside of his chin and stood. "For a fee I will take you into the villages and help you trade. You can take your chances with whatever you have to barter. The Malekula are very business-minded and shrewd. They think we Westerners are all feeble-minded and practically blind." He set his coffee cup down. "Meet me on the beach at sunrise if this is agreeable to you."

They entered the village just after dawn, Bernard leading the way with his pistol in his waistband. Giles, rifle slung over his back, trailed with Dickey in the rear, carrying a tea chest of trade items between them and pulling a sow up from the sandy beach. Jethro had managed to convince Terrapin and the cook to part with one of the hogs in return for a commitment that he would purchase two pigs at the next supply stop with his own funds. Despite the fact that this furthered Owen's trading agenda, Owen resented the interference. Bernard had implied that a sow, although inferior to a boar, was better than no livestock at all, so Owen had agreed to bring it along. Jethro gathered a few specimens in a muslin bag on the way into the settlement—a dusty moth, a tree frog, a skink, a horned beetle.

The village was set back from the beach and shrouded by a riot of cycas and tree fern. Beds of yam and taro were hacked into the junglescape, the swidden plots overhung with breadfruit. They moved in single file, the footpath narrowed by a gorge choked with wild cane and umbrella palm. As the native village appeared up ahead, Bernard explained its design. The dwelling houses for the women and children were made from thatch and bamboo, and the men's clubhouse—the *amel*—was at the other end of a central clearing and was more elaborately decorated. The men all slept and ate together according to rank. A series of carved wooden gongs stood in the middle of the clearing. The gongs were used during the men's secret ceremonies and rites, when the women were banished from sight behind the hedge fence. The villagers were milling in front of their houses, smoking and preparing food. They seemed indifferent to the arrival of visitors.

As they came into the clearing it struck Owen that the men outnumbered the women by two to one. "Are the women out gathering?" he asked.

"This island is overrun with bachelors. Why do you think Camille was so expensive? And now the missionaries want to stop the village wars in the name of the Virgin Mary. How do they expect to ever trim the male population?"

They stood and waited, the sow snuffling in the dirt. Bernard told them to wait in the shade. Giles placed the rifle at his side and leaned back cautiously on his hands. Jethro set his muslin specimen bag in front of him and sat cross-legged, pinching the knees of his trousers. He was glad to still see two faint pleats from their last proper laundering.

An old man with closely cropped hair came forward and squatted on his haunches in front of them, setting his spears on the ground beside him. Another man came from the *amel* clutching what looked to be a scuffed leather briefcase, its monogram lettering faded to tiny shards of gilt. Like the first man, he wore a boar-tusk armlet and a strip of bark around his waist that was tethered to his penis by a woven sheath.

"Shoremen bring the sheath straight up and tuck it under the belt while the bushmen come up on the diagonal. A matter of style," said Bernard to a snickering Dickey.

Rather than carry the briefcase by the handles the approaching man clutched it in front of his chest and joined them on the ground. He snapped the metal fasteners open, then removed and spread a yellowed edition of *La Gazette*. Jethro noticed that it was five years old and bore the headline *Guerre Afrique Atroce!* Giles Blunt took his eyes off the bare-chested women for a moment and said, "Jesus, he's taught them to read French," with simple wonderment. But then the two villagers began to tear one of the newspaper pages into strips and proceeded to roll cigarettes from a pouch of tobacco. They handed out perfect newsprint cigarettes and Bernard passed around a silver lighter. They sat in the dirt smoking silently, a hazy nimbus climbing above their heads. The rest of the village went about its unhurried morning ritual. To Jethro the tobacco tasted a little stale and leggy.

When the Malekula men had finished their cigarettes, Bernard introduced them as Bonum and Nagolo, brothers and headmen. Jethro extended his hand in greeting and it hung there for ten seconds before he cleared his throat and brought it back to his lap.

"Merry Krismas," said Bonum solemnly.

Bernard spoke to the two men in a combination of pidgin and monosyllabic French. They called him *man-oui-oui*. Owen saw him gesture to the tea chest and the sow, his voice emphatic. The Malekula men clicked their tongues and laughed, shaking their heads. Bernard said something scoffing and the men laughed with renewed vigor.

It was arranged that they could move about the village but they were banned from entering the *amel* directly. Anything they wished to barter for could be brought into the clearing and a reckoning would be done at the end. Jethro took Giles to help him gather specimens and received directions to a snake-riddled grove of bastard cotton trees behind the village. Although Owen had prevented him from bringing along his 12-gauge birding shotgun—the trading party didn't need to look like a militia— Jethro had smuggled a small pistol into his wicker creel and intended to use it if he spied unusual plumage. Dickey tied the sow to the hedge fence and several young boys came forward to inspect its snout and flanks. Bernard said, "The men won't eat a sow. It is beneath them. A boar has value in relation to its tusks. You have brought them a little tub of bacon grease for their wives."

Owen walked toward the dwellings, where householders were already bringing out belts, baskets, boar-tusk armlets, clay masks, bows made from arched roots of mangrove. The goods were laid on leaves of ivory palm. Owen took several armfuls of artifacts down to the clearing. Dickey peeked into the sleeping rooms of the houses but was shooed away by an old woman in a banded headdress. She took him by the arm and led him into the center of a group of women and girls who immediately began touching the kinked blond strands of his hair. Dickey had endured countless taunts on account of his woolly head of hair and he'd neglected to have the cook-surgeon-barber trim what Terrapin called the most unseamanlike pelt he'd ever laid eyes on. While a commotion gathered around Dickey's unruly hair, the girls twining out strands between their fingers and whistling through their teeth, Owen went to look at the chest-high gongs and drifted over to look partway into the clubhouse.

At the far end of the murky interior he could see a mummified effigy—three feet tall, the limbs tightly coiled in cobweb and clay, the smoked skin mottled and roughed over the skull. The mouth was harrowed through with jagged teeth, the eye sockets empty. It brought to Owen's mind the apocalyptic menace of the sharks at the Columbian Exposition aquarium four years prior, of staring into the maw of something otherworldly and desolate. He knew it was the item worth collecting above all others and wondered what would induce the villagers to give it up. It wasn't on Hale Gray's list but only because he'd not known such a thing existed. The Field Museum would also go to great lengths to have such an item behind glass. He walked over to Bernard, who was eating a bowl of laplap pudding. "Did you ask them about the effigy?"

"You would need a whole ship full of boars and virgins."

"Is that so?"

"And even then they might not oblige. That statue is some long-dead headman and they think he still breathes somewhere inside that ghastly head."

Owen said, "Would you ask them what it would take?"

Bernard shrugged and kicked a pig-bladder ball back to a band of playing boys. "They call us ghost skins. We're the walking dead to them. I'll ask them politely but I won't haggle. I'll still be their neighbor long after your ship sails on."

Jethro and Giles came bursting out of the bush at that moment, the insurance heir with his finger raised in anguish and Giles carrying a bag of writhing snakes and lizards. "He's been bit," said Giles, repositioning the rifle on his shoulder.

"As I said, not poisonous," Bernard responded calmly.

Jethro came forward with his finger lacerated and purpled. A few drops of blood had gathered on the fingertip and he was squeezing it. "Best to bleed it, I think," he said, wincing. "I didn't have the stomach to kill the snakes but I suppose that will have to be done before too long."

Bernard picked up the muslin sack of shifting forms, swung it nonchalantly above his head, and let it thwack against a coconut tree. He placed the bag back at Jethro's feet — "Nothing damaged, I hope" — and returned to his impromptu soccer game with the village boys.

Jethro took the bag and emptied its dazed, reptilian contents onto the dirt. He began arranging the snakes and lizards by size with his one good hand, holding the other limp at his side. He tossed several damaged specimens into nearby bushes, the dogs setting on them immediately, and placed the better ones into the creel for later curing. Bonum came over to tend his finger, rubbing some bark and leaves into the wound.

Owen returned to look at the effigy in the clubhouse, staring into its inscrutable face. Nagolo noticed him and took him by the hand, leading him behind the *amel*. They walked toward a lashed bamboo lean-to that stood under starbursts of wild orchids. Nagolo removed some of the leafy camouflage at the entrance to reveal a pyramid of yams, shoulder high and a dozen feet deep. On a planed piece of hardwood at the base of the pyramid was an assemblage of rusted tins of meat, the sun-jaundiced lettering in German and French and Malay, a lineage of HMS *Liverpool* brass buttons, and a Civil War musket lying in pieces, a cupped leaf of gunpowder at its side. A pinned and torn broadsheet presided above it all and depicted Santa Claus — sparsely bearded and a little too thin — holding hands with Parisian children on the Champs-Elysées in a glitter of dusky snow. Owen wondered what all of this meant. Was there a deity involved? An offering? Had the man in the red suit and patchy beard been mistaken for an exiled ancestor? He'd heard passing stories during his last voyage of cults centering on Western goods, of native militias marching under a threadbare Union Jack, pigeon rifles and broomsticks over their shoulders. Were they saving tins of meat for a future day of reckoning, a day when they would take their rightful share of ghost-skin spoils? Nagolo pointed at the broken musket, then at Owen, then touched his own chest. He squinted one eye as if looking through a gun sight. Owen nodded and they returned to the clearing. It was time to barter and apparently the women had already decided that in addition to the fathom of calico they wanted all of Dickey Fentress's golden curls. He sat upright under the deliberation of a bone-handled knife, wielded by an old woman who sang as she severed one lock after another. The Frenchman turned to Owen and said, "We have begun to trade without you. As you can see, your shipmate has made the first payment."

That night, Owen had the shorn apprentice row him ashore to trade a rifle for the rambaramp. He waited until the lantern at the trading station was extinguished and told Dickey to hush the oars through the water. Nagolo was waiting for him at the beachhead, the effigy upright in the sand beside him. Owen gave him the rifle and a box of ammunition. Nagolo helped him load the rambaramp into the boat while Dickey looked on warily. "Face it the other way," he said. "I'm not rowing back with that thing lookin square at me." Owen obliged and turned to make some gesture of thanks to Nagolo but the headman was already walking up the beach with the rifle aimed at the onrush of stars.

In the morning Captain Terrapin spent an hour tossing coins for the diving Malekula boys. The seamen watched them rise through the tessellated depths with silver in their teeth. Half a dozen villagers launched fishing kites from their outriggers. The crew prepared the sails aloft and waved goodbye, waiting for Terrapin to give the order to heave short. Main and mizzen trimmed, the captain patrolled the boat for native stowaways, Nipper at his side, wind at the starboard beam. With the topsails set and the windlass manned, he boomed to break her out and it wasn't long before the *Cullion* was under a nice press of sail.

Owen watched the shores of Malekula diminish in the distance. He thought of the rifle and the damage it might wreak on the island; trading it had been a moral failure, to be sure. Somehow he'd felt powerless to stop the transaction, even though it was of his own devising. He wondered if there wasn't something defective in his personality, a calculating instinct and competitiveness. He thought now, with Malekula diminishing, that he'd paid more than necessary for Bernard's services. As far as he could tell, the Frenchman was more of an impediment to negotiations than anything else. The expedition needed to retain a native guide and translator if they were going to keep costs down. Future expedition funding from Hale Gray would depend on it. By maximizing the gain on every trade, Owen thought, he was securing a livelihood and therefore benefiting his future family.

He planned to spend part of the day writing a fresh letter to Adelaide, having mailed the first one in Fiji. He would write about the bamboo store of yams and tinned meat, about the image of Santa Claus hanging like the patron saint of tubers. He tried to picture her life and routine—taking dictation in one of the narcoleptic meetings at the museum, or reading in the streetcar—but what came to him, leaning against the Baltic fir of the mainmast, was the image of her making love during their final night together. Against all convention and propriety she had given herself over and there she was on his Chinese junk of a bed frame, naked, a traveler out of her depths, eyes peering through a curtain of her own hair, looking back over her shoulder with a mixture of flushed indignation and total surrender.

Jethro sat in the orlop with his dead birds and reptiles. His snake-bitten finger had been bandaged by the cook and it pulsed now in the fetid, submarine air. There was work to be done and he'd given the bulkhead over to Owen's trading items and settled for the would-be sick bay. He'd had Giles rough together some bookshelves, a workbench, a stool. He sat with a lamp burning and his microscope gently swaying a beam of light from its mirrored disc. No one bothered him down here and he'd managed to rid the orlop of some of its briny reek. His glass vials and hand lenses were resting on velvet; his jars of algae and starfish were arranged on a makeshift shelf. There was so much to do—compile a seaweed album, a fern case, a rack of eggs prepared with gum arabic. There were countless ways to arrange and distill nature's breathing plentitude.

Open on the workbench beside him was William Muttridge's *Taxidermy and Methods of Preparing Natural Specimens,* its spine broken and pages heavily underlined. Lately he'd become enthralled by its wisdom and practicality, though he'd also borrowed some ornithological points from Robert Ridgway, curator of the Department of Birds at the National Museum. The only point of disagreement between the two scientists was what to use for poisoning the skin of a bird—Muttridge recommended arsenical soap while Ridgway insisted on mixing pure arsenic with oil of bitter almonds to repel insects. The soap was safer for handling but less vigilant against ants. Jethro found himself unable to make up his mind and shifted from one poison to the other.

On the matter of procedure and equipment they presented a unified front and Jethro had wholeheartedly adopted their regimen—set off birding early in the morning and with a field kit containing sharp- and blunt-pointed scissors, heavy cutting forceps for breaking the leg and wing bones of large birds, cartilage knives, raw cotton for stuffing, tow, needles and thread for repairing incisions, a variety of scalpels, a tin box to keep scientific kills cool before fuller preparation. They were very particular in recommending a firearm—a 12-gauge, double-barreled, breech-loading shotgun, one barrel choked and the other barrel cylinder-bored. They insisted on rimfire shells filled with American wood powder, grade D, and buckshot ranging in size from No. 4 to No. 12, depending on the size of the prey. Jethro carried all of the above into the field but also a small pistol for its ease of handling and concealment. Technically, he was forbidden by the ship's articles from possessing a firearm but—if the captain should ask—he would affirm that the oaths of science and art demanded separate allegiance.

He sat preparing a Royal Parrot Finch for its second life. He'd spent the morning cleaning it and working the skin from the carcass with cornmeal to prevent adhesion. He made a small incision with a scalpel in the bird's blue neck and introduced a gouge using the handle of a teaspoon. He used the orifice to tweeze out the bird's brain, about the size of a cranberry, and then cut away the tiny, pallid tongue. The most delicate procedure was removing the eyes intact. Jethro placed some cotton between the tines of his tweezers and plied each eye from its socket. They were like rolled beads of mercury.

The scientific technique was in the procuring and preserving but the art was in the resurrection of form, of trying to capture the very mind and wild spirit of the bird. The goggle-eyed stiffs of inferior bird-stuffers had always made Jethro wince. He knew he was an amateur naturalist but nonetheless wanted to achieve something lasting and artful. He could still remember the day when his father and he were in London a dozen years prior, Hale on some business at Lloyd's, and Jethro had spent an afternoon in front of the hummingbird case in the British Museum. In his memory it was the size of a railcar, glass-fronted, and he'd stood before it, half horrified by the desiccated forms. The hummingbirds were lifeless and wizened, petrified on their little twigs and branches. But he'd also been entranced by such variety—the swordbills, sapphires, ruby-breasteds, starthroats—the promise of nature's infinite forms.

A ripple caught his eye as he wadded cotton inside the upper body of the Royal Parrot Finch. Something shifted among the lifeless, coiled snakes. He moved the direction of the lamplight and saw the plumage of a Glossy Swiftlet faintly rising on its darkened chest. Jethro became aware of his own breathing, of a pinched feeling at the bottom of each inhalation, as he watched the bird, its eyelids slightly parted, squinting. There was no gunshot wound in the feathers and it was possible that when he'd fired into the nested cliff face that he'd dazed but not killed the bird. He lowered his face to the bird and could hear a delicate hook in its breath, something vaguely accusatory. He straightened, paced, returned to the workbench. It was still breathing, one eye shut. He looked around for a humane weapon, something to snuff the avian life with efficiency. He might hold a handkerchief over his fingers and clamp its short beak shut or twist its neck, swiftly, like a cook breaking a head of lettuce. But both options required manhandling and he preferred an instrument between him and a specimen. Science was the intermediary. He settled on a drop of pure arsenic and pried open the swiftlet's beak with a pair of tweezers. The bird twitched its wings, the underfeathers curling, as the liquid coated its throat. Jethro smoothed its breast with his bandaged hand. In his bitten finger he felt a renewed throbbing, a pain that was high and brilliant and radiated along the entire length of his arm.

IV

LINES AND LATITUDES

14.

Several times a week, Hale Gray took his lunch at the Prairie Club, a hallowed gentlemen's club in a converted mansion on Michigan Avenue between Adams and Jackson. Many of the members were Hale's neighbors from Prairie Avenue—six blocks of turret and sandstone that controlled the mercantile fate of the city. Philip D. Armour (2115), the meatpacking giant; George Pullman (1729), the ailing railroad magnate; John G. Shortall (1600), the realtor who, after the Great Fire, produced thousands of property deeds and covenants from his bricked-out basement; and Marshall Field (1905), the emperor of retail. The Grays lived at 1903, directly adjacent to the Fields. Over the years there had been squabbles about the upkeep of a common fence, Mrs. Field's mania for bird and squirrel feeding, and responsibility for removing a blighted elm. Hale could remember bellowing over the side fence at the chittering war cries of squirrels or standing with his shirtsleeves rolled up, fists clenched, as he stared down at the Fields eating breakfast in what amounted to a backyard aviary. In earlier years, they had been neighborly, even fraternal. Their children shared the same music and archery teachers, their wives served on each other's committees. The husbands—elm blight and bird menace aside—sat shoulder to shoulder at the club's million-aires' table or idled smoky talk from the divans in the sun-sheeted reading room. They were brothers of a sort, had framed the club's bylaws and points of order, helped to police the visitor sign-in book, enjoyed a bit of sport with the Negro hallboys—dressing them up as Nubian slaves in leopard skins and sandals for the annual Twelfth Night festivities—and yet their curiosities for each other's lives ran more to potential downfall than triumph.

Hale kept up with all the woes at the millionaires' table. George Pullman, who'd become widely hated after his handling of a railway strike, was said to be at death's door and would be buried beneath concrete in a lead-lined casket to avoid being plundered and exhumed by angry unionists. Hale was relieved that he had declined to carry Pullman's life insurance policy. Philip Armour, who preferred boats to trains, had attempted to dynamite a passage through the frozen lake one winter, trying to get a shipment of wheat and pork out east on time. This had guaranteed him the undying enmity of every sailor, bridge warden, lock keep, and shipping clerk in Chicago. Hale had no such enemies and was grateful for the quiet and dignified line of insuring a man against fire, maritime mishap, and untimely demise.

But Hale reserved a special curiosity for Marshall Field's life. That he had given a million dollars to found his namesake museum of natural history was, to Hale, showy and distasteful, the kind of puerile vanity that nowadays bloomed everywhere in America. Money could not buy character and giving it away—Marshall had also teamed up with Rockefeller for the University of Chicago—was a misplaced desire for status, an ornate label on a cheap bottle of wine. Marshall Field had never gone to university and knew nothing about the charter of a museum. He was a farm boy and dry goods merchant made big, didn't know a piece of Baltic amber from a sliver of Malaysian jade. Hale had peerage in his bloodline, members of the House of Lords, and even with that endowment—or perhaps because of it—he hadn't felt the need to inscribe his own name on the world's tallest building. A legend on the translucent windowpane of his office door was good enough for him. The totemic spire was a company gift to the skyline, to the children of the city so that they might aspire to something lofty, and it was born of civic pride, a social dividend from the simple calculus of hedging one's bets against God's unknowable plan. Civilization's highest point had for centuries been reserved for pyramids, cathedrals, and monuments, but now it belonged to this business of wagering against divinity.

The talk in the club reading room this Wednesday was about the suicide who'd plunged to his death from the Masonic Building that morning. Headfirst, arms trawling the air in front of him, the well-dressed clerk fell sixteen stories from the rooftop atrium, through the center court of the Masonic Temple, hurling past office windows in a downpour of sunlight. The shock of impact, said Horace Wells, a lawyer, was akin to an elevator in freefall. As a freemason and Worshipful Master, he had seen the body shuttle past his office window and thought one of the office boys had dropped a large bundle of newspapers as a dangerous joke. He held forth as the authority on the matter, leaning forward in a circle of armchaired tycoons and industrialists.

"The clerk hit the fourth-floor landing and went through it like it was butter, gentlemen. A scrubwoman discovered his body a story below in a tangle of wooden and iron balustrade. His shoes were found sixty feet away, the soles blown off."

"I heard he was down-and-out, living in a ten-cent lodging house on State Street," said Francis Cooper, an iron and lumber baron.

"Used to be," said Sinclair Tipton, who owned ice fields in Wisconsin and had been awarded lucrative city contracts, "that the suicides took their leaps from High Bridge in Lincoln Park. One a month or so. Or the south side of the Rush Street Bridge, until they stationed a constable there. Now the self-mutilators have their eyes set on the skyscrapers. This chap was said to have gone first to the Chamber of Commerce but was driven out by the building engineer. So he walks next door and sprouts wings. If I were you, Hale, I would make provisions against this sort of thing."

The hemming circle turned to face him with a rustle of newsprint that sounded to Hale like the weft of carrion wings.

"Already done," Hale lied. "I have a watchman posted on the rooftop around the clock." He would make said arrangement upon his return from lunch.

Marshall Field, prematurely gray, his eyes and complexion bright, spoke with his customary self-containment over the rim of his *Tribune*. "That's the least of your problems, I imagine, Hale. I've been following the stories in the paper and they say that most of the tall buildings have insufficient foundations." He turned his eyes on a column of newsprint, set his jaw. "All that deep blue clay, you know. And then there are the claims that the rush and backroom dealing to cheat the height limit resulted in shortcuts being taken. Substandard materials and whatnot."

Hale cleared his throat and ran a finger along the edge of his raised newspaper. They were like battle shields, these sheaves of broadsheet. "As a matter of fact, it's the heavy masonry buildings that are doing all the settling into the clay. Take a walk around City Hall and the courthouse and you'll have to keep one heel six inches higher than the other because the sidewalk inclines so badly to the façade. The steel-frame building doesn't have this problem, you'll be glad to know, Marshall." Technically this was untrue. It all hinged on the way the foundation met the floating concrete raft. Hale wasn't about to tell them this, nor was he going to tell them that most of his windows, over a thousand of them, were purchased from a foreclosed Canadian glassworks after the American combines threatened to delay his construction schedule. Hale changed the subject with: "Marshall, my wife wants to return a vase to your store but she's already used it for a dinner party. Our house smells like roses, I assure you, but I told her she cannot return an item once it is used. Am I correct on that score?"

Marshall crossed his legs. "Stop terrorizing the poor woman, Hale. Unconditional refunds is our motto."

The running joke at the club, which Hale was proud to have started, was to repeat Marshall Field's winning retail catchphrase—*give the lady what she wants!*—whenever he ordered another Scotch from a passing waiter.

Marshall continued: "I'm sure the notion of a refund is unfamiliar in your line of trade. Send her down to the store."

Hale flat-toned: "A man is dead or he isn't. Either his house burns to the ground or it stands. Refunds are strictly a retail notion. I will agree with you on that point."

This back-and-forth chuffed the circle of men and, like a Greek chorus, they enjoyed making statements about theme and content, inserting points of narrative clarification in this unfolding rivalry, in the century's run-off between old money and new, between American come-from-nothingness and the English sense of entitlement. Granted, Hale had been born in Boston, but it was to British parents who'd taught him all the words to "Rule Britannia" and "God Save the Queen." Francis Cooper, who performed the office of club historian and wrote member obituaries, adjudicated with "I call that round a draw, gentlemen. Pace yourselves. We have a luncheon lecture starting upstairs and it's sure to spark another round of disagreement. What's the topic you ask? The influence of food on character. That should be riveting. Are we to be told that boiled potatoes will make a man compliant? Good grief!"

They racked their newspapers and stubbed their cigars. Hale removed the dottle from his pipe with a silver penknife and walked into the domed vestibule. In twos and threes they climbed the carpeted stairs that led to the auditorium, the oil portraits of notable dead members sombering the walls. The millionaires went to their assigned table and both Marshall Field and Hale Gray eyed Pullman's empty place, the silverware crossed to signify his absence. Here was Armour coming to bolster their numbers, crossing the room as if he might toss a stick of dynamite at anyone who got in his way. He sat with a curt nod and took a sip of iced water.

The waiters emerged with trays of hot lunch—porterhouses

from Armour's stockyards served on china plates from Field's department store. It was a tidy arrangement, Hale thought. Was the club's silverware milled at one of Francis Cooper's concerns?

The guest speaker came to the lectern after a mercifully short introduction by the club president. The visitor, a portly fellow in a white suit, asserted that after eating, the blood left the brain for the stomach. "No good brain work can be accomplished after a heavy meal and the body falls into distemper. This accounts for the high incidence of apoplexy in after-dinner speakers and I assure you, gentlemen, that I will be eating a small meal at the conclusion of my remarks. Postprandial speakers are advised to be abstemious on this front."

This elevated drivel continued for an hour while Hale worked on his steak and mashed potatoes, followed by a slice of plum cake. He sat there listening to Marshall Field breathing too loudly—the brash modulation of his very existence—and thought about foppish Jethro at sea, about the imported windowpanes that clad his building, and whether he would stay for a round of billiards after this agony was over with.

At the conclusion of the lecture he hurried back to the office, bounding down Adams past the awnings and flags of the Fair Department Store with its rabble of window-shoppers. He turned north onto La Salle with the tolling bells of the Board of Trade at his back, then the overlay of his own clock tower bronze—which was fast and which was slow?—before coming to an abrupt halt in front of the First Equitable façade. For a full minute he stood staring down at the place where the terracotta and brickwork met the sidewalk. A quarter-inch fissure ran along the building's seam.

15.

Adelaide had kept Owen's unopened letter in her pocket all morning. Things were tense at the museum and she wanted to read the letter as an afternoon tonic. Ever since Franz Boas had been ousted by one of the museum's trustees, she had been shunted from one assistant curator to another, between botany, zoology, geology, and now back to anthropology again. Her new boss, George Dorsey, had recently been promoted to acting curator and was waging a campaign to retain the position permanently — he'd given up his predecessor's large office and converted it to a workroom, taking a small room near the east court so he could be nearer the exhibits. Dorsey was also enlisting a small army of clerks and typists to overhaul the flawed card catalogue, cross-referencing collections and donors, duplicating each accession in a set of inventory books in the department office. Adelaide had so many cardstock and paper cuts on her thumbs that she kept a pair of thimbles in her desk drawer. For all his efficiency and curatorial acumen, Dorsey could not escape scandal. He'd recently returned from an expedition to the West Coast and the stairwell gossip was that he had been arrested for disturbing Indian graves. A month later, he was called to give testimony as a physical anthropologist in the murder trial of Adolph Luetgert, attesting that the bone fragments found at the defendant's sausage factory were indeed of human origin. The case had led to a nationwide decline in sausage sales and had earned Dorsey a new nickname at the Field: the *wurst-wife inspector*. This amounted to humor at the museum.

Adelaide thought the whole affair, from the witness-stand testimony to the grave-robbing, tawdry in the extreme. She'd imagined some measure of respectability when she took employment with the newly formed museum but now she was finding her post to be no different from the typing pool and secretary jobs in the skyscrapers—doctoring the men's coffee with a dash of whiskey when they were out of sorts, curtailing her lunch to buy a bolt of silk for somebody's wife, sewing buttons between dictation and filing. She enjoyed typing exotic memoranda about burial customs and ghost dances. But for all its rarefied scientific aura, its stone lions and sun-spanned rotunda, the museum was sometimes a vaulted arcade of drudgery, backbiting, and petty revenge. Battle lines were drawn along discipline boundaries and there were daily clashes between geologists, botanists, and anthropologists in the lunchroom. The plant and rock men were always feeling slighted by the "gravediggers" and the zoologists feigned neutrality at the frayed edge of a debate about who had brewed the last pot of coffee. The model makers, preparators, and taxidermists who assembled the deer and bird dioramas were enlisted in these tribal skirmishes. The salaried men, both the curators and their minions, loved to play practical jokes on each other—pinching a femur and hiding it in the lavatory, inserting sheets of copied hieroglyphics into an herbarium case as if they were Egyptian ransom notes. Countless acts of sabotage could be found in the galleries, if only one knew where to look. Franz Boas, Adelaide thought, had been much too earnest for this place.

Adelaide drank her third cup of coffee and returned to her typing. She had just finished correcting an ill-worded missive about the upcoming Saturday lecture series whose topics included *How Plants Travel, The Beetles of Chicago and Vicinity,* and *A Visit to Queen Charlotte Islands*. The subtitle to this last lecture could have been *How George Dorsey Sacked a Bag of Native Bones and Was Subsequently Arrested by Local Authorities*. He was down in the bone room, preparing his osteological loot for display, and would emerge some hours from now in a mumbling fog. Maybe she was just having a bad day. She took Owen's letter out, smelled the envelope for hints of pressed flowers, and propped it under her desk lamp. She could see the place where Owen had rested the ink nib after writing her name. If she waited until lunchtime, she might take it onto the west steps and sit overlooking the stand of elders or take it up to an unused alcove and sit beneath a slighted display of Persian chain mail. These were her favorite spots for removing herself from the museum's piddling rivalry. But lately Dorsey had been taking mid-afternoon strolls by the bronzed Roman bathtubs—was he plotting his ascent?—and she couldn't afford to run into him up there.

She spooled a catalogue card into the typewriter:

Accession: 25
Object Number: 13124
World Area: North America
Country: Greenland
Description: sledge, etc.

It was the *etc.* on the last line that was giving Dorsey so much grief. The winding-up of the fair and the frenzy to inventory the masses of newly acquired objects had led to a cataloguing system that was both vague and incomplete. Hundreds of description entries simply read: *implement.* After his promotion, Dorsey had walked among the cataloguers and said: "But what kind of implement? Was it used for skinning or sewing or cooking? When we visit the library do we find a catalogue card that says *a story about a milkmaid's life in rural England* or does it say *Tess of the D'Urbervilles: Hardy, Thomas*?" At one point, fresh off the witness stand in the Luetgert sausage-murder trial, Dorsey had walked among them, hands butterflying behind his back, and had actually declared, "I hear something heroic in the clicking of those Remingtons, ladies." Adelaide could think of a dozen causes more heroic than revamping the museum's card catalogue—the neighborhood programs of Hull House, for example, or the Audubon Society's anti-bird-on-the-hat campaign.

She typed another card:

Accession: 25
Object Number: 13859
World Area: North America
Country: Greenland
Description: harpoon head

Did they use harpoons to catch whales in the South Seas?

She took up Owen's letter and walked out into the corridor, slipping the envelope into her pocket. She made for the ladies' restroom but, when she was sure no one was watching, climbed the stairs and passed quietly into a wing containing Etruscan objects of earthenware and bronze. She stood by a bone-and-ivory funeral couch that had been excavated from a tomb at Orvieto. A handful of coral sand and a dried frangipani dropped from the envelope when she opened it.

My Dearest Adelaide,

I began this letter not a day out of California, writing it in loose-leaf sections, and it soon became a rot of words and tangents. So I'm beginning again and plan to dispatch this version to a mail steamer in Suva. If winds and boilers and tides are favorable, then you'll be reading this within a month. I can hardly wait to hear from you. We are now westering out from the placid Honolulu Bay where we spent close to a week. The ship is watered and fueled and the men have seen to their business on dry land. While they killed off the days and nights in taverns and houses of ill repute, I consigned a few artifacts—fishing hooks made from human bone, stone lures, mortars and pestles. The

men came back to the ship looking as if they'd returned
from battle. I sometimes feel as if my work collecting
among the savages of the South Seas could be done on
board. The crew and captain are a rowdy lot. Captain Baz
Terrapin has a penchant for former inmates and rough lads
from the steel mills of San Francisco. He's really something.
Cantankerous doesn't even begin to describe it. Lewd,
calculating, womanizing, creative and barbaric with the
mother tongue, burlesque—I'm not positive about this
last word but you can call me out on it with your pocket
dictionary. I expect you are deeply immersed in activities
at the museum and hope that the savage curators aren't
making you slave at those catalogue cards all day and
night. Keep your eyesight for those chapbooks on the cable
car! And then there are the Sunday concerts at Hull House
and tutoring the illiterate immigrants and such is a life
filled with virtue. I sometimes hardly believe you wish to
marry me. My kindness toward others consists of avoiding
them when I'm feeling surly. Much to learn from you
in the years ahead. Hope the marriage preparations are
going well and not turning you into a nervous wreck or
one of those formidable lace-hunters on State Street. I'll be
honest, the thought of meeting your father intimidates me.
In that daguerreotype you have by your bed, he resembles
an English vicar with a case of burning gout. You'll forgive
my jesting as a kind of sea sport. As I sit here in the shade
of the topgallant sail, the wind finally gusting out of the
east, I'm watching a pair of seamen argue about the
virtues of homemade bitters as prevention against syphilis.
Despite the blather within earshot, the scene is worthy of a
watercolorist. The sky is the color of pewter and iron and
the ocean is a moiled dark green.

You'll remember the curious Jethro Gray from our
farewell at the train station. Here is another ephemera—

or do I mean enigma?—who can only be described as
unwonted. In the span of a week he managed to have a
banker's son pull a pistol on him on the train and to have
every mariner, the captain included, decry the gilded day
he was born. He seems unable to get along with ordinary
men. His privilege, the way he disports himself, the
stammering face and flinching hands, all of them get the
hackles up and make for discord wherever he ventures
or speaks. Things came to a head when he challenged a
stocky Irish kid to a boxing match and managed to win
with a king punch. Since then he has won the men's silent
and begrudging respect. They don't like him much better
but appreciate his combat. They leave him to his manhunt
for nature's curios—tropical birds of scarlet plumage, blue
parrotfish, enormous jellyfish, flying insects, lizards. He
spent the whole time in the Sandwich Islands with his
magnifying glasses and pillboxes and nets and he's taking
up too much of the hold and I've barely begun to collect
a thing. It smells like a briny zoo of dead animals down
there, which is exactly what it has become.

I have, however, charted a trading route, a jagged
horseshoe that cuts through the islands from east to
west and north again. We'll supply at Suva in Fiji before
heading for the New Hebrides and the Solomon Islands,
perhaps north to German and Dutch New Guinea from
there. There might be a few sundry islands thrown in
for good measure. Fortunately I made notes during the
previous voyage and I see now that it was a kind of
preparation.

I know of your reluctance that I should be at sea but
I firmly believe this is the trip that will allow me to make
the transit into middling society. I can't shake your father's
hand knowing that my sole property is an inherited
junkyard on the South Side. With the contracted payment

we can afford to take a mortgage on a modest house in
a good neighborhood. I picture grass in the backyard
instead of crushed stone and pig iron. What do you think
of that? I might even trade the Chinese junk of a bed
frame for mahogany or teak. You've made every display
of tenderness and understanding toward my position and I
will always be grateful for that. But I want something for
myself as well. My father smoked the cigars of a wealthier
man, always assuming his hard work would vault him
upward, that if he smoked the right brand then the shoes
and hat and house would follow. That didn't come to
pass and I don't intend to leave this world by the same
reckoning. Some of the objects on my cargo list will be
difficult to obtain but I feel up to the task. There must be
a reason why I hoarded all those things from a time before
my voice broke. Whether supernatural will or the material
grappling of a wrecker's son, I can't speculate, but I do
know my life comes to this enterprise with a sort of natural
ease. I am gifted at this trade, have an eye for detail, see
the way a stone implement can be a storehouse of a man's
soul and hopes, but also his hellgate visions. Forgive the
metaphysics; as you know, I am not much for religion,
though rest assured I would gladly baptize all of our
twelve children (six of each sex would be fine) as long as
we could name them all after ships: Enterprise, Republic,
Constitution, Beagle, Endurance, Fram—and those are
just the girls' names! All joking aside, I pray you'll have
the patience to endure this disposition for the remainder
of our days. Voyages such as these will be enough to float
us for years at a time. I promise to be more at home than
anywhere else.

With deepest affection—
Owen

Adelaide reread choice selections. She particularly liked the phrases *every display of tenderness, forgive the metaphysics* and *I promise to be more at home than anywhere else*. If she were going to catalogue this letter according to Dorsey's new system it might have read:

Accession: 25
Object Number: 13860
World Area: Pacific
Country: between Hawaii and Fiji
Description: letter from fiancé in which he refers to future wedding plans and jitters, chides himself humorously, makes oblique promises, uses several words incorrectly but nonetheless charmingly

She folded the letter, emptied the palmful of sand back into the envelope. Already composing a response in her mind, she hurried down the stairs, noticing from a wall clock that it was almost eleven. She'd been gone for half an hour and her stomach lurched when she saw Dorsey standing by her desk, a grim look on his face.

"I'm not feeling well," she said curtly.

He held a hand over his stomach in distress. "We've been looking for you everywhere, Miss Cummings," Dorsey said. "A Western Union boy came looking for you."

Adelaide walked toward her desk, edging the letter behind her back.

"I signed for it," Dorsey said, pointing with the back of his hand.

Adelaide took up the cable, and in her mother's frugal entreaty felt her life recede:

YOUR FATHER STOP PLEASE COME HOME STOP

16.

The island of Djimbanko was unclaimed territory, lying in the ferrous-blue straits between the New Hebrides and New Caledonia. It was too barren for yam gardens and the population too motley to be of lasting interest to the Anglicans, Presbyterians, or Lutherans. It was a trading outpost, black market, way station, and island brothel. For decades it had been a sanctuary for escaped convicts from the French and British colonies and for kanakas banished from their own islands. It was populated by lepers, syphilitic Spaniards, exiled shamans, Malay pirates, Indonesian jewel smugglers, beachcombers, highland pygmies. Courtesy of the island's founding fathers—a band of British mutineers—the language was a strange mix of pidgin and eighteenth-century alehouse slang. The whores were *blowsabellas,* the pygmies *minikins,* and *crinkum* was the sort of venereal shanker that drove men into the smoking mouths of volcanoes.

The island contained several French families who had escaped the failed expedition of the Marquis de Rays in 1880. The nobleman and self-proclaimed King of New France had enticed hundreds of followers from Marseille to Port Breton, where they were expecting a coral-garden utopia but instead found little fresh water and sandy soil. A bishop on board blessed the sea and hung a portrait of the marquis next to the Virgin Mary and the journeyed believers died in droves of hunger, typhoid, malaria, and despair. The land of the new empire was so inhospitable that the New Ireland natives had long ignored it and thought the Frenchmen were gods sent back from world's end to suffer in eternity.

There were still tattered copies of *La Nouvelle France* floating around Djimbanko. It was the utopian newspaper that circulated in French churches and spoke of Melanesian cathedrals and aubergine gardens and which now lined parrot cages and stuffed pillowcases. Its masthead said it was printed in the Pacific colony of the devout but in fact it was printed in a Marseille warehouse and continued to appear long after the last pilgrim had died, escaped, or been rescued, and long after the Marquis de Rays had been arrested in Spain for fraud.

Several French escapees of this failed religious expedition now held sway over Djimbanko's attractions. A family of Manouche gypsies ran a small native sideshow and petting zoo. It was an entertainment designed for visiting ships and took place the first Saturday of the month outside hurricane season. There was a makeshift bamboo arena with an acrobatics display by the eldest daughter, a gymnast and high-wire artist. She tumbled and twirled batons while her younger brothers juggled flaming torches, led wallabies on catches of twine so that drunk sailors could put shillings in their joey pouches. One of the brothers played a clarinet with broken keywork before a pit of venomous snakes while another lined up the highland pygmies with their broad noses and girlish voices and made them dance to a Russian waltz.

Terrapin had promised such whimsy and exotic delights to his men, told them he could vouch for the nubile whoring on the island. The crew was due a luff-day before Owen Graves took the ship southwest and north for a torrent of trade in every malarial port and tumbledown yamhouse. But the sailors would have to earn their reward by scrubbing the *Cullion* until she smelled like chalk. Ever since the equatorial crossing, Terrapin had been on a cleaning binge, lighting brimstone fires to clear out the fug and towing the men's foul laundry astern with the naturalist's dredge net of bolting silk. Lately the ship had taken a fetid turn—cockroaches, red ants, centipedes, spiders, house crickets, horseflies, and mosquitoes on the fly, scurry, and crawl. There were rats as

big as alley toms living in the hold and they were hungry enough
to eat hobnails. When seamen put their boots on in the morning there was a fine sod of mold growing on the toe hub. Everyone suspected that the vermin were breeding in the gloomy lair
of Jethro's laboratory—in the darkened theater behind a row of
scientifical books, perhaps, or in a tub of albumen extracted from
the eggs of native birds. It was a filthy practice, Terrapin told his
men, this poaching and pickling and offal-gathering.

Giles Blunt, as carpenter, was in charge of greasing the masts
and blocks and he sent Dickey Fentress aloft with a tub of slush
from the cook-surgeon. The boy moved with simian pluck, arms
stretched, nimbling over the ratlines. If there was one lesson the
apprentice had to learn it was never unclasp a spar or crosstree
without first securing a handhold on some other piece of mast
or rigging. Terrapin bellowed this cardinal rule up at the boy and
went to check on Jethro's progress in washing down his filthy
little orchis-house. Terrapin nodded approval to the sudsy-armed
seamen who had trawled in the towline of funked laundry like
some grizzly beast yanked from the depths. He went below calling, "Mr. Gray, I am coming to see if you've cleaned your room
like a darling."

Owen was cleaning out the bulkhead and the space beneath
the forecastle-head. Now that they had lost a pig to trade there
was only one sow, a hatch of chickens, and the rather seasick
ewe competing for stowage. They had anchored off one of the
islands southwest of Malekula and he'd picked up some low-
grade weapons and adornments from the natives who paddled
out in single-hulled canoes. When Owen refused to part with any
rifles, they'd settled for two knives, a box of wax matches, and a
pouch of navy tobacco. He was eager now to press on, perhaps
find a people or place untouched by mainstream trade. He wiped
the rambaramp down with a chamois cloth but couldn't look into
its gaping, hideous mouth. It amused him to think of Hale Gray
having this mummified effigy with its smoked human skull sitting

in a glass case on the twenty-eighth floor of the insurance skyscraper. He pictured secretaries not unlike Adelaide taking dictation in the mortuary pall of his office or executives coming to ask
for a raise while having to stare down this ancestral ogre. Would
it act as a souvenir of a savage and distant tribe or was it a totem,
a grim reminder that every man dies alone, powerless to govern
what becomes of his person? God help the widows and children
without a policy on their dead man's head. It struck Owen that
perhaps every relic in that display case was an advertisement for
insurance, a statement about the precariousness of life itself.

He didn't want to go ashore on Djimbanko because it sounded,
at best, like a native circus and flea market. On the other hand,
Jethro had threatened to go birding and he wasn't to be trusted
among the local rabble-rousers. Owen could easily imagine
Jethro being shot or bludgeoned for slighting a leper, pearl diver,
or jewel smuggler. Ever since his snakebite he'd taken to wearing
a white fencing glove on his left hand and claimed it offered protection when gathering tide pool mollusks. Aside from the question of how he happened to have a fencing glove aboard a ship at
sea, this addition to his person undid all attempts at camouflaging
his upbringing with workpants, broadloom shirt, and serge cap.
It announced his pedigree like a heraldry seal and Owen couldn't
help wondering what else he had down in the orlop that might see
him murdered—a pétanque or croquet set, a falconer's gauntlet
and polo mallet?

Three whaleboats went ashore, carrying most of the seamen. The
sailmaker was laid low in the hold with the Johnny-trots and the
Dutch cook, Hendrik Stuyvesant, stayed behind on the premise
of preparing a batch of scouse but was said to be sleeping off a
hangover in a hammock between-decks. The captain stayed in the
chartroom with Nipper and his gramophone. The sailors' laundry
flapped from the rigging like Irish pennants.

Owen rode with Jethro, who sat in the prow with his birding

kit and sketchpad. What exactly he planned to draw or catch was
a mystery; from what Owen could see the island was a treeless
clay bed skirted by coral. As they rowed across the honeycombed
reef heads, the smell of volcanic sulfur was everywhere. The oarsmen rowed in unison, singing lewdly in anticipation of the coming pleasures. Harvey McCallister sang the loudest and dirtiest
and had been restored to respectability despite his crushing defeat
in the deckside boxing match. Dickey Fentress was assigned the
job of watching the whaleboats to make sure they weren't stolen
but insisted he wanted to go whoring like the rest of them.

"Captain says hot black nubies is the best way for a man to
lose his cherry," he offered at the end of an oar stroke.

"When you can slush the skysail mast without dribbling pig
grease everywhere we'll worry about dropping your trousers,
little Dick," said Harvey, eliciting a delighted chuckle from the
seamen.

Owen watched Dickey blush and bite his lower lip. He saw
some of himself in the young apprentice: Dickey was orphaned
and had been forced to make his way in the world; he was unsure
of himself but also impatient to prove his mettle. His main downfall was distraction. Owen found himself dispensing advice to
the boy. One watch he'd told the boy that if he learned to box a
compass and bend a new topgallant the captain might give him a
trick at the wheel. He told him to steer clear of the shirkers and
the ship's deadweight. Dickey seemed to take this to heart for a
few days but then his enthusiasm fell off and he became absorbed
by some mindless and vulgar prank. A handful of ordinary seamen were always trying to corrupt and sabotage his training and
Dickey lacked the will to chart his own course. He would find
out the hard way, Owen thought, watching him put his back into
the oar stroke.

They dragged the whaleboats up onto the sand and left Dickey
to stand watch with a rifle. He propped himself in the shade of a
dory sail and whittled a piece of driftwood with his pocketknife.

The men started up the beach, adjusting their clothes and hats as if calling on their own mothers. The forlorn sound of a clarinet came from up ahead and, from the rear, a staticky aria broke from the ship's charthouse. Jethro trailed behind the group, blinking in the sun, looking for signs of collectible life. Owen slowed and cast a wary backward glance just in time to see him delicately pick up a snarl of kelp as if it were a weed from Lincoln's grave. He waited for Jethro to catch up, but when it became clear he would be some time on the beach, Owen joined the others.

They walked along a blackened path and Owen noticed a long-abandoned chapel up on a blighted hillside. Against the caldera it was an odd landmark, a listing shed with a white cross. The volcanic smoke fuming five hundred feet above was an advertisement for the furnaces of hell. They passed through a corridor of shanties and lean-tos and up ahead a band of Tapiro pygmies danced in the bamboo arena. Instead of an island corroboree of spears and foot-stamping, they were taking small, dignified steps in drifts of silt, waltzing in couples, the men in top hats and penis gourds and the women bare-breasted and bibbed in shells. Along the way there were all manner of sorry handicrafts laid out on sawhorse tables—gaudily painted masks, crude weapons hacked from stone, shoddy necklaces, and mud-daubed shields. Owen couldn't tell whether the artless trinkets had been made by banished natives or English castaways out for a dollar. He shook his head at the men and boys smoking pipes behind the tables and walked toward the din.

A pole-fence corral had been built around a dead banyan tree and a European woman with black hair was hanging by a roped ankle, spinning slowly. The seamen began applauding and tossing coins as the pygmies took leave and a team of animal keepers came out with exotic beasts. A native clown in vermilion facepaint entered the pit juggling fire sticks. Like the rest of the men, Owen rested on the fence and took in the spectacle. It reminded him of a tramp circus and ox-drawn sideshow his father had taken him to as a boy. Somewhere on the outskirts of Chicago, out beyond the stockyards, they stood in the rain and entered darkened canvas tents that smelled like snakes to see bearded ladies, serpent charmers, pinheads, men who smashed gravestones over their heads. His father had called it a mudshow and pushed Owen through the Congress of Strange People by the shoulders. At each freakish display his father said nothing but there was the insistent hand at Owen's back, as if this were a bearing witness to life's cataclysms, standing before the vaudeville and dime museum Stations of the Cross. His father smoked a cigarette and joked with the sideshow barkers and the venerable old circus barber with a wooden leg and it was all meant to show Owen the razor's edge that kept them from the brink, the godless maw that waited out in the tenements and stockyards. Owen, at nine, knew he had been spared but didn't yet know from what. For months after, he dreamed of the freak-show Siamese twins and woke terrified of seeing a brother's congenital ear next to his own or feeling the double thrum of a shared pulse, the lapping tide in the same hemisphere of blood. This feeling of dread came to mind now as the gypsy woman hung from her teeth and a midshipman pantomimed the humping of a kangaroo for his shipmates. One of the Manouche animal keepers called to the showoff to step back behind the fence or he'd have his whore-pipe culped. The sailor obliged, his shipmates guffawed, and the rest of the vaudeville passed without incident.

When the corral floor was covered in coins and the gymnast climbed down from the banyan tree to take a bow, the whores were brought out in single file. "Mine'll need a leash just like that wallaby," called Harvey, producing a wad of banknotes he'd borrowed from the sailmaker on account of his garnished wages. There were half a dozen Melanesian girls in filthy cotton dresses and ill-fitting girdles, brassieres visible beneath. Their faces were painted as gaudily as the shoddy tribal masks. The gypsy brothers were not only zookeepers but pimps and began haggling with the men, itemizing each girl's portfolio of carnal tricks. Deals were brokered while the *fusty-luggs* and *mackerel-backed madonnas* toed the dirt, the gypsy boys riffing in French and an English so strange and archaic it hadn't been uttered in a century.

Owen drifted back among the flea market stalls and, more from boredom than anything else, bought a boning knife of unknown origin. The boy who sold it to him said they took dollars, francs, English pounds, and rum prog as payment. He said his name was Roger Billy Smith and he sat on a wooden crate, chewing betel nut and dribbling its juice into a rusted oyster tin. Owen found it hard to believe that in the span of a few years the Pacific had become so debauched and overrun with Western influence. During his first voyage there had been plenty of interaction with copra planters and traders, mercenaries living at the strandline of the tribal world, but the native settlements had seemed intact for the most part. Had Captain Bisky steered them a course through untainted territory, knowing just where to anchor, or had something shifted these last few years? New Caledonia—which he'd decided not to visit—was now more European than Melanesian. The French prison colony had just closed down and a nickel mine had opened somewhere in the interior. The white pimps and hagglers of Djimbanko were probably extradited French pickpockets who preferred their lawless island inferno to the prospect of returning to the barbarous streets of Paris.

One such beggar came bundling down the pathway in a Panama hat and trousers hitched with a length of halyard. He walked in laceless shoes, shambling along with a hardwood cane, singing to himself. As he came closer Owen saw that he was a native boy of about eighteen and that he was carrying both a Bible and a leather-clad edition of *David Copperfield*.

"Boy that humboxes from the hill church," said Roger Billy Smith, gesturing with his chin and spitting into his can. The native stopped a few feet short and could no doubt see the surprise in Owen's face. Surely the Dickens novel was nothing more than a sheaf of cigarette papers, just as the French newspaper had been on Malekula? But then the boy looked him square in the eye and said, "Excuse me, sir, is there a doctor aboard your ship?"

Owen took him in. "Where are you from?"

The boy ignored the question but explained what had befallen his sister, claiming that she needed an operation. She would not let him near her buttocks with a syringe and had taken opium tincture every day to help the pain but the vial was nearly empty. All of it was delivered in a colony servant's English but with near perfect pronunciation and inflection.

Distracted by this linguistic display, Owen said, "What's a hum box?"

"They call the pulpit that. We are living in the old chapel since we rowed ashore. I am from another mission island and on Sundays a few of the men come up for hymns and a sermon."

"Are you a preacher?" Owen stifled the surprise in his voice.

The boy said, "I can lead you to her. Will the ship's doctor see her?"

To call Hendrik Stuyvesant a doctor was a wild stretch of the imagination. Granted, it was common slang to refer to the ship's cook as *the doctor*, so technically it wasn't a lie, but that designation in the wider world seemed to imply formal training and a thorough understanding of the body's mechanics and living systems. Terrapin claimed that the wiry Dutchman knew how to suture a wound, pull an abscessed tooth, administer laudanum and prescribe a mercurial ointment if a gonorrhea-addled seaman was pissing pins and needles, but the former prisoner and counterfeiter barely knew the names of bones or the vein-ways by which blood returned to the heart. Everything he'd gleaned about medicine had been on a ship and under bloody duress and it wouldn't have surprised Owen to learn that he had no more studied a medical treatise than read the *Iliad*. His one saving grace, and the only hope this native preacher boy had in the world, was that Hendrik, outside the kitchen, had a counterfeiter's precision and tenacity. Then again, Owen wondered, why had he spent a decade in jail?

Owen looked at the boy clutching the novel to his chest. He tried to imagine him in native garb, without the ragged shirt and trousers. But it was just as easy to imagine him in freshly pressed linens with a cravat around his neck. There was poise, something like dignity in his bearing. "Yes, the ship's doctor will see her if she comes aboard."

"I will have to come with her."

"Of course."

"Please, follow me to the chapel now. My name is Argus Niu."

He held out his hand stiffly for Owen to shake. Outside of some barely civilized traders and some men of the cloth, Owen hadn't shaken hands since leaving San Francisco. He shook Argus's hand and followed him down the path. As they came up the igneous hillside where the broken chapel stood rotting, Owen saw that Jethro was still down on the beach trawling for seaweed and plucking up sea anemones with his fencing glove. Dickey was helping him drag tentacles of weed out of the surf, the rifle slung over one shoulder.

The chapel was a Calvinist clapboard affair, not much more than a shed with a steeple, roughed out with ship's planking and sawn through with paneless windows. It had weathered at least a generation of neglect and Owen wondered what heathen uprising had seen the mission wane. From his years of wrecking he could tell the entire building was ready to topple. It read in the list, in the cracked soil around the foundation posts, in the wind singing through the joists and rafters. It was what his father and other wreckers used to call a Christmas present—a few hours' work for a day's pay.

Inside, the boy removed his hat and led Owen forward. There were alternating columns of shade and slatted sunlight through the glassless windows. An acrid breath blew down off the caldera and into the battered nave. A couple of pews made from planks and cartouche boxes had been pushed into the shade and the sister lay hallucinating on one of them. One hand was raised as if she were reading an oracle in her knuckles or fingernails, her mouth stricken and full of tremors. She moved her head slowly from side to side and her lips were caked white. She was older than the boy, though by how much was hard to tell due to the fever and opium. Owen stepped closer, peering into the bolt of deep shade where she lay supine. The heat and the smell of the volcano didn't disguise the necrotic stench. He'd encountered sepsis during his first voyage and the smell was something he could live without. The boy leaned down and spoke to his sister in their tribal tongue.

"Can she walk?" Owen asked.

Argus shook his head.

Owen said, "We'll bring a stretcher and treat her on the ship."

Argus said, "I've been praying for a ship but it's been almost a month."

Owen left the chapel and walked down to the beach, where Dickey and Jethro were frolicking like a couple of honeymooners on the shoreline—running through the waves, splashing each other, tossing a waterlogged coconut back and forth. Owen saw that the rifle was unattended by the whaleboats and he hurried to take it up and fired it three times into the air. The two of them couldn't be trusted to spot their own shadows. Dickey came running up the beach, his face already filling with shame. Owen could remember felling buildings with his own adze, being trusted with a box of dynamite at the age of twelve. Three shots was the signal for all-hands during a landing and soon the men would trudge reluctantly down to the beachhead.

Dickey stopped short and looked up, waiting for his lambasting. His hair was growing back in quills and spikes and it toughened his demeanor.

"Row to the ship and tell the cook we're bringing a patient aboard. If he's drunk in his hammock go to the cookroom and hot up some coffee. Understand? And bring back the stretcher in the boat. Be quick about it!"

Dickey began for the boat, earnest-faced, but turned when he heard Owen speak again.

"I won't tell the captain that the rifle was lying in the sand but consider that a loan of confidence. If you want to be an exquisite and splash about in the waves instead of standing watch then you better get rich and go to Harvard like your girlfriend over there." They looked off and saw Jethro loading his birding bag with seashells. Owen tightened the rifle strap and handed it back to the apprentice. He heard his own father in the admonishment and didn't mind the sound of it. Give the kid something to nail to the masthead. That's what Porter Graves would have said.

When the clay men bore her aloft on stretched white canvas Malini thought she was dead and crossing over. Long-departed uncles and cousins had come back in their white spirit guises to carry her. The old ones were gray and their hair was straight except for a boy who was plumed like a fledgling. She wanted to see her mother, who waited somewhere out on the ocean. She wanted her body to be returned to Poumeta for proper burial and so that someone might weep over her. For five nights she would haunt the lagoons, she thought, rousing the children and the dogs and the shamans before swimming out to meet everyone else. There was an island out there with fruits she had never eaten—grapes, green apples, the blue berries her brother had told her about.

They placed her in a whaleboat and she felt the ocean plinking against the wooden hull because it was trying to get to her wound. The oarsmen crowded over her with their green eyes and ruddy cheeks. The pain swam up into her stomach and spine when the oars rocked; she could hear their trousers strain against the wooden benches. Argus was sitting beside her singing and praying with her hands in his. The canvas stretcher smelled bitter and she wanted her brother to touch her head. *Was the Bible written in heaven?* This was a question she wanted to ask him. Their breathing was like a monsoon cloud as they rolled over the waves. The wound had its own heartbeat and she had to protect it. They pulled into the shadow of a ship. Two ropes were lowered and attached to the stretcher. She felt herself rise.

Owen and Terrapin watched Hendrik Stuyvesant walk unsteadily toward the orlop, a glass of soda water in his hand. He pushed his way through a wall of curious seamen who'd come below to watch him operate on the feverish savage.

Terrapin said, "A dead native is bad luck on a ship, Doctor. Get her up and able so we can weigh anchor from this little Babylon."

"I'll do my level best, Captain," said Hendrik. "What's the presenting complaint?"

The captain looked to Owen.

"A boil on her ass," said Owen. "It's turning septic or gangrenous or otherwise stinking and rotten."

Hendrik winced faintly. "Glad I brought my soda water. I'm feeling all-overish just at present."

"You will still prepare mess tonight, I assume," said Terrapin. "I expect the men are quite hungry from their debauchery."

"Of course," said Hendrik, put out.

Owen suspected Hendrik was the only man aboard with three jobs. Terrapin summoned him at all hours for food, like it was hotel room service, or if he wanted his sideburns, neckline, and nose hairs trimmed, like some mogul about to be martyred in battle.

The captain bellowed at the seamen to clear out so that the doctor could do his work. Owen went above while Argus and Jethro remained with the patient. Hendrik came into the orlop proper.

"The brother refuses to leave and I thought I might lend a hand," said Jethro. "I've cleared some of my specimens so you have room to work."

Hendrik took a sip of his soda water and set it down beside the abscessed buttocks. There was a row of glassed jellyfish and a mound of tropical bird pelts on a nearby table. "Suit yourself."

"Will you put her to sleep?" Argus asked.

Hendrik paused, looked at the native's clothes and shoes. "Not sure I see the need."

"She's in a lot of pain," said Jethro. "You must have some chloroform."

"What I have in my medical kit is my concern."

As if on cue, Dickey Fentress appeared with the leather kit and placed it on the workbench. The bag was monogrammed and this made Argus relax a little; they were in good hands. Hendrik began removing items from compartments and sleeves—a tub of jalap, a vial of mercury, cough syrup, laudanum, lousing kerosene, a scalpel, bandages, quinine, needle and thread, a stoppered glass jar of chloroform, a forger's loupe that doubled for surgical magnification. From out of the cavernous bottom he produced a coil of steel wool and a bone saw with a brocade of rust stippled along one side. Argus felt his heart drop.

Hendrik ran the scalpel through the candleflame. Malini moaned and turned away. "You gents may need to restrain her."

Jethro said, "We can purchase more chloroform if that's the matter."

"I like to keep it in case of emergencies. Hard to come by, it is. One time I had to take off a man's leg at sea. You want that poor bastard to go without the tide of mercy so this kanaka can take a nap while I lance a boil on her black rump?"

Jethro looked at his hands and then at the terrified woman on the table. "I don't think lancing is required." He paused, folded his arms. "I have a syringe I use to empty bird eggs. If you drain the boil from the inside it might heal without fissuring."

Hendrik licked his bottom lip. "Didn't know I was in the company of a royal physician."

"I've studied science and I understand the body somewhat."

Argus said, "The syringe might be better. I saw a doctor use it on the Reverend Mister one time. We are very grateful."

Hendrik removed the scalpel from the tallow flame and in one fluid movement sliced down the patient's filthy skirt, exposing her coppered nates in the browning light. The plum-sized boil was marbled and the whole offending buttock was taut and blowzed. Dickey Fentress swallowed hard as the black woman brought a hand to cover her rear and the cook inched the candle closer. Jethro grabbed his wrist and said, "Please. I insist on anesthetic and a syringe. I'm prepared to pay for both."

Hendrik let the scalpel go limp and looked up. He sighed and said, "Dickey Fentress, get above before I kick your freckled ass." Dickey fled the orlop and instead of recounting a boil the size of stone fruit he told the midshipmen that he'd seen his first black snatch, a lozenge of brown quim glimpsed in candlelight and from behind.

Argus began murmuring a prayer with his eyes clenched shut—*Dear Heavenly Father, thank you for these men's Christian spirit and for the vapors of the Holy Ghost which will be breathed into my widowed sister's lungs so that she might be healthful again . . .*

Hendrik angled his wrist, the scalpel poised. "Twenty greenbacks and you can have a kerchief dipped in chloroform but it's too late for your birding syringe. This mess will fester and even after I lance it the melon will drain for days on end. You or the brother will have to bathe it in salt water three times a day and she won't be able to walk for a week. It smells like rancid meat down here for Christ's sake and I have to go make scouse and bean soup. Can we get this over with? My eyeballs hurt."

"We will tend the wound very promptly," said Argus.

Malini wept, her nostrils flared in terror. Jethro handed Hendrik a clean linen handkerchief from his pocket and the cook removed the stopper from the chloroform. A moment later Malini's eyelids fluttered shut and her body went limp. They turned her fully on her side. Hendrik fitted his forger's loupe into his left eye socket and bent to the task. The brother continued to pray and hum but looked away as Hendrik placed two fingers on either side of the boil, gave it a slight squeeze, and made a V-shaped slice across the top. A liquid tree of blood and pus burst from below and Jethro held a beaker to the wound to let it drain. There were several ounces of expellant in the glass beaker before Hendrik prodded and squeezed the wound to work the core up to the surface. Something like an apple seed pipped into the beaker and there was a narrow black chute of air extending down into the wound.

"That's got it," said Hendrik, teeth bared. "Wash it with salt water and keep it covered with clean gauze. Call me if she isn't awake before long. You can give me the money at dinner if you like but don't let the captain or the men see." Hendrik packed his kit and left.

Argus brushed some hair from his sister's forehead and tried to wake her in a whisper. Jethro took the beaker over to his workbench. He placed the jar of native blood and suppuration on the shelf right next to the embalmed anemones and the hummingbirds stuffed in mid-flight. From behind he heard the native's voice: "I am very grateful to you, sir."

Owen intended to query the native lad further as a potential guide and translator. Once the sister was got ashore he might help out the cause in the Solomons and beyond. Owen was behind schedule and needed a trading coup. It was a pity the boy and his sister were wide of the mark as Chicago imports. He was pretty sure Hale Gray had something else in mind entirely—some wood-backed noble savages, tattooed and dreadlocked, wielding tomahawks instead of leathered editions of Robert Louis Stevenson and Charles Dickens. But here was also a chance to prove an ethical point—that his collecting mission and kindness toward the natives weren't mutually exclusive. And he had brought the girl aboard out of common decency, he knew, not just to further his own scheme.

Owen came into the orlop and set down a tray of steaming soup. The sister was still on the table but was now covered in a white sheet. She stared up at the joists above her, oblivious to the men. Jethro and the native—was it Argot or Arganus?—were crouched over a taxidermied fruit dove. The boy said softly, "It looks like it will fly away at any moment." They turned and faced Owen, Jethro a little flushed.

"I brought you all some soup. How is she feeling?"

The boy picked up the tray and handed Jethro a bowl and spoon before taking it over to his sister. He placed one hand under her head to tilt her chin up but she turned her mouth away. "She is sickly and confused. She has never been in a ship before. We are like the inside of a pickle bucket with all this wood around us."

Jethro sat down on a stool, threw one leg over the other, and took a few spoonfuls of soup. "It's only natural for her to be nervous, Argus. To be expected, really."

Argus, that was it. Owen leaned against a workbench and ran one hand against the grain. "Argus, where did you learn your English?"

The boy gently placed his sister's head back down on the cotton pillow and looked over. "The Reverend Mister taught me English. He was a missionary from Scotland but he died on the verandah before breakfast. I was his houseboy. But also he taught me to know Jesus and the Holy Ghost. I am a catechist."

Jethro smiled into his soup. "Your English is excellent."

"Thank you. Transitive verbs used to give me grief but now they don't bother me."

Owen laughed and said, "I'm not sure I even know what a transitive verb is."

"A verb that desires an object to go with the subject. Like I *give you* the book," said Argus.

"That explains it," said Owen. He watched the sister touch the sides of the table with her fingertips. "What is your sister's name?"

"Malini."

"And does she speak English?"

Argus shook his head, his mouth brimming with soup. "She is heathen but I try to teach her hymns and Bible verses. She wants to become a governess in a mission because she is barren and likes babies. Will the doctor look at her again?"

"If he needs to," said Jethro. "But you and I can take very good care of her. Wash her wound three times a day with salt water."

Argus looked at Malini. "We are very grateful."

Owen placed his hands together. "Where did you come from before the mission?"

"Poumeta. Up near the Bismarcks."

"Are there lots of your people still back there living in small villages?"

"Not my village but on other islands."

"We are headed that way on a collecting expedition."

"To collect birds and snakes?"

Owen shook his head and noticed Jethro's smug grin. "No. To collect artifacts. Weapons and art for a private museum in America."

Argus nodded extravagantly. He knew about America and museums.

A full minute of soup spooning.

Owen said, "Maybe you want to work for us to help trade in the villages. Do you speak other native languages?"

Argus looked up. "Many languages," he said definitively. In fact he spoke three: English, Poumetan, and a strain of bastardized pidgin that was only good on a handful of trade route islands. "I also cook and clean and can mend clothing such as coat buttons."

Owen said, "That might please the ship's master. I would need to get his approval, of course. Perhaps when you aren't trading you could help the apprentice. Would you like to learn how to sail?"

Argus thought of the infernal rowing he'd endured and wished to never feel the ocean beneath him again. "Very much," he said.

"A general sort of trading hand and cabin boy," said Jethro. As soon as he'd seen the native siblings he'd hoped to study them, to measure their bones and write down their customs.

Owen said, "He's not for helping you collect wildlife. Understand that. Objects only. Don't get any designs, Mr. Gray."

"Of course." He'd been *mistered* into place.

"And what will my sister do on the ship?" asked Argus.

A quiet fell over them and they were suddenly aware of Malini's fitful breathing.

"A ship isn't much of a place for a woman," said Owen finally. "We can arrange safe passage for her to anywhere you like. When she's better, of course. But I am offering you a job. Twenty shillings a week plus meals and clothing."

Argus let his soup spoon rest at the edge of his bowl and Owen couldn't help recalling Adelaide in all her midday refinement. The boy had a womanly introspection and grace about him.

Argus said, "I must decline."

"Why is that?" asked Owen.

"Poumetan sisters are like mothers. They must be honored by the brother. This is proper conduct. I promised I would look after her and find us both jobs. Our parents are dead. We are orphaned like the two Davids."

Both white men looked confused by this reference.

"How old are you and your sister?"

"I am just eighteen years and I think she is twenty-five and one-half years."

Owen said, "This would be a good job for you. Just for a few months."

"I am declined," said Argus. "Unless the sister can come on

the collecting exposition." His English faltered and he sounded flustered.

Owen worried about the ramifications of having the sister aboard but admired the brother's loyalty. He pushed off the workbench with two hands and headed for the door. "The captain says we can anchor here one more day. I will speak to him before we leave. That's all I can do. It's his choice to make. But either way, we'll make sure your sister is on the road to recovery."

Argus nodded and Owen turned for the hatchway ladder that provided a shortcut to the main deck. They watched him disappear up the ladder one rung at a time.

Dreamily, Malini saw a pair of clay hands and black boots ascend through a timbered canopy.

17.

Jethro came knocking on Terrapin's stateroom door just before ten that night, when he knew the river of rum and brandy would be ready to brim its banks. From inside he heard Terrapin's vespertine piano playing. He was admitted by way of a distracted voice and entered to see the captain in a floral sarong, sitting naked to the waist at the old church upright. The piano, like Terrapin's face and chest, showed the ravages of age and life at sea. The lid was ajar and it was split along the uppermost rail, exposing hammerwork that was both frayed and bowed. Terrapin trebled into a morose refrain, his eyes brimming. Through a wedge of rosiny light Jethro could see dust motes cascading off the dampened piano wires and hitchpins. Terrapin lifted his hands slowly from the keyboard and took a sip from his mug of liquor, two-handing it like a goblet of mead. "Is there a duel on the foredeck?"

"How's that, sir?"

"The fencing glove."

"Ah," Jethro said, feigning amusement. "Ever since the snakebite I've felt the need to keep it covered."

"Let's see it then."

"Excuse me?"

"The snakebit finger."

Jethro hesitated before slowly working the glove off his left hand. He was standing a few feet away.

"Closer, please," said Terrapin.

Jethro came forward and Terrapin couldn't resist playing a

dramatic progression on the left side of the keyboard. He smirked while the purplish finger edged into a cone of kerosene lamplight. After a moment of squint-eyed consideration, Terrapin said, "I take a great deal of ownership for my men and what goes on above and below decks. In some ways I consider a man's bodily parts to be extensions of my very own corpicus. We is all one organism and such. A metaphorical illusion you can appreciate from all your botanizing and taxidermy, no doubt. May I touch it?"

Jethro blinked. "Very well."

Terrapin ran a finger tenderly over the rucked tip. "If you are not careful with this turnip it will end up topped and pickled in one of your jam jars. Ha! Consider collecting your own digital whatnot in some of that glassware. That would be a turn. Keep it away from the cook and ventilate the ghastly bugger or it will fester like the Moroccan clap. Understand me?"

Jethro pulled his finger from the light. "I'd rather keep it hidden from the men but I'll air it at night. The glove helps protect the injury when I hoist or reef sail."

Terrapin smiled, belched, puckered. "You almost sound like a sailor except there's still a hint of eastern custard in your voice. Have a drink."

The captain handed his own mug to Jethro, who, sensing this was a test, took a sip and returned it. Terrapin got up and went to water a tendril of leaf that sprouted from a pot under the foremost porthole. "I also enjoy a spot of botanizing. Sweet potatoes is about all that will start in this gloomy fug. The other darlings died off. I understand your father has built the world's tallest skyscraper? Ain't that a thing! That air must be sweet and Himalayan up there. You could bottle it, I reckon. I've always been partial to mountains. In Tassie we've got mountains."

Jethro rested a hand on the top of the piano. "I've come to talk to you about the natives on board."

Without turning from his potted plant, Terrapin said, "Do we need another round of delousing?"

"No, sir. Mr. Graves has offered the boy a position as guide and translator for the purposes of trading, but the brother won't leave the sister. They are very close and he wants to protect his sister. Admirable, really."

Terrapin turned on his heels. "First I've heard of it. Nice if somebody kisses the bloody papal ring every once in a while." He came forward. "That aside, what business is this of yours? Do you have lusty designs on the carbuncled sister? A little basket-making in the orlop, hmm, is that your campaign?"

Jethro was taken aback, his temper idling below a tight-faced smile. Then he realized he'd beaten Owen to the captain's door and saw an opportunity. "I just think we could help them and proceed with the trading at the same time."

Terrapin hefted onto the piano bench. "We ain't runnin a fuckin quarantine or malarial hotel here, lovelace. Who knows what pox and plague those two are carrying. Don't misunderstand me. I've loved many a native woman and borne fruit by such labors and erudition. But they turn when you cage em up. Their souls rot from the bowels up. Give a native a piece of cheese and see what Armageddon looks like."

Jethro looked at the list of children's birth dates running down Terrapin's forearms. "Blood families are very close on their island. Brother and sister is a sacred bond. More sacred than husband and wife and father and child."

Terrapin folded his arms. "And how do you know so much about island life, Illinois?"

"I've been speaking with the boy. He speaks English exceptionally well."

"Christ, sometimes you sound like a tabernacle boy what's been castrated and taught to sing high. Naturally, the Irishmen and San Quentin blokes take offense up top and sometimes you curdle my breakfast. I won't lie to you. The fact that you can punch a man flat is one of the lasting mysteries on this green and blue earth. You look like you'd tucker out trying to open a box of chocolates."

Jethro pulled his shoulders tight. "I'd like to study the natives as the ship's naturalist."

"A woman on a ship is like a dog that chases a mud wagon. Sooner or later the show ends with blood and entrails."

Jethro pitched his hands into his cotton trousers. "I am willing to pay for the opportunity to study them both. I can personally guarantee the girl's safety because I will guard her myself. And as for the brother, when he's not trading he can help the apprentice. He'll be paid out of Mr. Graves's trading allowance. I believe that's the proper accounting for it."

Terrapin ran his calloused hands along the edge of the keys. "Aw, pikelet. Not everything can be bought with hempen paper. Do you realize that if your father weren't funding this seagoing jaunt that you would have been keelhauled by now? Fish would be feeding on your pasty parfleched hide. You may be able to knock a spud to the ground fair and square but those seamen have a burning genius for revenge. It's what keeps them alive out here—thinking about the scores they'll settle back in port. The ocean is a playground for slighted men on the comeback. So much time for doggery and bucket-shop plotting." Terrapin belched some brandied air between his lips and appeared startled; he'd tarried out beyond his own moorings. "Where was I headed?"

Far from feeling slighted or wary, Jethro wiggled the fingertips of his left hand into the fencing glove and said, "My father always taught me to put things in writing. So if you decide on the requisite amount I'll be happy to fetch the ink bottle."

Terrapin said, "As captain and maritime luminary I'm in favor of the advancement of science—three hundred dollars, I believe, is the correct figure." He played a big fat chord with his left hand.

They anchored two days in the bay at Djimbanko before heading north toward the Solomons. The men had been sated, the wind was abeam, and the *Cullion* was fully clothed, the sails trimming out over the waves like a hundred silken pitchtents. Owen didn't know of the retained natives until the ship was about to weigh anchor and the captain made no attempt to get them ashore. He'd planned to talk to Terrapin that morning, when he knew the captain would be sober and distracted by the routine of departure. Owen went to find Jethro amidships.

"You talked to Terrapin, then?" asked Owen. "About the natives?"

"A few words," said Jethro absently, leaning on the rail. "I told him you needed the brother's help for trading and that the sister wasn't well enough to go ashore."

"It wasn't your place to do that."

Jethro looked up from the churning waters with a blank expression. "My apologies. I was only trying to help the cause."

"Which cause?" Owen asked, anger rising in his voice.

"Trading, of course."

Owen saw that the heir was undaunted, possibly even sincere, in this last statement. Perhaps he was being unnecessarily harsh with Jethro. Softening, he said, "I'm glad we can ensure the sister is properly healed. I will need the brother to work, though. Perhaps you can keep an eye on the girl. Keep her away from the men as much as possible. You know how they get."

Jethro nodded with vindication. "I'll do my best to keep them at bay."

Sixty miles out of the bay and with eight bells sounding the end of the forenoon watch, the wind died off and the sight lines bent with a mirage. They sailed into a bowl of warm, moist air that played havoc with the helmsman's sense of direction. A blanket of atmosphere hung above the water. Islands shimmered, hazed in front of the horizon even though the charts showed them to be a hundred miles off. The riffled, blue expanse became a sheet of murrhine glass, distorting the helmsman's view. It was as if the *Cullion* were sailing under a bell jar, into a dome of vapors. Terrapin came onto the deck and told the helmsman to heave to. The foresails backfilled and she pointed toward the wind, idling up from a close-reach. "Are you sailing by feel or by chart, Mr. Ricketts? Because the bark is backing and filling like a frigid bride peeling back the bedsheets."

The helmsman released his grip on the wheel, ran a hand over his whiskered face, plumbed the horizon for new information. "We are hove to, sir. The wind is flukey."

"Answer my question."

"The islands are springing up where they shouldn't," he said. "I'm seeing double."

Terrapin said, "Don't trust what you see unless we're about to hit one of them, and rest assured I'm not about to resort to the steam engines on this account. Stick to the charts, because they have been vetted with my own hands and eyes. Now stop luffing into the wind and keep her trimmed. Are we agreed on this front?"

The helmsman nodded and the first mate yelled at the men to take their places. Terrapin walked on the foredeck, Nipper at his side. Odd-looking shadows then amorphous shapes emerged from the ropy groves of rigging. Owen watched the captain as he discovered that the ship was run amok with Djimbanko stowaways — the sailmaker with a mongoose on a leash, the apprentice with a green parrot on his arm, a large tortoise eating chunks of pineapple below the bulwark, a blue-eyed Siamese cat drinking from a bowl of condensed milk, a wallaby eating oats from the carpenter's hand. Terrapin put Nipper down and let the terrier run a yapping circuit around the ship until he backed the tortoise into its shell.

Terrapin called for the first mate. "Pym, what are the ship's rules about pets on board outside a captain's personal hound?"

Pym straightened and brought his hands to his sides. "I believe, sir, that pets, like livestock, are at the discretion of the master himself. As far as I know, the only animal expressly forbidden on a ship is a monkey . . . and that might only be on a surveying ship, come to think of it. Somewheres I heard a story about a monkey destroying a map that was being drafted and now the admiralty has written a ban into the laws of the sea."

Terrapin called off Nipper from the terrified tortoise and the dog scampered up, wheeling and nuzzling at the captain's pant leg.

Owen couldn't resist a little dig. "Strange cargo we have, Captain."

Terrapin winced. "You worry about the collecting, Mr. Graves, and I will worry about the fucking petting zoo we seem to have acquired." A dozen men were listening from the rigging. He continued loudly, "Pym, inform the men on your watch that if these beasts so much as shit or piss on my deck they will end up eating parrot soup and wallaby meat loaf before the day is out. Or I'll set these mammal and amphibian demons in a dinghy and watch them drift away in a squall. There's no end to the invention I have for these kinds of turns. Furthermore, make sure the men know that the orlop is strictly off-limits and that the natives are to be treated fairly or I'm not above lashings. I don't care if it is nearly the twentieth fucking century, I'll flog a man sixty times and would be within my nautical rights for doing so." He picked up Nipper and walked toward the chartroom muttering every expletive he had ever learned or invented—*fuckhorse mother, bitching louse, barnacled slut, shit-faced canks*—while the men relished the scene from behind the cover of sailcloth.

What Argus thought about in the hold was Noah's Ark, about animals paired and saved. But were the stuffed and cottoned birds or lizards going to come back to life at sea? The man named Jethro—a good biblical name belonging to the father-in-law of Moses who lived near the Dead Sea—was kind and patient. Argus didn't understand who had the higher rank, Owen or Jethro, but the skinny, tall one wore a fencing glove on one hand and tended his sister's wound and wrote things down in a leather notebook. He gave her medicine called laudanum, which was another name for opium tincture, and it eased Malini's pain but also made her drowsy. Argus slept on a cot in the corner of the orlop and on a few occasions woke to see Jethro trimming his sister's fingernails, or cutting a piece of her hair, or measuring Malini's arms with a tape measure while she slept. The nails and locks of hair were bottled and shelved and more notes were penciled into the book. If Jethro were an islander, he would be accused of sorcery because only shamans took such an active interest in the sprouting and residue of the human body. It was never-ending and the Reverend Mister hadn't liked it at all, the constant battle against unkemptness, the calcareous civil war that raged in nails and hair and teeth. Argus carefully watched Jethro empty Malini's bedpan into a slop bucket to be taken above and made sure nothing was retained. Storing excrement was a sure sign of devilment.

For Jethro's part, he was applying what little he knew of anthropometric and craniometric methods to the study of the native girl. There was a correlation to be made between head and nose form, stature, and skin color, though he didn't have the books he needed to bolster that view. Something about Camper's facial angle came to him, that if you drew a line from nostril to ear and another line perpendicular from upper jawbone to the prominence in the forehead you could ascertain the angle. Europeans had something like an 80-degree angle and Africans 70 degrees and orangutans less than 60. The body, after all, was a map of consciousness. But he was a Darwinist at heart and stayed skeptical of any method that lent itself to a polygenic theory, to the idea that humanity came from separate lines instead of a single ancestor. Why, then, was it so satisfying to measure the architecture of her bones?

They shared an interest in sketching and, while Malini rowed on the tide of laudanum, Jethro taught Argus new techniques—how to cross-hatch his shading, how to leaden the clouds in his landscapes. He gave him a knife-sharpened pencil and showed him how to capture the essence of a specimen. Jethro brought out his japanned tin box of watercolors—viridian, burnt sienna, pale cadmium, carmine, bistre, Chinese white, and a dozen other tints that could capture any hue found in nature. They outlined then painted a series of marine creatures that had been built on a radial plan: sponges, sea anemones, jellyfish, starfish, sea urchins.

"The great wheel of life seems to be sewn into their very structure," Jethro said, holding his page at an angle to the lamplight.

Argus considered the sketchbook and the idea. Was life a wheel?

Jethro looked at Argus's pencil-and-watercolor of the starfish and said, "You can draw the structure of what you see inside as well. Imagine if you took the roof from a church and looked down from above." Jethro took a scalpel and sliced down one of the legs of the starfish.

"Why do you want to know the insides?" Argus asked.

"So we can determine how it works. The structure reveals its nature!"

This didn't make any sense at all; wouldn't you watch a starfish or jellyfish swim if you wanted to know how it worked? Nonetheless, Argus took up a new piece of paper and began to sketch the struts and filaments of the dissected limb.

Jethro stood and went over to the brass microscope he had lashed to a workbench. He clipped a glass slide onto the mounting stage.

"Come over here," he said. "I will show you what I mean."

Argus went to the workbench. "Who are Bausch and Lomb?"

"Look into the eyepiece."

Argus bent to the vulcanite eye-rim and Jethro lit a candle near the base. At first he saw nothing but when Jethro told him to close his other eye a ring of light shimmered into view. Translucent specks floated across a pale moon.

"You are looking at a single drop of sea water."

Argus repositioned his eye and said, "Are they germs or tiny fishes?"

There was no end to what this boy knew; next he would be talking Pasteur and Thomas Huxley. Jethro said, "Think of them as sea mites. Tiny creatures dancing and swimming for our amusement."

"And what do they do when we are not watching with amusement?" Argus asked.

Jethro wiped a fingerprint smear from the brass pinion but did not answer. The boy sometimes spoke in Confucian riddles.

The sister began to moan and Jethro felt in his trouser pocket for the vial of laudanum.

Argus straightened from the workbench. "No. Let her wake."

Jethro kept his hand in his pocket.

"I think the pain has fled her," Argus added softly.

They crossed to the table where Malini was wrapped in a flannel sheet and cushioned on a bed of wadded cotton. Two wooden boards had been nailed to the table sides to ensure that she didn't topple while the boat was under sail. She held a hand in front of her face and seemed startled to be in the boat.

"Sister," Argus whispered in Poumetan. "Are you hungry? We are in a boat and sailing to some islands where I work as a guide. We are safe."

A weight was pushing down on her chest. Her eyes felt swollen and she was glad for the dark wooden cave. Like kava, the medicine had numbed her tongue and lips, ribboned its way into her stomach before banishing the pain. It felt like a soft silver voice speaking inside of her. She had drifted in and out of dreamless sleep, half glimpsing thoughts like a swimmer coming to the surface before plunging anew. Where were her children? This is what she thought now, looking at the back of her hand as if for the first time. Then the old gnawing sadness swelled again, all her childless days, and she remembered the rowing and the husband who must surely be dead. She had been cursed after all.

"I will wash her wound again," Jethro said. He cut some gauze and went to unwrap the flannel sheet but Malini pushed his hand away. "Tell her I need to make sure it is still draining."

Argus spoke again to her in Poumetan.

She heard his voice from very far away. Were they all dead? She said, "Why are we beneath the ocean?"

Argus said, "She says she will clean it herself if you tell her what to do."

Jethro tightened his lips and set the roll of gauze on the table. He explained that the wound needed to keep draining, that it should be covered with gauze but also exposed to air for a few hours each day. "Tell her those things," he said. "She will need to press it until nothing more comes to the surface."

Argus said, "You will need to let it weep and clean it with a piece of cloth. He says it also needs air."

Malini closed her eyes. "I don't want to stay under the waves."

"Did you hear what I said, sister?" He gently shook her shoulder.

Her eyes stuttered then settled on his face. "I will do it. I am in charge of it. Leave me so that I can clean it."

"She wants us to leave so she can have some privacy."

Jethro paused, swallowed. "Yes, of course. I'll take you up on deck for some fresh air. Perhaps your sister can join us if she feels up to it. Ah, that reminds me, we'll need to find her some clothes and I know just the place to look." He hesitated, smiled reassuringly, then took up Sir John Herschel's *Manual of Scientific Enquiry* and led Argus toward the companionway.

Owen was about to come off the first dogwatch when the siblings emerged from the hold, Jethro at their side, a pair of placental forceps hanging from his belt loop like a cutlass. The brother appeared with Dickens under one arm and had been decked out from the slop chest in a broadloom shirt and sturdy trousers. Then the sister, incredibly, came forth in the silk evening gown that Teddy Meyers had used to win the equatorial beauty pageant. There was a slight hobble in her gait as she favored her left leg, but she was undeniably radiant, her dark hair hoisted above the mizzen of a bare neckline, the sorrel ridge of her shoulders against the scarlet gown. A few men of the dogwatch came down out of the rigging to gather around the trio, Dickey Fentress in front, awed by the sight of so many dark and womanly parts packaged in silk and frocking.

Malini breathed in the southeasterly, moved unsteadily to the rail without giving the men a second glance. She could hear the waves slapping against the wooden hull of the ship. Her bare toes gripped the deck planks and she could feel the throb of the wound dimming away. It was almost dark; she saw a sliver of mackerel sky along the horizon like a glimpsed river. They were heading north, she could tell, and the hurricanes would be coming before the next full moon. She turned and looked up into the rigging, where a few faces stared back at her. The sailors were perched like tree-dwellers, some ghostly barefoot clan with knives between their teeth. One of them flagged his hand through the air as if it were on fire. She had seen this violent greeting before and she wasn't about to respond. She turned for the rail and watched the sun wink then disappear into the sea.

Owen didn't know the particulars of how Jethro had persuaded the captain to bring the natives along but he suspected that, as with everything else, it involved bribery, begging, or both. Jethro followed the sister to the bulwarks and Owen came up beside the boy.

"We're heading to the Solomons. Do you know anyone on those islands?"

"No, sir. But I have passed through the Solomons before and know they are headhunters."

"Excellent."

Argus adjusted the book under his arm. He said nothing but the confusion read in his face.

Owen said, "If they headhunt then they probably also make artifacts to celebrate the rituals. That's what we're after. Objects."

"There is an Anglican mission there and smallpox fever." Argus also knew that the Bishop John Coleridge Patteson had been killed on Santa Cruz but thought it best not to mention it.

"Then prices should be coming down," said Owen. He didn't mean to sound callous but he couldn't help the feeling that some kind of conspiracy was being plotted in the hold. What in God's name was Jethro showing them down there? And he didn't like one bit the way the heir looked at the sister. If his interest was scientific it was a low-grade brand, the kind of zoological bent a man shows at a horse auction. Here he was, circling her chestnut flanks at the rail, warding off the seamen with a proprietary hand. "Do you speak the language?" Owen asked Argus.

"They will speak pidgin because of the mission and traders."

"We're all set then. You can help me negotiate a fair price. We have a lot of beads and calico. Think we can steer them away from the tobacco and guns?"

"We can try."

They turned to see Terrapin descend from the poop deck with a sartorial swagger, Nipper cradled in his arms. The bright plumage of a cravat drew attention to his ponderous chin and jowls. The sleeves of his undersized peacoat were too short and his stomach surged against the line of gilt buttons. "Mr. Gray, are you and your guests ready for dinner in the stateroom?"

Jethro performed something that approached a Regency bow. In that moment Owen could envision dragging him behind the ship in one of his dredge nets. The captain's eyes drank down the sister in several slow gulps. She took a step forward, much to the amazement of the men. Maybe the captain's self-proclaimed prowess at the stern of a four-poster bed or his command of the unsounded waters of coital union were, in fact, true. But then the real motive of her advance was revealed. The first time any of them saw Malini smile was as she put a gentle hand to the dog's ears and Nipper raised his black nose to lick her fingertips.

Owen watched the diners go below. If Terrapin claimed the girl, marked her in some way as his own, then the ship was doomed. The *Cullion* would become a hen frigate, only the hen was a tribal widow. Between the lusty seamen and captain, the protective brother, the pike-hearted naturalist wanting to pin her like a beetle, nothing good could come of her presence.

Owen took a lamp up to the foredeck and worked on his next letter to Adelaide. Before leaving, he had instructed her to send her first dispatch to the government station in the Solomon Islands and he prayed the mail steamers had favored their correspondence.

18.

The *Cullion* spent two weeks trading in the southern Solomons, anchoring off San Cristobal, Ulawa, and Malaita. They weren't the untainted islands Owen had hoped for—they were part of a newly formed British protectorate, and Roman Catholic priests had been in Makira Harbour since 1846—but the villages were resilient and steeped in their own culture. Away from the coastline, where smallpox had wiped out a sizable swath of the population, the clansmen were eager to trade with the landing party—Owen, Argus, Jethro, Giles Blunt, and Dickey Fentress. Argus agreed to let Malini remain on the ship after much deliberation; he reasoned she was better off under the captain's questionable watch rather than run the risk of her being snatched for the local bride market.

The well-armed trading party headed out each day at dawn, to avoid the heat but also to afford Jethro ample collecting opportunities. They trekked along ridgebacks of chert and limestone, along clifftops that overlooked the coast. The sea was striated in bands of green and the sun rose a smoky gold. They came upon villages fortified by stockades, riven by trenchlike fosses designed to keep enemies at bay. They stared into bamboo pitfalls staked with human remains. The highland settlements consisted of four or five taro-thatched houses on rocky knolls. At each cluster of dwellings they heard elaborate tales about the infidels over the hill, translated from the bastardized pidgin a few elders had acquired long ago in Queensland cane fields. Stories of infanticide abounded, women who suckled pigs, men who ate the flesh of serpents, a tribe of hermits who lived above three thousand feet and used only dew for drinking and bathing. Their acrimony was so dramatic that Owen wondered whether they weren't protecting their brethren in the hinterland. Was there a village up there that had never smelled a body gone to the ruin of smallpox?

Owen led the way through stands of canarium and milkwood, sometimes wielding a machete to hack a path. In the clearings he used a spyglass to survey the escarpments and stony valleys that reminded him of the Colorado canyons seen from the westbound train. Jethro trailed in the rear with his creel and 12-gauge, eyes worrying the tree crowns. He brought his cinématographe along and captured the sight of a hawk whisking a village chicken from the ground. On Argus's advice he refrained from shooting the bird—plumaged in black and white, at least fourteen inches head to tail—for fear of offending the locals.

The villagers disliked giving their names directly to the whites and they regarded Argus with suspicion, calling him their word for the twice-fruiting Malay apple. Despite their general wariness, they traded, albeit at spear point—relic-house figurines, elaborately carved gongs, ceremonial bowls of l'ao shell, in return for tobacco, wax matches, calico, sharpened tomahawks, and bush knives. Owen gave Argus credit for not trading a single rifle in the Solomons. The villagers asked for Martini-Henry rifles and breechloaders—the preferred murder weapons of the New Georgian headhunters—but Argus said they only had the rifles they carried and that firearms did not fare well in the bush. He sermonized on the maintenance and care of steel or iron adzes and tomahawks and within fifteen minutes the topic of guns had been all but forgotten. He was also responsible for their biggest trading coup—swapping a spyglass and some incidentals for a festoon of decorative skulls and a prized single-hulled canoe. Owen had no idea how he was going to get the canoe back to Chicago, let alone into Hale Gray's private collection, but he was hoping its workmanship and audacity would win him a handsome bonus from the insurance magnate.

The canoe and skulls were obtained on San Cristobal. They arrived there on the morning of a burial ceremony for a chief, and trading looked like a remote possibility at best. They contented themselves with watching the proceedings, Jethro working the handcrank of the cinématographe. A boy sounded a conch shell and the villagers prepared themselves as if for war, gathering adornments and favored weapons, streaking their faces with lime and arranging feathers in their hair. Young warriors rushed shouting into the village square, sham-fighting and throwing spears. The chief's body was washed by his relatives, painted in turmeric, wrapped in the heated leaves of the pandana. The corpse's big toes and thumbs were tied with rattan. Argus learned that this practice was designed to puzzle the ghost so that he would leave the villagers alone. They wanted the chief's ghost to swim out to the island of Maraba, the Hades of the Arosi clansmen, without lingering.

The dead man's property was destroyed—his trees were cut, his nuts and yams thrown into the bush, his feasting bowl broken, a favored pig or dog slaughtered and buried alongside him. The women began the lamentation and Argus extracted the meaning from an elder—*Ancestor, my mother has come, I come back to thee, through the deep sea*. The dead man was taken away. His relatives would shave their heads and fast for twenty days. *Water, my mother*. Argus heard the elder say that a youth would have to be bought as a *ramoa* sacrifice for the chief's death and that his body would be cooked and eaten . . . *taboo of the dead, I rest from weeping*. He did not offer this information to Owen and his men; although these heathens were alien to Poumetans and God, he liked their graceful bearing, the way they sang lamentation and observed custom. He thought of Jeremiah 9:20 and the instruction to teach your daughters wailing. He was sure if they were offered the *Catechism of Christian Truth* correctly they would come to embrace it, learn to trade their winged serpent *Hatuibwari* for the Holy Ghost.

After the burial ceremony was completed there was a feast and the landing party prepared to depart. Jethro returned the ciné-matographe to its case and began looking for reptile and avian trophies. Owen sat with Dickey and Giles, passing a cigarette back and forth, admiring the dead chief's canoe. It was slender-hipped and inlaid with pearl. The smell of tobacco brought a few onlookers but Owen failed to interest them in trade. Argus watched Owen mime, point, gesture with his hands to a circle of implacable faces. He remembered the exact moment he had won the Reverend Mister's affections. Not five days into his post as houseboy, after studying the ritual of a palmful of Darjeeling into the china teapot, of counting the minutes for the steeping of boiled water, then the sequence of stirring, kneading, and baking flour that resulted in soda-scones, he had come out onto the verandah one morning with the preacher's breakfast on a lacquered tray. The fleet Scotsman was pulled by gratitude to his feet, the closest thing he knew to Calvinist joy registering in his features. *Ye cannae know how you've pleased this ol' Glaswegian, boy.* It was a brief but definitive anointment and Argus never looked back. Now he wanted that same recognition from Owen. He didn't understand all the stations and offices aboard the ship, but he knew now that the trader was higher in rank than the tall, single-gloved one, that his own future was somehow bound up with service to this man.

An idea came to him as he listened to the villagers argue about whether the chief would return in malice. There were itemized grievances, occasions listed when the chief might have felt slighted. Argus picked up Owen's spyglass, told several of the dead man's relatives to follow him, and walked down to the beachhead. The villagers flanked him as he pointed from the shoreline, raised the telescope, and glassed the horizon. He was unsure whether the island of Maraba was a physical atoll or a mythic transit for dead souls, so he scanned a series of distant coralline islands with the spyglass. The pidgin phrase for telescope was *glas blong look-look big* and he repeated it as an incantation each time he glassed the blued distances. The old widow stood by with her shaven head, squinting into the east. Slowly he positioned the telescope for her and covered her left eye so that she could make out the shimmering atolls in the circle of light. Several times she plumbed the distance with her naked gaze, then raised the spyglass to the horizon, her mouth opening in skepticism or awe, it was hard to tell which. The chief's brother, of some political clout, took the telescope and repeated the process.

Soon there was a delegation of elders on the beach. A shaman was brought in for consultation. Argus knew they had seen spyglasses before but perhaps they had never found a metaphysical application for the instruments. Other villagers wandered down to see the pilgrimage route of the dead magnified and brought under scrutiny. The telescope was handed down a line of bereaved relatives. Argus suggested that the spyglass and other goods could be swapped for the chief's canoe and the skulls on his clubhouse. It sounded ridiculous, even to him, but there was no denying the revelation on the shoreline, the sense that they might steel themselves against supernatural whim. Owen, Dickey, and Giles listened from the periphery as the new headman and shaman held forth. Argus could tell from the undercurrent of Melanesian cognates and pidginized slang that there was some advantage in his proposal. The canoe, like the rest of the chief's property, was slated for destruction, the prow was to be removed and placed as a headstone, and the skulls were kill trophies from a previous generation. The headman was happy to be rid of them, to gather a festoon of new skulls that might seal his own reputation. Argus chimed in with enticements of additional goods. To the white men, he gave the impression of deft salesmanship when, in fact, he mostly repeated key phrases and arguments of the lobbying shaman. He felt Owen's approving regard at his back.

By nightfall a deal had been brokered—the canoe and skulls in return for the spyglass, three fathoms of calico, six tins of wax matches, and half a dozen tomahawks. Dickey and Giles paddled the dead chief's boat out to the *Cullion* like Polynesian warriors, shirtsleeves hitched, hamming it up in the slender prow and stern with full-armed strokes and bloody war cries. She was tippy and lean over the swells. Dickey put his back into it, his hair diamonded with spindrift in the falling dark. Giles picked up one of the skulls and raised it to eye level in the stern. He botched a rendition of Hamlet's "Alas, poor Yorick" speech—a mash of *gorge rims* and *infinite jests*. Jethro winced from the other boat. Why was it that the common man always yammered, *Alas, poor Yorick, I knew him well* instead of *I knew him, Horatio*? Jethro watched the native boy rowing with considerable gusto, facing Owen with a smile. Some shift had occurred. He had hoped to make a naturalist of Argus, to bring him onto the confluent streams of art and science. Perhaps there was still time. Unlike the traders, Jethro's day had been a bust, a few desiccated insects and skinks in his creel.

They arrived back at the ship and the crew took turns paddling the canoe through the light swells. Owen consulted with the captain and Terrapin pronounced that due to lack of space on the quarterdeck, the canoe would have to be towed astern. Jethro went below to drop off his equipment before going to check on Malini. On his way to the poop deck he passed Argus, who was carefully loading the skulls into the bosun's store. They exchanged a careful glance. Jethro could see Terrapin standing at the wheel, a slouch hat pulled low and Malini at his side, reclining in a wicker deck chair with Nipper asleep in her arms. She was dressed in a frock made of muslin and gingham, eating a stick of saltwater taffy.

Just as Jethro put his hands on the railing and started to climb the stepladder, Terrapin said, "Officers only, cupcake."

Jethro stopped, dropped his hands by his sides. "I was just coming to check on the girl."

"Sure you was." Terrapin cast a glance back at Malini. "She's in fine spirits. I had the sailmaker hem her up something from the slop chest offcuts and he's quite the seamstress, don't you think? I'm calling it Bush-and-Bodice . . ."

"Very nice. Perhaps you can have him make some extra blankets. It's awfully dank in the hold at night for the native girl."

Terrapin turned the wheel to port with his extended thumbs. "No need. I've asked first and second mate to share a cabin so the kanaka princess can have her own quarters. That seems like the proper and Christian thing to do, wouldn't you say, Mr. Gray?"

Jethro turned to the weather side of the boat just so the captain wouldn't see his face blanch. "Indeed."

Terrapin jutted his chin to windward. "All up, a nice little agreement we made the other night. And let's just say that when you wants to study that dark race behind me that it's by appointment only. Due process, it is. Good day, now, Mr. Gray." Terrapin threw a cracker into the air and caught it in the enormous grotto of his mouth.

One of the skulls in the bosun's store was larger than the rest and contained a gold tooth. The first mate claimed it belonged to an Englishman from the Royal Yacht Squadron who'd gone missing several years prior. The gold-crowned maw had been perched under the binnacle and Mr. Pym gestured to it with his foot as he lobbied the captain from the leeward side of the poop deck. He wasn't happy about sharing a berth with the second mate. Owen waited for his turn to speak.

Pym said, "We should be weighing the mudhook, captain. Before them savages come at us one midnight. Sitting targets we are in this bay. Ruddled as sheep before slaughter."

Terrapin looked up at the high, cirrus sky and considered. "I'm as superstitious as the next mariner, Pym . . . I know that seabirds are the vanquished souls of dead sailors, that the bark lightens under the magnetic draw of a full moon—so of course an Englishman's gold-toothed cranium augurs bloody ruin." He looked at the skull, then at Owen. "But these waters are proving tradeworthy, so let's linger a while and reinforce the middle watch, Mr. Pym. As a precaution against night ambush."

Mandrake squared his jaw into the easterly billows and gave a curt nod.

"And Mr. Graves," the captain continued, "three more days should do the trick. You should think about where we'll be heading next."

"We'll work our way north through the island chain. But we'll head next to the government station in Tulagi. I'm expecting some correspondence."

"Ah, yes, I've seen you writing letters in the moonlight . . . must be a beloved. Any man who pines in the epistolary form has yet to have his life plundered by a woman. They wait for us ashore, like goddesses juggling severed heads . . ."

"I'll keep that in mind."

Terrapin told the first mate to have the topgallants trimmed.

Jethro overheard all this from the quarterdeck railing, a sketchbook in his hands. He was elated that they would be visiting Tulagi. The Resident Commissioner, Charles Woodford, was the author of *A Naturalist Among the Head-Hunters,* a first edition of which graced the little orlop library. What a boon to have a naturalist reach such a distinguished government office. If there was going to be a collecting frenzy in the next few days, Jethro wanted to be a part of it. So far he had managed to gather a good supply of reptiles, birds, and marine life but he was sadly lacking in the way of mammals.

As if willed by the thought of mammals, Malini came down from the poop deck with Nipper trotting and panting at her side. He wondered if he might gain her interest. Wasn't he owed a debt of gratitude? After all, it had been he who'd stood up to the sous-surgeon with his medieval bone hatchets and knives. He'd given her the civilizing tonic of laudanum to ease the pain. And the captain—now her seeming protector—had been ready to kick her off the ship before she could walk.

The seamen were whipping lines aloft and they watched her

descend to the quarterdeck as if she were a doe edging out of a copse of trees. The hobble was gone and she had been returned to full, sorrel-skinned health. Part of her daily regimen was feeding the native stowaways. She crouched beside the wallaby and fed it oats from her hand. When it was done eating she rubbed the hem of its pouch and the marsupial nuzzled her arm. The men watched this display of tenderness and thought of their mothers and girlfriends, of sisters with a soft spot for lapdogs. Nipper was learning restraint: if he growled or barked at the wildlife, Malini removed the hibiscus flower from behind her left ear and tapped him on the end of the nose with its stem.

She placed some sliced mango onto the deck for the turtle and saw Jethro's long shadow spread over her. Along with the ship's brass bell, his shoes were among the shiniest objects on board—twin suns winking on burnished leather domes. The shoes were called Balmorals, which was also a place, Argus had told her. He made some lines in his notebook and handed it to her. It was a likeness of the turtle, down to its sharklike eyes and granulated skin.

"A present," he said.

She knew that word because the captain had been teaching her English—*I am full, thank you, swimming is good for the heart, you are very pretty.* Then Jethro said some things she did not understand. She could remember the sight of him and her brother sketching and painting in the hold. But she could also remember him spooling a strand of her hair and pressing against her wound with his nail-bitten fingers. He was like somebody's unmarried uncle come up from the coast for a feast, staying too long and eating too much; the Poumetans used the expression *gives pebbles but wants stones* to describe his sort. She chased after Nipper, who was trying to corral the mongoose, a sport that would not end in his favor. Argus was arranging things at the front of the boat and she went to talk to him, the dog in her arms.

"Whose heads are these?" she asked, peering into a tea chest.

"From the islands."

"What do they want with them?" She ran her fingers through Nipper's fur.

"They will take them to a museum in America."

"What is *museum*? A kind of church?"

"It is like a clubhouse with many tools and weapons. You can look at other people's things." Looking square at the dog, he said, "What does the captain tell you?"

"Nothing."

"I see you have moved into a cabin."

"He gives me presents and teaches me English. We listen to a woman singing in his wooden house. I like the sound of her voice."

Argus reached into the tea chest, his words sounding hollow. "Make sure he does not touch you."

The mongoose had retreated to the forecastle and Malini set the terrier back on the deck. "You have never been married or initiated, little brother, but you give me advice like an elder. I am widowed and childless and he likes to give me things. There is nothing dishonorable about that. He is old and fat but also kind."

Argus straightened to look at her, but before he could say anything she was retreating for the shade of the chartroom.

Owen went to inspect Argus's stowage. He was wrapping skulls and artifacts in muslin and newspaper, tagging each with a square of cardstock that listed the date along with the island and tribe of collection exactly the way Owen had demonstrated. The boy was methodical and thorough and even the roughened seamen had taken a liking to him. One evening Owen had come from below to find Argus reading *David Copperfield* aloud to the starboard watch in the forecastle, an emphatic hand marking the orphan's trials in the salty air while the seamen listened rapt and boozy in their tiered iron bunks. Whether they saw him as an apprentice or ship's mascot, Owen couldn't say, but they made their affections known with hanks of cloth, cigarettes, nips of brandy. It was also a statement: that this tribal deckhand was much closer to being a brother than the Harvard dandy could ever be.

"You're doing a fine job, Argus."

"Thank you, sir."

"Owen."

"Owen."

They smoked a cigarette together, Argus producing a tin of Bryant & May wax matches from his trouser pocket.

"Do you think my sister is safe with the master of the ship?"

Owen hadn't brought this under full consideration; he'd been too distracted by the business of trade. He wasn't sure if Terrapin's interest was lascivious or paternal, simple lust or some misplaced desire to be a surrogate father, to summon an ill-begotten native child from one of his tattooed forearms. "I'll keep an eye on her and make sure she's not dishonored. Her cabin is right next to mine."

"Thank you."

"We are heading on in three days. Be sure to get plenty of rest. It will be a lot of work."

"Where will we go next?"

"North through the islands but then to New Guinea."

Argus forced a smile. Since boyhood he'd been told that the New Guinea highlands flowed with rivers of blood. But perhaps he could read the villagers psalms while trading for basketry and shields.

Owen said, "First we have to go to Tulagi for some mail."

Argus smiled. "Are you expecting a letter from your wife?"

"Fiancée."

"You are betrothed. What is her name?"

"Adelaide." It was the first time Owen had spoken her name at sea. Naming attachments made you vulnerable among seamen.

"I was supposed to marry a girl but I left Poumeta."

"Maybe someday you will marry. You're still very young."

"First I will need brideprice. The islanders say that one

eyetooth of a dog is worth fifty coconuts. Maybe you should give your fiancée a dogtooth necklace instead of diamonds or pearls. It would be like giving her a forest of coconuts."

"Porpoise teeth are more her style."

They laughed at this. Owen was surprised whenever Argus enjoyed a joke, never at anyone's expense but sometimes in gentle disparagement. And he seemed to know Owen's mood at a hundred paces, the way it registered in his face or hands or gait, ready with a comment to lighten or augment what was already there. Owen handed him the half-smoked cigarette and went below to consult the island charts.

Argus continued his winning streak among the Solomons in the days to follow. He always seemed to hold something in reserve, knew when to stand his ground. Not satisfied with merely listing the items of trade, he evangelized on their relative merits, the way things could be put to better use. There was the usual exchange of calico, beads, wax matches, knives, and tomahawks, but he also managed to swap clothes for handicrafts and tribal weaponry. The local term for whites was *men with the body of a parrot*; this referred to the colorful peacoats and weskits that spilled from the anchored brigs and missionary sloops. Since clothing for the villagers was more ceremonial than practical—there was a hinterland chief who wore a ragged admiralty jacket to annual festivals—it stood to reason that its value depended on the need for status and prestige. Owen had Fennimore Jauss, the sailmaker, tailor a range of gaudy attire from the slop chest and they took it ashore. Argus convinced one of the shamans to model the clothing, dressed him in patched gingham and retired sail canvas. The elders and the children, anyone not working the taro gardens, made him parade around and doff his plug hat like some tribal court jester. Argus told the elders that trousers ensured a better price during trade negotiations with whites. Then they all watched as Argus taught the shaman how to shave with a hand mirror and soap, the old man nicking and bleeding his way through the afternoon to delighted cheers. Mirrors had other applications as well, Argus reminded them. A man could use them to see who was walking behind him on a pathway. For every objection to trade he had a prepared response, just as the Reverend Mister had an armory of fixed rejoinders for every flavor of heathen doubt. The trick, Owen saw from the sidelines, was to imbue each item of trade with an expanded significance. Wax matches were more than a convenience; they could be used to light funeral pyres or conduct sorcery so that the brand of Bryant & May could be spoken aloud like an appeal to the twin ancestral gods of fire and light.

The running luck petered out their last night in the southern islands. Jethro, on the premise of needing to collect nocturnal animals, convinced Owen to overnight on one of the islands. Owen agreed, partly because it meant more hours of trade. He brought Dickey and Giles along and the landing party camped at the edge of a mangrove swamp on the periphery of a coastal settlement. The villagers agreed to let the clayskins stay, as long as they kept to themselves. The people were overrun with ague, their children riddled with ringworm. The few hours spent in the settlement, before heading a mile up the coast, yielded nothing. A young warrior was having chevrons tattooed on his face with the dismembered claw of a flying fox, the clan's totemic animal. Jethro hand-cranked several minutes of the tattooing ceremony with the cinématographe before they were asked to leave. They were escorted to a beachside grove since the village couldn't risk further infection.

Argus built a fire in the triangle of pitchtents and made a pot of coffee. They ate beans and hardtack while Jethro prepared for his night-time expedition. They heard the throb of tree frogs and the surf breaking on the coral reef. Thunderheads scraped in from the south, low and bruised, blotting out the Southern Cross for the first time in days. Owen barely looked at the stars back in Chicago but out here he found himself constantly looking skyward, leaning against the mizzenmast during a watch or roped to a yardarm.

The fireside talk ran to cursed ships and the perils of the South Seas, the barquentines, clippers, and yawls that lost men on each and every voyage, the widowmakers of the Cape, the *British Enterprise* and the *Annesley,* rammed by steamers or scuttled on uncharted reef heads. Or stories of escape and shipwreck, of the Aberdeen woman who was taken captive by the Mulgrave Islanders, kept for years as tribal pet and clan princess until the HMS *Rattlesnake* delivered her from that fate. Dickey held forth on the discovery of a human tooth in a tin of Malay beef, leaning forward to spit in the fire.

"At least it wasn't gold-crowned," said Owen.

Giles drank from his flask of rum and passed it around.

Argus could remember many a night of glass-eyed reminiscence with the preacher and wondered if these stories would also end with nostalgia and self-remorse. Would they run aground on the shores of a blighted boyhood? In the case of the Reverend Mister, single-malt whiskey was the sea for that particular voyage.

Giles wiped his mouth with the back of his wrist. "No man would ever sail if he took the time to read a boat's charter. About the only demise those articles don't mention is pinching into the mouth hole of a sea dragon. We are dust mites to the underwriters. Fucking lice on a rat's periwinkle."

"The captain read them aloud when I signed on," offered Dickey. "Like he was giving a speech."

Giles raised a palm to the fire, indicating a change in subject and that he had the floor. "One time I able-bodied on a limejuicer round the Cape and the Brit greenhorns were all up in the high rigging, trial by fire and all that, and fuck me if it didn't rain vomit for a month. Deckwash of bile and ankle-deep!"

Dickey hawed and spat again into the flames.

As the talk continued they watched Jethro ready himself as if for some obscure battlefield commission—placental forceps hanging from a belt loop, the fencing glove cinched, the collecting rifle with its extended auxiliary barrel, a chest of copper tanks for batrachians and reptiles. He'd camouflaged his coveralls with dead leaves and branches and smeared his face with mud in the manner of the New Georgian headhunters. He checked the muzzle and bore of the rifle, removing his glove so that the aggrieved finger appeared fat and yellowed in the fireglow. Absentmindedly he pointed the rifle into the bowl of firelight by the tents.

"You'll want to point that away from us, Mr. Gray," said Owen.

"Forgive me," Jethro said, aiming the rifle into the harkening woods.

Giles said, "Mudface won't hide you tonight if these clouds open up. Looks like it's going to piss down horses and cows. What are you collecting this evening?"

"I'm hoping for some mammals." Jethro strapped the chest of tanks onto his shoulders.

"Possums and rats more like it," said Dickey. "You look like you're going to sell ice cream cones at a ball game."

Owen gave the apprentice a look that told him to ease up. As much as he wanted to, he couldn't let Jethro sally out into the bush dressed like some deranged ancestor back from the brink. The skittish clansmen would shoot him or pinwheel a tomahawk at his head just as soon as look at him. "Which way are we headed?"

"I won't stand a chance with the night wanderers if you all come along."

"We'll be quiet and stay back," said Owen. "And since you're on my docket it's not much up for discussion."

Argus kicked some ashes into the fire and they headed out, Jethro in front and the men fifty yards behind. They watched the hurricane lantern bobble through the darkened thickets up ahead and heard the slosh of the copper tanks. The cordage and drapery of the bush made it slow going, Jethro deciphering a narrow footpath that led alongside the beach. Robber crabs and rats scurried underfoot, albino possums with pink eyes and hairy white tails. The din of the frogs in the fig trees was deafening, punctuated here and there by the guttural calls of a lone bullfrog. Luminous beetles flurried between branches and there were platforms of fungi, serried and glowing, like banks of phosphorescent cloud in the dark understory. Dickey and Giles took turns throwing areca nuts at Jethro's back when Owen wasn't looking. Argus brought up the rear, hesitant in his dead man's boots, his chest on edge against the memory of the night he trekked up the caldera to find his sister. He'd led the tree-dwellers into battle against the shipwrecked Englishmen, but the whole time he'd tasted his own fear like blood in his mouth.

They came to a clearing and saw the reef houses that were raised on pilings of coral and driftwood, their hearth fires visible through the chinked bamboo walls. Earlier in the day Owen had learned that the householders here were exiles of a sort, disgraced widows and shamans, adulterers and the mad, all of them spending their days fishing for mullet and making stone-shell money. The inhabitants were brought in for feasts and ceremonies, their canoes laden with currency and fish. It might not work in a city like Chicago—to let the inmates of Dunning Asylum run the local branch of the U.S. Treasury—but on an island it was an ingenious solution. The insane and socially blighted were isolated while given an important job to do. Besides, they were also the first to go if a flotilla of enemy canoes paddled into the bay on a night raid.

Just as Giles had predicted, the sky opened up and torrential sheets of rain drenched them to their bootlaces. A river of mud sluiced at their feet. Skeins of lightning backlit the coastline, turned the treetops skeletal. Undeterred, Jethro pressed on, collecting a grounded possum, a cuscus, several frogs, a number of glowing beetles. He wrapped the larger kills in muslin and folded them into his creel. The frogs were embalmed in the tanks, legs first. The other men slowed and took shelter in a grove of ficus and coconut trees while he forged ahead. The animals of the night stopped moving for a stint and Jethro felt a thousand eyes on him. He wondered how they saw him, this strange figure moving in a cone of lantern light. Or was he shifting and phosphorescent and in that way utterly unremarkable to them?

He heard the flying foxes chirping before he saw them, stepping over a rise to see a mango orchard being devoured by a colony of giant bats. They wheeled above the treetops in slow arcs, flapped between branches, hung inverted to gorge themselves on fruit. He could hear their teeth against the mango skins just below the snare drum of thunder. It was clear this was a seasonal feeding ground—even in the salt fog and rain the stench of guano and rotting mango flesh was overwhelming. He stepped into the orchard, slightly stooped from the vampiric racket overhead, and loaded two 12-gauge shells of wood powder and buckshot into the collecting rifle. A seam of rainwater bled off the chamber onto his finger, forcing him to recoil then relax against the trigger. As he fired the weapon he was glad that the gloved injury was on the other hand.

Six shots in succession—separated by rapid reloads—brought the others running, Owen yelling at Jethro through the monsoon. Like the rest of them, Jethro had been there when it was explained that the clansmen held the flying fox to be sacred, that they sponsored annual festivals in its honor and used its claws for tattooing only after its natural death. There were stories of wayward children being led back to the village by a camp of bats, a woman who gave birth to a flying fox in an ancestral cave. Unlike their sacrilegious neighbors, they didn't use the wing bones for sewing needles or for making barbed spears, but carved bat effigies into the prows of their canoes. This had all been made plain to the naturalist who now knelt beneath the furious, roused colony, the beat of their wings like broomsticks on leather hides. Jethro was already field-dressing a female in the pall of the lantern, the rain hissing off its hot tin cap. The men ran into the orchard then slowed, stunned and silent. Half a dozen bats lay dying and flapping in the guanoed dirt, their wings augered with buckshot. Jethro used a scalpel to slice down the bat's gullet and began to swab out the intestines with cornstarch and excelsior. Then came the grim surprise of an infant coiled and wobbling in its mother's viscera so that Dickey Fentress began to weep audibly. Giles swallowed, said, *You've killed us all, you fucking sodomite,* and charged Jethro with his fists swinging. Jethro took a punch in the back of the head and dropped his scalpel onto the carcass. He crouched forward, covered both ears with his hands. Owen pulled Giles back, breathing hard beneath the Babel of shitfire and terror. Argus watched, stupefied, certain now that he had backed the right man.

They heard the clansmen pounding through the bush in the downpour, running through ravines on the narrow, hidden footpaths. Owen tried to wrest the rifle from Jethro but they struggled, dancing with the weapon between them. The gun went off inches from Dickey's ear and he doubled over, clutching his head. Owen freed the weapon and yelled for them to all run for the boat. Dickey looked up, dazed. The naturalist began grappling with his chest of tanks and Owen yanked it to the ground. They took off running for the beach, Dickey stooped, Giles and Owen firing their pistols into the air above the trees to give the villagers pause. The tribesmen flushed out of the woods with spears and tomahawks but also Confederate muskets and Winchesters, a front-runner bearing down on them with a revolver like a frontier sheriff. The seamen sprinted across the beach and dragged the whaleboat down to the water, returning fire across the gunwales. Dickey steadied the prow while the others scrambled to get in, Argus pinioned against the oars to make traction in the surf, Giles and Owen firing at the sand in front of the rampaging kinsmen. Dugouts were already being dragged down to the beach. For a moment Jethro sat motionless, still as a monument, and Giles used him as a shield before Owen shoved the naturalist onto the boards.

The *Cullion*'s middle watch saw the chase unfold across the wavetops, the native outriggers cutting through the high swells while the whaleboat dipped and yawed. Gunsmoke and musket gas flared on the wind. Already the second mate was rousing the captain from his cabin, where Terrapin was teaching Malini card tricks and playing sonatas. The captain bristled onto deck in his dressing gown and gave the order for the bosun to unlock the small armory. Rifles were handed out and the watchmen gave fire over the leeward railing. Terrapin let the seamen do the shooting, as he leaned against the shrouds in silence. He gave the order to weigh anchor and for all hands to stand by to wear ship. The first mate relayed the order up into the crosstrees, but the watch was already unfurling the sails. The whaleboat rowed to port beneath the smoky fusillade. The hemp ladders were lowered and the boat brought up on davits. The traders went below and the bark heeled on a broad reach, fully canvased and armed like a Spanish galleon of another century.

19.

Jethro Gray, now confined to the hold, would not be getting his first edition of *A Naturalist Among the Head-Hunters* signed by its author. Terrapin granted Owen two hours at the government station in Tulagi and the trader rowed the dinghy onto the beach without passengers. The makeshift station was patrolled by five Fijian policemen and a sergeant from Guadalcanal. Even if Jethro had come ashore in hopes of flattering his fellow scientist into a personalized inscription, it was unlikely that Charles Woodford would have received him. He was preoccupied and not taking visitors just at the moment. The Anglican mission of Siota looked set to be placed under quarantine and there had been a spike in outbound correspondence. Among his other duties, Woodford sold New South Wales stamps to the Europeans in the islands and arranged passage for postal items on government steamers. The missionaries, all those strapping English lads and freckled Australian girls eager for Christian service, were now brought down by every strain of milkpox, cottonpox, and Cuban itch, so that the mailbags were filled with deathbed epistles and codicils, entreaties for forgiveness and reconciliation, strands of hair coiled inside feverishly licked envelopes, night poems filled with remorse. On the mail hut wall, next to a portrait of Queen Victoria, there hung a tintype of missionaries flanked on a beach, sunhats fastened, gilded King Jameses in their hands. Owen stared up at it while a Fijian policeman dug for Adelaide's letter in a canvas mailbag.

The envelope was spattered and torn, looked more like a prison letter from the Congo than a love letter from Chicago. Owen was puzzled by the Boston postmark and wished he could read the letter at once. He placed it in his pocket and was already thinking about half an hour of solitude on the foredeck. Or maybe he would take it up into the rigging, amid the flying kites and moonrakers, rolling the words in his mouth to better hear her voice.

Although he had to be back on deck in a little over an hour, he couldn't help wondering whether the Resident Commissioner might be interested in selling some artifacts. Owen knew that he had once collected for the British Museum, technically making him the competition, but he'd also heard from the grumbling constable that the government station had a single whaleboat and five pence in reserves. Maybe the commissioner could be tempted into a quick and haggle-free sale. Owen sent word of his interest with one of the constables. What came back was a politely worded declination and a cup of English tea on a china saucer. Owen drank it down in the hot sun and returned to the ship, watching the envelope square his trouser pocket as he rowed.

On board, Owen avoided the commotion of the crew weighing anchor and unfurling the sails. He retired to his cabin and lit the hanging lantern above his small desk. It sputtered to life, a wavering blue-yellow in the noxious atmosphere. He crossed to the porthole and opened the glass hatch. The letter was thinner than he expected and disappointment registered faintly in his thoughts. There was something about every letter he'd ever received that made him expect surly creditors or bad news. He smelled the folded edges for traces of roseships and steadied the pages in the disc of daylight.

> *My Darling Owen,*
>   *You will notice from the envelope that I am sending this from Boston, where I have come, it seems, to bury my father. He has been taken ill for some time but it was only when my mother wired me in Chicago that I*

*realized the extent of his duress. A train brought me east
and I'm writing this while a host of visiting aunts and
uncles pay their last respects in the room adjacent. I find
it difficult to stand by his bedside for fear of having to
say goodbye. Although he is a stern sort, he also possesses
deep veins of kindness and a philosophical turn. He was
forever handing me books during my childhood, much to
my mother's dismay. She thought I should be learning to
cook and dance and generally finessing the art of snaring a
husband. It was he who encouraged me to attend college
for no other reason than it might provide me with some
interesting reading and conversation. On the topic of
charity to one's fellows and rights for women, we never
saw eye to eye but we also never argued. He had a kind of
decency that seemed to cut through disagreement. There
were only three things that made Gerald Cummings
angry: wastefulness, greed, and badly behaved dogs.*

*Oh, Owen, I miss you terribly and feel a great sadness
that you will never shake my father's hand. Undoubtedly
he would have given you a thorough going-over but he
knows resourcefulness and depth of character when he sees
it. He would have taken you fly-fishing and tested your
seamanship on his little ketch; the two of you would have
argued at dinner about rope flemishes or whatever it is
sailors argue about. That meeting will have to exist in my
mind. Before he goes I will tell him all about you. He has
already asked me about your voyaging and lamented that
he never made it to the end of the St. Lawrence or all the
way up the Hudson. Mostly he wants to know that I will
be in good hands and I assured him of your vision for our
life together.*

*I received your letter with great glee. I must have read
every word a dozen times by now. Whenever your absence
is too much I take another look at it. My letter was*

supposed to do it justice but if I write past a few pages you will find yourself in possession of a treatise on mortality and I'll spare us both from that gloomy fate. We made a pact at the train station to remain sensible and I swore an oath not to sob or throw roses at the moving locomotive. I was true to that pact and I have been remarkably sensible these months of the voyage. However, love, I do want to say that our life together is about to take a turn. My father has been a prudent and cautious man his whole life, made sound investments, and it appears mother and I will inherit a considerable sum. The majority will be hers, of course, but even allowing for her keeping the family house and other properties I will be receiving a significant consideration. More than I will rightfully know what to do with. It holds the promise of transforming our lives. I know that these last years you have worried about how to make your way in the world and provide for me as your future wife. You are far too proud to want to live off your wife's dead father's estate, I know, but this windfall will allow us the luxury of having you at home while the children are young. There won't be any monetary need for voyages abroad. And as for me, I don't know that I will continue on at the museum forever. I will, however, always keep up my affairs with the women's committee and Hull House . . . I'm getting ahead of myself.

Mostly I want to say that we are fortunate and the future looks bright. I'm already feeling the sadness that will come from my father's passing, but he demands that my mother and I live at the very marrow of life when he is gone—he's read too much Henry David I suppose. I love you and miss you so. Be safe and return as quickly as possible. My father might live a day or a month, we cannot know for sure. If by some chance you could come home early it would mean the world to me. Wire me when you

make American landfall. I hope I haven't botched that
maritime usage!

Your loving, future wife—
Adelaide

Owen folded the letter and stood by the open porthole. Outside and above he could hear the first mate bellowing orders and the captain stumping on the windward side of the poop. With the anchor weighed, the bark heeled to leeward and headed down. Owen had told the captain to sail toward New Guinea but that was before he'd read the contents of the letter. A stint in New Guinea—the German or Dutch territories—would mean another six or eight weeks before turning back. It was already December and they'd been gone three months. He couldn't make sense of the complicated emotion battering through him. Tenderness, longing, an eagerness to see Adelaide, to comfort her, that was all there, but so was a flickering scheme in which he would adhere to the New Guinea trading course and simply tell her that he'd never received the letter. He felt a wave of self-loathing at how effortlessly this idea occurred to him.

Slumped on the iron cot with the letter still in his hand, he lit a cigarette and watched the smoke siphon out through the porthole. The thought of marrying a woman of independent wealth terrified him. It felt too easy, like cheating. Before, he supposed now, there had been the threat of a family inheritance, but he'd envisioned years of relative scrimping, the boom and bust of life between voyages, before the golden hammer came down. He was braced to endure the summer-house visits in Maine and the old blood horse's New England condescension—how else would he feel about the son of a housewrecker from the prairie states?—but he was also, or had been, resolved to quietly stand his ground. There would be months at sea, an intermittent hermitage that prepared him for the seasonal role of loving husband and devoted father. Now the future rushed to meet him and seemed intent on cutting him off from his own vision. What he feared most was being unmoored, of not living up to his father's pragmatic example. Without the combustion of needing a livelihood, of plying a trade, he might turn to laziness or vice; as it was the taverns of Little Cheyenne seemed to hold his interest when he was back on land. How to explain that he lived like a monk at sea, barely fraternized with the men, but found it necessary to be among their rowdy, drunken cousins when at home. Did he belong entirely in either of these worlds? And how would he justify leaving for months at a time if they didn't need the money?

The tone in Adelaide's letter—he reread some of the passages to affirm this—contained something new. Was it wifely insistence? God, was she pregnant? No. She would have written it plainly and issued a summons. Nonetheless she was firmly staking her claim, marking the channel with red and green buoys to bring his ship home, and she had every intention of keeping it there. There was no choice but for the *Cullion* to head north and east, to begin a winding course home. Whatever trade could be salvaged would have to do. Owen got off the cot and studied the island charts that were tacked to his cabin wall. He began circling his index finger east of the Solomon Islands, making small orbits around the equator to find mentionable specks of land. Argus would have ideas about where to go for homebound trade, but heading northeast would also mean saying goodbye to him and his sister.

He drew on his cigarette and ran his gaze along the map's equator.

What were their chances now of recruiting a family of Melanesian tribesmen to return to Chicago, especially if the ship made only perfunctory trading stops? Maybe he should settle for the Christianized boy and his muslin-frocked sister. He entertained the idea that had floated somewhat dimly until now. The contract demanded *a number of natives, preferably related by the bonds of blood,* and *two* was certainly a number. Would it be less morally repugnant to Adelaide—*and to himself?*—if he brought back two already-tainted natives rather than a family of purebreds? This would fulfill the collecting contract, secure his own independent windfall, a reasonable sum, while diminishing the moral transgression. Adelaide's conscience hovered above his own, like a hand above a tabletop.

Looking into the circle of ocean outside his berth, Owen wondered whether Argus and Malini could be persuaded to come. Perhaps Argus could act more tribal than Presbyterian, wear a loincloth instead of starched trousers, and Malini might wear a grass skirt. Hale's planned exhibit demanded an indigenous spectacle—dreadlocks and tomahawks and all the rest of it. But Owen would present it to the siblings as a business proposition, not as playacting. Six months to a year in Chicago with a monthly retainer and guaranteed steamer passage back to the islands. Surely it was infinitely better than going to the sugarcane plantations in Queensland . . .

Owen ascended to the deck and told the captain to luff up a while. Terrapin gave him an imperious stare followed by a sunward squint. Owen apologized, told him he would have a new course by evening and to bear northeast. The first mate stood by, already filling his lungs to boom directions and insults aloft. The seamen trimmed the sails and the *Cullion* headed up into a close haul. Owen scanned amidships for Argus and climbed down to the quarterdeck. On his way he passed Malini. She was standing by the railing and looking out at the diminishing islands, a Japanese parasol shielding her face from the tin-white sun.

Jethro had been confined to the orlop for two days and he was lightheaded from its drowsy, high chemistry—formalin, methylated spirits, camphor oil. A lock on the companionway served the same purpose as it did in times of quarantine: to keep the malodorous funk from the rest of the crew. This had been the captain's proclamation as he and Owen Graves colluded to keep

Jethro down below. Technically, he was told, he would be allowed on deck when the ship was under sail but so far that hadn't proved true. Couldn't run the risk of the naturalist slipping ashore, no, as if he were some larcenous criminal and most of the crew weren't San Quentin parole jumpers. An awful lot of fuss, he thought, over a field specimen. And it was beyond ironic that he was being kept prisoner on a ship that his own father had underwritten. Perhaps Hale was in on it. Another of the old baron's attempts to teach his son the ways of the world. Jethro chafed at these would-be lessons; they were levied by an aristocrat reared on foxhunting, who'd read at Oxford, but nonetheless—Jethro suspected— thought the word *rectitude* referred to a kind of hemorrhoid. His father might have committed swaths of Keats and Coleridge to memory but only so he could crib a line for an anniversary card or a club member's eulogy. Knowledge was opportunity for Hale, nothing more. Jethro couldn't help the white rage that clamped over his thoughts when he closed his eyes. As a distraction, he returned to the journals of Joseph Banks, spreading them before him in the tallow candlelight. The audacity of the young and wealthy Banks continued to impress him. Here he was at sea, collecting and naming his way across the Pacific in his mid-twenties, already the overseer of a large estate back in England, blending batches of *Sower crout* to protect the seamen against scurvy. But there was also a sense of absolute entitlement in the journals, the hunger of a noble touring his realm for the first time. On one page he spoke of copulating species, recited bird kills like a Latin prayer ("Calm this morn: went out in the boat and shot Tropick bird *Phaeton erubescens,* and *Procellaria atrata, velox* and *sordida*"), and a few days later he spoke of the island girls with that same hint at possession. Anything could be obtained; it was merely a matter of logistics.

Our cheifs own wife (ugly enough in conscience) did me the honour with very little invitation to squat down on the mats close by me: no sooner had she done so than I espied among the common croud a very pretty girl with a fire in her eyes that I had not before seen in the countrey. Unconscious of the dignity of my companion I beckond to the other who after some intreatys came and sat on the other side of me: I was then desirous of getting rid of my former companion so I ceas'd to attend to her and loaded my pretty girl with beads and every present I could think pleasing to her: the other shewd much disgust but did not quit her place and continued to supply me with fish and cocoa nut milk. . . .

Was this what the captain had in mind with the native sister? Was he plying her with gifts to weaken her guard? No doubt he was making inroads and it was a grievous affront to Jethro. Maybe it was the bottles of embalming fluid all around, or the etherlike cloud seeping through a hundred cork stoppers, that made him envision, in vivid detail, the hundred ways by which their pairing might occur. There was the question of morality, of course, but more than this the thought of the slobbering captain spreading her coppered thighs kept him awake at night. If anything *he* was the savage and held the potential to ruin her native innocence. He'd stared into the man's porcine face the night his personal belongings were ransacked and seen the lechery there like a cancer of the soul. Smelled it like the blackened, mucked bowels of lust so that he couldn't help picturing Malini astride the captain's blotched, paunchy middle or him pounding behind her like a ramrod, her face pressed into the Turkish pillows but her bottom swagging in the air like a tupped ewe. Nature, especially in the spring, brimmed with this kind of bestial ravishment but Jethro liked to think it was the ghastly exception to the rule. He closed Banks's journal and removed his glove. His finger throbbed. It was a poisonous blue around the tip and there was a warbling line of pain that backlit his every thought, like a seam of lightning behind a cloud.

He got up, cinched the glove, and retreated to his specimen shelves. The birds had vigor, that special inflection of flight in the weft of their wings. He was gifted at taxidermy. It was obvious. The bottled subjects were less impressive—coiled snakes without eyes, inverted frogs with separated hind legs, starfish and jellyfish floating in miniature seas of brine that were littered with particles of their own strange flesh. The fern case and the blotting sheet of desiccated beetles, the moths colored like chaffs of dead wheat, were nicely ordered and well labeled. All told, it was a middling collection, but Jethro felt sure that he could end up with something distinguished. First, he would have to sort out this nonsense about being shipbound when the *Cullion* was at anchor.

He returned to the swabbed and splayed bird specimen on the workbench—a Rufous Night Heron. The inversion of the skin had taken place; he had carefully detached the delicate membrane of the ear from its cavity in the skull and cut through the nictitating white membrane of the eye socket. The wings had been skinned down to the wrist joints, the leg tendons cut, the oil gland removed from the base of the tail. He'd been careful not to damage the feather roots as he worked. He prised the skin from the body and placed it wrong side out in a shallow tray of powdered arsenic, working the poison into the denuded wings and the base of the bill. This procedure required the removal of his fencing glove from his left hand but he kept the injured finger above the fray. The arsenic could easily be absorbed into fissures and tiny cuts and this demanded caution—although the powder was mixed with enough alum so as not to be fatal in its present form. Luckily for the captain the poison was in a muted form, or he might find his rum tasting like bitter almonds one evening. Jethro shook his head in the sputtering candlelight; he was no more suited to the role of assassin than he was to the role of insurance company president.

A set of footsteps stopped outside the companionway and Owen Graves came forward with a lantern. "Are you still alive in there?" The unlocked door let in a shaft of slightly cooler air.

"Is this amusing to you?"

"Not really. But neither is the thought of five men being killed in the islands because you failed to observe the local warnings."

Jethro washed his hands in a clackdish of bloodied water. "Am I free to go above? I haven't seen the sun in two days. I admit I acted a little hastily on the island."

Owen edged into the orlop proper, the museum of dead and pickled animals. "I've come with a chance for you to redeem yourself."

Jethro pretended to busy himself with dissecting instruments. "Is that so?" He wiped his hands on a cloth, working his fingertips.

Owen watched him daintily dry the injured finger. "Has the doctor seen that?"

"The barber, you mean? The culinary genius who turns maritime flesh into bonemeal? I'd rather lose my finger than let that blunderbuss come at it."

Owen pressed his lips together, stifling a laugh. How was this man ever going to get on in the world? If he someday helmed the insurance empire there would be a policyholder revolt, not to mention striking file clerks and secretaries. "We are heading northeast, beginning the trip back."

Jethro was surprised to hear this and felt briefly overjoyed. The house on Prairie Avenue, the thought of entire Sundays reading in bed, the breathtaking image of Danish pastries arranged on a paper doily, all these things seemed suddenly within reach. Then he remembered his mission and what did or didn't wait for him back in Chicago. It was from this stronger burning sentiment that he spoke. "Why so soon? We've barely begun. What do we have to show for our efforts?"

"Actually, I've already amassed a sizable collection that I think will please your father. And we'll make a final stop before heading up to Hawaii. Argus has told me about an island about two hundred miles east of here. His father and other Poumetans made annual trading pilgrimages out there when he was a boy. It's an outlier of the Solomons, past the Santa Cruz group, at the cusp of Melanesia and Polynesia. From a collector's standpoint it sounds promising. Remote enough that it's had very little contact with whites."

Owen watched Jethro cover the skinned Night Heron with the hand towel like some avian coroner.

Jethro noticed his stare and said, "Keeps the mites out until I finish the preparations." He arranged some implements on the table. "What you're describing is also a naturalist's dream, Mr. Graves. If you think I'm going to sit idle in this suffocating lair while you go ashore then you're sadly mistaken."

Owen looked around the orlop, took in the spread of specimens. "That is something we can discuss."

"Ah, I see, I am to be placed on probation."

"Something like that."

Owen took out a cigarette—his fifth in the hour since reading the letter—and held it at bay. "I'm afraid to light up for fear of an explosion."

Jethro didn't give in to the slouching, pally tone.

Owen said, "You mentioned at the beginning of the voyage that you had some reels of Chicago."

"Nothing really. Some footage taken inside the Loop and elsewhere before we left. I was trying to fathom how the contraption worked."

Owen blew smoke into a pause. "I'm going to ask Argus and Malini to return to Chicago with us."

Jethro folded his arms. "I see."

"This was part of your father's proposal, to bring back some natives. I had hoped for better samples, as it were, but we've had to cut the trip short on my account. A family crisis." He looked at the backs of his hands.

Jethro had no choice but to appear sympathetic. "I'm sorry to hear that." Of course there were arrangements with his father to which he had not been privy. It had always been that way.

"I take it you didn't know about the native cargo."

"My father has a habit of not confiding in me. But I'm surprised you've been taken in by one of his schemes. Are you bringing back the savages like a couple of tomahawks?"

Owen hesitated. "I believe it can be done ethically."

"I've been studying them in my fashion, their bearing and culture. But sooner or later, as with all live specimens, the choice is simple—put them behind glass or release them into the wild."

"You make them sound like wild birds."

A brief silence. They regarded each other.

"I haven't told the captain or the crew either. We're idling at the moment until I ask Argus and Malini outright if they'll come back."

"And what are you waiting for?"

"Some enticement. It would be a way for you to gain some much-needed goodwill from the crew and the captain if you showed some reels of Chicago. We've been at sea long enough for them to be homesick. And if Argus and Malini saw it for themselves, the glitter and bustle, maybe they could be tempted to come back with us. Of course, I'm expecting they'll need to play-act a little to fit with your father's designs."

"And what designs are those?"

"A rooftop exhibition. He has some notion of displaying a tribal village up there."

Jethro smiled ruefully. "Two people is hardly a village, Mr. Graves."

"True. But better than nothing. Will you show the reels?"

Jethro considered; the entire ship had been alive with secret dealings from the get-go. The cook bribed to administer chloroform, the captain to allow the primitives to sail, and now this wager that a few minutes of film could inflame the native mind as if it were a nesting magpie before a shiny spread of coins and tassels. He would happily study the natives further, even back in Chicago, but he resented being caught up, pawnlike, in some larger design of his father's. Would he ever be trusted in his own right? "I'm the salesman, am I? Show the blackies a few skyscrapers and they'll be champing at the bit to come along? I'm not so sure." He circled the workbench, rising to a theme as vaporous as the fetid air, elbows jutted. "I'm certainly not going to stand in the way of my father's wishes. That would be irresponsible of me. But, in due course, rather soon, actually, I will expect a return favor."

He turned on his heels and it was cheap vaudeville to Owen, who blew smoke at the ceiling.

Jethro said, "You'll give me permission to come ashore when we get out to this satellite island. Think of the species that breed in such a far-flung place. It's a scientific duty. Not even Banks went out that way."

"It's not just my decision. The captain will have to agree to it."

"The man is a servant of the expedition. You devise the route and my family funds the wake."

"Nonetheless, under maritime law, he is in charge of our collective well-being. He must serve the ship and the men. And I'll be asking him to use the engines for the last leg, so I need to stay in his good graces."

Jethro ran his hands along the edge of the workbench. "You will do your best to represent the interests of science, however?"

"I'll do what I can."

"Fine, then. Tell the captain and the men that I will show a reel in the messroom tonight. Have the cook mangle together some refreshments and let the natives sit up front with their mugs of hot cocoa. And I take it that I am now free to go above and breathe some fresh air?"

"Of course."

When Owen had left, Jethro practically lurched for the companionway and used the vertical hatchway to ascend to the deck. He shielded his eyes from the blinding light of the sun when he got above. Red orbs and swirls blotted his vision. The wind blew fresh and from the southeast. He hobbled forward, took the glove off, felt the air graze his finger. Somehow, he felt his awareness swing open, like a door flung wide, and then it came back with a sudden jolt of pain. The snakebite was poisoning his mind, he thought, a tide of tainted blood rising up his arm, lacerating his thoughts.

He watched the men gather around the forecastle where the captain and Owen addressed them. Through cupped hands Jethro caught sight of Argus and Malini by the mizzenmast, chatting in their ragged hand-me-downs, and he thought, God help them if they come back to Chicago, the merciless crowds and the canyons of brickwork and the plumes of soot, a world infinitely stranger than any tribal afterlife could deliver. Then he thought of Malini in a downtown teahouse, dressed in taffeta, and how he would personally teach her to put a napkin on her lap before taking her to a symphony. All was not lost.

At ten o'clock the *Cullion* sauntered into a light breeze, close to fully clothed and fifty miles from the nearest island. Terrapin told the helmsman not to take any sail off her then went to his stateroom to dress for the spectacle. Six men from the port watch stayed on deck to navigate the bark while the rest went below to sit on stools and kegs or cross-legged on the floor of the mess-room. Jethro had set up the cinématographe on an upended crate, the canvas of a retired topsail clewed taut across the galley as a screen. The seamen watched him tinker with the contraption's fidget wheels and gears, peering from behind a candle lantern into a brass-plated recess. He carefully threaded a spool of film, his hands shaking, a blinkard defusing a bomb. "It doubles as projector and camera," said Dickey Fentress, a little too loudly. His left ear was bothering him, he said, so that he had to swallow to ease the buzzing of the room. A nearby seaman said he'd seen the device exhibited by a Frenchman in a San Francisco dime museum—seen a horse race, a gaggle of factory girls skipping rope, a Parisian dog pissing on a lamppost. Argus had been told to sit up front in one of three wingback chairs brought in from the captain's cabin. The seamen ribbed him for his elevated position, pretended to be shoeblacks and buff his shoes, joked that he should recite passages of *David Copperfield* if the moving pictures were bunkum. Argus waited for his sister and the captain to join him, nervous about his place of honor. Hendrik Stuyvesant had cooked up a batch of duff and Argus watched the hardboiled pudding being rushed around as quickly as a collection plate among heathen pewfellows. Owen leaned against the aft wall and gave him a reassuring nod.

Terrapin arrived with Malini on his arm and instead of his usual eventide sarong he wore something resembling a coronation cape, silk lined in scarlet, and in the dimness there were either honeybees or embroidered stars on the trim. He carried a pair of opera glasses and since Malini was in the evening gown that had once belonged to Teddy Meyers's mother, it wasn't hard to imagine them stepping through the din to reach their Rossini box seats. Malini sat next to her brother without comment and Terrapin eased himself closest to the wall. He crossed his legs, drew the silk proscenium of his cape across his girthed middle, and gave a hand flourish that indicated the projectionist could begin the show. The hanging slush lamps were snuffed and Jethro began to turn the hand crank, the projector bulb straining to life. He'd spent several hours splicing footage into some semblance of a reel. He let a brown tail of film warm the machine through before he removed the lens cap, by which point the seamen were throwing pudding currants at each other and pretending to kiss and fondle in the nitrate-smelling dark.

When the cap came off, the grainy light startled into blue pales then dissolved into a silent, underwater gouache of the Chicago streets—pyramids of oranges at the South Water Street Market, the shipyards of Goose Island, charcoal baking under clouds of steam, women with parasols on the pier at Cheltenham Beach,

Swedes and Germans reclining under elms in beer gardens, a line of telegraph boys racing their bicycles, fleeting down the canyons of the financial district like a slender-legged cavalry. There was a marching band with trumpets glinting in a municipal park, squatters' shacks drowsing woodsmoke from the shoreline, the civic façades of the Art Institute and the University of Chicago, in which Argus recognized the tintyped images of Oxford and Cambridge, the sandstone cloisters from the Reverend Mister's college days.

Owen was pleased that Jethro had gathered so many amusements of the city as if he had anticipated this particular sales pitch—the wooden toboggan slide and ice-skating rink near Forty-second and Drexel, the sight of couples gliding hand in hand, their reflections muted and amorphous on the frozen pond, the cable cars barreling into soundless turns, the Irishmen playing handball in front of South Side saloons, the carriages priding out of the livery stables as if a monarch ruled the city instead of a mayor, the river with its drawbridges up, steamers lugging for the open lake, and then the skyline itself held in reserve, almost an afterthought, the camera scanning the sooty perches of terracotta and glass, panning up from the curbstone, jittered and harried, to see the shirtsleeved office managers smoking cigarettes by open windows twenty stories aloft, then back down to the brass doors swinging wide to feed the noonday streets with lunching secretaries. The seamen cheered, drummed the floorboards, recalled the monuments and warrens of their own beloved cities. Out here it was inconceivable that a million people had built their houses and paved their streets in the middle of nowhere, driven pilings into Indian marshland and settled a port a thousand miles from the sea. Owen tried to gauge how Argus and Malini were receiving the filmstock but their faces were concealed by shadow. Malini held the opera glasses a few inches from her face. Suddenly nostalgic, Owen watched the city of his boyhood unfold, a patchwork of street corners and stoops that recalled days spent with his father's wrecking crew. He wished to see it again for the first time, envied what Argus and Malini might feel as they stepped into the tumult from the rail yards. But would they see the promise and perdition that lurked in every doorway? Or would it be merely a chaotic wall of noise? From this distance he felt a strange kind of tenderness, something familial, for the city. It had taken both his parents, in its way, but now, looking up at the screen, it seemed like his only living relative—an irascible old uncle waiting for him to finally come good.

From what Malini could see, the men of this distant island all wore hats and the women wore gloves and there were people with black skin selling fruit and carrying tall drinks in shaded gardens. Her eyes feinted over the canvas where the light broke in waves. It was a kava dream. If Melanesians traveled the nightlands in their dreams then the clayskins had found a way to coil their own sleeping visions into a lamplit machine. Argus whispered *Chicago* aloud, repeating it after one of the men, as if it meant something to her, then said *America, America,* then *they are asking us to come* and she had to tell him to hush. It was hard enough to see what was what without his hymn voice. Cliffsides with many windows, the sky a divided blue field in their reflections. High-perched caves of smoking men and everyone walking so quickly in their clothes, almost running between the giant shadows. There were lurching animals everywhere, horses or mules she'd seen in sugarcane photographs, pulling wooden boxes with people huddled inside. So many hats. Where were the gardens? What did they eat? The women traveled in pairs, headdressed in bird feathers, not an inch of skin visible to the sun. She liked the flounce of their skirts and the tidy hair twists and the way the men stood by to watch them pass.

Argus stopped counting after twenty-two church sightings, all of them steepled and most with stained-glass windows and bell towers. This was a city of the devout, a godly keep by an inland sea, and they were being asked to come. He thought through his conversation with Owen on the foredeck a few hours prior, the suggestion of a proposal in his manner, and felt the wingback chair now as part of that same conversation. Would there be a letter of employment? Was he to be a butler or a ministry houseboy? How many bishops called this city home? He saw himself walking the bitumen streets in leather shoes, an overcoat slung over one arm, saying good morning to pedestrians and eating a green apple. There was a tailored suit in that shimmering future and pinstripes no wider than a hairbreadth. He would teach Malini how to make her way because he was ahead on this front of acting civilized and she would work as a nanny because that is what they called a governess in America. He watched the frozen pond, couples gliding on steel blades across its surface. The canvas seemed to move toward a girl's bright face and she was waving and smiling at Argus, a scarf wrapped around her throat, her breath like mist off a lake, beckoning to him with one hand and the other poised for balance.

Every seaman saw their own beloved in this waving Chicago girl just as the weather turned and the *Cullion* pitched to leeward. Jethro managed to grab the cinématographe before it fell to the floor. The reel shuddered then stopped. The canvas went black. Without the soft pales of projected light, the messroom was all but dark and the men began scrambling to their feet. The swing tables flapped on their hinges. A seaman from the watch appeared in the companionway and called to the captain that the barometer had been plummeting for an hour. "Squall's come up," he hollered. "Helmsman says he's done his level best not to take any sail off her, just as you ordered, but now this, sir." Given the heel of the ship, the men falling sideways over each other, this was a little late in coming. Terrapin waited for the gust to subside, the messroom to level out, and gave the order for all hands to wear ship. The sailors heaved themselves off the floor and dashed for the companion ladder.

On deck Terrapin saw a dome of weather hanging low and

malignant, winds gusting from the west at fifty knots, seas already breaking over the lower rail. A wall of rain advanced, fissured by lightning. The darkened fetches of water were churning and the air smelled like iron. Terrapin braced himself against the windward shrouds as the crew scuttled onto the mid and foredeck, shouldering uphill on a pitch, already clambering up the ratlines in their oilskins. The ship was overcanvased and he told the helmsman to head down to ease the tension in the sails. A wave broke over the prow and sent three men sliding across the deck on their backs. As the bark groaned to change course he roared at Mr. Pym to have the men haul down the outer jib and bring down the main and mizzen topgallant staysails.

The seamen grappled with the clewlines and buntlines, the canvas bellying along the yards. Owen worked the foremast with the other port watchmen, helping to stow and clew and brail, one arm cleaved against the drenched Baltic fir. The squall came all at once and he felt cold needles of rain against his face. He could see the bowsprit plunging in and out of the swells and a surge of seawater top the windward rail. He looked below and saw Jethro watching the mayhem from a hinged hatch cover like an Elizabethan stage prompt. With the river of deckwash the open hatchway was an invitation for flooding but there was nothing to be done. Owen took in the rest of the deck—Terrapin skirling beside the helmsman and Argus helping to unravel the sheets from the belaying pins near the mizzen. Terrapin was pointing at the foremast and Owen turned his attention upward where the royal sail was flogging in the wind. His watchmates had failed to furl and gasket it properly and now Dickey Fentress was climbing up the ratlines to stow it. He was nimble in the upper sticks, partly because of his weight, but Owen followed him aloft. There was no way the apprentice could secure it on his own. The bark pitched into a bowl of turbid water and Owen could feel his finger joints loosen against the ratline. As the bark yawed he felt his stomach drop away. He could only climb a few feet at a stint before another roll forced him to brace the shrouds. Dickey made better ground, edging closer to the unmuzzled sail with its flailing lines and wrenched canvas.

Terrapin pointed beyond the unruly sail to a quadrant of sky that was turning a poisonous green. The *Cullion,* her record unblemished, was sailing at the leading edge of a hurricane front and from the southwest funneled three storm spouts, glimpsed in sheets of lightning, each one a mile high and attached to a separate cloudcap. They were in the offing but the bark was bending in that direction, caught in the eyewall of the storm. Terrapin sent for Argus and his pigskin Bible because he wanted benedictions right beside the binnacle. The seamen could hear the sucking of seawater in the full dark between verses of lightning. The sound terrified them as the greening cloud continued to spawn overhead. Argus scrambled onto the poop with his Bible and started in with Jonah, preaching, *All the sailors were afraid and each cried out to his own god. And they threw the cargo into the sea to lighten the ship. But Jonah had gone below deck, where he lay down and fell into a deep sleep.* Apparently, this was not the kind of comfort the captain had in mind and he yelled to Argus for a hymn instead, something big on hallelujahs. Argus sang about Christian glee and making the Promised Land and that was better. But then the bark refused to be diverted. They were on a broad reach through a wilderness of vapors and wracked cloud, attempting steerage on a helix tide. Terrapin moved to take the wheel, O-mouthed at the wall of oblivion.

Owen trailed Dickey up the foremast. The apprentice was standing on the footline beneath the royal sail that wailed in a fifty-knot gale. He stepped out onto the yard. He shook his head side to side as if he'd taken a punch. His balance was shot. Since setting sail Owen had been waiting for young Dickey to flash to the surface, to stop slouching with the pranksters of the forecastle and this was finally an article of proof. No one had told him to come aloft and repair the shoddiness of his watchmates but here he was, keeping his head down to avoid the brunt of the royal sail. Neither of them saw the cyclonic front taking its turn. Each man occupied a universe two-foot cubed, a sphere of hemp and handholds. Dickey hauled in one corner of the sail from the head but the tension made his nail beds bleed on contact. He bellied over the yard, face struck with terror as he stared down the hundred-foot sheer drop to the roiling deck. Owen made eye contact with him and yelled for him to wait. It was crazed to attempt to lash the sail on his own. As it was, they might need another three of their watch. Owen made it to the upper yard and edged out along the footline. The weight of his body brought Dickey down from the head of the sail and he saw immediately that the apprentice had soiled himself through. "Pull together!" Owen yelled. Dickey nodded, eyes wide. They each took a fathom of sail and hauled it in. The footline whipsawed and fell back and all the furled sail was let go. Other seamen were climbing aloft; Owen could see them through the wedge of space between his feet.

Then Dickey righted himself, craned up, mouth open. Owen hollered at him to bear down on the sail because he'd seen the swirling clouds in his periphery a moment before, but Dickey blinked and straightened as if all hearing and sense had stripped away. He stared into the underbelly of the clouds. His head tilted back slowly and by degree, as if it were the blue depths of the middle watch and he was drunk on starlight.

Then a trait that was an error of handling—his habit of unlatching a handhold before securing another—expanded in this state of disbelief. He simply drew both hands off the yard and royal and reached for an imaginary line directly in front of his face. For a moment he was stooped, still leaning to counteract the wind, then he was straightening as if getting up from his knees but with his eyes closed against the needling squall. Owen would remember this, an image flashbulbed into the scene, the apprentice's eyes squinting shut against the terror of the fall before he'd even begun his descent. When Dickey fell his hands continued to rake for the imaginary line, the invisible halyard beyond his grasp, and Owen had the curse of seeing his face as the apprentice fell all the way down to the deck. His arms winged up then buckled out on impact. The watchmates huddled over his rigid form. Owen took out his knife and slashed along the clewlines and buntlines, letting the royal loose in the wind. He climbed down the ratlines and heard the engines rumble to life. Terrapin was trying to force his way out of the eyewall.

When Owen got to the deck, Giles Blunt was holding Dickey across his lap and a pool of seawater was mired with blood. The captain was struggling toward the foredeck, still in his Napoleonic cape, his legs bent and his face ashen. He joined the semicircle of men and saw that the body was threatening to wash overboard. Above the welter, he told Giles to take the corpse below and for the others to continue wearing ship. "I'll burn all the coal we have to get us on the outer edge of this maw, mark me, but I need you to get the canvas reefed and snugged. Dickey will get his hour, I promise you that." The wind stalled for a moment, as if in sympathy, and Terrapin said gravely, "What day is it? For the log." The seamen looked at each other, braced to snatch block and mast, and not a single man could recall that it was December 7 in the year 1897.

V

BEYOND THE STRANDLINE

20.

The word *crizzel* passed among the window-washers of the First Equitable. A nineteen-year-old Norwegian named Anders had spent time in a St. Louis glassworks and said it was the proper name for it—an opaque roughness on the surface of the windowpanes. "Clouds its transparency like a filmy eyeball," he said to the others. "Cheap windows with too much sand and not enough flint. They brought the plates in from Mexico or Canada on account of the American glass combines. No doubt about it." He was holding forth at the lunchtime gathering of workmen in the sub-basement room they called the cave. It was a staging area for repair work and for storage, but each noontime it was their clubhouse, the head janitor presiding with a metal rod as his scepter of office. They sat on nail kegs and broken chairs and barrels, eating from their tin pails as each man gave his opinion on the topic at hand—evolution, electricity, magnetism, airships, the merits and burdens of marriage, the tariff on tinplate. Today it was the building's imperfections. Subordinate janitors, window-washers, elevator men, steamfitters, gasfitters, electricians, stokers, carpenters, the sign-painter, thirty men who tended every aspect of Hale Gray's colossus. For many of them, the building was a living thing—the pneumatic arteries that carried paper instead of blood, the electricity that passed blue and silent through the thin walls like nervousness in human skin.

The building was fickle, they all agreed. Now that winter was nearly upon them, the windows frosted and jammed and the elevators ran slow on cold mornings. Design flaws, they said. They knew her like an intimate. The lairs and crannies, the architectural hollows that were a wink from the draftsmen to the workmen, the cavities for smoke breaks and a hand of cards, the hidden nook inside the rooftop clockworks that was just wide enough for a mattress. A fifteen-minute nap, wedged between churning clock gears and the quarter-hour bells, was better than nothing, they all agreed. And since the bells stopped pealing at dusk, a man on the outs with his wife could spend a restful night directly above Hale Gray's office, 350 feet above the dime flophouses of Van Buren.

Thirty-four hundred sheets of plate glass, Anders said, and half of them faulty. The blend of soda, lime, and silica botched and now baked into the terracotta walls. The window-washers were being blamed for the murkiness. The eldest window-washer, a Swede, got up to acquiesce. They risked their lives, he told them, strapped themselves in with a leather surcingle not much more than the girth strap on a horse saddle. It was criminal, he said. The scummed double-sashes were ruining his reputation in the city. The reflection of city and sky was glimpsed in the windows as if on the surface of a millpond instead of an alpine lake.

Hale Gray had assembled a panel of experts to determine whether the building was settling into the blue clay beneath Chicago's streets so soon after its construction. A structural engineer, the architect, a soil expert, a geologist, none of them could agree. He sat at his cherrywood desk each afternoon, in the bleak Canadian light, waiting for a definitive sign. Part of him expected to feel the slippage, as if a few inches—that was the disputed figure—would register as a mild earthquake, a gentle tinkling of glassware. He watched the inkbottle on his desktop, waiting for a miniature black tide to ebb toward him. But none came.

On Fridays he made his habitual descent to the basement strongroom for an inspection of the various deeds, policies, and treasury notes that made up a good part of the company's assets. It wasn't that he didn't trust bank vaults, but rather that he was comforted by the thought of a stanch of his wealth lying in the core of the building, the beating heart of the enterprise like a boiler in the iron hull of a steamship. The strongroom, the latest Chubb, was made with foot-thick walls of steel-reinforced concrete and a wafer of explosives wedged inside in the event of drilling. As an insurance man, Hale kept abreast of the trends in larceny and bank heists, knew that safecrackers boiled dynamite and skimmed off nitroglycerin to pour into the hairline cracks beside safe doors. Chubb, like Otis and his elevators, assured him that all design flaws had been eradicated.

Benny Boy took him down in the express elevator. The sub-basement required an elevator key and Hale watched the operator produce a brass keychain from his breast pocket. He liked Benny for his conversational instincts—he knew when to keep quiet and when to hazard a joke.

"Seems slow today, Benny," Hale said, glancing at his fob watch.

"Some wind in the shaft, sir. Maybe ten seconds off."

"Not so bad. Will you wait for me while I check the week's takings?"

"Happy to, sir, take your time. I'm here till seven."

The elevator rocked to a stop and Benny held the door for Hale. He passed along a narrow corridor of thick brown brick. Down here the building's secret commerce could be seen plainly and Hale always felt he was walking backstage. The walls were girded and massive, the heating pipes clanked, and the tradesmen's shops were littered with repairs. The subterranean world smelled of mechanic's grease and burning coal. The strongroom was next to the little room where the workmen met each lunchtime. Hale knew about these ragtail proceedings, knew they called the strongroom *the chapel* out of deference but also as a dig at the hallowed money of the Grays. It was all right. Let them have their little broomstick parliament. A man was won over by degrees and Hale suspected even his vice presidents sometimes fantasized about throwing him out a top-floor window. He would take respect and fear over chummy regard any day of the week.

He used a small brass key that was attached to a lanyard around his neck and opened the outer door, passing into the next chamber. He applied the combination to the second door—the scrambled birth date of his grandfather—and went into the inner chamber. The smell of paper and gold was as unmistakable as iron railings after a rain. It was the smell of safety, something sacramental: yes, let them call it the chapel. He opened the wooden box of policy duplicates and fingered down the stack alphabetically. The company's chief accountant brought them down each Friday in preparation for Hale's ritual stocktaking. It would have been easier, but not as satisfying, to read a tallied sheet of newly added policies. But one of the lessons learned from Elisha Edmond Gray was to treat the business, no matter its size, like a corner shop or lunchroom. Touch the money and paper receipts yourself, keep your fingers on the till and lockbox. For this reason, every one of his employees, from typing-pool girls to his top salesmen and managers, received a personalized, signed card on the anniversary of their joining the fold. Make the business personal was Elisha's advice. He counted 162 new policies—most of these for life coverage. The economy was on the rebound and men wanted to prepare for the next catastrophe. He clasped the iron box and returned it to the shelf. The fire had taught him the virtues of catastrophe-proof record keeping. The goldenrod triplicate of every policy was sent off site to a brick warehouse.

He stood in the strongroom, a lion's share of his assets on the steel shelves flanking him. Somewhere in a file was the deed to the ancestral estate in the north of England, a piece of property that had been in the Gray bloodline for three centuries, but also his marriage certificate and last will and testament and the carbons of every dismissal letter he'd ever written. He heard the low rumble of the La Salle Street tunnel and he closed his eyes, listening. Chicago may not have had catacombs like Paris but it had cable car tunnels and sewers, a network of basements set in the clay bed below the lake. The city's root cellar was the janitor's store and the furnace room. He listened to the building whirr, clatter, breathe. None of it sounded like three hundred feet of bridge-work steel sinking into an ocean of blue clay. He opened his eyes. He believed in Providence, in timing. This was his time. A stranger could see it in the cuff of his pant leg or feel it in the consular handshake he reserved for acquisitions and mergers. He'd built them a vertical city, a tower of Babel for the Bohemian mail boys and the prairie girls in cotton dresses. Pullman might have built his railway workers a town out on the plain with varnished municipal bandstands but Hale had built a cathedral of glass.

21.

At her father's funeral, Adelaide couldn't help thinking about Indian burial customs, about certain letters Franz Boas and George Dorsey had dictated to her at the museum. There were tribes along the lower Columbia that built hutlike structures for the dead on little river islands. The body was wrapped in a blanket and lowered into a shallow pit, sometimes in a sitting position, then covered with slabs of wood and bark. Sitting would have been a better position than supine for her father; he'd spent his life reading in armchairs or settling accounts and drafting correspondence at his Wooton desk. Part of her wished that Episcopalians favored an open casket. Perhaps the sight of his silver halo of hair, the drawn cheeks pinked with mortician's rouge, perhaps these would have brought her into the room and the moment of his death. He'd died midwinter, in the dormer nook with the window cracked, basset hound at his side, a view of the river slurried with ice.

The cascade of bright flowers in the chapel and the organ grinding below the Twenty-third Psalm, not to mention the eulogies for a man she'd never known, someone glimpsed through a barrage of civic business and committee work, all these felt decorative. Where was death itself? There was Gerald Cummings the occasional philanthropist, the business owner, the churchgoer, but no one spoke of the man who recited sonnets to his dogs, a lineage of hounds all named Peggy, one after the other, and who vowed a day of silence when Lincoln died. Wrap Gerald Cummings in a blanket and lay him in the stony cold ground, she thought. Let someone wail over his body. Adelaide held her mother's black-gloved hand as the pallbearers shouldered the casket out into the wintry day. They followed the coffin and she felt Owen's absence in the sharp, cold air. They buried her father beside his own parents and one brother lost to the Civil War. Adelaide didn't break down until she threw a handful of dirt down into the pit. She saw that the coffin was the exact same hue of briarwood as the pipe her father smoked after dinner each evening.

A week later Adelaide returned to Chicago with her mother. They came by railcar, a library of inherited books—all of them rife with marginalia—trailing in the luggage compartment. Adelaide had been named the sole beneficiary of Gerald's bookish dominion and she was delighted, even if she had nowhere to store the thousand volumes. Her father had given her the courage to annotate a poem or novel directly on the page, to fill the Doric-like columns of white space with penciled musings. Join the conversation had been his entreaty; never worry about how daft and sophomoric those notes will seem ten years hence. But she was sometimes appalled to come upon some nugget of her own supposed insight—*marriage imminent* scrawled in the middle pages of Austen or *inner turmoil* in the conflicted tailings of Eliot or Hardy—and on several occasions she had erased the entries altogether, wearing the paper gutter to a carbon smudge.

Adelaide was surprised to find that her mother, Margaret Cummings, was a strangely stoic widow. If anything, she seemed angry, put out. Margaret watched the fields and streams flit outside the carriage window, saying, "It seems quite absurd that your father is lying in the ground in his best suit . . ." She said it with a tone of disappointment, as if Gerald had done something inconsiderate. By the time they reached Chicago, she had found distraction in devising plans for the wedding. She said she planned to spend a month in the city and Adelaide saw a vision of her bustling between dressmaker and stationer, killing off the hours and weeks, pouring her stunted grief into lace and cardstock selections.

They sent the crated books to a railway warehouse for storage and took a hansom cab to the ladies' entrance of the Palmer House. Margaret, who had traveled to Europe and Montreal, seemed to find the hotel lacking. The barbershop floor was tessellated with silver dollars, the dining halls were gilt-mirrored and marbled, but everywhere came the foot pounding of telegram boys and beery guffaws from the men's smoking lounge. Almost thirty years after the Great Fire—which had destroyed the original hotel just thirteen days after its opening—there were still signs claiming the Palmer was the world's only fireproof hotel. "Like they discovered iron and brick," Margaret said dismissively.

The bellhop showed them the third-floor room and drew the curtains. The uniformed boy waited next to the door, eyes up, waiting out his tip. Margaret handed him a coin and lay back on the bed, exhausted. She closed her eyes then opened them. "The room's stifling."

Adelaide stood by the window and opened it slightly. "You have a view of State Street."

"So much noise," Margaret said, her voice almost a whisper. "You should be getting married in Boston . . ."

Adelaide turned but said nothing.

"Your father, on his deathbed, had an idea."

"He was full of ideas. Which one was this?"

"That you should buy a house in your name before the wedding. It would be yours to bring into the marriage."

She was offended by this notion but forced her voice to remain even. "We'll be buying a house together."

Margaret took out a handkerchief and dabbed her eyes, but Adelaide mistrusted this sudden display of tearfulness.

"It was your father's wish. After all, we've never met this young man."

"You'll meet him soon enough." Adelaide looked out the

window. State Street was its usual chaos of wagons and imperiled pedestrians. "I'll leave you to rest, Mother. I have to be at the museum tomorrow."

Her mother sat up. "But I thought we would begin the preparations. I made some lists on the train." She began ferreting through her purse.

Coming toward the bed, Adelaide said, "I can meet you at lunchtime tomorrow and then we have all day Saturday. The museum is busy at the moment."

Margaret looked into her compact mirror and gave a considerable sigh. "Tomorrow at noon, then? I'll wait in the lobby." She looked around the room. "I expect I'll take my dinner here tonight." She raised a hand. "Do you feel that? No fresh air at all. On the way out, ask the porter to send up dyspepsia tablets, if you don't mind. All that buffet car food . . ."

Adelaide leaned at the bedside to kiss her mother on the forehead. Without looking back, she said good night and went out into the carpeted hallway. She took the stairs for the sound of her own footsteps and to avoid a polite exchange with the elevator operator. She found a porter and delivered her mother's request for dyspepsia tablets and was then out the door. Any daughter of merit would have stayed for dinner but she felt the weight of the funeral and the train trip and the endless days of conviviality. There was an hour of reading in a hot bath in her future. She had kept aside a dozen of her father's books for immediate consumption, had carried them apart in a brown paper sack, and more than the verse and prose itself, she wanted to feel Gerald Cummings's mind written into the page margins.

At noon they soldiered through the department stores, Margaret taking notes on fabrics and ribbons and lace. She stopped in the cutlery department of Marshall Field's for no other reason than to admire the sharpened, gleaming knives. Kitchenware was something that held her imagination. She questioned haberdashers and seamstresses and wholesale buyers, cross-checking and verifying prices. Pursuit of a deal demanded that they obtain prices and quotes by the yard from three stores.

Margaret seemed to find the stores pleasant enough—Tiffany-domed, windows as big as swimming pools—but she winced when they got out to the curbstone. There were snowbanks turning to ponds of browning slush, crippled girls cupping for nickels, street preachers bawling with apocalypse. She pulled Adelaide into each store, barreling through the heavy storm doors to get away from so much motley need.

Adelaide trudged behind her, trying to spot the store detectives in the press of shoppers. There had been a rash of shoplifting, and if she believed the papers, the mink-stoled woman trying on the diamond ring at the jewelry counter was about to turn and make a dash for the exits. Adelaide had been at the museum all morning, typing letters and cataloguing while the curators uncrated a new collection. Apparently, in the three weeks she'd been gone, no one had typed or filed a letter. It was a miracle the museum men knew how to make a cup of coffee without her. She was prepared to let her mother battle against the dressmakers of the world so long as it all passed without incident. When Margaret was bent on a task there was no use getting in her way. And she was clearly avoiding her own grief with her infantry tactics. As the housewives marauded around them, as the world blurred with ruffles and corsets, all Adelaide could think about was Owen's return in the coming months. She gave her mother a thin smile at the proffered bolt of white satin, white—the color of surrender—but she was thinking about their last night together in the junkhouse emporium, about the oily dark smell of grease and metal as Owen kissed her neck and shoulders before snuffing the light.

They moved down State Street with tied packages. It was snowing, a light glitter off the lake. On La Salle Street they hit a wall of wheat brokers and secretaries coming off their lunch hour, bundled and cinched with wool scarves, bounding along in the brittle air. *Like an army of madmen,* Margaret was saying, *and all I want is to find the stationer the head porter recommended, did you know, Adelaide, that head porter is quite a lucrative position in the better hotels and the man at the Palmer told me something curious, George or Bernie if I recall, that all the hotels have housecats and the bigger ones have a cat on every floor. Brings them luck, he told me.* They walked under an awning and Adelaide realized they'd come upon the First Equitable. She'd taken to crossing the street to get away from its self-involved splendor, but here it was, reared up before her. Through the big frosted windows she could see a cigar stand with a carved Indian standing sentry and salesmen having their shoes blacked in the aura of blown lights and brass. The clerks and typists were filing in through the double doors, in from the cold, their faces falling a little. She'd half believed that they weren't allowed to leave the building during daylight, that management patrolled the cafeteria for jailbreaks. At the far end of the building's endless frontage hung a large sign that killed her stride. Two native men stood on a beach with spears and very little clothing, facing each other as if in battle. Below the image:

Rooftop Springtime Spectacle Opening Soon!
Highest Building in the World!
Soon to Arrive, Savages of the South Seas!
Come Enjoy Refreshments and Observe Island Customs
in Genuine Re-created Village
And Don't Forget to Consult Your Friendly Life
Insurance Broker!

Margaret yammered something about the wind at such a height and perhaps they should abandon the quest for the stationer because there was always tomorrow. Adelaide felt her shoulders harden in the cold. She'd suspected this might be afoot and had offered Owen a chance to confess on their last night together. Now here was the proof. That Owen hadn't told her about bringing back natives was a betrayal, a deceit. He'd lied to her face, knowing that she would be dead against such a thing. She'd even mentioned something about Boas, her former boss, persuading Robert Peary to bring back Inuits from Greenland. The six Esquimaux were studied in the basement of the American Museum of Natural History in New York, but all had fallen sick and ended up at Bellevue Hospital. In a letter from Boas's new secretary—a woman with whom Adelaide had struck up a correspondence—she'd learned that the wife of the museum president planned to adopt the recovered seven-year-old Inuit boy as an experiment in educating the uncivilized. The rest were expected to die before the year was out. Hadn't she told Owen all of this?

She saw her face next to her mother's in the window's reflection. In the hard set of her jaw, in the imperious regard she now weighed at the sign, it was Margaret's long-suffering countenance settling over her. It was not the first time she had been angry with Owen but it was the first time she'd felt hollowed out by his deceit, furious over his absence and the way she would have to nurse this hurt until he returned. He was implicated in this, regardless of who was funding the voyage. She turned from the giant window, shopping bags swinging wildly, and hailed a hansom in the slushy street. "I'll pay if I have to, Mother, but I am not walking another block!" she yelled above the bustle.

22.

For days the *Cullion* malingered without a glimpse of sun or moon or stars. The wind had died off but the sky remained a blighted gray. Without view of the celestial bodies, Terrapin couldn't take his sightings and angles and was therefore ignorant of the bark's exact latitude. They were adrift. At dusk and at dawn he paced the poop with the sextant still in its case, waiting for a break in the ulcerous sky that would allow a shot at the sun burning above the horizon. The twin chronometers were running perfectly in the hold—one with Greenwich and one with local time—but without angles their location was a hundred-mile wedge of ocean on the map. Terrapin fell back on dead reckoning, studied the current, leeway, wave action, and the helmsman's yawing to get some sense of their position. He consulted almanacs and admiralty charts, cross-referenced his own deck logs from previous voyages. None of it gave more than a pale illumination of where they were.

On the second day adrift Terrapin ordered a sea burial for Dickey Fentress. Regardless of the ship's ghostly latitude, proper custom had to be observed, the apprentice committed to the deep for fear he might haunt the ship and worsen her luck. Sailmaker Fennimore Jauss and carpenter Giles Blunt had taken the body below for due preparation. Jethro offered up the orlop for the funerary preparations and they found themselves scrubbing the jeweled blood from the boy's crown with muslin rags used for wrapping dead birds. Dickey's face was waxen and pale, his lips parted as if in speech. Jethro stood by with embalming fluids and tins of excelsior cotton, but the sailmaker insisted that he was following, under captain's orders, the procedures outlined in the Anglican Book of Common Prayer circa 1662. They lifted the body onto a shroud of retired sail and Jauss placed two lead weights by the feet. He sewed the shroud, starting at the feet, then up the middle above the sternum. As per custom, he hooked the final stitch through Dickey's nose because this assured the seaman was really dead. Giles Blunt wept openly at the sight of this maneuver. When he regained himself he went above to signal the body was ready.

Eight seamen carried the canvased body on a mess table. It was draped with the red ensign but also decked in flowers from Terrapin's stateroom: hibiscus and frangipani and something resembling a native rose. In matters of funerary rites, as in all observances of religion, philosophy, and inebriates, Terrapin took a blended approach—leaned on the Anglicans for wherewithal and procedurals, stole from the Hindus for their flowers and oil lamps, borrowed a few ceremonials from the U.S. Navy. This was only the tenth man he'd buried at sea in three decades—a low trade average he was proud of—and he liked to think each seaman had been dispatched with tenderness and form. The bark was hove to, the topgallant yards were a-cockbill, topped up in mourning. The bosun and the mates stood at the head of the lined-out men, dressed in their church clothes, the entry port open on the starboard gangway. As the body came out of the hold, the officers held burning cressets at the incline of parade swords. The seamen clutched rifles brought up from the armory.

Argus and Malini watched from the quarterdeck, apart from the official assembly. The body came forward. *I am the resurrection and the life, saith the Lord: he that believeth in me, though he were dead, yet shall he live,* Terrapin said. Argus recognized the prayer as St. John's and mouthed the words *and whosoever liveth and believeth in me shall never die.* Malini held the captain's dog in her arms but was stone-faced, wondered why guns were part of a ceremony to bury the dead. Poumetans and the Kuk would never bring a spear to a funeral. Terrapin said, *He brought nothing into this world, and it is certain we can carry nothing out.* The bosun ordered *ship's company, off hats* and the seamen doffed their serge caps and broadbrims.

The captain read psalms in his best oratory but Argus couldn't help cringing at Terrapin's dry inflection, the way he chewed over *quickening spirit* and *sown in weakness* and *raised in glory* like so many stale crackers. At the conclusion of the psalms, as the pallbearers prepared to upend the mess table and slide the canvased body overboard, Argus began to sing a Presbyterian hymn. They all turned to hear his voice climbing the notes of "Take My Life and Let It Be." Far from being affronted, the captain raised a palm to cease the pitching of the corpse.

> Take my life and let it be
> Consecrated, Lord, to Thee
> Take my moments and my days;
> Let them flow in ceaseless praise,
> Let them flow in ceaseless praise.
>
> Take my hands, and let them move
> At the impulse of Thy love . . .

Standing beside the tearful carpenter, Owen reflected on the boy's life cut short. He remembered Dickey's face as he plunged to the deck, a look of apology in the startled eyes. In falling, Dickey had wanted to say he was sorry for not being more adept in the upper rigging. He was more afraid of the men's faltering opinion of him, of being called a lubber, than of the afterlife rushing from below. An orphan on a ship full of men and none of them had been the least bit fathering. Owen had extended a timid hand to the boy, offered him a smattering of advice, but had waited for a sign of true worthiness. He withheld his affections out of some wager with his own past, revisiting his thirteen-year-old self on the grimy stoops of Chicago tenements and feeling, anew, that he'd been abandoned by God and life. Did he expect Dickey to climb out of that same pit without help? He imagined Dickey's self-pity and kept him at arm's length. To make amends, Owen came forward to offer a eulogy. The seamen nodded, glad that he would say some words on their behalf.

"We all failed him in a way," Owen said, surprised by the tone in his voice. "We all assumed that he was already fully raised, capable of shouldering against the driving day on his own. What was he? Fifteen? None of us extended an example. Least of all me. He was ripe for guiding. Wanted it, in fact. Anyway, he should never have been up there with his hearing shot. We should have looked out for him."

The seamen looked down at the deck timbers.

Owen continued: "I'm sure in his own time, Dickey Fentress would have become a first-rate sailor. Someday a captain, perhaps, if he applied himself. But he's gone now and we commit him to these waters with our gratitude and blessings. Rest easy, Dickey. And forgive us."

The seamen looked over at Owen, uncomfortable with the sudden air of culpability. One of them stepped forward and added, "Goodbye, Dick. We'll miss you, little mate!"

Argus finished the hymn's last verse with a flourish, arms held to the heavens and rigging above, his voice at the edge of wavering. The men waited a beat and the captain gave the signal for the body to be committed to the sea. *We therefore commit his body to the deep, to be turned into corruption, looking for the resurrection of the body*. They retained the ensign but the canvas sack slid into the waves. The body turned, sank, and was gone. The sky was still cancerous and brooding. From the foredeck the ship's bronze bell sounded and the seamen fired their rifles three times into the air. Teddy Meyers played his rusty old bugle and the men were dismissed, half of them reporting for the afternoon watch and the other half going to the forecastle to get soused.

All that night the weather stayed ominous. Owen leaned against the mainmast halyard during the middle watch and saw the sky fissure with lightning. The seas stayed calm but the monsoon was clearly in the offing, the hemisphere's turn for the wet. He could see Jethro holding on to the rail of the foredeck and wanted to stay clear of him. Dickey's fall, he knew, had been partly caused by his dulled hearing, which in turn had been caused by the close discharge of Jethro's collecting rifle on the island. A sailor's sense of hearing was everything, part of his instrument for fathoming windshift, for deciphering the barked orders from the first or second mate. It gave him balance in the rigged treetops. Owen pictured Dickey aloft during the storm. The kid had heeled to one side, faltered on the ratlines, ignored Owen's calls from below. Perhaps that look of dismay just before Dickey fell to his death wasn't an apology after all but him feeling the ship's auditory pulse slip away. Perhaps for Dickey Fentress the world went silent before it went black.

Sometime in the small hours of the night the main and mizzen-masts gave off an electrical discharge and the captain was called above. He insisted on being roused for any display of unusual weather or nature and St. Elmo's fire was no exception. The atmosphere was thick with electricity. The trucks and spar-ends of Baltic fir were alive with corposant flares and this was further proof, Terrapin told the men, that they were under the auspices of a metaphysical Dog Star. Whether it was the apprentice's stymied soul or the humors of a poisoned latitude didn't much matter. The result was the same. He took a tin cup of rum on the poop and did not sleep the rest of the night. "I feel another blue funk coming on," he told the helmsman. "Taste it like an iron hobnail on my tongue . . ."

Meanwhile, in the doorway of the forecastle, Argus recounted the trials of St. Erasmus, now called St. Elmo, to the men of the watch. They regarded the flickering spars with unease. It was fortunate there were no winds to be caught, because none of them would go into the rigging with the masts seemingly ablaze. Argus spoke of Erasmus, the patron saint of sailors, who was persecuted by Roman emperors, spat upon and besprinkled with foulness, thrown into a pit of snakes, boiled with oil and sulfur. "Erasmus went on thanking and loving God, this man of big forbearance, and then the angels sent lightning and his torturers were electrocuted. Then came another emperor who put him into a pan seething with rosin, pitch, and brimstone lead but he did not shrink from his punishment and continued to say the Gospel in a high preaching voice."

Harvey McCallister hollowed his cheeks and made a sucking sound through his teeth. "Tough son of a bitch, that Erasmus."

The others agreed.

Argus did not encourage the blasphemy with a glance. He continued, "His teeth were plucked out of his head with iron pincers and they carded his skin with metal rods and roasted him upon a gridiron."

"Sounds a little like sailing round the Horn," a veteran offered.

"But the angels saved him in the end," Argus said. "Some scripture books say he went to Mount Lebanon and survived on what the ravens brought him to eat but Reverend Mister used to end the story with the holy man having his intestines stripped out and wrapped around a windlass. Reverend Mister Underwood didn't like happy endings."

"And he protects all men at sea?" asked one of them, suddenly earnest and rum-flushed.

"Yes," said Argus. "He also looks out for colicky babies and women in labor and old men with rotgut, which is why the Reverend Mister knew all his woes. Stomach of sulfur and pitch is what he used to say when he had the Johnny-trots. One time I heard him praying to St. Elmo when he was resting a long time in the outhouse."

This got a big laugh and the men craned up at the flaring masts with more wonder now than fear.

In the days that followed, the cloud dome broke apart and the wind freshened. Terrapin confirmed by sextant what they had all suspected—that they were back in the Doldrums and had drifted badly off course. The island of Tikalia, a cashew-shaped spit of land on the charts, was two hundred miles to the southeast. With Terrapin's bonus hitched to the final leg of trade, the captain agreed to head south for the island. Besides, Owen suspected the captain didn't want to part with Malini anytime soon. They ate dinner together at night in the stateroom and she had begun to laugh at his ribald jokes. The *Cullion* came about and headed south and Terrapin told Owen that he would anchor no more than three days at Tikalia.

"And then we'll engine back directly?" asked Owen. The need to head south again reminded him that he was failing Adelaide in her hour of need.

"Last time I checked, the hatch was full of coal and the engines were greased-up nice. We can trot through the unwinded Doldrums and Horse Latitudes like a bitch in heat if you give the word. Mind you, we're in full hurricane season now so we take our chances. Only madmen and pirates are out here this time of year. Coal by the yard is the contractual arrangement for reimbursement, I believe."

Owen turned to descend from the poop.

"And Mr. Graves, there will be no more savages coming aboard. Two is plenty with all the menace they might bring upon us. Heaven forbid if one of them gets sick. I know these people and I know my maritime jurisdiction. I should have been informed from the outset what was intended."

"My apologies."

"Well, the skyscraper magnate will have to be satisfied with the brother and kanaka princess. Understood?"

"Of course."

Owen left the captain and went to take inventory of the remaining trade items. He'd already justified that two natives was a lesser crime than a whole family, but wondered if he might have erred without the captain's edict. Would he have been tempted to find others on Tikalia? He stood at the rail for a moment, watching the bark ply through the swells, the men singing overhead. He remembered his father, swallowed by debt, a man so burdened by the past that he could speak only of the present, of meals and weather. The kissed fingers that touched the daguerreotyped wife on the way out the door each day—this was the only gesture toward the wreckage that lay behind them. They lived in a bare room on the South Side, their clothes in packing crates. They lived, it seemed to him now, as if they had just emerged from a burning teardown and were expecting the same calamity to befall them at any moment. He knew where his material hunger came from. And not just for objects or money, but for respect, acknowledgment, a foothold. He was a gambler making a calculated bet—that the potential yield on Tikalia was worth the risks, that the delay would mean nothing to Adelaide in the long run, that two natives could be brought to America and safely returned. He would fill his children's mouths with food from his own endeavors, at the very least. He understood that the bet had been placed some time ago; he was merely waiting for the cards to be turned over. He pushed off the rail and headed toward the foredeck.

He found Argus and took him on a tour of the bark, scouring for trade items, for objects that would strike the tribal fancy. Argus had showed him how to see the second life within an object, how a candle or mirror held more value if it could be traded as sorcery as well as for illumination and reflection. They walked all over the ship, from the underworld of dank compartments to the painted deckhouses. They stood in the orlop, Jethro somewhere above, and stared at the Bausch & Lomb microscope with something that could only be described as object-lust.

"He would never let us have it," Owen said. "Even if we paid what it was worth."

"No matter. If the Tikalia thought their seawater was swimming with invisible animals all the time they might give up fishing and live in the jungle forever."

For now, they left the brass instrument and continued to forage for trade currency throughout the bark, begging and buying trinkets from the seamen and the idlers.

They tacked for three days across a southeasterly headwind, the air swinging north in short, turbulent bursts. Fifty miles from Tikalia, the skies turned crystalline and china blue, a rarity for this zone of sail and time of year. With the winds bearing fifteen knots and the *Cullion* on a close reach, one of the men in the high rigging sighted another ship. Terrapin took up his spyglass and winced. It was an iron-hulled clipper uncanvased down to the lower topgallants, dragging fathoms of seaweed from her stern, the mainsails torn and billowed to rags. She lacked steerageway, idled to leeward. A drowsy strip of white smoke came from the foredeck. Terrapin told Mr. Pym to bring her abeam and the *Cullion* headed down. The seamen crowded at the bulwarks, already speculating about the ship's predicament: that she'd been pillaged by murderous Algerines, or quarantined on account of some tropical malaise—never mind the lack of white flags—or the cannibals of Tikalia had stocked their bamboo larders and sent the empty brig out into the voided ocean.

Owen and Argus waited at the rail with the rest of them as the broadside of the *Stately Hope* edged closer. They secured lines and boathooks to steady her prow, turning her into the wind, back-winding what was left of the ragged jibsails. Terrapin came down onto the quarterdeck. He said the sight of the unmanned ship made him nervous and he suspected the mariners lay in the hold with their throats slit or their tongues bloated white with pox. The clipper eased up into the wind, the *Cullion*'s hull flush and groaning beside it. The white smoke continued to draw up from the forehatch.

Terrapin knotted a kerchief around his mouth and nose and prepared to board. He asked the second mate to join him and they began to climb onto the bulwarks. There were captains who sent their seamen on errands such as this, but Terrapin prided himself on having come to the stateroom with calluses on his hands. Owen volunteered to join them. One leg over the side, Terrapin stopped short. They all felt the heat rising from the *Stately Hope*'s hull. The captain crouched down and placed a palm close to the ironclad siding. Straightening and casting his eyes amidships, he said, "She's on slow fire from the coal inside her guts. The whale-boats and dinghies are gone."

The seamen held out their hands to the iron hull as if warming themselves by a hearth.

Terrapin said, "Flares deep down in the cargo bay is my estimation. Probably carrying her cargo from Sydney to South America when it caught. Coal will rumble along for months sometimes. Captain and crew must have abandoned ship too soon and let her drift. They panicked because they left most of her sails up. Poor bastards might have rowed to Antarctica by now. She's so fuckin hot I bet she glows at night. You could cook omelets on that skillet of a hull. They couldn't take it no more."

"What should we do, sir?" asked Mr. Pym.

"Let her drift. She'll end up beached or reefed somewhere or maybe the coal will burn a hole straight through her crotch. Release at your leisure, Mr. Pym."

"Shouldn't we make sure that no one is left on board?" asked Jethro, emerging from the group of men with sudden indignation.

"Be my guest," said Terrapin. "I have all the information I need to know that not a living soul is on that smoldering scow. Mind you don't burn your slippers when you clamber aboard, lovelace."

The men scoffed at the suggestion of boarding the smoking brig.

Owen said, "He's right. We should make sure no one is left aboard." It was the right thing to do, the moral thing, but he was also aware of a thought running parallel—that the ship was filled with left-behind trinkets if all the men had abandoned ship. Couldn't an action be both moral and expedient? "I'll go along with him."

"And me as well," said Argus.

Owen added, "There might be provisions we could use."

Terrapin formed a big, sarcastic grin before turning for the charthouse. "Let me know if you find any victims or rheumy wayfellows, gentlemen. I reckon they might have a spot of fever by this point."

Owen steadied a plank between the two decks and asked one of the men to hold it. He balanced his way forward, followed by Argus and finally Jethro, arms out like a tightrope walker. The smell of charcoal was overpowering and they felt the heat through their boots. It had once been an elegant ship—carved bulwarks and flemishes on the coiled lines, oiled timberheads, the deckhouses painted and trimmed in oyster-white. All of it now in varying degrees of spoil. They walked toward the smoking forehatch and Owen told them not to touch it. "If you let the outside air in there the whole thing will blow. There might be fifty thousand pounds of coal down there." They entered the forecastle and saw the abandoned iron bunks and the sailors' lockboxes unhinged. Whatever could be grabbed had been taken en route to the whaleboats, but countless personal items remained—nickel shaving dishes, decks of cards, birthday telegrams, coins, framed photographs of wives and children, pocketknives, compasses, journals, monogrammed handkerchiefs, ditty bags with needle and thread. Owen told Argus to load it all into a pillowcase.

Jethro turned and looked at him. "Stealing from the dead?"

"They might not be dead," said Owen. "But they won't be coming back for any of this."

"All the same," Jethro said, blinking.

"Are you going to lecture me on proper conduct? After all I've seen you do on this trip?"

Jethro stooped through the forecastle doorway in reply.

They continued to the main hatchway and climbed down into the tween decks and the hold. The farther they penetrated the hotter it became. They wended through the companionways, the berths and cabins like smoldering wooden grottoes. They found the armory, its metal doors flung wide and empty down to the last cartridge. In the galley a pot of ancient coffee sat blackened and smoking on the swing table, the air so stifling that the paint was beginning to flake off the walls. They retreated deckside to approach the captain's stateroom from above, glimpsing the room first through its brass-framed skylight as if looking down into a murky, frozen pond. They went below and came through the companionway. Inside, it was the kind of master's cabin Owen had imagined all those years ago, standing mesmerized in the stacks of the public library—a pilastered bed, scrollwork on the maple walls, maps of antiquity hanging above the massive, iron-legged desk. In the extreme aft, a pair of French doors opened onto a balcony that cantilevered above the gudgeon and stern-piece. Through the doorway, Owen could see the clipper's errant wake written across the sea, a veering, undulant line.

Inside, the captain's orderly possessions were relatively unscathed by the heat—being as far from the forehatch as the ship's length would allow—except for an uncorked bottle of blue ink giving off a cloud of vapors. Owen opened a mahogany armoire, a nag's head carved into its crown, and saw two sets of clothing—the captain's jackets and trousers, but also a number of frocks and blouses. Either the captain had a secret or his wife had been aboard. It was a hen frigate. Owen looked around the cabin for feminine adornments and saw empty vases and china figurines, could feel the marriage battle that had played out in the weave of the rug and the tasseled bedspread. It was clear that no one had won the battle decisively because the décor remained democratic, hedging between masculine browns and lacy, effeminate fringes. The thought of a woman fleeing the burning ship changed the clipper's predicament in his mind. It struck him now as sadder somehow, more poignant. There was a Japanese parasol hanging forlornly from the hat stand, its rice paper edges curling from the heat. To lift his mood, he imagined Adelaide rocking gently in her sleep under a stateroom skylight, saw her waking beside him to watch the stars dot westward. He wondered if she would ever come aboard a ship. He told Argus to load whatever he could manage from the stateroom and they came back out onto the deck, their arms laden with clothes and their pockets full of foreign coins and porcelain dogs. Jethro was made to carry his share and he almost toppled into the swells as he wobbled back across the plank-bridge between the ships. He managed to drop several items, so that when Owen crossed he looked down to see a flotsam of ladies' undergarments and loose-leaf papers floating among the dredge of seaweed.

23.

Where does night come from? Why do marsupials sleep in caves? Why do women no longer have beards? These were among the riddles of Poumetan mythology, the stories woven into Argus's childhood memory. Every myth began with *long, long ago* and ended with *this is how it came to be.* The stories about their distant cousins, the Tikalia, were no different. Long, long ago, there were two brothers and their two wives. All were banished and went to sea. They paddled a single-hulled canoe for many weeks but no other island would take them in. They paddled a month more and finally reached an island so remote it was uninhabited and bore no name. They called it Tikalia, the Poumetan word for *far away,* and built bamboo huts on the white beach. There were limestone mountains that rimmed a deep lake and freshwater eels with eyes that glowed at night. Food was so abundant, and the needs of the four so basic, that mangos and coconuts rotted where they fell. Bonito fish schooled into the shallows along the coastline and allowed themselves to be caught with bare hands. Wild pigs slept on the beach at night and were easily killed. Because the outcasts didn't need to work for their food, they began making bark paintings and music, necklaces and babies. Soon there was an entire village of people who had rarely hunted but knew how to make tortoiseshell armlets and bamboo panpipes.

Word of Tikalia's plenty traveled back to Poumeta and, after a hundred years, it was decided that some of the warriors and fishermen should see the island for themselves. A voyage was mounted and it lasted a season. When the party finally returned they carried hundreds of ornate armlets and necklaces, pearl-shell bracelets and amulets. They told stories of sheer white cliffs that dropped into a lake a thousand feet deep, of open fields of bread-fruit and canarium almond forests, of clans living in cave houses with floors of tawny hibiscus. The island was very beautiful but for six moons of the year it was ravaged by terrible hurricanes. The Tikalia, who now spoke their own language and barely understood Poumetan, took shelter in their caves and didn't seem to mind the storms a bit. There were no yam gardens to rebuild and they sat by their hearth fires, making handicrafts and telling stories, while outside the world broke apart. Only twenty of the thirty Poumetans returned from Tikalia and the villagers didn't know whether the missing warriors were dead or now dwelling in caves with their distant cousins. The mystery remained but every two years a voyage to Tikalia was made anew. The Poumetans loaded their canoes with items of trade up from the other islands and set out. The circumcised boys went along with their fathers, and each time some of them did not return and were never spoken of again. In this way there was always an excess of Poumetan brides, enough to trade with the tree-dwelling Kuk. *This is how it came to be*.

Argus mulled over these myths in his mind from behind the bulkhead, the *Cullion* plowing through the brilliant field of waves. Tikalia specked the horizon between swells, a chalky ridge blinking through the morning haze of salt. There were the legends of the past, spread like vellum pages of scripture, and then there was the living dream of the past, the moments he carried, as real as the silver napkin ring in his portmanteau — the smell of his father searing white wood for a canoe, or the taste of guava and wild meat during a feast. He had failed his father long before being invited to make the voyage to Tikalia and it felt strange now to be approaching the island in a pair of trousers and leather boots. He wondered if he might encounter all the boys who did not return from the voyages of his youth. Far from being dead, they might greet him on the beachhead with music and garlands of mimosa and he could teach them, as a sideline to trade, the catechisms of truth and veneration. Like the earliest missionaries in medieval Scotland, St. Ninian or St. Columba, or the New World brethren with Mohawk Bibles wrapped in their saddlebags, cantering across the ungodly American plains, he might be the first to bring them the good news of the Son and the Ghost. From the prow he also thought of David Copperfield going to London and wondered what they would find in Chicago. Instead of ending up in a blacking factory like David, he might work in a bishopric with a rose garden and his sister might nanny in a mansion of singing children. The future *was* different from the past. The reverend had written that it was all the same to the islanders, that clansmen swam in a broth of eternal present, but Argus knew the future by the way it made him feel. The past was sealed in envelopes, pockets, memories. It had been picked over, the Almighty's plan already revealed and known. The future, though, was still being made and furrowed into the minds of heathens and catechists alike, and Argus could sometimes feel the plowshare as God pulled him along, the revelation of who he might become. A different life was being sown for him.

He wasn't sure his sister saw it this way or that she understood the point of the moving pictures in the messroom. They had been invited to America, to the city of Chicago, which was a thousand miles from the sea. He sounded these words in his mind. They had the same revelatory bent as *Whether I shall turn out to be the hero of my own life, or whether that station will be held by anybody else, these pages must show.* If the white men in Chicago couldn't pronounce his surname of Niu then he might call himself Argus Copperfield. Or maybe Argus Blunderstone or Argus Trotwood, names that carried within their open, flowing sounds some hint of rookeries and hamlets and forests of English camphorwood. They had been invited to America and before they could answer formally the storm had driven them east. Argus had seen Owen tracing their course on a map in his cabin. They were now closer to Fiji than they were to New Guinea. It was written into the charts—the answer was *yes*.

He turned from the approaching island and went to find his sister. As usual, she was tending the menagerie of stowaway animals on the quarterdeck—feeding a handful of oats to the wallaby, dried apples to the tortoise, a paste of dried fish to the Siamese cat. The mongoose had taken to climbing the rigging with the men, catching dragonflies and moths in its snapping jaws, but was also taken by the sailmaker into the belly of the ship to catch mice and rats. As a consequence, the mongoose, now named India, was never hungry and skulked a wide circle around the other feeding animals. Terrapin and Nipper watched the feeding from the elevated poop, the dog's bark growing perfunctory.

"We are almost there," said Argus. "Our father made the voyage here many times in his life. Now we can see where he went and what he saw."

"It is taboo for Poumetan women to set foot on that island. I am not leaving the ship," she said. She let the wallaby nuzzle into her skirts.

"Do you know where we are going next?"

She straightened and beckoned to the cat. "And I will not live inside a museum with dead men's skulls and poisoned arrows. I want a house to work in if we go anywhere."

Argus watched the Siamese purr around her bare feet. It was even more occult looking than most cats—eyes that suggested supernatural malice as well as cool indifference. "Who told you we would be living inside a museum?"

She glanced up at the poop deck, where the captain squinted, slack-mouthed, into the bright morning. There was no word for *captain* in Poumetan except *headman* or *chief,* so she called him *chief of the big canoe.* "He says that they will keep us behind glass windows so that clayskins can put us in their books. He says that he can get me a cooking job on another island."

"He wants to keep you, Sister, behind his own window. He has halfblood children all over the ocean. Owen Graves told me this. Their days of birth are written on his arms."

"You don't know him. You are not allowed in his cabin without an invitation. He has never touched me."

Argus closed his legs so that the cat couldn't circle through them. He said, "Did you see where they want to take us in the pictures?"

"I saw too many lights and fat women with ostrich feathers on their heads. I am not for that place. You can go because you are already half made of clay and Bible song. You want to be in their books."

"Only for a short time and then they will bring us back. You will work in a mansion, which is a house of many rooms."

She said nothing further but they watched the mongoose emerge from a shadowy nook with a mouse in its teeth. It was apparently too full to eat; it left the tiny corpse for the cat to investigate. The cat did little but paw at it and, after a few minutes, Malini threw the dead mouse over the railing and into the ship's wake. For the second time since the sea burial she thought of Dickey Fentress in his body sack, twirling and spinning his way to the bottom of the ocean, where he would rot or be eaten by whatever dwelt there. What a grotesque ritual, she thought. He wasn't even important enough to burn, not even a finger bone was nailed to the ship's tall trees up among the fluttering canvas. He had been forgotten altogether. The sea was deep and filled with bags of sailors' bones and there were sharks and whales with strands of human hair coiled inside their stomachs. This was something she would never understand.

The *Cullion* skirted the island, looking for anchorage. Terrapin leaned at the helm with Owen at his side. There was a wide fringing reef, a series of brown coral ramparts that extended for a quarter-mile. On the leeward side, the sheer cliffs plunged into a volcanic bowl, the lake suspended cuplike over the white beach. Above the massif a rim of stunted trees bent seaward before the slopes gave way to jungle rioting—stands of Tahitian chestnut, tree ferns, casuarinas, coral trees kindled with scarlet flowers.

"Not more than fifteen square miles is my guess but she's a fuckin fortress," said Terrapin. "Skirt of gnarling coral and not a channel or place to find bottom." They held a starboard tack, rounding the northern tip. Without the caldera's wind shadow the bark sallied into a gust and was pushed leeward, closer to the fissured heads of coral. Then, beyond the point, they saw a boneyard of shipwrecks hulked on the windward reef—a nautical museum of broken brigs, sloops, and barks. "Come about!" he yelled to the first mate and within seconds the *Cullion* tacked through the eye of the nor'easter and away from the wreckage. When they had passed about eight boat lengths toward the open sea, Terrapin drew breath. "The charts are wrong, Mr. Graves. There is no island at this latitude. Just a graveyard for scuttled ships. The *Lady Cullion* will not anchor here."

Owen regarded the angled masts of the wrecks, weathered and pale as driftwood, the spars and sails long gone. He looked amidships, where Argus had prepared their trading cargo for loading. Owen said to Terrapin, "Can you get us near the edge of the reef and we'll row from there?"

"Because you intend to join the shipwrecked and the drowned, Mr. Graves? What's my payment if I come back without a trader? A kick in my corpulent arse?"

Owen looked off into the blue-white distance. He found himself on the verge of confiding in Terrapin and then he was saying: "I don't know when I will be able to come to sea again. My livelihood depends on whatever I can get off this island." It sounded true enough, though there was the small omission of a looming inheritance. That would never seem like *his,* though.

Terrapin handed the wheel to the helmsman and took a step toward the cataclysm of yawed hulls. "Nine," he said. "I count nine ladies hogged up." He stood with his hands clasped over his ponderous belly, a bootlace untied, a fazzolet knotted around his ruddy neck as if for dinner. His breath was redolent of aged cheese. "You must really want a bamboo harp, Mr. Graves, because this is lunacy of the empirical order."

"Come back for us in three days, at noon. We'll take our chances."

"And where am I supposed to take the ship for three days?"

"Half a day north there's another island. The men can rest before the trick home."

"Yes, and that island was probably shot out of the same cannonical mud-dick as this one. Understand that an island without anchorage is no use to me. A ship likes to sleep in bays, sandy bottoms, channels, that drift of thing."

"We can row from here," Owen said in a tone of appeasement. "It's just Argus and me, and the rowboat can be lowered quickly." Since waking that morning he had been aware that Jethro would be jettisoned from the trip to Tikalia. His unpredictable behavior would hamper their odds of success. No, if he was going to attempt a final boon, he was going to do it in a precise and ordered fashion. Everything needed to be under his control.

Terrapin nodded, letting the trader's scheme settle over him. "I imagined that the carpenter and the dead-bird collector were going along on this jaunt. That's the precedent that's been struck. 'Course, with the apprentice dead I wasn't going to give you another seaman. Does the wraith know he's not going along? Seems he might be a little miffed . . ." A smile played on his lips.

"I can't risk it after the run-in on the last island. It's just me and the boy. No one to slow us down. I would have liked to take a whaleboat because I can fit in more trading supplies. Any chance of that?"

Terrapin puckered and leaned forward against an invisible weight. "Like you, Mr. Graves, I'm hedging my bets. And after the weather I've seen pissfiring out of this particular sky, I can't risk being caught short on lifeboats. You and the kanaka lad can have the dinghy and that's all. But if you want extra stowage, I recommend hauling something in the rear. The carpenter might have some old planksheer or something you can float behind to carry more loot." He stepped back to the helm. "Mr. Pym, bring us on a skirting line, six boat lengths from the edge of the reef so the trader and his boy can row ashore. Noon three days hence, then."

Owen nodded, retrieved his duffel bag, and descended to the quarterdeck to help Argus load.

In the fug below, Jethro was preparing his field kit, waiting for the definitive jangle of the anchor chain against the cathead before going above. The trip was winding down and at this final island he would go after something unusual, a gun-gem of the tropics. He was coming to think that Nature, in all her thrashing abundance and delicate recoil, was governed by a secret language. A cryptology that murmured just below human perception. His finger throbbed in the lamplight; was it trying to send him a message with its metronomic insistence? The body pulsed with electricity and it seemed his moods, even his thoughts, emanated from that poisoned blue tip. If it thrummed angrily, he was surly. If it fell into spasm, he was erratic. In the middle of a meditation on, say, avian flight or the armature of a wing, the finger would cut him off like an impetuous guest—*I am here, I am here*. And like some muzzled dog, more and more the finger objected to being imprisoned inside the glove. It wanted air, attention. He covered it with a piece of cloth and tried to run free with his thoughts. Consider the silkworm, he said to himself, aloud, surprised by his own voice. There was a half-written poem on the workbench that described a white mulberry with its thousand silking tenants. He took up the poem and found a pencil. He had been trying to finish it for days but it evaded him just before the last stanza, at the point where he compared the tree to an ancient citadel. What about the Chinese Tree of Heaven? Could that be in the next line, and then the stanza could continue:

Living inside their filament-spun caves
Then every cocoon plucked and boiled
Lest the worms sprout moth wings and ruin the harvest

It was passable, for now, even showed promise. He sometimes wondered if his poetry wasn't better than his ornithology. Then his finger burned through with pain and he was on his feet, pacing, practically loosed from his senses. He wanted to scream obscenities. He waited and waited for the ship to come about, for the clanking river of the anchor chain.

24.

The Tikalia lived in wattled huts and limestone caves. They burrowed into sea cliffs on the windward side of the island. There were chieftains and headmen on both sides of the island but no dogs. Women held sway over the gardens—Poumetan mythology was wrong about Tikalia's lack of agriculture—and the forests were patched with yam and sago plots, fenced in by poles kerfed with whale teeth. The beardless men rubbed their faces smooth with pumice and cut their hair with shards of flint. The children, unlike their distant cousins on Poumeta, were among the best artisans, their small hands adept at stringing bows or pulling wefts of barkcloth through a loom. The broad, surrounding reef had led to more than a century of shipwrecks and the Tikalia had never suffered for lack of contact. They borrowed or stole whatever improved their lot. Over the years, the Chinese and Malay traders and the white men had all been rescued by passing ships or found a way to decamp the island but the sugar slaves, the hundred kanakas on their way to Queensland in the bosom of the *Sea Foam* in 1875, had mostly stayed on. As a result, Tikalia was a crucible of cultures and languages and innovations. Pidgin was the lingua franca but there were ornamental styles from every region of Melanesia—the New Hebrides, New Caledonia, Santa Cruz and the western Solomons, the Admiralty Islands, even the New Guinea coast and highlands. The immigrants were mostly men but also a few women. Long ago they'd passed themselves off as boys to go caning, lined up for the blackbirders with their flat chests and shaved heads.

Because of their isolation and lack of safe harbor, the Tikalia had never been raided or missionized. There was no smallpox, typhoid, or malaria. For these same reasons, the population had spiraled to over a thousand, all within sixteen square miles. Far from being a Pacific idyll, its populace lived at the brink. They schemed ever-new ways to trim the island's inhabitants, sponsoring dangerous trading voyages far afield, elaborating complex marriage rules, allowing garden plots to pass only to firstborn daughters. There was a village perched a thousand feet above the lake that prided itself on no new births in ten years. The last nubile woman was only a few years from barrenhood and this was cause for great celebration.

So when the Tikalia saw two men—one black, one white— dragging a laden dinghy across the mudflats at low tide, they were less than welcoming. Households were rationing their sago during the early monsoon season and the wait at the communal oven houses was obscene by any measure. Not being accustomed to warfare—their own fledged weapons, outside of trade, being more decorative than martial—there was no flotilla of warriors paddling out to deter the uninvited guests. Instead they gathered on the beaches by the hundreds, staring out at the damage that was being done to their weirs, to the stone pens that caught fish at low tide without an hour of human enterprise.

Argus saw the kinsmen flank the beach, more people than he'd ever seen assembled in one place before. They waited gloomily for the next thing to happen, entire clans and lineages, bare-chested and girdled in barkcloth, more of them sifting through the trees in pairs. They waited in the slatted blue shade of the palmwoods, chewing betel nut, or they stood in the blaze of exposed sunshine, squinting through cupped hands. Even the children were immovable; they toed the sand, calabash gourds in hand, implacable at the sight of two grown men hauling through the mud. Argus had tied a rope through the iron ring of the small wooden bow and they had plowed a deep groove across the flats. It seemed like miles but was no more than a few hundred yards. Owen turned to see the mud-wake and noticed the damage they'd wrought to the islanders' fish weirs and stone corrals. This was not an auspicious beginning. He saw the *Lady Cullion* in retrograde, glimpsed through the rotting prows of the shipwrecks, heading northwest on a run, already a tiny apparition on a quieted sea.

When the rowboat was on actual sand, monstrous footprints and the boat hull swaled in the mudflat behind, the islanders walked down to meet them. Owen was caked to his rib cage and Argus had fallen facedown on their final heave-to. A wide circle formed and a few villagers ventured farther to inspect the contents of the boat, the begrimed seafarers more of an obstacle to inspection than anything else. Argus reached for some pidgin, fingering the pages of the reverend's phrase book in his mind, but all he could commute was the word for low tide—*draiwara*. The obviousness of the statement didn't seem to warrant a reply but then a child piped up with *draiwara dripmen*, which, ported into English, meant *low-tide vagabonds*. There was general agreement, languorous nodding, something like the murmur of bees. Then, finally, the crowd erupted into laughter. Part of the problem, Owen thought, was that there seemed to be no one in charge. If he could find the chief he would ask for permission to land with due ceremony and a doffed, muddy hat. But no chief was forthcoming and therefore they were not officially guests.

Owen, in desperation, said, "Tell them we have lucifer matches and calico. Show them a deck of cards."

Argus complied and held up an ace of spades like a stage magician. The children clicked their teeth in disgust. Then one of the older boys stepped over to the dinghy and held up some tinned food—peaches then beef then mussels. This drew the circle in, though not for the reasons Owen assumed. The Tikalia had no direct interest in the tinned food but were relieved that the strangers could feed themselves. Argus asked them where they might set up camp and whether they might venture into the villages for trade. The responses were tepid and contradictory—*sleep on the beach, sleep up the mountain, there is no wood for fires, rent payment levied for all guests to the island and extra for coming into the villages.* Argus scanned the faces as different voices rose above the heads of the front-row children. He wanted to find a familiar face, a cousin from his days of reed spears and fish-poisoning. Instead he heard a series of complaints about foreigners who showed up looking for trade with nothing but matches and mirrors.

"What did they say?" asked Owen. The mud on his forearms was drying to a second skin.

Argus tried to summarize their welcome by saying, "They want us out of the way and we have to pay a fee to enter the villages."

"Hospitable, aren't they?" Owen muttered. "Tell them we'd like to trade for handicrafts."

"I told them already. They said it depends on their mood, our luck, and what we have in the boat."

Owen slicked some mud off his forearms and said *Jesus* low enough to avoid Argus's prudish stare.

Argus summarized some more: "Many islanders come here for weapons. The Tikalia do not go to war themselves but they make excellent spears and shields for other islands. In a month there are men coming from far away for daggers and arrows. They will be bringing a giant raft of chickens and yams. They want to know why we didn't bring chickens or pigs?"

Owen turned to regain sight of the departing ship. The tide was still receding and he could feel his drive ebbing with it. The rules changed on every island and all of them were designed to vex and confuse the white trader. No wonder curators and private collectors were willing to pay a premium to avoid the penance of going into the field; anything to avoid its moiling rituals and fevers. He summoned a tight-lipped smile and told Argus to relay their thanks and their determination to be invisible until the ship picked them up. This last sentiment faltered and was relayed as a promise to remain as ghosts for three days.

Darkness fell and the fishermen took to their outriggers with coconut-sheath torches. The tradition was to burn the torches on the night tide and collect the flying fish as they leapt toward the light. The fishermen chewed sandalwood and gingerroot while they worked but never jinxed the catch with song or whistling. The competition was fierce and only the quickest hands could fill a canoe before morning. The closest the Tikalia came to blood-shed was a rammed prow if someone violated an ancient fish-ing protocol, the ornate tribal laws that determined who fished which reef head. Owen and Argus watched the canoes float in haloes of torchlight as they moved out past the breaking waves. They had set up camp by an estuary that flowed across the sand. Because they wanted to preserve the tinned food for trade they ate hardtack with jam and dunked it into bowls of sweet coffee. The cookfire was small for lack of wood—the beach and fore-shore had been thoroughly picked over. Argus arranged the trad-ing items by size and type. He had a methodical mind and Owen liked that. The canvas pitchtent was square in the corners with the floor pulled taut. He'd driven the stakes deep into the sand with a stone.

Owen let his mind slacken, alternating his gaze between the embers and the white starlight above the horizon. He thought about Adelaide's deathbed vigil in New England and wondered why it seemed so remote to the course of his thoughts. He missed her terribly, but he had to remind himself to consider her impend-ing grief and not just the way in which his fate was being decided in a house with a widow's walk somewhere in Boston. Papers were being signed, perhaps. Tracts were being deeded. The father was either alive or dead; it was a simple equation. Nonetheless, Mr. Cummings's death felt like an abstraction, a conjecture. He should have been wondering about Adelaide's well-being instead of his own fate. But here he was—a housewrecker's son sitting on a beach at the end of the world. A workingman whose fear was not that life would turn ruinous at any moment but that it would turn comfortable and plush without his own effort. His father was always peering from the pauper's grave. His scuffed, steel-toed boots, retrieved from the entombing rubble, still sat on a high shelf in Owen's wardrobe, no less powerful than a warrior's calcified heart in the rafters of a tribal longhouse. In this regard he was exactly like a Melanesian clansman—his days were forever being scrutinized and judged by a dead patriarch.

Argus spoke, wrenching Owen from his meditation.

"In Chicago, do you know of jobs of employment for me and my sister?" Argus said.

"The man who paid for this voyage would like you to work for him."

The fire sputtered in the light breeze.

"Doing what?"

Owen took up a stick and reorganized the scant embers. "He would like to set up an exhibition." He paused. "So that city people can learn about your ways."

"I have two ways now."

"Yes, and I think he wants to see the island way more than the Christian way."

"He does not love God?"

Owen considered that for a moment. "I'm sure he loves God but he thinks people will want to see you in traditional costume and speaking your own language."

Without a hint of indignation, Argus said, "As a savage?"

"I suppose so."

"But I am no longer a heathen."

"I know. Here's the thing. Have you ever heard of acting? It's people pretending to be something they're not for a show on stage. Entertainment."

"The theater. Strutting the boards, he called it. Reverend Mister said it was godless and pagan."

"He may have a point. Well, you'll be like an actor. Then, after the exhibit, we can find you a job or arrange for you and your sister to come back." The thought of this conversation had been weighing on him for some time. Grow your beard and shed your Christian, civilized skin was essentially the upshot. He couldn't meet the boy's eyes.

Argus followed Owen's gaze into the fire. How would a bishop hire him as a servant if he didn't wear any shoes? How would he meet a Christian wife if he could not walk down the street in a suit and straw hat, a green apple in hand? "For how long do I have to be savage?"

"Maybe a few months. In all honesty, you'd be doing me a favor and I'll make sure you're treated well."

Argus asked, "Will there be a salary?"

"Room and board and a stipend. Not sure I would call it a salary."

"We will do it if you will watch out for us. I would like to serve a holy man and my sister would like to be a governess. Will I meet your bride in Chicago?"

Owen nodded but was caught off guard. "I suppose you will."

"You said she works in a museum. Does she clean the weapons?"

"Something like that. She keeps track of things and types letters."

"What is the name of that job?"

"Secretary. This is a job that girls can do in America."

"Ah, yes, I know it. I remember now." A silence, then Argus said, "My sister likes children because she cannot have any. How many children will you have with your wife?"

"Lots," Owen said. "As many as she's willing. I had no brothers or sisters."

"Good. Because that way it won't matter if my sister doesn't have any. May I read to you *David Copperfield* to pass the time until we sleep?"

"Please," said Owen.

Argus stood by the fire and held the book like a hymnal. *I know enough of the world now, to have almost lost the capacity of being much surprised by anything; but it is a matter of some surprise to me, even now, that I can have been easily thrown away at such an age . . .*

Owen stirred the fire again and looked out at the fishermen, their nets held wide like jibsails on a run.

. . . I became, at ten years old, a little labouring hind in the service of Murdstone and Grinby . . .

Above Argus's voice, Owen could hear the tiny plinks as the fish arced out of the darkening waters toward the fishermen's torchlight, toward the certainty of an airy death.

In the morning they began to explore the island, disregarded for the most part, but waved off if they violated the treaty between wary host and uninvited guest. They carried sample trade items in bulging rucksacks but left most of their goods at the makeshift camp, under the shelter of the overturned rowboat. Unlike the other islands, there were no children trailing behind them with sharpened sticks and mangy, hairless dogs. The Tikalia had no use for dogs but had imported cats over the years to help diminish a plague of rats. The rodents were kept under control but the cats—the kinsfolk called them *long-tails*—had bred voraciously and had killed much of the island's birdlife. There were calicos and tabbies of every stripe, sleeping and idling on the trails, slinking and mewing in the thickets. Argus thought of the disagreeable Mr. Nibbles, the mission cat who'd spent his existence licking himself between naps and petulant stares, and wondered whether Tikalia cats had found their very own Eden, the feline equivalent of heaven on earth.

Stepping across the well-worn pathways, Owen and Argus noticed the sheer volume and variety of houses. The crowded villages had no clear boundaries but bled together, stippled among the dense foliage of the forest. There were dwellings of every sort—daubed huts of yellow cane and palmetto thatch, lashed bamboo lean-tos, caves hollowed into the limestone karst of the mountainside, treehouses of driftwood perched up among the orchids and honeyeaters. The Tikalia slept wherever they could, three and four to a room, curled on the beach in the dry season. They buried their dead beneath the floors of their houses or in graves topped with stone dolmens. When the grave plots were full or the departing spirits were particularly malevolent, they interred the corpses in the shipwrecked hulls, wrapped and laid out in the derelict holds like pharaohs.

Away from the shoreline the vegetation thickened, the ironwoods draped and corded with vines. The trail zigzagged up the massif, streams flowing out of the high lake and washing across the narrow footpath. There were brief vistas of riparian garden plot below, little arcadias of irrigated croft and groves of shaded canarium. Argus had insisted on carrying the heavier rucksack up the hillside and he thought of atonement and English fenlands in old photographs as he climbed. The reverend had told stories of Scottish summers spent in the Highlands as a schoolboy, navigating a yew maze on the family estate. Each time he got lost, he dropped to his knees and asked for God to light the way. And each time the yew hedges revealed an exit because they were collaborating in divine proof. Later, preparing for bed, he would stand at the high windows of the manse and look down on the maze, a boy of ten, and see the intricacies of the hedge walls, the mandala-like geometry, and he would be struck by the unlikelihood of accidentally solving the puzzle six times in a row. *God is everywhere,* he would whisper to Argus from the captain's chair half a century later, *waiting to be drawn down by worthiness revealed.*

The sense Owen had as they picked a trail up the mountainside was that the whole population was watching from depths of shade. Their rucksacks bounced with goods as they hiked but no one emerged from the jungle to trade. They continued up to the lip of the extinct caldera, where the stunted trees bent seaward, and looked down into the buttressed lake. Pied cormorants stepped through the shallows and gray ducks floated in a wide V across the lake's surface. This vantage point gave a reminder of the island's smallness and isolation—a cup of tranquil water, a volcanic rim as delicate as bone china, and the ocean spread on all sides like a bolt of Persian blue silk. The shipwrecks and the dugouts on the fringing reef were the only things to give dimension and suggest human scale. Argus prayed quietly at the immensity of it all, wondered if it was the first place to see the sun each day, while Owen threw a rock into the fulgent eye of the lake.

The clansmen emerged as the visitors began the descent. Those interested in trade brought their items to the pathway so that the strangers wouldn't have to be received in the village. Sanctioned guests had to be fed and offered tobacco and kava, but only if they entered the communal square itself. A party of villagers assembled at a switchback and Owen saw that they had laid out their goods on banana leaves. Owen and Argus trudged farther down the trail and the kinsmen began to play music, not so much in greeting but as a display of hardware. Every island style and technique was represented in the band—flutes and double-row panpipes from the New Hebrides, a bamboo jew's harp and reed flute from New Caledonia, drums from New Guinea that changed pitch with a smear of wax, wood trumpets from the highlands that were generally only played during nights of tribal bloodshed. Whether the myths Owen had heard from Argus were true, that the Tikalia were renowned for their artistry and received trading parties from as far away as New Zealand, that they once took in wanderers of every denomination, any outcast who muttered the pidgin phrase for banishment— *rausim i go longwe*—was hard to say. Certainly, white men were not very welcome here and he thought the music had an off-kilter staccato that was filled with menace. A caramel-skinned boy played a friction gong, looking straight at them, refusing to smile.

The music swelled and subsided. The visitors unloaded their rucksacks and set the items on the ground. To Owen it had the feeling of a long-held ritual, this chess match of competing inventories. Before the haggling could begin in earnest they arranged the brightly colored clothes the sailmaker had sewn from the slop chest as a kind of backdrop, placing porcelain dogs and music boxes and steel knives on top, as if on a velvet-lined display case. Everything had to be first glimpsed in the best possible light. Owen had packed as diverse an array of objects as he could think of, hoping to cover every angle and to give Argus ample opportunity to appeal to their supernatural concerns. Mirrors, candles, whale-tooth amulets, photographs of dead men who might be enlisted in hexes and curses. Owen had decided to leave the guns and ammunition and some of the more elaborate goods in the overturned rowboat, to keep these in reserve. If the islanders saw the depth of your pockets too early, he believed, then it was all over.

The two trading parties swapped places and inspected each other's array. Owen knew immediately that he'd underprovisioned. The tribal spread was miraculous in its diversity. It was as if the previous months had been wasted, that he could have just come to Tikalia from the start and cut the trip in half. The island was a clearinghouse, whether accidental or not, for a hundred far-flung places. Pearl- and mussel-shell scrapers, a rasp of wood covered with sharkskin that he'd been unable to purchase near Santa Cruz, another covered with the skin of a stingray, some kind of bludgeon, cordage from the Carolinas made from paper mulberry and the aerial roots of pandanus, strung across mangrove bows, the corresponding arrows fletched with egret feathers, Polynesian baskets of woven rushes with carmine trim used for carrying babies, a spoil of awls and axes and basalt adzes, bamboo beheading knives and carriers with a special loop for passing through the windpipe of a severed head, strings of old Solomon shell-bead money, pearl bridal ornaments, entire outfits of cuirass and plaited cane armor for Bismarck chieftains. The objects came from every region of

Melanesia and Polynesia and it occurred to Owen that the Tikalia were as trade-minded and mercenary as he was—that for the right price they would trade anything with anybody, would supply highlanders with cutting rasps that would someday be used to garrote their distant Pacific cousins. How many colonial muskets had been traded only to be fired against the descendants of the gun's original owner? Part of his mind was already clicking over with possibilities. If the *Cullion* had been anchored nearby he would have bought the captain's piano and rowed it ashore in the hopes of a trading coup. He would have traded the four sticks of dynamite in the armory, the explosives the captain kept on some strange and personal reckoning with his past. He was doomed by this hunger and felt galled by the spread before him; he'd been outclassed and outmatched and the islanders knew it. Already he could hear their mouths tsk-ing, feel them wondering why the vagabonds of the mud tide had bothered to climb the hill.

Owen tried to save face. He told Argus to suggest a later meeting on the beach. They were welcome to inspect the rest of the articles. This was merely a sample.

Argus translated this and they stared at his scuffed boots, skeptical. Wanting to test the waters for their eventual conversion to godliness, he said, "Do you want to be washed holy? Because I know the teachings of Matyu and Luk." They chewed ginger and he could smell it on their breath. They said nothing but quietly packed their things, avoiding eye contact. "Will you come to see the rest?" Argus repeated. Still no response. The instruments were put away and the ornaments wrapped in cloth. The island traders disbanded and Owen watched them descend the hillside, their sniggering restrained until they rounded the first switchback.

They set up camp under a gibbous moon while an expedition of cats trotted down off the caldera. They mewed for scraps and lay in C's by the fire. Argus tried to chase a few of them off with a brandished stick but they started then wheeled, circling back to their original positions. The smell of baking fish and breadfruit wafted down from the village ovens while Argus heated up some beans, salt onions, and coffee. Owen laid out the rest of the goods on a tarpaulin. He would not be caught off guard again. The Tikalia seemed fickle and skittish to him and he placed a douceur of rice with as much care as the steel fishhooks or the meerschaum pipes acquired from the forecastle of the burning coal ship. Argus lit oil pots of citronella to keep the few mosquitoes at bay and they ate standing, arranging and rearranging the articles of trade until they were satisfied.

After dinner, Argus read aloud, this time from *Kidnapped*. Owen had always been fond of Stevenson—he was part of the reason he first went to sea. The letters that Stevenson published in the *Tribune* years earlier had suggested that cruising the South Seas was harrowing but filled with pleasures. One account described the author's ship picking its way through a bedlam of coral reefs and atolls for days but the reader never lost sight of the green mountain-islands cowled in cloud or forgot the ocean-river of the Trades. After a visit to the leper colony on Molokai in Hawaii, Stevenson sent a gift to the disfigured children he'd played croquet with—a $300 Westermeyer grand piano with instructions to the Mother Superior in charge of their care to administer music lessons. This had always stayed with Owen, both the thoughtful, extravagant gift and the fact of his visit to this far-flung place. Stevenson, he knew, had gone to the Pacific on the pretext of his ailing lungs, had brought along wife and stepson, mother and maid, but what drove him to shake hands with lepers, to envision them playing sonatas in their hermitage? What made him sail to the remotest islands on earth? Failing health, surely, but also, it came to Owen now in the coals of the fire, a kind of intractability. He shuffled his family from one island to the next, looking for an idyll, eventually settling in Samoa, where he died at age forty-four. Clearly, the isolation and weather hadn't cured him.

Owen knew himself to be capable of such relentlessness. There were few islands more remote than Tikalia and in two days they were headed home, but Owen couldn't help wondering what lay further afield. Was there an island remaining that no white man had visited? He scoffed at his ruminations, thinking them no better than Jethro wanting to haul spiny sea monsters from the deep and give them Latin names. As he listened to the missionized boy read *Kidnapped* in his butler's English, with the righteous lilt of scripture, he couldn't help wishing for communion with something wholly dark and primordial before his rebirth into civil society and his bearing up into marriage. Argus was a proxy for what had brought him here outside of a paycheck—a chance to step beyond. He'd always known the periphery of life, ever since his father and he had watched theatergoers on State Street as if they were as strange and exotic in their frock coats and gowns as Tapiro pygmies. Objects—found, excavated, traded, sometimes stolen—had been his way to bridge the gap. Or was it a way of forging the gap? He couldn't be sure. *No man is an island* was a phrase the nuns at the Tabernacle School for Boys were fond of repeating to the orphans and he continued to doubt the veracity of the sentiment. Almost twenty years later, still prone to romanticizing his own sense of isolation, he'd failed to discover that the quote belonged to John Donne and not the Bible.

Some hours later, the Tikalia traders descended to the beach. They led an ancient piebald mare down from the mountainside, a hackamore of woven green saplings around its neck. It hobbled forward, unshod and wary, its flanks painted vermilion and pale in the moonlight. Instead of being laden with goods the horse moved unencumbered, strands of sennit and cowries braided to its mane. Owen was surprised to see the men carry the trade goods on their own backs instead of using the horse. They patted her rump tenderly as she hoofed across the sand, fetlocks wrapped in tapa. Was it a clan god painted and decorated for festivals? Did the old mare live in the valley by the volcanic lake, half blind and dim-witted, sequestered like a mendicant until she was bridled and led down under a full moon to dispense oracles? Owen stood and opened his hands in a gesture of welcome. The traders brought the horse forward and the cats looked up momentarily from their fireside naps. The mare proceeded to shit in the sand and nobody spoke.

The goods were laid out as before but this time the traders showed no interest in examining the visitors' spoils. They crouched in the sand and held their hands to the fire. The horse was allowed to wander along the beach, its hackamore untied.

"Tell them we have everything on display now," Owen told Argus.

Argus did so. "They have decided to welcome us as guests."

"What a relief," Owen said, sarcastically.

"They have brought the chief for this side of the island."

Owen looked at the man leaning forward on his haunches — he was taller and older than the others. Owen had wrongly suspected this was a chiefless society, some egalitarian chaos ringed by coral. Perhaps the chief had balked from coming forward earlier because it meant claiming them, bearing responsibility for the vagabonds.

Argus said, "He would like us to drink kava with them." A moment later, he added, "There is a mission ban on kava so I cannot drink it."

Nodding at the delegation, Owen said, "Do whatever it takes to make the trade."

Argus went quiet and stirred the fire.

The chief took out a bundle of dried kava root, removed a stick, and passed it to Owen.

"What do I do?" Owen said, shrugging in self-mockery.

The chief chewed the tip of the root and, after a minute, swilled a stream of dark saliva into a wooden bowl at his side. He handed the carved bowl to Owen and waited for him to do likewise. Owen took the bitter root in his mouth, chewed it to the count of sixty, and trailed a line of nut-brown spittle into the bowl. The taste was about what he expected — woody, bitter, tannic. The roots were handed around and each man spat into the bowl until it was brimming. It was then that Owen realized that he would be drinking other men's saliva in his new role as sanctioned guest. The bowl came to him and he drank with his eyes closed. Now he could taste the peppery root and the swill of spittle gave it a fermented reek and bite on the tongue. It was akin, he felt sure, to chewing wood from old doors and then sprinkling the mouth with Chinese pepper. He watched Argus take a tepid sip at the rim of the bowl, his jaw set against all heathenry. After several sips Owen felt the dull narcotic rise through his system like a pale balloon. It started with a gelatinous feeling in his legs. He nodded appreciatively and stirred the fire even though it didn't need it. The traders produced clay pipes and began to smoke tobacco. Owen rolled several cigarettes and handed them out. They passed an amused ten minutes watching a clansman try to light his cigarette by the campfire. He singed his dreadlocks and eyebrows.

The Tikalia chief half pidginized something and Argus clarified. "He asked whether you can hear the ocean from your land?"

Owen said, "We have a lake almost as big as an ocean. But we are very far from the true ocean."

"How far?" the chief asked.

"From here to New Guinea."

They all considered this in their pipe bowls and in the red eyes of their cigarettes. "What is in between?" the chief asked.

The man's face was smeared with something like kohl and tattooed beneath the eyes—delicate lines of cross-hatching—and in the smoke-filled gloaming Owen thought it looked like fishnet stockings. He could feel the distortion of his own mind in the afterbite of the kava, some kind of playfulness he knew was not native to his mold of thought. He licked his lips, accepted that he had not changed his clothes or bathed in five days, thought briefly and a little guiltily of Jethro in the *Cullion*'s hold and how he had led the heir to believe he was coming ashore, all of it passing in an instant, before saying, "Land. Great gardens of beans and corn as tall as a man."

The chief puckered with amazement. "We belong to the sea,"

he said. "When a man has something on his face we say the sea-ward cheek or the landward cheek. This is all we know. The tides and the big winds. We can teach you these things."

Argus said in a quiet voice, "I can teach you gospel songs to help protect the island from hurricanes." In his inebriated state his pidgin came out with a slight Scottish brogue.

The kinsmen ignored him. They had heard about and dismissed the clayskin god long ago. "We want to know the names."

Argus said, "This is Owen Graves and I am Argus Niu."

One of them said, "No. We want to know names of the big-fella's place. We change names depending on the houses we live in and the gardens we work. A man can have ten names during his lifetime. His name changes when his father dies."

Thus began a brief lesson on Tikalia nomenclature and the rules for naming children. It was places, not people, that bore permanent title. Men belonged to houses and gardens and reefs. Children were named after streams and trailheads. And every Tikalia word sang with embodied meaning so that the word for wheel was itself a sonic revolution—*takiri-karika*. Argus knew the term for this was *onomatopoeia* but kept this recognition to himself. Next came an introductory course on Tikalia obscenities and curses, and the clansmen all agreed that *may your father eat filth* was the best and most flexible form of profanity. They asked Owen to say the names of places he knew and he began with the names of American states and presidents but soon got down to the curbstone poetry of Chicago streets—Adams, Monroe, Jackson, Polk, Van Buren, Madison, La Salle—so many of them named after men of note, ancestors and patriarchs now that he thought of it.

"Do you name your children after the big chiefs?"

"Yes. I know three Madisons and two Monroes."

They all appraised the dying fire. A few Tikalia legends were offered to the flames at this point, one about the woman who gave birth to an eel, another about the ocean-dwelling ancestors who roamed the seafloor and kept sharks as doglike pets. Owen, still emboldened by kava, thought of Chicago's finest myths, of the slang fables George Ade put in his newspaper column—*Once upon a Time there was a slim Girl with a Forehead which was Shiny and Protuberant, like a Barlett Pear,* or *Once there was a Bluff whose Long Suit was Glittering Generalities,* or the baseball fan who arrived home every summer evening to tell his wife that the Giants made the Colts look like a lot of Colonial Dames playing Bean Bag in a Weedy Lot back of an Orphan Asylum, and they ought to put a Trained Nurse on Third, and the Dummy at Right needed an Automobile, and the New Man couldn't jump out of a Boat and hit the Water, and the Short-Stop wouldn't be able to pick up a Ball if it was handed to him on a Platter with Water Cress around it . . . Owen knew there was no way to translate any of this. The stuff of city legends was as inscrutable to an outsider as Oriental philosophy.

A moment of silence passed.

The chief said, "Are those all your goods or do you have more in the big canoe? When is it coming back for you?"

"In two days. This is all we have to trade. From here we are going home."

"To the land with the lake as big as an ocean?"

"Yes."

"Do you have things from other islands?"

"Yes. Weapons and handicrafts."

The chief said, "We need more feathers for making weapons for other islands. The long-tails have killed many of our birds and they have stopped flying here. Rats or birds. This is the choice we have."

"We can get you more feathers," Owen said. He was thinking of Jethro's dead-bird aviary in the orlop.

"And the kanaka. Is he going back to the lake? His tribal scar says he is Poumetan. One of the great canoe voyagers and our cousin."

Owen nodded. The Tikalia looked at Argus's shark-toothed wrist and then at his face with a mix of admiration and pity.

The chief gestured to one of the men to bring forward a woven saddlebag. It was set beside the chief and he produced a rusting typewriter and laid it on the sand. A sheaf of papers was produced and a list of typed names. From what Owen could tell it was the names of visiting and wrecked ships, their crew itemized, some with an *X* beside their Christian names.

"Who typed these?" Owen asked, pointing to the *X*'s.

The chief ignored him as if this were a rhetorical question. "I want you to masin the names in my clan. The chiefs of the island and also the garden and house names." He moved the typewriter toward Owen and stood, preparing to dictate his lineage. Owen wondered what use a genealogy of typed names was to tribesmen who couldn't read but nonetheless complied. He took the typewriter in his lap and began to hunt and peck his way through an incantation of chiefs and dwellings, the ribbon dull and powdery with old ink, the headman circling the fire with his hands behind his back. The others corrected him if he misspoke or skipped a generation. Argus looked on, slightly appalled that Owen didn't know how to play the typewriter keys the way the Reverend Mister had taught him. Owen's fingers halted across the keys.

After an hour and six typed pages, the chief told the other clansmen to fetch the horse and bring it forward. The mare hobbled over and lay again in the sand, its eyes filmed with cataract. It was breathing heavily, ringed by cats. If they thought he was going to trade for this decrepit animal they were sadly mistaken. Surely the gift of recorded genealogy was worth something. He was just about to have Argus convey this idea when the chief said, "We have been keeping one of your gods for you."

Owen double-checked the translation. The chief squatted to caress the haggard mare on the flank. "Many years ago the animal swam ashore after a shipwreck. We did not know the word *horse* then and called her the *big hog*. Now we know. We have kept her beautiful and fed her but she is old and of no use to us. She is worse than a dog and it's time you took her away. We will give you everything on the barkcloth in return for your goods and if you will take the animal from this place. We think the horse god is ready to die and it will be bad luck for her to become a ghost here. We have poured the kava libations to the ancestors and asked for this."

Owen saw that the typewritten names and the ferrying of the horse were the real asking price. The traders had little interest in what he'd assembled on the tarpaulin. They wanted some feathers for fletching and little else. He told Argus to agree to the terms of trade but insisted on walking them through his inventory. As the traders loaded their woven bags with zinc pails and snuff boxes and rifles, with a hundred trinkets and tools, he told them that the kerosene lanterns would draw many more flying fish from the waters at night. They nodded politely, said they'd already tried this but ran out of fuel, and took their leave. They packed their typewriter in its bag and left the god-horse on the beachhead in the custody of their welcomed guests. For a full fifteen minutes Owen ran his fingers over the bartered goods, taking inventory of his boon through the eyes of Hale Gray, keeping the thought of removing the horse from the island as distant as possible. Terrapin's gall at having to transport a glue horse would be a revelation. Finally he turned and saw the mare strain to its feet, saw the whites of its walled eyes in the moonlit night, then watched it follow in the direction of the vanished kinsmen. Argus followed behind and led it back by the fire. They tethered it in a copse of trees where it could feed on tufted grasses, but the animal brayed all night like a god bereft of worship.

25.

It was dusk already and Jethro—still fuming from being left on the ship—came into the apprentice quarters to finish out the workday. He'd spent most of the daylight mounting insects and reading about the fertilization of orchids in the orlop. But the fug below had made him qualmish and he'd come above in search of fresh air. He opened the cabin porthole and spread his books and blotting paper on his iron cot. He lit the slush lamp and it rocked and swayed with a jaundiced flame. He tried to pin a brown beetle but, after three attempts, pricked his snakebitten finger so that a dot of blood broke to the surface. He punched the wall in a burst of anger and momentarily enjoyed the camouflaging pain in his left fist before the finger reasserted itself. His mind was not right. The taste of sulfur and iron was the first indication that he'd placed his bloody finger in his mouth. He thought he could taste the poison. He turned back to his woefully pinned beetles. How could any naturalist be an expert in ornithology, entomology, conchology, and all the rest of it? He was a dabbler at best, he thought. A tourist of the sciences and arts. Where was that resolute self he'd glimpsed in the early days of passage? The poems of ascent. Did every man come to sea in search of some figment?

The Karlsbad pins were too long and flimsy—German skewers where an English short pin was required. And anyway, when pinned through the thorax of a Hymenoptera specimen—an ant, wasp, or bee—the pins were eventually overcome by verdigris, corroding with the secretion of the insect's bodily acids. Or maybe it was Coleoptera and Diptera specimens that turned the pins gangrenous. If only he'd brought along short, japanned pins for this particular use. His preparations now seemed hasty. At least he'd had the foresight to visit a Chicago tinsmith and commission field containers of various dimensions. This ensured the separation of insects by size and species; otherwise the bigger ones devoured the smaller ones within hours. And he'd taken the time to make a cyanide bottle, which he picked up now, removing the cork. The ingenuity of this killing device could not be overestimated—a two-ounce quinine bottle with cyanide of potassium in the bottom and mixed with plaster of Paris. The word *Paris* made him think of organdy ribbons and bunting and he imagined for a second that cyanide had penetrated his body via the pinpricked finger, saw a flashing vision of his own sea burial, then somehow thought of Keats writing tubercular poetry in Rome, before the briny taste of his own blood brought him back to the cabin. He removed his finger from his mouth and held a vibrating honeybee with a pair of tweezers. He placed it slowly into the cyanide chamber. If you left them in the bottle too long the yellows of the Hymenoptera turned reddish and were ruined for the display case.

Through his open porthole he heard the seamen on watch talking about their exploits with women. The mating habits of hominids, he thought. Harvey McCallister, with his brawny shoulders and clipped Irish accent, was talking up a sexual typhoon. The recounting of bestial acts on foreign shores. Coital plunder north and south of the Line. The ravaged divas of Asia Minor and so on. Jethro remembered the surprise in Harvey's eyes as he'd socked him in the jaw, sending him to the planks; he would have liked to frame that incredulous grimace behind glass. He set the insects and blotting paper aside and turned to Darwin's *The Various Contrivances by which Orchids are Fertilised by Insects*. But instead of being a distraction from the escalating bawdiness outside his porthole it seemed to augment the general slant of talk. Darwin sometimes gave over to botanical descriptions verging on the sexual; more than pithy aphorisms and the refrain of *Nature's beautiful contrivances,* he spoke of the orchid's surging labellum with its secretions of nectar, of the way the flower courted flying insects and trapped them in its darkly folded lips.

One of the seamen said, "Tonight's the night. Odds are six to one in favor. Which way are you going to bet, Harvey?"

"I already bet."

"Which way?"

"That the kanaka gets her sails reefed tonight. Five dollars on landfall credit. Captain's been circling for weeks but I see it in his eyes. What with the brother gone and the trader, too. Full moon tonight, lads. With a bit of luck we'll hear them howling like alley cats sparkin it hot."

They moved amidships and Jethro couldn't bring himself to turn another page; suddenly he was holding in his shaking hands a pornographic treatise on orchids. Something had been happening all this time. The corruption infecting the ship, radiating from the stateroom just as poison issued from his own rotting finger. A kind of savage lust had taken hold, blooming like verdigris on a straight pin. Who would take a stand to protect the native girl's station? Here was a chance, he thought now, for resoluteness, to become the figment evoked in those early poems he'd written in the crosstrees. Wasn't character ultimately a question of action? History was full of fledgling men who reached across the way with a single act of defiance. He waited until he heard the seamen go about the business of the anchored watch and went below to the orlop. Unsteadily, he lit the lamps and unwrapped his collecting pistol from its muslin. He loaded two .32-caliber shells, each filled with the mixture of grade D American wood powder and buckshot that was ideal for larger birds, for hawks and eagles and herons.

Terrapin played a sonata with all his big racehorse heart, his ham-knuckled fingers lighter and quicker than they had any business being. Malini danced in slow circles, eyes closed, moving through a cloud of ambergris. The perfume was a present from the captain—from the dark of a whale's stomach he'd told her—and she was wearing somebody's dead mother's frock, something red and too big, but she didn't care. For dinner she'd had bacon and pudding and tinned cherries. Terrapin watched her dance, nodding in appreciation, swelling beneath his cotton sarong. He stopped playing and handed her the jug of rum. She drank up, like she really meant it.

Somehow they ended up on the piano bench and he was teaching her "Chopsticks" or something else for children. He watched her fill with girlish delight as she tapped it out. Looking at the relief of her breasts against the neckline of the frock, her slender, sun-bronzed arms, he said, "Here's church if you want it." Malini shrugged, moving her fingers into an atonal scale. He stood up, nodding again, providing encouragement for the two-fingered playing. Standing behind her he looked down into the dimming abandon of her brown cleavage, his calloused hands resting on her shoulders. He began rubbing her shoulders while she chopped away at the black sharps and she angled her neck to one side, the piano slurring a little. He inched a hand down her neck, running over the lamplit gloss of her collarbone, the tinkling still in motion. It wasn't until he had a breast cupped in one hand that the piano stopped. It went dead silent in the stateroom—the hush of all those Bedouin draperies and carpets. Malini swallowed against the crook of his arm, against the tattooed list of begats and halfbloods. The pause that followed was complicated. His hand went limp and he said in a whisper, "You're a lovely thing . . ." She sighed and played a handful of bass notes to indicate that her allegiance was to the music, and the piano wires were still humming dark when Jethro Gray burst into the cabin with his long-barreled pistol. Terrapin straightened and let his arms go loose. The naturalist was red-eyed and rabid with something. The captain saw that he was clearly out of his head.

Terrapin took a step back from the piano bench and Malini adjusted her dress, face down. "Steady on, lovelace, let's ease into this together."

Jethro advanced, the pistol aimed at Terrapin's chest. The bulbous finger was biblical in its fury and proportions. He said, "Everyone has turned a blind eye, until now. The girl is coming with me."

Terrapin set his jaw. "This is mutinous, understand that. You have entered the master's stateroom without permission, wielding a firearm. This won't look good in the log, peanut."

"I'm tired of the way this ship is being captained."

"And do you intend to relieve me of my office, Mr. Gray? Because if you intend a mutiny you better find a man who won't come with me in the whaleboats. Those men would have shoved a golden rivet up your arse if it wasn't for me. Ungrateful fucking dandy! I will wring blood from your spleen for this little trick. Mark my words." Terrapin's voice wavered in anger.

Jethro kept his voice low. "This is not mutiny. I intend to protect the native girl in the orlop for the duration of the passage home."

Malini could feel humiliation burning in her cheeks. She took a step back, furious that her brother had left her behind in this mess. Her choice was between a lecherous old man, who could probably be persuaded to keep his hands to himself, or a ghost of a man who now stood with a gun, blinking wildly.

"Go on then, love," Terrapin said to her.

Malini picked up her shawl and wrapped it around her shoulders. She petted the sleeping dog and went to stand beside the skinny bird-killer, her eyes down. Terrapin smiled at her and said, "Don't worry we'll work this all out in a jiffy." Jethro backed out of the stateroom, gun muzzle raised and pointed, Malini at his side. Terrapin didn't bother following. He took his time putting on his favorite peacoat and belting a pair of trousers before going to consult the first mate in his cabin. He told the bleary-eyed Mr.

Pym that he wanted to discuss the strange and supernatural pleasure he would take in Jethro Gray's downfall. It was like a prayer
on his lips, he said, brimming with a vengeance so pure it was
holy.

All the way down the long run of companionways Jethro kept
telling Malini to hush. But she wasn't making any noise. A few
sailors noticed the pistol and backed away. He flashed the weapon
through the underworld of the ship, spinning crabwise. He
grabbed Malini by the arm and led her into the orlop, barricad-
ing the door with workbenches and sawhorses and the wooden
faldstools the carpenter had made him. Malini hadn't been in here
since her recovery from the lancing of the boil and it reeked of
dead birds and lizards. There were stuffed and hanging corpses,
white cotton bulging from their mouths, frogs limp in briny jars,
ferns pressed and mounted, jellyfish bobbing with the ship's rocking sway. A horned beetle, pinned in place but still alive, was trying to scratch its way up a sheet of white blotting paper.

He made her a bed of wadded cotton on the floor and
smoothed it out with his hands. The gun was still at his side when
he handed her a drink of brandy. She knew she was still drunk
from the captain's rum, could feel it buzzing away in her arms
and legs, but she took the drink because all she wanted now was
sleep. It tasted funny, more bitter than the captain's bottle. She
drank it down and went to lie on the cotton bed. She wanted
the dog in her arms and wished her brother would return at
once. The wooden cave of dead things started to move all around
and she couldn't feel her body. She closed her eyes and thought of
treehouses draped in wild flowers.

Jethro watched her on the floor, her legs crossed at the knees,
the dress slightly splayed in the rear. She'd been at the point of
nervous prostration, he told himself, and the laudanum in the
brandy would ensure a restful sleep. It would be a long night and
he would stand guard by the door. He sat by the bed on a stool
and alternated his gaze between the blocked companionway and

the bed. He listened for the sound of footsteps, for Terrapin's cavalry, the gun square across his legs. After some time he dozed off and woke with a start, a single lamp burning. Still nothing. He got up and placed a glass beaker on top of the furniture blockade so that it would announce a forced entry. He took up the lamp, quietly removed his shoes, and lay down on the bed next to her. The dress was unbecoming and he draped her legs with a square of blanket. Her breathing was easy and light. He thought of all the anthropological measurements he'd penned in his leather notebook—the circumference of her head, the incline of her forehead, the breadth of her mouth. He thought of the way Nature kept receding. This game of advance and retreat kept him off balance. What was it to know a thing with absolute certainty? A poem allowed doubt but natural history required something declarative. He ran his hands across the plane of her back, scientifically, across the dark skin that overlaid an armature of bone no different to his own. He blew out the lamp and felt something mount within him in the tallow fumes. It was so quiet beneath the waveline. The ocean pressed against the ship's gently groaning ribs. He thought of Darwin and his orchids full of nectar, of the proposition that a flower's extravagant beauty served nothing but insect courtship. In the dark he felt invisible, unmoored. Slow-wheeling thoughts moved through the submarine dark, loosed, somehow, from his own mind. His hands edged beneath the blanket and he searched out everything that was obscure and unknown, everything that Nature was keeping at bay.

26.

The *Cullion* did not return at noon on the third day. They waited all afternoon on the beachhead, the boat loaded with trading spoils, ready to walk the ancient piebald out onto the tidal mudflats. From there it would be a matter of coaxing the mare into the swells and towing her behind the rowboat. Owen knew that horses could swim—he'd once seen a palomino ford the mire of the Chicago River during a stable fire—but he also knew this hack could barely walk, never mind dog-paddle. He didn't let his thoughts eddy beyond the image of the horse flanked to her ribs in seawater, did not plumb the proposition of getting her aboard the bark. The skeptical villagers looked on from a distance, watching the sun transit the quadrants of clear blue sky, waiting for a ship to speck the horizon.

By late afternoon, Owen began to speculate about the reasons for the delay—faltering winds, flukey tides, a mishap in navigation. If the *Cullion* had forayed half a day north, to the anchorage of the nearest island, then it was hard to imagine a botched return. The sky was a high blue and the wind was blowing fresh from the west so that the clipper could easily zag its way south. The hours passed without sight of the bark and a band of clanswomen appeared on the beach as a distraction from the waiting. They collected fish from the mudflat weirs and urchins from the silvered tide pools, gathered up an array of cowries and cat's eyes and cockles from the wet sand. Owen and Argus watched them in silence. Carnation and hibiscus garlands around their necks, bandeaus of leaves and myrtle blooms in their hair, girdled in paperbark, they picked across the sand without haste, singing and calling to one another. The word among traders and colonialists was that whenever you saw the women you were safe. Tribal attacks never occurred with women present; this was the inherited wisdom. The Tikalia trusted the two clayskins now that a deal had been struck, it seemed to Owen, but he could feel his tongue coat with thirst as he stared out at the younger clanswomen's bent, lithe, and near-naked forms. There were sylphlike girls and old crones with breasts as pendulant as eggplants, daughters and sisters and cousins of the same bloodline, judging from the familiarity between them.

More than anything, it seemed to Owen, the extremes of life felt a part of the natural order in the islands—the vigor of youth and the plainness of death was everywhere. It reminded him of a plot of ground out by the Livestock Emporium where a full-bloomed pear tree and a burned-out byre flanked each other on the same hillside. He thought of polite women in Chicago, about their fruit-laden hats. *Wasplike waists and with tempers to match* was the saloon refrain. Adelaide was wholly different; well-bred but also earthy and decent. He imagined her teaching a daughter to sew, pictured a sunny kitchen with a dog curled at their feet. He needed, suddenly, a diversion from the twilit haunches and jostling breasts before him. Those visions of the future anchored him, promised a kind of safety. From what? he wondered. From his own flawed character? From a trader's hut on a lonely far-flung beach? He heard himself swallow and it felt like his mind blinking over. He was ready to surrender wholly to his future, however it unspooled.

Argus watched the native women a little distantly, as if from a height. In the falling light he thought their flower coronals made them resemble English wives of title and dominion, like aristocrats walking in a dusky rose garden instead of godless women gathering shellfish at low tide. A lone woman walked apart from the others, some distance behind, and Argus wondered whether she was childless. A native woman without children was adrift, invisible. He thought suddenly of Malini and hoped she was safe aboard the ship. He had been a negligent brother, gone six years and now letting her fend for herself. He felt a pang of guilt and quietly said a prayer for her.

The women departed and Argus made a pathetic fire with coconut fiber and scantling washed up from a wreck. The flames flickered and sputtered. It was barely enough light to read by, and anyway Argus felt much too hungry for orphans flung out. They had traded their tinned food and rice and fishing supplies, and the Tikalia had led them to believe that catching bonito or barramundi would be an intrusion. As a small gesture of good-will and hospitality a few villagers brought down a clay pot of fermented breadfruit and left it in the sand by the campfire. They said it had been buried in the earth for a year and was eaten in the caves during the big wet. The sticky, glutinous compound— yellow and formidable as bookbinders' paste—required a swift finger to spool it mouthward before it was retracted by the rest of the brimming compote. They ended up still hungry, with their shirtfronts and trousers strung in fermented breadfruit.

Owen retrieved a flask of whiskey and a scrimshaw knife from his rucksack. He sliced crescents of coconut from a shell that was woody and slightly green. He placed them on a hank of cloth. "Dessert," he said to Argus.

Argus took up a piece of coconut—thin and curled as a wood shaving—and popped it into his mouth. He hesitated when Owen passed him the whiskey. He didn't like the heat and smoke of whiskey but didn't want to be impolite. A small sip was enough to make his chest and windpipe burn. He handed it back to Owen, who took a long pull.

"Do you think the ship will come tomorrow?" Argus asked.

"I'm sure of it," said Owen. In fact, he was far from sure. All afternoon and evening he'd been playing out various mishaps in his mind—the ship had been scuttled on a reef or had caught fire, had been involved in an act of mutiny or piracy, or Terrapin had simply decided to take what trade items had been stowed in the forehatch and bulkhead and steamer for home. In any event, his meditations saw him and the mission houseboy stuck among the unyielding Tikalia for many months before a frigate happened by. In one vision, Adelaide would give him up for lost or dead and marry her blue-blood dentist, a man named Erasmus Plimp. Such was the mockery of his thoughts. And it could all be justified, he thought, these events flowing in the wake of his object obsession. He should have steamered for home as soon as he got her letter. The word *monomania* came to him before he quelled it with whiskey.

"I have the sickness of worry about my sister," Argus said, taking another little nip of liquor. The heat led to a kind of singeing in his chest.

Owen had noticed that Argus's English faltered whenever he was nervous or anxious. Properly drunk, the boy might start up in tongues. "I'm sure everything is fine. Tomorrow the clipper will come and we'll work out how to get the horse off the island."

"And bring back feathers for the Tikalia," Argus reminded him.

"Yes, the feathers as well."

After a while the fire all but died, but the moon came up full and bright. The old mare chewed in the broad-bladed grasses up from the beach, black and white as a Holstein, its ponderous head dipping in and out of the leafy shadows like a derrick.

"Is it true a ship's captain can marry lovers at sea?" Argus asked.

Owen smiled at the turn of phrase. "Technically, I suppose that is true."

"This worries me. What if Master Terrapin decides to marry himself to my sister?"

Owen took the whiskey flask in mild disparagement at the idea. "In the first place, I don't think the fat old sod wants to marry your sister. He just wants some company in the stateroom. And in the second place, I don't think a captain could marry himself. It wouldn't seem right. The admiralty wouldn't stand for it."

Argus leaned forward conspiratorially. "The captain's head is very large. Have you noticed?"

Owen grinned. "A ghastly thing! The ship heels to leeward on account of that enormous crown."

Argus shot out a laugh, part of it through his nose. "Will you have a very big wedding?"

"If it were left up to me it would be the two of us, a preacher, and two civil witnesses dragged in at random from Michigan Avenue. But it seems Adelaide will have her way with a big wedding and my side of the church embarrassingly empty."

"Your family will not come?"

Owen shook his head. "All dead."

"Mine too. Sister is all I have."

With mock gravity Owen declared, "The world is full of orphans," then, a moment later, "I must be getting drunk."

"My heart is fighting with my ears."

"Good. That means it's working. An empty stomach does the trick." It felt good to be drunk again. How odd that he kept himself sober among the bawdy seamen but gave himself license to drink freely with the pious houseboy. There was a chastity to Argus that demanded resistance in the same way that a month of Adelaide's charity and altruism demanded at least one alehouse bender. The smell of saloon sausages and eggs on the skirt of a Sunday morning had kept him sane all through their courtship, this secret communion of the damned. He would give her nine-tenths of his body, mind, and soul, and keep the remainder for himself. That seemed like a fair proposition.

Argus said, "My blood is all smoke and whiskey. It makes me want to pray to the Holy Ghost."

Owen said, "Don't get religious on me. I was partially raised by nuns and they left me sore about God."

"I can't help it. I am drunk with God also."

"Steady now. A man should never say exactly what he's thinking when he's drunk. Least of all about religion or politics."

"Oh. I see."

The night fishermen were dragging their dugouts through the surf and the two watched them paddle out beyond the breakers. The torches were lit and the nets ghosted over the waves like clouds. They spoke more about Chicago and America, about doughnuts and underground trains and tall buildings. They spoke about the way Argus would meet his future wife in a department store.

Owen said, "She will be shopping for lacy undergarments and you will buy her lunch in the cafeteria."

"What will we eat?" Argus asked.

"Ham sandwiches and cake."

"That sounds very good to me at present."

They stared into the dying fire for a moment, hungry and smitten with the thought of real food.

After mulling it over for a few moments, Argus said, "Or I might meet her in a big church with carved pews. Imagine taking communion in a cathedral of stained glass. That is something I would like to do."

"Let's go swimming," Owen said, standing. He threw the empty flask by the fire.

Argus followed him down to the water's edge and watched as Owen stripped naked and plunged into the waves. The sight of a white man's body had always been unnatural to Argus; the spackled limbs and luminous buttocks seemed to demand coverage. Owen began swimming out through the surf, his face in the ocean. The fishermen watched the naked clayskin from their dugouts, cursing him for scaring the shoaling fish. Argus took off his shirt only and folded it neatly on the sand. He waded into the surf and let it break around his stomach. The water was warm and it made the air feel cooler than it was. He had always disliked putting his face underwater; the salt burned his eyes and mouth. Owen was waving to him and hollering. Argus held his nose, pinched his eyes shut, and dived beneath an oncoming wave. The surge of the ocean in his eardrums turned the drunkenness into something leaden and dark. When he came up for air, he felt horribly afraid that he was not going to make it back to shore. He tried to call out to Owen but the trader was already mid-stroke into an Australian crawl, his legs and arms thrashing as he rose up the face of a wave. Argus let the waves pummel him back into the shallows so that he could stand again. He shivered slightly, exposed to the cooling air from the waist up. He watched Owen swim wildly past the breakers then return to shore on a single wave. Naked, invigorated, Owen jogged up the sand from the ocean and for a moment, with his arms raised and his head back, he looked like a man resurrected.

The *Cullion* finally appeared the next afternoon on the leeward side of the reef, her canvas quarter-set and drawing. The tide was coming in and the weirs were filling up. The bark took in sail as she approached the coral skirt and came onto a broad reach and prepared to heave to. In silhouette, Owen could see the entire crew on deck and the chief's canoe being towed astern. It looked as if additional cargo had been placed in the pull-behind, perhaps some of the naturalist's spoils. Good, because he would need all the room he could get for his windfall. Argus broke camp and they dragged the laden rowboat down to the water's edge. They looked back at the tethered mare, still eating in the copse of trees, and for a brief moment Owen contemplated leaving the animal behind. Then Argus trotted up the beach and led it down to the sand with the sapling hackamore, its eyes walled, nervous in every hoof-step. Owen steadied the wooden prow into the knee-high waves. The decorated and braided nag stood indignant at the waterline and Argus came in front to pull hard. Owen tossed him a rope, ten fathoms of old halyard, and Argus attached it to the hackamore's crosspiece. Without a metal bit in its mouth the tow-line was going to pull mostly around the creature's sinewy neck but it was all they had. Owen backed up the boat, keeping the prow into the surf, and they took the rope together and began to haul.

A few of the Tikalia gathered on the beach to watch the white man and the Christian kanaka reclaim the god-horse. They were leaving as clumsily as they had arrived. The horse got its front fetlocks wet and flexed its haunches in defiance. *Come on now,* Owen was saying. They wrapped the rope around their waists and shouldered out onto the sandbank. The mare snorted then buckled forward. All four hooves were now in the water but the horse reared its head up and began to sink into the sand. For good measure, it pebbled out a few pounds of dung when it flexed in terror. Owen told Argus to get up behind it and whack its hind-quarters but the resulting slap was more conciliatory than any-thing else. Owen untied the rope from his waist and let Argus take the boat. He took up an extra length of halyard and went behind the mare and whipped it sheer across the rump. In a show of temper and dexterity, the horse shot out a hind leg like a piston and caught Owen full in the stomach. He fell back, swearing and burning for air, drenched to the hat felt.

Argus called out but Owen told him to keep the boat pointed into the waves. He strained up, clutching his rib cage. *Bitch of a horse* was all he could manage to say. The horse turned its head to keep him in its periphery. Owen knew as much about horses as he did about dogs, which was very little. Some inherited idea of showing them who's boss and not looking too deeply into their uncanny bay-brown eyes. He skirted round, considering the dilemma from all angles, ready to flay the animal bloody with the halyard.

"Let me try," said Argus, calling above the surf.

Owen spat and waded forward to take the prow of the boat while Argus advanced upon the creature. The boy leaned into the horse and started voicing hymns and rubbing its flank like a lover so that Owen could barely watch. The grizzled old mare snarled its lips, bared its big yellow teeth, thrashed its tail in response. Undeterred, Argus kept combing its hair and shell-braided withers with his hands and that gospel voice gushing quietly into one pricked ear. Some little clicking noises with his mouth eventually moved the horse a few feet forward, the seawater now to its shanks. With the water girding higher, Owen was able to find some traction as the waves shifted the sand beneath the horse's hooves. The rope strained around his waist and Argus pulled close to its mane. In this fashion, a few feet at a time, they managed to get the mare to its dappled girth and barrel, its nostrils flared and snorting. Owen jumped into the rowboat and pulled on the oars, the rope still attached. A big wave shoaled off the reef and forced the mare to break free of the sand in order to keep its muzzle dry. It rode up the wave, braying madly, and Owen pulled on the oars and the god had no choice but to swim. Argus scrambled into the boat and kept a hold of the towline.

They rowed into the narrow channel through the heads of coral, Owen turning now and then to sight the *Cullion*'s broadside. The old mare snuffled and gurgled with unnameable humiliation but continued to paddle forward, doglike, ears back, wild-eyed. The trade items were wet but intact, cinched to the gunwales and partially covered by tarps. They made it out past the breakers and the reef's serrated edge. Argus held the towline tightly, his hands burning with the rope, but he almost let go when he saw the tall, skinny naturalist sitting in the tribal canoe that trailed the ship. Owen saw something register in the boy's face and he stopped rowing to turn and take it in. Jethro Gray sat hatless in a grimy oiled guernsey, his face horribly sunburnt, dead birds and stuffed lizards and bottled frogs piled high on all sides. For a moment Owen thought of the effigy in the hold, the sculpture of smoked human skin and the taut, bloodless expression in the eye sockets and hinged jaw. The insurance heir did not move but stared back in a stupor, mouth open like a thirsty cat, apparently incurious that a slavering horse was being pulled behind a rowboat. Owen called out to him and waved but he failed to stir from his trance or show any sign of comprehension. Something moved in the prow of the canoe and Owen saw the mongoose, then the wallaby, then the Siamese cat and the clip-winged green parrot. The Djimbanko stowaways had also been banished.

Whatever had occurred while Owen was on the island would require his immediate intervention, that much seemed obvious, but for now he had a horse to load. He pulled the boat amidships and told Argus to take the oars. The horse was exhausted and rasping for air. One of the crew dropped a rope ladder and Owen pulled himself up to the deck. The seamen were equipped with armory rifles and all eyes turned to Terrapin stumping down from the poop, Smith & Wesson in hand, an affable sort of aspect about him, like a man coming out of a chophouse after a good meal, not so much a smile for Owen Graves as a proclamation of right order composed with his whole massive face.

"Things took a turn, they did. Lovelace went south on us and I had to isolate him, put him in the tow-behind with the animal stowaways. Restore some semblance of calm. He can come back aboard just as soon as the carpenter finishes his commission." Terrapin pointed with glinting gunmetal at the man-sized wooden cage that was taking shape on the quarterdeck from pallets and tea chests and crossbeams. The captain had gone mad, perhaps the whole ship, that much seemed apparent. Then came a boyish scream from below and they all went to the bulwarks to see the horse foundering and Argus in a state. The mare thrashed, struggled for breath, went under, threatened to take the rowboat down with her.

Owen yelled for Argus to untie the rope from the stern and he did so but there remained the spectacle of drowning, of the god-horse kicking along an invisible beach before submitting to the maul below. Terrapin, in his keen and fragile state, discharged

the Smith & Wesson and put the glue-horse out of its misery—
straight into the diamond of white on its forehead. It sank bodily
and at peace, filaments of blood climbing to the surface. Terrapin
said, "These latitudes are poisoned, runneled with cyanide clouds
and gas-blue ether that passes for air . . ." He turned to the first
mate and said, "Fire up the engines, Mr. Pym."

Owen prepared to broker and summon common sense, but
the seamen were already hauling the rowboat up on the davits, the
mission boy rising with it like a stage actor on a rigged-up scow.
Malini came running from somewhere and the siblings embraced.
What is happening? Argus wanted to know, but Malini already
carried the weight of the silence and knew that things would run
their course. She understood now about America. The engines
rumbled to life, coalsmoke billowing in the sails, the air rattling
and choking with soot as the *Lady Cullion* surged north, its wake
ten fathoms wider under a head of steam. And beyond that trailing wrack of foam, beyond the towed canoe plowing the glazed
waters, the dead horse resurfaced and rode the incoming tide,
across the skirting coral, floating back to its little Elba of twenty
years, where it had lived like a ruminant. The Tikalia found it
beached and half hacked by reef sharks and they cursed the clayskins for all eternity—*may your fathers eat filth* repeated with the
devoutness of prayer.

VI

HOMECOMING

27.

If Hale Gray had believed in omens instead of destiny he might have been unsettled by the steamship foundering on the lake. It was full of uncrated Steinway pianos, concert grands hewn from rock maple and spruce, and they were being hoisted, one by one, onto a narrow shelf of ice for fear the steamer might sink at any moment. The ship had struck the ice in the foggy dawn, her horn bleating for hours like some animal dying out in a field. One of his vice presidents had called it to his attention and they stood watching on the rooftop in the early light, a viewing party of six or seven bundled men, opera glasses poised and someone narrating the rescue's progress: *That makes three floating on the island of ice . . . now the winch hooks are going back to the deck for another Steinway.* They watched as if it were a kind of calculated violence, a lynching or firing squad execution. They smoked cigars in muffled fur caps, tycoons of the upper drafts.

As it turned out, Hale carried the insurance policy for the Lyon & Healy Music Store, the concern attempting to import this particular shipment of pianos from out east. The store was a favorite sanctuary from the din of State and Clark, a showroom of gold-crowned harps and ebony-glossed pianos, where the salesmen all had the handshakes of diplomats and the smell of sheet music and French walnut was hypnotic. As far as Hale was concerned—and he didn't mind telling his underlings this— the pianos, though paid for in advance, were in the official care of the factory until signed delivery at the storefront had occurred. *Expect no losses on this account, gentlemen.*

Just then the ship listed and yawed. *Now she's rolling like a sperm whale,* the narrator announced. The harbormaster and the fireboats had rescued most of the crew but two men remained in charge of the derrick. Five pianos had been lowered to the ice but the steamer appeared to be going under with several instruments in the hold and one suspended in midair, now lowering, its black legs dipping into the lake. The two derrick operators jumped as the ship went under. Bubbles rose and broke on the surface; the men were plucked from the icy waters. After the steamer had disappeared from sight, the insurance executives watched and smoked in the cold. An aura of filmy residue formed in the steamer's watery footprint. Hale watched the black Steinways drift on the little ice shelf and then a grain barge looked set to haul them aboard. It was an occasion for hope, he thought, not because several grand pianos had corkscrewed and trilled their way to the frigid lake floor, but because the size of the shipment showed the economy was on the mend. He couldn't help wondering who was buying all those pianos.

The viewing party dispersed and Hale took note of the preparations for building the native set. He imagined this was how a stage director might feel in his contemplations—there was a growing sense of theatrical possibility mounting beside pragmatic concern. For example, the trade-off between how much space to devote to the staging area and how much to the audience. Should he include a photographer's concession so that visitors could have their likeness taken beside the South Sea Islanders? Where would refreshments be served and should they have a native theme? Coconut milk in frosted glasses? There was a platform erected in the foreground of the clock tower and the frame for a single hut. Where were they going to get bamboo at the end of February? Or sand and palms, for that matter. On the other hand, an opening day of May 1 gave him plenty of time. He'd received a telegram from the trader in Hawaii indicating that artifacts were plentiful but that only two islanders had been contracted. That was better than nothing, but now his plans had to be scaled back. A brother and sister hardly comprised a village but he would have the designer capitalize on that diminished number, set a tone of savage siblings marooned at the top of the world. *From the ends of the earth to the top of the world.* That was a phrase the marketing department might use. If a potential policyholder didn't think his life was worth insuring after such a sight then he was beyond redemption.

He took the stairs and decided to complete one of his impromptu tours of the building, wending his way from management and sales to clerking before bottoming-out in typing and filing. He enjoyed the look of submerged terror among his employees as he walked the floors in his rubber soles. They never heard him coming until they were ambushed and had to thrust out *good morning, sirs* like bayonets. As he walked, he listened to the tenor of the desktop conversations, tried to gauge the view from the ground, like a general eavesdropping outside a barracks. In this way he heard about infidelities and secret lunch dates, about babies and christenings, about baseball defeats and horse-racing wins, but also about the speculation that the blighted windows of the First Equitable were ready to pop their frames. The rumors were becoming mythic: the colossus was sinking and leaning into a field of clay, a foot a week if you believed the stories, the Pisa of La Salle Street, and pretty soon the windows would explode from their casings and the elevators would tilt and spark against the darkened shafts. Hale had sent memos, invited an eminent engineer to deliver confident remarks during a luncheon, made official announcements to quell the rumors, but all of it to no avail. People feared in droves—a boon for the insurance game—and no amount of reason could dissuade them.

He soft-shoed across the floor and caught a whole tribe of clerks studying one of the ill-glazed windows. They traced their fingers across its opaque mottlings as if they could divine the future. "Gentlemen," Hale called from behind, "the murkier windows are merely designed to prevent distraction at every turn, so that you don't spend the day watching clouds or your own reflections." The clerks straightened, coughed, retrieved pencils from behind ears in a burst of industry. Hale enjoyed the look on their faces. Walking away, he said, "Someone bring me the Lyon & Healy policy."

28.

Malini watched the world freeze over from her window. The flatlands banked in white, the blueless sky. Ever since leaving the ship, the sun had moved like a dull rumor behind an ocean of cloud. Incredulous, she saw signs of human life in the cold barrens—smoky-breathed animals shambling in icy fields, men cutting fallen trees with enormous hatchets, yellow light coming from neat wooden houses. There were bridges across swollen rivers and level, wide roads. Most of the trees were as bare as driftwood and it made her lonely to look at them. She recognized pigs and dogs, knew about horses and wagons. People and animals trudged through the dull landscape, fell away, came back someplace else. Some things moved faster than others; fences and trees rushed by close and whirring while frozen fields floated along the horizon. If she looked at the whirring her eyes hurt and she felt like throwing up. It reminded her of looking at the moving pictures in the belly of the ship. She cinched her heavy coat about her shoulders and felt the cold against the rattling windowpane. This was civilization, the big fella's place, so cold you could barely breathe. An oven was going in the back of the clattering room on wheels, *carriage,* and the air brimmed with farting and burning coal and wet clothes, just the way the ship had smelled in the final weeks of the voyage. She was glad to be off the ship. Once ashore, she had accepted the captain's apology and he'd told her he would no longer go to sea. One of his halfblood children was coming to visit him, a Tahitian boy, and he had a letter waiting in dock to prove it. She told no one about what had happened in the orlop, had banished it from her thoughts.

The heavy smells of cooking filled the carriage. Half of what was being eaten around her she did not recognize or acknowledge as food. Old whitefellas with beards spooned up something brown and smoking while others, families of tired women and bleak-faced children, ate gristled cuts of meat. The captain's food had been unfamiliar but came in tins or on plates; what she saw before her now was wrapped in pieces of greasy paper or skewered on flimsy wooden sticks. Something the color of taro rolled in a husk and drizzled with bloodred sauce. She recognized pig's feet but could not overcome the Poumetan bias against any part of an animal that trod the earth. The snow continued to fall like white leaves outside her window.

She was hungry but refused to eat. The people who shared the wooden benches with her offered some of their unsightly food. No thank you, she told them, proud of her English. She knew more than fifty words by now but Argus had told her to act like a highlander in Chicago, a Kuk tree dweller come down for the first time. This would be their job of work. But she had no intention of parting with the wool coat—it was like a blanket sewn up with buttons. While the parents across from her ate, she took their baby for a stint, patting its little rump and letting it look at the white whirring outside the window. They were black people like herself, even darker, and she liked seeing so many different-colored faces in the crowded carriage. She had never before seen Chinamen or Africans or Mexicans and found herself studying their mouths and eyes and hands when they weren't looking. Their languages and accents filled the carriage with clipped words and singing phrases, with hushed arguments and nighttime whispers, with murmurings so soft and liquid they sounded like a river flowing by. She'd heard the uniformed ticket man call the bustling carriage a Zulu Car and she wanted to ask Argus what that meant. She touched the baby's head with the tip of her nose as it stared and blinked out the window; it smelled like sun-warmed clay. After some minutes, lulled by the rocking motion, the baby snuggled in her lap and she felt a ball of heat spread across her middle. Sometimes, when she held babies, her breasts throbbed and ached and it made her cry. She patted the baby's back and a belch shot out from its mouth. The parents shrugged, smiled, ate. Malini began singing it to sleep. She sang about a mother turtle coming ashore to lay her eggs and die and soon the baby's body went limp. She saw Argus watching from across the aisle, where he sat with Owen Graves. The tall, skinny one, the ghostskin, rode in the back of the train with a bed made of feathers and boys serving him brandy. Malini had not seen him since the ship but knew he was back there. She closed her eyes, feeling the baby's milky breath against her neck. She thought about all of these people moving together, about sitting on her bum at such a speed—as fast as any man could run, mile after white mile. Somewhere in the back of the train, boxed and tied up in string with all the suitcases, were the dead birds and lizards from the islands, the bottled jellyfish and starfish, the honeybees pinned to sheets of paper. Some had been lost and ruined in the canoe, where the captain had banished the tall one, but many had been saved. She thought of them coming back to life, of the carriage door opening in Chicago to reveal a shrieking flock of gold-breasted birds, a flurry of angry wasps, a swarm of stinging jellyfish living in air.

It was just after dawn when they got to the outskirts of Chicago. Argus and Owen stood smoking in the vestibule between railcars, watching the sun strain up through a cloth of weather. In the windy gaps above the coupling head they could see the rattling undercarriage, sparks flinting against the gunmetal rails in the early light. The train slowed in the vicinity of the stockyards, a mile or two shy, and Owen watched the boy's face sour as they got their first premonition of the city—the ammoniac anthem of the feedlots and slaughterhouses, a stench of animal dung and charred fur and beef tallow. Then there was some hint of lime or cinders as they passed a tanning yard and saw butchery wagons unloading, their beds piled heavy with steaming bones. A man in coveralls was spreading ash over the fetid ground.

"Smells a bit like the *Lady Cullion*," Owen said, grinning.

Argus pulled the lapel of his greatcoat over his nose.

"My dad used to bring me out here when I was a kid. All of America practically gets its meat from here." It was a boast and only half true; he could feel his hometown pride coming in.

Argus saw pigs and cows lowing behind fences, enough animals to sponsor a lifetime of feasts. He asked about butchering and keeping the meat fresh because he wanted to understand everything about America. Owen told him what he knew, about railcars stacked with ice and the migration of steak and pork chops. Argus would study their customs like a foreign language. The first rule was to mimic, but before he could imitate he would have to put on a tribal show. *Strut the boards.* He could do that, he knew, imitate someone savage and godless for three months, bend to their expectation of a heathen, a wily kanaka. Him and his sister dancing and chanting tribal oaths on the rooftop, if that's what it took, but in the end he was destined for something entirely different. God was at work, seeding the field of his future—a bishopric with oriel windows and a garden of antique roses came again to mind; he would be of service and study the scriptures at night, become a seminarian, take to wearing spectacles and ale-colored weskits, find a Christian wife, a black girl who also felt the call, whose life had been riven, like his, by a fervor for the Holy Ghost. The skyline came into view—hard-edged silhouettes jutting against the formless sky, the soft diffusion of daybreak mirrored back, squared-off in the countless windows, then, as the train rounded a bend, the sun broke through in a glassy flare, a burst of Orient gold. They watched the light glint and quake off the buildings, silent for a full minute.

As the train approached the Loop, Owen began to reminisce, yelling to be heard—his father shooting deer on the south branch of the river, within living memory, near the west side of the gasworks, an ex-minister to Persia, the honorable F. H. Winston, riding a white horse, same as Napoleon's, every morning along the lakeshore, the very word *horse* like an expletive in his mouth after the business on Tikalia. His stomach was still on the mend from the animal's kick and he had a hoof-shaped bruise just below his sternum. As the city drew them in, he told Argus about hitching rides from wagons in the lumber district during his Tabernacle days and about stealing a slab from the iceman (who carried a long-handled axe!) midsummer, keeping the cake of ice like a foundling in straw and sawdust for weeks, concealed beneath the dormitory piers, unwrapping the muslin when no one else was around. It was all in secret, the block of ice like a giant, embezzled diamond.

He hollered such memories at Argus, who feigned interest even if he didn't catch every word above the train's clatter. Owen realized, by listening to his own booming voice, that the stories were a way of talking himself back, of preparing to be with Adelaide again. He was nervous, chatty, winded with anticipation. He wanted to talk and smoke off the nerves so he could come to her with some presence of mind. He would have to tell amusing stories and recount the strange islands over dinner. For months he'd been accountable to no one, showed up to meals and traded, but he'd shared nothing of his inner hopes and ambitions, had guarded them closely. She would want that and much more; he would have to begin again. The slow seduction of lapbound napkins and hearing her recite poems or the lilting immigrant songs from Hull House; most of it entailed listening but some of it, he recalled, involved the revelation of innermost character, of *selfhood,* as if that were anything more than a cipher, more than that scintillation off the windowpanes as the sun surged and fell back in the east. He pointed out the tallest building to Argus and told him that was where they were headed. To the highest mountain of glass, Argus said, tossing his cigarette out into the rushing cold.

It was a Monday morning and there was no welcoming party at the train station. This was Owen's doing—he'd neglected to telegraph the details of their arrival, either to Hale Gray or to Adelaide at the museum. He suspected it was an oversight, but perhaps it was by design. He wanted to first see his fiancée in private and the memory of the Gray family during their departure was still fresh in his mind, the convoy of teary aunts trailing behind Jethro's mountain of kidskin. That same luggage was returning in tatters, cankerous with salt and little starbursts of sea-green mold. The son had not fared much better. From the platform, Owen watched him step gingerly down from the hotel car, the fencing glove on his left hand, an insomniac and drawn look on his face. His face was sun-scalded and the eyes, coldly distant, held the febrile blue of child-hood illness. The dandy's nerves were shot and Owen suspected a loud handclap might send him over the brink.

There was a distance of a hundred yards between them and Owen had no intention of bridging the gap. He had intervened on Jethro's behalf, brokered a treaty at considerable expense with the manic captain, in return for the heir's cooperation. There would be no divulging to Hale of the native siblings' true station in the tribal world, that the brother, outside a few faltering phrases, spoke a scholar's English. Jethro moved uncertainly down the platform toward the baggage compartment, apparently to oversee the unloading of his specimens. The porters hefted the boxes and cases and tanks, began lugging them onto dollies and carts. Suddenly animated, Jethro scolded them to be gentle with his cargo. The arti-facts, along with the canoe, were packed in a separate compartment so that Owen could avoid standing beside him. Argus and Malini alighted in the exhausted flow of immigrants and they joined him on the platform, already shivering in the cavernous station.

Owen arranged for all the artifacts, the canoe, as well as Jethro's taxidermied spoils to be transported to the insurance building. He would find a hansom for himself and the siblings, but Jethro could fend for himself. Owen was hours away from completing this colossal errand—receiving payment and getting a foothold on a new life—and he was suddenly impatient to be unyoked from the feckless son. He would simply tell Hale that

Jethro was in good health, perhaps a little fatigued, and would be along shortly with his seaweed albums and bottled seahorses. That ought to get a single-malt chortle out of the old baron.

The hansom pulled into the frenzy of the streets and Owen couldn't help feeling as if he were crossing a threshold. A native son to this city, he was returning under changed circumstances. By the end of the week he hoped to look at houses where he and Adelaide might live after the wedding. The trade payment would put a sizable dent in a mortgage, especially if they found a fixer. His own house. He did not take up the thought of her father's possible death or the threat of a looming inheritance. Instead, as they rode into the din, he thought *Here comes Porter Graves's kid*, raised as much by doormen and demolitionists as by his own father and the whey-faced nuns. He missed that time, longed for communion with the boy who, at age thirteen, had a smoker's consumptive laugh and was a confidant to dog fanciers and druggists airing grievances out on their stoops. Adultery, larceny, gambler's remorse, nothing was held back from their confessions to the orphan on the lam. Could a man pray to his boyhood self, send back worship like a telegram, reassure the little sniveler that all would end well? A pretty wife, a promising house on a third-acre plot, take heart. He was drunk with his own return and wanted to launch a Sioux cry out the window of the cab. He loved this town in a way that confounded him, caught in the back of his throat—the bawling, mongrel side streets, the midwinter offerings of the curbstone vendors (meat, hothouse flowers, blankets), the singing blind man hawking pencils from a tin box on Washington, the big-bayed windows of State Street, as if the city couldn't get enough of her own brash reflection. He turned to see if some of this wonderment was lit into the faces of the native brother and sister but he saw nothing but cold and wincing confusion. He pointed his stupid grin out the window to let them have their moment of bracing contact.

Argus felt sick riding into the wall of noise and traced it to a wedge of cheese he'd eaten on the train. Cow's milk didn't agree with him, he knew that now, and he would have to develop a tolerance. Perhaps a constitutional piece of cheddar each night before bed, just the way the Reverend Mister had taken sulfonal for wakefulness. Owen sat next to one window and his sister had the other, so everything Argus saw of the chaotic city was above dreadlocked, black hair or crowned around a felt hat. He looked at his shoes when a wave of nausea threatened to brim the banks of his stomach. He counted his breaths, first in English, then in Poumetan, then in pidgin. The cold ached in his bones and he wanted to bathe. He'd spent six years hearing about distant lands and imagining cities, but there were things he could never have guessed—dogs on leashes, dray horses feeding from nosebags, bicycles dusted in snow, placard advertisements for dentists and undertakers nailed to tree branches, the view of the enormous lake choked with ice, the clay-red buildings as tall as cliffs, their hundred postage stamps of windowlight. He couldn't discern, for now, what was beautiful and what was ugly but knew that it all moved too quickly and with too much noise. Malini had her hands over her ears as a delivery wagon blocked the way and their own driver incited a tirade in the street. Every driver and pedestrian within a half-mile radius began screaming blue murder at the wayward wagon, an assault of such profanity and violence that Argus feared someone might actually get killed or injured, feared pistols and bloodshed, but then there were big guffaws and belches of belly laughter from the box seat above their heads and ridicule came hurling with laughter from open windows on all sides. Even Owen leaned out his window to lend a hand in the humiliation. He pulled his head back inside, wild with good humor—*Welcome to Chicago!*

First Monday of March and Hale Gray was getting his monthly shave-and-trim in his office. The white-smocked barber, a man with the demeanor of a jeweler, of someone who spent hours bent at close work, went at the ruffle of unsightly neck hair with something like religious devotion. The straight razor made a few scratches at a time before being wiped free on the hand towel. Hale was in his singlet, the doors were closed, his face still stinging with the ablutions of a hot lather shave. This tradition of ushering in the month with personal grooming always made him hungry for a substantial lunch, a steak so rare it made him consider his own mortality. Insurance was a great, pragmatic philosophy to Hale; a wager against God but also an acknowledgment that death could come hurtling through at any moment, bloody or benign, slow and grueling, or, with tremendous luck, merciful and swift. He had his head down to let the barber razor his collar line, eyes closed, the smell of lather and tonic a bit thick for his liking—was he being embalmed or barbered? When he opened his eyes he saw them enter under the shambling auspices of his frumpy new secretary—Owen Graves and two savages buttoned up in wool coats, eyes averted, the lot of them, as if this ritual of barbering were a single rung above bloodletting.

"You've caught me in the throes of the monthly trim. Don't worry. We're almost done here. Please have a seat and I'll be right with you. Fetch our guests some coffee and cake would you, Miss Ballentine?"

The underwriters called her type a lumpy dresser and Hale watched her shuffle out of the room. Could an Iowa girl with a first name of Lulu be trusted with company letterhead? Some scrolled papers arrived for signature, the document capsule thucking in the pneumatic tube behind Hale's desk.

The sound reminded Argus of a dog clearing its windpipe.

Hale continued to study the savages and on several occasions the barber had to adjust his head back down. "I take it we're all in one piece?"

"All things considered, we're in fine shape, sir. Your son is tending to some details at the train station and should be along shortly."

"Very well. How did he fare?"

"At the very least, he had an adventure."

"Did him good, no doubt. And tell me of the collectibles."

Owen produced a handwritten inventory from his coat pocket and brought it forward.

Hale took it and began reading, head still down, the paper in his lap. He made a series of nods and murmurs before speaking in a cryptic tone: *And how am I supposed to get a canoe into my office, Mr. Graves?*

Owen shrugged, stalling.

The barber wiped Hale's collar line with a steaming towel, dried it briskly, made some whisking motions with a neck duster before releasing the insurance baron to a standing position. Hale buttoned up his pressed shirt with a half-turn away from the black girl. Tucked in, buoyed, and close-shaven, he shook Owen's hand with slow, emphatic movements. "This is something," Hale said, pumping. "You've bettered the Marshall Field collection and then some. South Seas ethnographica is now my niche, I would imagine. Maybe I'll turn the whole building into a museum. Ha! I knew you were a top-notcher when I laid eyes on you the day of the opening. Picture me in that chief's canoe on the sooty river in June. Or down at the yacht club for the commodore's amusement. No, it'll be preserved and hoisted somewhere. Bravo!" He still had hold of Owen's hand as he directed his attention to the siblings, their stiff woolen backs turned at the glass-fronted display case. Behind the glass doors Argus recognized some tribal weapons from the island of Poumeta.

Owen pried himself free as Hale continued: "Now, let me get a good look at our guests. Will they take their coats off? Never mind. Must be chilly for them, no?"

Argus and Malini turned to face Hale but kept their coats buttoned. Owen introduced them by name and said that Mr. Gray was Jethro's father and the man who funded the voyage. Argus nodded, smiled, but knew better than to shake hands. Malini was surprised by the old man's solid build and athletic bearing; he was nothing like the fence post of a son. Hale deliberated, took a few paces toward them like a theater director about to dispense insight to thespians, then stopped short: "I assume there are, what, grass skirts and loincloths, that sort of thing?"

Owen couldn't bring himself to answer and the room fell quiet, the slate sky darkening the high windows. Miss Ballentine returned with a cart of clattering refreshments and Malini thought again of the train, of sitting on her backside for days without end. She was beyond hungry and would eat whatever they offered. The curdled feeling she carried in her stomach from the elevator—a flying room not much bigger than an outhouse—was beginning to subside. In the slight commotion of tinkling spoons and china and water glasses, Hale seized the barber's scissors from a metal tray and caught Malini off guard. Lulu Ballentine brought the cart to a full stop, asked whether the darkies drank tea or coffee, but as she did so they all turned to see Hale holding one of Malini's dreadlocks between thumb and forefinger, raising it in the air like a kitchen mouse. Stunned, they watched Hale take the dreadlock over to the barber to ask his professional opinion. *Not exactly lustrous,* was the quip he offered, *but very sturdy and thick.* A second later Malini crossed the room to snatch back her stolen hair, gripped by the idea of clayskin sorcery, by the memory of the old man's son counting and measuring her teeth to what end she couldn't tell but knew it to be dark. Hale arched his freshly pruned eyebrows, then shot Owen a glance. Again, as on the ship, Owen was the intermediary. "Sir, the natives don't like their bodily parts touched, especially the hair. Has to do with black magic."

Hale folded his arms as Malini returned to her brother beside the display case. "Ah, I see, then, well, should we have our refreshments and take a tour of the exhibit I'm building on the rooftop? I think you'll be pleased. The first of May is the scheduled opening. Should be a spot warmer by then. Black magic, you say?"

And then, with his own kind of black magic, the barber packed up his shears and straps, the ivory combs and unguents, all of it cinched neatly into a leather case, like a physician's bag, and with such precision that Argus couldn't help thinking of customized luggage, of how much he wanted a Gladstone bag with his own monogrammed initials blazed in gold. The barber took a piece of cake for the road, holding it in a paper serviette with his free hand — "In a month, Mr. Gray, just like clockwork."

Hale turned to his guests and gestured to the sitting area. "Most barbershops are underground in this city and I refuse to be lured into their dank lairs. I gave Bart a concession and storefront in the lobby and he's played it up strong. Our clerks and managers get a discount, of course. He comes up here by special arrangement. Cake?"

They drank coffee in cups that sat on little white plates. Malini had a second piece of cake and didn't regret it — it tasted of nuts and honey. The coffee, on the other hand, was so strong it felt like a wasp was trapped and buzzing in her chest. The white men were talking about the weather in Chicago and in the islands; *snow* and *typhoon* were two of the English words she knew. Her brother sat quietly, studying the things in the big glass case, pretending not to know anything. After a while they were taken to the roof of the tall building, this time on a staircase. They were outside again and the sky was so low she could have touched it with her fingers. There was a policeman walking around, shoulders up against the weather. Again the cold; it felt like her bones might shatter. She squinted against the snowy glare. The hair thief was pointing this way and that, yelling to be heard above the wind — a monsoon bearing ice instead of rain. When she widened her eyes a little she saw something that resembled a bamboo hut, made poorly and tied with twine instead of rattan or sennit. The roof sagged and there were no eaves. Some brownish wet sand, clumped with snow, had been piled outside and above it all was the biggest clock she had ever seen, a pale moonface rimmed with giant numbers. Weather and time; she was beginning to understand that these were two of the clayskin gods. And then the way her brother started poking around the bamboo hut and gesturing to the white men as if he were a Kuk clansman gave her to understand that this was why they'd been brought here. This was the job. Live in a hut that looked as if it had been built by a child—a stupid one at that. In Poumetan, her brother told her that for now they would be living in rooms in the tall building. He said the sun would be out in two months and that's when they would be moving to the hut. She told him that they had better make a decent hut first, with separate rooms, and that the sand smelled like cat piss. He turned back to the whitefellas and a second later the son appeared on the rooftop. Her whole body shuddered. She couldn't hear or understand what they were saying. The father and son shook hands and Jethro took off his glove to display his mutilated fingertip.

They all walked over to the place where the sky began. Malini had been aware of the high, churning air in her peripheral vision but walking toward it she felt her legs blunder at the knees. She had been on top of volcanoes many times but for years had lived among the nearsighted Kuk, in a village where a thirty-foot clearing constituted the horizon. If you wanted to see the ocean you had to climb to the uppermost branches of a teak and only the children bothered. She slowed and let the others go ahead. They stepped up onto a wooden platform and Argus showed off by taking two connected glass tubes, one for each eye, and looking through them, as if the unpeeled sky and the stony chasm weren't close enough already. They beckoned to her with smiling faces but she stayed put. As it was she looked up and felt an unbroken thread between her stomach and the swirling clouds and then, moving her gaze out toward that sea they called a *lake*, she felt the dream where she was out of her body but somehow walking across the ocean floor. She felt the heaviness of deep water. The wind blew hard against her face; the sky was going to fall on her and she wanted to be inside again. Another piece of cake might do the trick. The wave of dread pinned her in place as she remembered, with clarity, the son's breath hot in her mouth and ears, the bruises he pressed into her wrists, the wavering candlelight and the burning shame that followed as she got up, trembling with poison, to clean his salt from between her legs. All the while he had sobbed on the floor as if he'd been the one wronged. She felt the weight of this memory like a stone lodged in her mouth.

According to Jethro there was a small glitch in the delivery of the specimens and artifacts. Owen had to hear all the variations of excuse as they rode down in the elevator. He'd made the mistake of letting the heir speak with the deliverymen. Jethro motioned and explained beside his father, trying to get an empathetic word from the tycoon, but Hale was all business, eyes front and center, done up in his Prince Albert coat and derby hat, warning Jethro that he'd better not be late for lunch at the club. Every now and again, as if to ignore Jethro by degrees, Hale exchanged a remark with Benny Boy, on the order of the day and the league team developments and elevator running times top to bottom. Owen suspected that Hale found it hard to look directly into his son's eyes, and he hoped to get his check before some State Street physician shone a light into that dead-blue stare.

"The deliverymen ignored my instructions," Jethro sputtered, "and they were very explicit, down to the letter. Workingmen with delusions of independent thinking, as if we need any more of that."

So far he had made good on his word to keep quiet about the savages. That was something at least. Was the check in Hale's breast pocket?

Malini pressed into the corner of the elevator, but Jethro was still close enough that she could smell his chalky breath. She wished him dead; it came to her with the simplicity of a pebble in her palm.

Argus was the only one in the elevator who commiserated with Jethro as he talked. He listened attentively, feigning incomprehension, a brute overcome with fellow feeling. Argus had been warming to him ever since he'd heard of Jethro facing down the captain to protect his sister.

"A step at a time, son," the baron was saying; "let's get to the loading bays and see what's what."

Jethro pushed forward onto the balls of his feet. "This is what I'm trying to tell you. Ben needs to take us to the lobby instead of the loading bays."

Hale looked directly into the tropical fever or whatever malady lingered behind that wavering regard. "What?"

Benny Boy, bent at the controls, brought the elevator to a gentle rest and into the chiming bells of the lobby. They all piled out and the commotion was already starting up from the cherrywood rotunda and the nookery of cigar shops, shoeshines, newsstands. Half a dozen men in coveralls were stacking wooden crates and a few of the containers were already open, a cotton-stuffed sea eagle emerging from a bed of straw, a tomahawk brandished overhead. Actuary clerks and secretaries were shoulder to shoulder in the lunchtime gawking, a gaggle of pedestrians also, in from the cold, following the hullabaloo to its source. Deliverymen were still bringing in crates and tea chests, the doormen holding the main entrance in an open embrace, and with the snow-spun wind and the debouching of people in through the doorway the chaos of the streets had taken root in Hale's marble lobby. He was powerless to stop it and rested a hand on the bronze bust of his grandfather, waiting for the racket to simmer down. More people—stenographers, typists, commission men—arrived by the elevator-load, straining and jostling, right there with the curious window-shoppers and housewives. Next through the doors came the chiefly canoe, carved with war gods and inlaid with pearl shell, carried like a coffin by four men. Its stately entrance brought a fresh round of jostling and murmurs.

It came to Hale in the commotion that this was something he could use. He didn't have nearly enough room in his office for all the artifacts and he'd never planned on exhibiting Jethro's mothballed specimens. But why not turn the lobby into a museum, at least through the summer, while the native spectacle showed on the rooftop? Keep Jethro busy and away from treatises and chapbooks, give him a chance to find his land legs. A curator of sorts. Why not? The genius of the idea brightened his mood and he went to tell the head watchman to post a few guards and leave the rest of the boxes unopened. He would inventory the items later. Tomorrow he would speak to his master carpenter about display cases. He was mounting another theatrical. The tradesman was probably incapable of museum-grade joinery but so be it; this would be a temporary display, just long enough to drive up interest in the building, pull in the crowds, and, of course, put a damper on admissions at Marshall Field's namesake museum. He donned his hat, buttoned his coat, shot through the cavalry of onlookers. Owen Graves was suddenly at his heels, wordless but clearly on tenterhooks. Ah, the check. Hale could hold out until all items had been properly appraised but he felt flushed with goodwill and found his fingers probing his coat pocket.

The sound of the crisp envelope grazing the silk lining—this is what Owen would recall thereafter. "Put it to good use," Hale said through a clenched, benevolent smile.

"Also," Owen said, hesitantly, "I wonder if I might ask a favor. I'm seeing my fiancée for the first time this evening and I wanted to make it something special. I was wondering if I might bring her to one of the upper floors and show her the view from the rooftop." Owen thought her bias against the building might be cleared away by the panoramic view but also wanted her to meet Argus and Malini, to see that they were being well cared for.

Hale agreed to the proposal and told him to speak with the building manager. And then Hale was at the curbstone, free of the mob, bounding along La Salle in the cold, thinking about lunch and recalling the title of today's noontime club lecture: *Recent Advances in Mesmerism.*

29.

Adelaide saw the driver waiting for her at the bottom of the museum steps, a placard held at chest-level and barely visible in the six o'clock gloaming—*Adelaide Cummings-nearly-Graves.* She knew at once, of course, but was already finding reasons to fan the anger she'd been coaling night and day. On top of the deceit about the natives, he hadn't bothered to telegram his arrival. She had half a mind to keep walking. The driver helped her up onto the covered seat and put a twill blanket over her lap. He poured her a mug of hot chocolate and handed it to her. "Where are you taking me?" she said.

"Strict instructions of secrecy, ma'am," he said, clicking the horse into a trot.

She expected the hansom to forge its way toward the South Side, to Owen's scrapyard, but then they were riding into the Loop, walled in by chiming streetcars, their interiors lit up, ashen faces and worsted coats full-pressed to the windows. She thought briefly that he'd had the decency to choose a good restaurant, but then the cab stopped in front of the towering First Equitable façade and her anger surged; she could barely move. The driver took the blanket and untouched cocoa and helped her down. The street was still thinning from the six o'clock exodus. The building doorman opened one side of the double doors, tipped his cap, told her to make for the elevator. She did as she was told and in her fury failed to notice the packing crates and the canoe that had been banked into an alcove of the lobby, a night watchman standing by with his truncheon. The elevator operator appeared also to be in on the conspiracy because he said, *Evenin', Miss Cummings* as he closed the doors. Adelaide said hello, folded her arms across her chest, settling into her warding-off stance. For what seemed an hour they rode to the upper floors; she stared into the mosaics at her feet, itemizing her complaints, deciding in which order she would bring them to light. Her mother was waiting to have dinner at the hotel and she would have to excuse herself after fifteen minutes. Let him feel some of the cruelty she'd been carrying. But then the bell rang in the lower twenties, somewhere between Underwriting and Management the man said, and her pulse thickened so that her whole throat was swollen with it.

The elevator doors opened onto a gloomy floor still under construction, the columns exposed and unpainted, an acre of drop-clothed desks arranged in rows. There was a hollow of candlelight somewhere up ahead and she had no choice but to walk toward it. The elevator closed behind her with a stutter, followed by a descending hum. She moved forward but refused to call out his name. The perimeter of windows hung washed with late twilight, darkening, a few stars and rooftop beacons pearling up against the chill glass. She thought of drab portraits and then of aquarium tanks, of seeing the shark knife through the underwater murk the day of their first meeting those four years previous. He'd been gone half a year. It astounded her. For an instant, she couldn't picture his face. There was something oceanic about the sky at this hour, seen from this height—she felt as if she were beneath a wave, breaking to the surface, the way the atmosphere poured into the alcoves and stone canyons, stippled faintly with gaslight, the way the boundary between the lake and the shoreline blurred in the near-dark. She was aware of her footsteps, her palms turned and facing forward. He emerged slowly out of candlelight, his shadow looming, and she found this overly dramatic. She dropped her hands by her side and looked at his silhouette. She didn't trust her voice but decided she would be the first to speak.

"My mother is waiting for me at the hotel for dinner."

He took a step forward. "And your father?"

She breathed, clasped one wrist at her waistline. "He won't be waiting anytime soon."

He tried to discern some sign that everything was ruined.

She looked at the darkening windows behind him.

"I'm so sorry," he said, finally.

"Months ago now. That's what it seems like."

"I should have come sooner. There were delays at sea." He made another step forward and took her hands in his.

She wanted to retract her hands or at the very least curl them into fists, but instead she let them go limp, brought her gaze to meet his. Suddenly, and infuriatingly, she wanted to be held, kissed until she felt thirsty and faint. Instead she turned her shoulders away. He let go of her hands and she moved to the windows, annoyed that now she was the one being overly dramatic. Was she going to fold her arms, stubbornly regard the skyline, the billows of smoke, the blackened river, while he explained, apologized, beckoned? Yes, apparently, she was going to do exactly that. She watched his reflection beside her, dimly aware of his words, her attention gripped by the way he held a flounce of her dress between two fingers.

She said, "He died peacefully, with a view of the river, his dog beside him. That's something at least. But my mother has come for God knows how long. I think she's afraid of being alone in Boston."

He touched her shoulders and she stiffened to fend off an embrace. She didn't like the predictability of this scene and realized the topic of her father's death was killing her anger. She put one palm against the cold glass and said, "I know about the natives."

There was a pause.

She continued: "You deliberately kept that from me. I suppose because you knew what I'd say."

His face fell a little in the window reflection.

He'd aged, she thought, something around the mouth. Perhaps it was the sun and salt air.

Their ghosts floated silently in the blackened plate glass.

"I meant to tell you and then it was too late. I didn't want anything to jeopardize the expedition. Our future was at stake."

"Where are they?"

"Who?"

"The natives."

"There's only two of them. Brother and sister. You were going to meet them tonight, here, but I think they're tired out from all the traveling. You'll meet them soon."

"These things don't end well, Owen. Do you remember the Esquimaux at the fair? They treated them like slaves or carnival freaks. Most of them burned down their skin tents and ran off to who knows where. And there were some others from Greenland in New York lately, living in the museum basement, dying by the day."

"This will be different. For starters they're islanders not Esquimaux."

"As if that will make any difference—they're going to freeze to death."

"I'll make sure they're well looked after," he said. "In three months they can go back if they like."

Suddenly appalled—with herself? with him? with the little scene animating the windowpane?—she turned and walked between the rows of covered desks. There were enough desks for a hundred clerks or typists. Insurance must be booming, she thought. Why not put a petting zoo on the rooftop instead of a Melanesian village built for two? It amounted to the same thing. She started for the middle rows, running her fingertips across the desktops—out there was a little dell of open space and more candles. Some rows in, she noticed a narrow desk converted for dinner service, covered with a white tablecloth instead of a drop cloth. Pewter candlesticks, brown paper packages, a bottle of wine. The smell of food was pungent and she wondered how she'd missed it.

He came toward her. "I went hunting for our dinner. Braved

the open-air markets, two delicatessens, even the building's cafeteria."

He began unpacking the motley spread—fried oysters, a tub
of cottage cheese, corn cakes, veal loaf, sweet pickles, a ham sandwich cut in two, a handful of peppermint wafers. He finished with
a volcanic island of mashed potatoes rising in a sea of gravy and
two tin cups of wine. As he pushed one cup toward her, she felt
the anger slipping.

"I have no intention of being wooed by your brown paper packages," she said. "I'm fuming. I really am." She took a step back
from the table, drummed up some fury. "I have half a mind to call
the wedding off and never see you again. I don't even have a ring,
Owen." She held her composure long enough to see the cruelty of it
register in his eyes. There was a moment where she saw him looking
into his own future and his face dropped, stricken and utterly bereft.
Somehow—she was certain she was a despicable person for this—
that glimmer of desolation in his face made her willing to soften.
She came back to the table, picked up the cup of wine, and took a
gulp. And like the night sky gushing at the windows, everything
came pouring out: "Oh, God, what a thing to say and I don't mean
a word of it. I just wanted you to confide in me. But already we
have secrets from each other. I missed you terribly, Owen. Here's a
secret: my mother almost convinced me to buy a house before you
got back. I was ready to do it, too. With my inheritance. And I was
afraid you wouldn't love a rich girl. It was going to be your punishment—an old regal lair not far from Prairie Avenue. A house with
servant bells and a library. My father gave me his books and I have
nowhere to keep them. You would have hated the house my mother
picked out. Me as well, probably. I don't know. It even had an attic
apartment where she was threatening to live for part of the year.
You really dodged a streetcar on that one, Mr. Graves. A big streetcar named Margaret. She would have made lists of things for you to
do because idleness is a terrible sin and she is the queen of lists. Do
you understand how close you came—"

He kissed her full on the mouth, her cup of wine poised mid-air. He wondered *how rich* but knew better than to ask. Her hand came up to the back of his neck, then took hold of his shirt collar for good measure. They leaned kissing across the table, across the street-vendor spoils, then she pulled him around by the shirtfront, their mouths still flush and brimming with wine, her hair tangled in the kiss. His hands thumbed the waistline belt of her dress and she murmured softly, but then he realized she was saying *my mother*.

He drew back, dabbing at his mouth with his wrist, breathless, as if he'd been punched. "Invite her up here. There's enough pickles for the three of us."

"She'd have a conniption."

She smiled for the first time and with such ease that he wanted to cup her jaw in his hand. Her mouth was an object in the world, no different than a jade figurine.

Owen collected himself. "Very well. I'll send a messenger to the hotel. Which one?"

"The Palmer House. But you can't."

Owen took her meager protest as absolute surrender. He walked to the elevator landing and pressed the call button. While he waited for Benny Boy—who was working late and for a handsome tip—he danced an off-kilter jig, stupidly and without remorse, for Adelaide's entertainment. She told him to stop, lifted the lid on something that resembled pork rinds, rolled her eyes extravagantly. A few minutes later the elevator arrived and Owen negotiated a relay of transactions—Benny Boy to doorman, doorman to delivery boy from the late-night druggist, errand boy on his bicycle through the slushy streets to the Palmer, only a few blocks over, deliver message of regret to Mrs.—what's her Christian name?—Margaret, tell Mrs. Margaret Cummings, a new widow mind you, so kid gloves, that her daughter is visiting with her fiancé just returned from the South Seas and must miss dinner. Very sorry. Repeat. Very sorry.

"She'll be miffed," said Adelaide. "The proper thing would be to all dine together and I'll hear that refrain for weeks to come. Maybe years."

Owen handed Benny Boy some more money, enough to disperse to the various parties, and strode back to the dinner table, feeling like a general who's just ordered soldiers to the front. "'Margaret' is a formidable name. Now I'm especially nervous about meeting her."

Adelaide was sitting, legs crossed at the knee, her hands folded in her lap; apparently the kissing was over for the time being.

Stifling a smile, she said, "You should be nervous, especially after what you've put her only daughter through." She picked up a fried oyster and put it in her mouth.

He sat across from her. "Eat up. We have a tour to take after this. Veal loaf, Duchess?"

Suddenly ravenous and relieved, Adelaide began eating everything in sight, spooning and slicing things onto the cafeteria plate embossed with the company seal. They ate and drank for an hour before he led her into the stairwell and they climbed their way toward the rooftop. What she said of the view was, "This building bothers me with its self-importance," and then she complained of the cold wind and that she couldn't see much for the descending fog.

So much for winning her over with the view, he thought, and so he took her into the tower and kissed her again, held her behind the illuminated clock face, the enormous lunar disc that was like a set piece for a musical. At least twenty pedestrians, confirming the hour from down on State Street, saw two amorphous silhouettes projected behind the white clock face as Owen and Adelaide kissed. The gears clicked over with their deadbeat lock and slide and she found herself, within minutes, unbuttoned and shivering. As with most things between them, Adelaide would concede in her own time and on her own terms. He was back along the strange coast of her affections, powerless and waiting for steerage. She told him to take her down to Underwriting or whatever it was and to make them a bed on top of the desks with their coats because she wasn't about to lie with him on an office floor. He chided that he was better prepared than that and they took the stairs back down, stopping twice to kiss, emerging into the cavernous space where a daybed had been made up with sheets and pillows and pushed into a corner of windows. She made him turn away while she undressed hurriedly, her fingers still trembling from the cold. Owen listened and counted the layers of underwear and lace as she unpeeled. He got down to his underwear and they pressed together under the blankets for warmth. Owen told her about the drifting ship burning with coal, about imagining her beneath the captain's skylight, watching the stars, and she said she would probably get horribly seasick. He kissed her again, marooned in her smell.

At some point during their lovemaking, Owen realized he was facing northeast and that through the windows he could see the lake and the department stores of State Street reared up like enormous passenger ships and somewhere over there were the sites where he and his father's crew demolished buildings, sometimes in a single day. They devoured the teardowns like titans, like warring Vikings or rampaging Huns, pickaxes and adzes thrashing and sparking through the daylight. All of them fall, eventually, and in the meantime are leased from gravity, his father used to say in his grave, substantial tone. Owen had lingered on the sidelines, a demolitionist but also bent on unlikely treasure. Oddly, with his life spread before him, partitioned into city blocks, with Adelaide's pliant body beneath him, her cold hands against his chest, he thought of his father's boots on a shelf at the scrapyard, worn into workaday combat with their laces frayed. They seemed like an admonishment not to trust his luck.

30.

They slipped out of the building under cover of dark, before the secretaries and clerks arrived for the day. Owen bought her hotcakes at a worker's diner and they idled with talk and coffee for hours, waiting for the sun to rise over the lake. At first light, they bought her a fresh blouse from a street vendor and she wore it over her dress to keep rumors at bay among her colleagues. They bounded along the shoreline in their coats, contemplating the long walk south to the museum. "We're quite the vagabonds," she said. "First we eat out of brown paper, then we sleep on a narrow daybed—incidentally, that was torture on my back—and now we're buying me clothes from a gypsy on the street. This isn't what I had in mind for us, Mr. Graves."

He smoked a cigarette, striding out, brazened by the cold and the sex. "I don't know what you're talking about. I'm living like a king. We slept up with the stars last night, didn't we?"

She took his arm, then his cigarette.

The lake was still and quiet. Windrows of ice clogged the shoreline, a field of white boulders and foot-high escarpments. A fishing boat moved beyond the frozen rim, pulling into a shroud of fog, the upstroke of its engine magnified and somehow forlorn in the stillness. Owen looked out at the wide skirt of ice and recalled the coral flanks of Tikalia. Already it seemed like a lifetime ago. In fact, it had been less than two months since he'd been sitting on that beach, wondering if he'd gambled everything and lost. He touched the corner of the check in his coat pocket.

Adelaide bristled with plans—there was dinner with Margaret, wedding errands, a fitting appointment for Owen at the tailor's, on Saturday if they could get him in.

"How far along are the arrangements?" Owen asked.

"With my mother in town, you can rest assured they are quite far along. She tried to convince me that we were getting married in Boston but after three days of not speaking to her she finally conceded. Now that means there will be trainloads of Bostonites coming in."

"I may be ill."

"Stop it. The church is booked, though the date will have to change now."

"Why? You never told me the date. I'm just a passenger on this train."

"Well, that was another reason why I was fuming. Hale Gray stole our wedding date when he chose the first day of May for his ridiculous rooftop event. I wouldn't want to compete with that. No, we'll go with the first of June. The weather will be nicer anyway, but that means my mother will be here the whole time."

"They're going to name a room after her at the Palmer."

She stopped walking and said, "It's more than four miles to the museum. I can't walk all that way. Not in these shoes."

"I thought you were intrepid. I met you in a room of bottled brains, remember? There was a brain belonging to a murderer on a shelf right behind your little desk."

"I can see Indiana down there."

"All right then."

She took his cigarette again and they headed for the road. Eventually a hansom came up from the south and they got in. Just before eight they stopped in front of the museum. Adelaide kissed him before she got down.

Standing on the sidewalk, she said, "I'd like to meet the brother and sister today, if I can. Lunchtime? Eleven-thirty? I'd like to see if they need anything. Which island are they from anyway?"

Of course, Owen thought, they're just another pair of newly arrived immigrants to her, no different to the Italians, Bohemians, Slavs, or Swedes at Hull House. He said, "Originally from Poumeta, off the coast of New Guinea."

"I'll look it up in the museum library. Eleven-thirty, then?"

"And then it's dinner with Margaret this evening? That's a full day."

She nodded. "Should I come to the eyesore to meet them?"

"Naturally."

"That building is ruining my life," she said, making for the steps.

"Adelaide?"

She turned.

He wanted to ask how rich but was afraid of the answer. "Have a wonderful morning."

"You as well."

He told the driver to wait a moment so he could watch her climb the stairs to the museum, ascending to its coppered dome and Greek pavilions, passing between the stone lions with the red collar of her gypsy blouse flapping above her coat in the wind. He watched her and suspected this was happiness. "She's something, isn't she?" Owen said to the driver. The man hummed his consent and roused the horses. They got back along the shoreline and he told the driver to head for the South Side. He'd had his luggage and a few private collectibles sent directly from the train station to the yard, before Hale could see what he'd skimmed off for himself. He would spend the morning getting his affairs in order—unpacking, finding some clean clothes, opening a bank account to house his windfall.

Hale had given the savages a corner office each on the floor below his, sending a signal to the press and his employees that these were his guests and not mere curiosities, but also because he wanted to see how they would react to living at such a height. Malini had covered her windows with newsprint because she disliked the view. It made her dizzy and cold. She'd placed the mattress on the floor and slept in her coat. She dreamed of ironbarks growing on the high rooftops, of her Kuk husband in a hammock, asleep and swaying through the clouds. Argus had gone to bed that first night watching the city blink its sulfurous light and had woken early to count church steeples. These were a God-fearing people and it filled him with hope.

The section of the floor they were on was still being finished out but they could hear voices—mostly female—on the other side of a dividing wall. Argus heard the rippling detonations of the Remington typewriters, the same company, he knew, that made rifles and pistols. Miss Ballentine brought them breakfast from the cafeteria—rolls and doughnuts and juice—and they ate together in a makeshift dining room, a table and two wooden chairs in plain view of the elevator landing. She brought them towels and they took their time bathing in the sinks of the hard-surfaced bathrooms, but their clothes needed laundering and they had to dress in things that smelled like the train ride from California. Malini's coat smelled like anthracite and bacon grease and this was Adelaide's first impression when she got out of the elevator on the twenty-seventh floor—that the poor woman was wearing a man's smelly old coat. The siblings were sitting in their breakfast nook, though you could hardly call it that, Adelaide thought, with six thousand square feet of steel columns and space sprawling on all sides. Owen made the introductions and Argus knew better than to extend his hand to a lady.

Adelaide pronounced a formal Poumetan welcome, hoping the museum's Melanesian phrasebooks had been accurate. She'd spent two hours trying to find a list of Poumetan greetings, all the while pretending to reorganize the library shelves.

The phrase was close enough to brighten their faces.

Malini smiled freely. She liked Adelaide's long, dark hair.

Nervous, for reasons she couldn't explain, Adelaide said, "Very pleased to meet you both. Welcome to America. You must be freezing!"

Argus shrugged politely.

"It's all right," said Owen. "She's one of us. You can be yourself."

"What are you talking about, Owen?" Adelaide said, slightly embarrassed.

Argus said, "I've heard a lot about you, Miss Cummings. And if I may say so, you are just as pretty as Mr. Graves said you would be."

Adelaide didn't want to seem shocked but felt herself staring. "Your English is excellent, Mr. Niu. Where did you learn it?"

She even pronounced his surname correctly. "From the Reverend Mister, madam. He was my employer until he died on the front verandah one morning. He had a heavy heart and the whiskey made it sink."

She laughed but instantly worried it came off as a patronizing giggle. "Oh, I see. And does your sister speak English as well?"

"She is still learning it."

Argus side-mouthed something to Malini in Poumetan.

Malini looked terrified for a moment, then said: *Here we are standing.*

They all smiled at this.

Owen said, "Old Hale Gray thinks they were found in the jungle. He wanted true primitives brought back. Truth is Argus speaks English better than I do."

Argus blushed.

Owen added, "And Malini there is fast on her way. Didn't speak a word of English when we left the islands."

"Amazing," Adelaide said.

There was an awkward silence.

Adelaide broke it: "Well, I wanted to see if you need anything. I know this must be a very big change for you both. What can I do to help? How about new clothes for a start? Owen, I'd think that Mr. Gray would be outfitting them with new clothing and personal items. He is their employer, after all. By the way, Hull

House did a survey of wages not long ago for the Near West Side. I hope he doesn't think he can get away with less than, say, twenty dollars a week. Each, that is. Perhaps I could take charge of clothing procurement." Was she prattling? she wondered, looking off at the empty expanse.

Owen said, "I'm not involved in the labor conditions, Adelaide. That's Mr. Gray's concern."

Her eyes came back. "Well, whether it's with his money or mine, they can't go around in those tattered old coats. And they can't just fester up here in this half-built colossus." She was aware of speaking about the siblings as if they were invisible. To correct her mistake she turned to them. "I would be honored to show you around the city, help you get settled in. We can take a bit of a tour."

"That would be very nice," said Argus.

"Perhaps you'd like to visit the museum where I work."

Malini felt her mind flinch at the word *museum*.

"I'd very much like to see a bookstore and a library," said Argus.

Owen said, "Now hold on a minute. All this needs to be approved by Hale. These people are in his custody."

"Yes, but they're not his property," said Adelaide, her cheeks slightly aflame. She didn't care for the word *custody*.

Owen knew he was being contrary—why was he protecting Hale's territory as if it were his own? Were future trading assignments at risk? She meant well but he was slightly taken aback by her insistence. "All I'm saying is that we need to go through the proper channels."

As if to adjudicate this discussion, the elevator doors opened and Hale Gray appeared in his double-breasted, affable enough in the face but his cane thrusting out violently; the handle—a silver dog's head—resembled gunmetal a little too closely for Owen's liking.

As Hale approached, Owen whispered, "Remember, they barely speak English."

Hale arrived, quietly, in his rubber heels. "Just back from a risk and provisions meeting and I thought I would check in on our guests. I trust everything is to their satisfaction. Quite a view from up here, no? Probably think the lake is the Pacific. Those corner offices are slated for vice presidents but I've been setting them aside."

Argus wanted to tell him that Malini had blotted out the view with sheets of newsprint. He had gone in there several times to read the pasted articles when he'd grown bored with the two Davids. He was hungry for new books and knew they were out there, like people waiting to be met. To see a library and a bookstore, to run his fingertips along the spines of green clothbounds and full-grain hardbacks, to smell bookdust as holy as frankincense, now that would be something. Miss Cummings seemed equipped to break them out of there, to take them out into the gorged streets. He was ready for another splash.

"Very comfortable," said Owen. "You remember my fiancée, Mr. Gray, Adelaide Cummings."

Hale bent at the waist, then continued down, almost into a Regency bow. He came back up, blood rising into his face. "Of course. We met at the train station. Delighted to see you again, Miss Cummings. When is the big day? Nuptials are the reason God invented spring!"

Adelaide couldn't help feeling a brief and vague liking for Hale—the dog-head cane reminded her of her father and the bow was overdone, the gesture of a man who plots grand gestures. There was something poetic about it. He was mostly bluster, she imagined, a strong handshake and quip, but a man who teared up easily during patriotic songs. But then she remembered the postponed wedding date, the specter of her mother in town for months on end, and she fell back on aloofness. "June first," she said. "Practically summer."

"Should be warmed up by then, I imagine," Hale said. "You two could always marry on my rooftop if you had the inclination. Ha! Might be a world first."

"No thank you," said Adelaide.

Hale turned to the siblings, then back to Owen. "Are they getting on all right? Any sign of altitude sickness? A change in temperament?"

Owen said nothing but wanted to remind Hale that Melanesia had volcanoes ten times taller than the twenty-seventh floor of the First Equitable.

Adelaide said, "I wonder if I might be of service?"

Hale found this a little impetuous and, as with Miss Ballentine and Miss Carver and the secretary before that whose name he could never recall, a splenetic woman with breasts of historic proportions, he would not reward the misstep with eye contact.

In response to Hale's question, Owen said, "For the most part, I think. Perhaps they need more clothing."

Adelaide said, "Forgive me. I know it's not my concern. But I would be delighted to help find them some clothing and toiletries. I volunteer at Hull House and have helped a lot of new immigrants get settled in."

"Immigrants?" Hale said, now pivoting, giving her the brunt of his attention. "Miss Cummings, these natives are here for a few months as part of an advertising campaign for the First Equitable Insurance Company. They're visitors, not immigrants. Come May, they'll be wearing leaves and bark up there."

Owen shot Adelaide a stare but she was unmoored. This was something he would have to accept about her.

"All the same," she said, smiling, changing tactics, "with due respect, seeing them properly clothed and entertained until then would be my civic honor. Really, I should love to show them around the city. The art galleries and museums."

Hale twirled a cuff link, a lion's head slow and gold. "Let me consider it." He knew when he was in the crosshairs. He saw that she had pluck, imagined she would be quite something in the marital department. Women like that said the most damnable things in the boudoir. Bravo. "You work at the Field Museum, do you not, Miss Cummings?"

"I do, sir. And I was suggesting earlier that Mr. Niu and his sister might enjoy seeing the collections. Perhaps you could accompany us?"

"Adelaide," Owen said, stiffening.

Hale stopped twirling his cuff link. "Marshall Field is a colleague of mine at the Prairie Club and my neighbor. We're rivals of a sort. Keep the objects in the hands of private collectors, I say. Not everything is for public consumption, Miss Cummings."

Adelaide summoned a tight smile.

"Well, I must be off," Hale said. "I have pressing matters above. Good day to all." He turned, swiveling on his soft heels.

He felt their eyes boring into his back as he waited for the elevator. After a minute he gave up and went to the stairwell. He climbed the stairs two at a time, blood pounding in his ears, his cane rapping against the iron railing. He came out onto the landing and walked toward his office. Miss Ballentine sat plodding away at the typewriter, a pecking monument to drudgery. Lately she'd taken to painting clear iodine on her fingertips, a protective shellac against typing cuts and splits, and Hale thought it smelled like a battlefield triage in her little nook. Ghastly. He'd give her until summer to right her ways. What separated Hale from his peers, he knew, was the way he embraced abrupt change. He could find opportunity in a puddle if it came down to it. Bring him a plate of horse dung and he would find a man willing to buy it. The fidget wheels turned in his head, no different than the escapement of the clock above, truing up time. He would let Miss Adelaide Cummings give them a tour, but with a twist. Her idea was a gift, he saw now, an offering from that puckered rose of a mouth.

Dictation, Miss Ballentine, quick as you like. Letter to the Chicago Tribune, *"Bits of the City" editor or whoever is the right man. Today's date. We wish to inform that we will be offering a sneak preview of our South Sea Island guests, in preparation for the first of May opening. First day over forty degrees. Preferably sunny, on account of savage constitution. Will advise. Send a reporter as the savages get a tour of our grand city. Exclusive to your newspaper. Use words to this effect, Lulu, and bring me a draft for correction before it's sent out. Hand-delivered.*

He stepped toward his office door, already imagining Marshall's reaction to the museum visit. One of the august institution's own employees acting as tour guide for the savage siblings. She'd probably get fired once Marshall found out. That was a good name for something—*The Savage Siblings.*

He suddenly needed a drink. "Oh, and bring me some ice."

He watched as Miss Ballentine—no, Lulu—neatly typed out these words.

She looked up, flummoxed. "Very well. Sir, your son is waiting for you inside."

Hale felt something in the back of his throat. He went inside and saw Jethro standing in front of the display cases, the fencing glove on one hand. "Hello, son. How are the arrangements coming in the lobby?"

Without turning: "Oh, just fine, Father."

"Are you keeping the carpenters in line? They'll build a fruit stand if you don't watch their work."

"Yes, it's coming along. I gave them some diagrams to work from."

"Excellent. Anything else?"

The boy stood there, staring into the velvet lining. "I've been thinking about Pythagoras."

This did not bode well. Hale took a nip of whiskey to settle his mood. How long did it take to fetch a pail of ice? "I see."

"We know so little of him. All those volumes of philosophy destroyed and mostly we have his work with triangles. Supposedly he lived in a cave and took vows of silence."

"Best to keep off the books just at the moment. You have work to do."

"Do you know what I was thinking?"

"I doubt it."

"We should have a *wunderkammer* in the lobby, right next to the display cases."

"A what?"

"You know, a cabinet of curiosities. A room of wonders. I got the idea from reading—well, from remembering Rudolf, King of Bohemia. He had the most marvelous collection of natural specimens, minerals and gemstones, mechanical objects, freaks of nature . . . that sort of thing. I could arrange my collection in there. Show strips of film—I did manage to take moving images at sea. Perhaps I could use the vacant cigar shop? Just for the summer. Taxidermy shouldn't be mingled with artifacts, you know." He finally turned from the display case, rubbing his bloodshot eyes with both thumbs. "I think I may need a doctor."

Hale swallowed, felt a smoky trickle of whiskey ease down his chest. "For the finger? Yes, by all means. Go see Dr. Jallup on Clark Street. Careful he doesn't bleed you, though. He's a bit Greek on that front. An old-schooler."

"No, it's something else."

Hale refused to ask.

Jethro clutched one elbow, his shoulders slumped. "I'm afraid I don't feel well. In my thoughts. Something happened on the ship. And now I can't sleep at night, even when I take the laudanum."

"Ah."

"I'm being punished it seems."

Miss Ballentine trundled into the room with a silver pail of ice. They watched her in silence as she set it on Hale's side table. The ice gave off a slight vapor and Hale wondered why he always craved ice, even in winter, why he always wanted to snuff part of the whiskey's heat. Constitution, no doubt, but also because it was elemental. He did it for the same reason he lit his own fires, stacked the kindling in the hearth, even though the house was teeming with servants. He looked at his son, the tremulous hands and vacant eyes; whatever he'd hoped the voyage would achieve had failed. The Gray line had ended. What stood before him was the bitter end of a frayed rope. Now it was a matter of riding it out, of planning for an eventual public sale, singling out a successor from the vice presidential ranks. Retirement seemed out of the question. Then there was the matter of keeping Jethro harmlessly engaged. Maybe he should be sent back east, let the boy take another useless degree in those ivy-ravaged lecture halls. Miss Ballentine withdrew and he looked at his son. "As I say, go see the doctor about your finger. Now, if you'll excuse me, Jethro, I have some telegrams to read."

Jethro said, "And the *wunderkammer,* Father?" He sounded eight years old.

"Very well. Use the cigar shop but keep the renovation costs down. Talk to the master carpenter. And just for the summer. I want a new tenant in there come August."

"Excellent," Jethro said, brightening. "You won't be disappointed. Thank you."

"Yes, but as I say, watch the budget. We may go public one day and the first thing a shareholder wants is thrift in management."

The boy grinned, oblivious.

Jethro walked out of the office, closed the door, and went to wait for the elevator. From somewhere above his head, unseen, the big clock made its baritone call for afternoon.

Dinner with Margaret. Owen took the streetcar from the South Side, his face stinging with aftershave, a new suit on his back. He met them in the Palmer House lobby, a vault of marble and chandeliers. His first impression of Margaret was of a sturdy woman, slightly guarded but also chatty, free flowing with opinions on practical matters. They were shown to a secluded table in the dining room and by the time the salads had been brought out Owen knew how lime water kept eggs fresh—one pint coarse salt, one pint unslaked lime, one pailful water—why New England rum was a first-rate shampoo, why honey mixed with pure pulverized charcoal was still the best recipe for cleaning teeth. She'd grown up poor, she told him; they made their own candles with mutton tallow and beeswax. Adelaide slumped in her seat, picking through her greens. She couldn't get a word in. Was Margaret prattling from grief? Owen wondered. Was it a sort of nervous distraction? In a nonwidow it would have been charity to allow the woman to go on like this. The merits of Makassar oil. The dangers of oversleeping. Margaret seemed afraid of silence, wary of conversational drag. She let the waiters fuss over her; she had been there more than a month and it showed in the way they brought her, unprompted, a cup of warm water with lemon—a digestive for her bilious stomach.

"I'm sorry to hear you've been feeling poorly," Owen said.

"It's this city," she said, letting the lemon-scented steam rise to her face. "Puts me on edge."

Feeling emboldened by her prattling, Owen said, "Well, it won't be long before you'll be back in Boston."

She eyed him through the candlelight, slightly imperious—an old girl with rum in her hair. She'd married well, that was all, he thought. The blue blood was on the father's side; Owen could see it plainly. Margaret regarded him slowly, taking him in like a burgundy of uncertain vintage. Owen reckoned she'd drink blackstrap if it came down to it, if the posh establishment suddenly ran dry of claret punch and lemon wedges. The disliking was, at first, instantaneous and mutual. They had come from similar workaday roots, only she'd turned her bleak childhood into a series of quaint and folksy tidbits for the amusement and edification of others. It appalled him that she left food on her plate. Probably ate on the hour and couldn't remember the ache of real hunger. He suddenly felt cruel. She had lost a husband of many years.

She said, "Yes, I suppose I'll be home soon enough. But I will come back once a year just to check up on you, Mr. Graves."

She turned the solitaire ring on her wedding finger so that the big diamond was crowned in candle flame, a corona of gem light. She was telepathic as well, apparently, because Owen could feel the ring box bulging in his trouser pocket. After the bank, he'd spent most of the day traipsing between second-rate jewelers and glorified pawnbrokers, consulting arthritic men with loupes on their foreheads, one eye magnified to Cycloptic proportions as they talked prices and installment plans. He'd settled on a middling ring of dubious provenance. Whether it had been stolen or not, he didn't know, but it fit the bill—big enough to get attention but not so brash it would leave him broke or offend Adelaide's modest tastes. He still had enough for a down payment on a house with promise.

He drained his glass of wine.

Margaret launched another stare through the fifteen-watt dusk above the table. Owen swore that the electric lights flickered every time his future mother-in-law opened her mouth, which was to say they never ceased flickering. She was just protecting her daughter, he thought, for herself and on her dead husband's behalf.

Adelaide said, "I'm so glad you two have finally met."

An eon of silence and eating.

"Me as well," Owen said, smiling. "I regret we haven't met until now, Mrs. Cummings."

"Well, you were gone such a long time at sea."

Owen could tell they were headed for a conversational abyss. She would skewer him, sentence by sentence, word by word, one folk remedy at a time, one slight against the city at a time, until he'd feel offended and become territorial as a junkyard dog, a stray pissing on lampposts. He'd leap to Chicago's defense, act as if butter wouldn't melt in the old rube town's mouth, all because she'd rile and back him into a corner. There was only one way to stem the tide of the inevitable. He got to his feet, slightly drunk. Why did he only overindulge in the company of temperance?

He'd practically been an abbot at sea, a saint amid the ribald, and here he was, sloshed, about to slur his good intentions to Adelaide's mother, promise his undying love and affection for her daughter. An errant thought flashed through his mind—*may God grant Adelaide grace in old age*—and then he got to one knee and fumbled the ring box from his trouser pocket. All eyes turned to him, the whole dining room drawn in. Suddenly it was theater and the waiters were ushers.

"Adelaide, I know we're already engaged but there has been something lacking. I feel ashamed thinking about our engagement without this formality. Will you take this ring and continue the promise of becoming my wife?"

Adelaide turned a delicate shade of fuchsia, nodded, kissed him to get him off the floor.

But Owen stayed in place and turned to Margaret. "And Mrs. Cummings, let me say how honored I am to be entrusted with your daughter. I can assure you I will do everything in my power to take care of her and our family. And let me say how deeply sorry I am for your loss. I hear Gerald was a tremendous man."

The dining room fell into sighs and then congratulatory chatter—look at him on his knees, asking for her hand in front of the widowed mother in epic peach silk.

Margaret thawed and became tearful. She ordered champagne and was laughing through her tears and nose in no time. They toasted Mr. Cummings and Adelaide's unborn children. Before dessert was out she was calling him *Owen* and *son* and they parted with genuine affection, Owen pulled into her bosomy embrace, a full bear hug that defied custom and dignity and left him dazed. Her final tipsy words of the evening were a recipe against offensive breath, whispered like an oracle—*Peruvian bark . . . in lime-water*—and then she was off, toddling, waving gallantly as if from a warship, dabbing at her blotched face with a white handkerchief. Owen decided he liked her after all; underneath all that folk wisdom was a rather fragile woman. She kept the world and all its brimming action slightly at bay with chatter but he'd managed to topple her. All it took was humility and sincerity on bended knee. He tipped a smirking bellhop to get Margaret back to her suite before turning to Adelaide. She was looking down at her finger. The ring was slightly old-fashioned, a sizable diamond raised above white gold and a series of swooped engravings. She thought it was beautiful but found herself saying, "It's too much."

"I can take it back if you like."

"Don't you dare," she said.

They held hands and went outside, into the blue glitter of an unseasonably cold night, the diamond, possibly stolen, enfolded between their fingers.

31.

The big day out was redolent of spring, brilliant with late March sunshine, the gutters awash in snowmelt. They set out from the First Equitable a little after nine, Adelaide in front, the siblings abreast, a *Tribune* reporter following behind with his notebook. The magnate would meet them at the museum in the afternoon and had sent word to Marshall Field that he was finally taking up his offer of an official tour. This ought to make its way into club lore—that sunny spring Friday when Hale Gray finally crowned the years of reading room skirmish with a decisive victory, when he whacked it free and clear with a St. Andrews full swing.

Malini liked the sun on her face, however mild. As they moved down the street she saw fat women staring at her from behind smoked, round glasses, their hats piled heavy with wooden fruit and stork feathers. There were pigeons everywhere, she noticed, defecating on stone ledges and swooping down for crumbs. She recalled the taste of roast squab and wondered if they ate these birds or whether they just let them shit on their heads all day. People walked quickly, shoulders up, elbows out. Men in suits slowed to gawk, unabashed, cigarettes smoking in the pale sunshine.

Into the big house of goods where all the world's objects had been poured into one place. Did people live in here, sleeping and eating in the roomfuls of furniture—chairs made of feathery plush and strange oiled woods, beds as big as reef heads, a jumble of clothes whose use she could not fathom . . . Miss Cummings took her aside and tried to teach her about underwear. Bustled into a tiny room with a curtain, she put on flimsy silk dresses, then more layers, then whalebone brassiere cups that pressed her breasts hard against her ribs. She knew about mission girls who strapped and mashed their *susus* until they got rashes from all-day cotton heat. But it was cold here so maybe there would be no cotton rash; she would try the brassiere for a day. *No breathing*, she said, handing back the *girdle*. Miss Cummings smiled and laughed, threw the contraption on the floor like it had just bitten her. The silk felt cool then warm against her skin and the woolen dress went all the way down to her ankles. Here was a *cashmere* scarf, gloves, a hat without feathers or painted wooden fruit. She went out into the hard light of the store, bundled, dimly aware of her body swimming beneath all that fabric; she had been wrapped and bandaged, mummified like an effigy. But she also liked the way she felt swaddled, as if the world could barely graze her through all that wool and silk. She held her chin forward to keep the itchy collar off her neck but every now and then, as if to compensate, a wave of silk warmed up against her bare thighs. Argus came out dressed in a dark suit and a tall, boxy hat. He had a new walking stick and an important expression on his face. White people dressed by rank and Malini wondered what position had been assigned to them with these clothes. Did the height of the hat on her brother's head mean something? Did the length of her dress? The reporter made a sketch of them standing together while a crowd of shoppers looked on.

Out into the river of people, the amazed stares. It was sport of a kind, to see the native girl with dreadlocks and a cashmere scarf, walking stiffly along, as if in damp clothes, and the black fellow strutting out like a duke of the underworld, that Malacca cane rowing him down the thawing sidewalk. They got cheers and whistles, welcomes, racial epithets, scowls. They passed through the shadows of the terracotta cliffs, the towering façades tilting down on them as the siblings looked straight up, into the heaving,

abyssal blue. Argus gave in to the street's curiosity and spread his
coat on the ground so that he could lie down, faceup, arms across
his chest, casting his eye up one of the endless stone walls. They
applauded this, though he couldn't think why. From this angle
the parallel lines converged upward, reaching out to the big blue
vanishing point, as if craving the benediction of heaven. There
was a time, he remembered, when his sketching had been free
from perspective, free from the lines that did not meet in life but
appeared to merge on paper. That was another person now, the
boy who'd seen the world rioting without pattern, flushed against
a single plane. He got up and dusted himself off, received several
pats on the back for his timely display of awe.

Adelaide took them to a lunchroom for morning tea and they
ate slices of hickory nut cake. Fellow diners watched as Argus
sliced up his cake with knife and fork, aping a fastidious Briton
they thought, both utensils in hand. Malini spread her cake with
apple butter and ate it like a sandwich. She wanted to take the
whalebone and fabric cups off her breasts so she could eat without sighing between bites. Argus had already noted the way that
Americans favored the fork, as if the knife were merely an accom-
plice, only to be used in a pinch, for navigating the outskirts of a
steak or breast of chicken, then promptly set down. He imitated
this style, putting down his knife and attempting to use the business end of his fork like a shovel. But then he noticed the reporter
looking askance and he suddenly remembered that he'd been *discovered in the wilds*! He fumbled the silverware, picked up the
cake with both hands. The reporter wrote something in his notebook and the neighboring diners looked away now that everything was in its place.

Back outside, into the mellow sunshine, a small attachment
joining the entourage as rear guard, a few tourists from Kan-
sas and a couple of housewives loafing on State Street. Adelaide
let them tag along, no harm done, so long as they gave a wide
berth. Adelaide took them into a venerable old Loop bookshop,

Hardwick's, a book depository that resembled a rail depot with its iron and glass-block landings and wooden benches, seating designed to keep potential customers on their feet. The shop was presided over by a slovenly monastic, a man who'd spent his life in bookish pleasure, and it showed by the way he ate with his mouth open, spitting crumbs, working his sack lunch while deliberating on sonnets and obscure European novels. He sat behind a rummaged desk on a raised platform, like a judge, interrupting his private reading to dispense literary justice. Adelaide had been coming for years, at least once a month, and each time he made his recommendations and pronouncements anew, calling her *young lady* and sending her into the hinterland of wood-rung ladders for a particular volume or translation. If she didn't return within sixty seconds to the register with said edition he was on his feet, indignant, chewing, telling her to hop out of the way. Today he stood watching the native boy climb in search of hardbacks. Some new books of marginal interest came down—*A Students' History of the United States* (cloth, with maps, $1.40 net) and *Where the Trade-Wind Blows* by Mrs. Schuyler Crowninshield, a novel set in the Spanish West Indies, for $1.50. Hardly Hardy, the book monk pronounced, seeming to enjoy the hard *H* up against his glottis. Adelaide saw the reporter study Argus as he perused the books so she moved the party to the register. "I'm going to teach him how to read," she said to the proprietor, loud enough so that the reporter would take note. Argus wanted to stay and linger in the fusty pong of endpapers; he hadn't even been allowed to enter the scripture section, an entire alcove walled in by kidskin.

They moved up along Michigan Avenue, the broad plain of Grant Park to the east, softening the enormity of the lake. They came to the new public library building and entered from Washington. It was a mausoleum dedicated to books, that much Argus knew, devotion worked into the Bedford bluestone and granite like faith itself, the Tiffany domes and Romanesque portal, the mosaics of Favrile glass and mother of pearl, the chief librarian, a supplicant with a hushed voice, giving the tour himself. They padded across the cork floor, noiselessly passing into the reading room with its oak tables and lamps. Argus was allowed up into the iron stacks and when no one was watching he opened several books in a row, bringing each up to smell its faintly fungal loins. The act was almost sexual in pleasure. He fingered the leather spines, thumbed along the parched bookblocks. One day he would have a library card and use the catalogue, use the saving shelves set aside for scholars. He would spend long hours in the reference room working on sermons—they were open thirteen hours a day, Sundays included—studying the history of knowing and loving God, yes, but also centuries of literature, history, art.

They were gathering in the lobby and he was called to join them.

Next stop was the Art Institute at the foot of Adams, a whirlwind of Egyptian and Assyrian sculpture, objects of the Italian Renaissance. They stood the natives in front of the old Dutch masters and waited for something to happen. The *Tribune* reporter sidled up, pencil in hand. Malini walked the perimeter of the room, feeling the oily gloom of the paintings weighing down on her. These were the clayskins' dead ancestors, she could tell, assembled in a longhouse for remembering but with no bones in sight. Argus came close to a Rembrandt and noticed the perspective was off, but to great effect, the girl looming in the foreground with her rouge cheeks and snub nose, her porcelain, globoid face and averted eyes. She was standing in contemplation, in a cataract of half-light, a tunnel of miry shadow behind her. It was too uneven to be sunlight; it fell marbled and daubed, white firelight cast through shifting muslin. *Chiaroscuro* the plaque pronounced and Argus repeated it aloud after Adelaide pronounced it for him. *Probably thinks it's on the menu for tonight,* said one of the Kansan tourists, playing to the others. Adelaide didn't bother with a reply and they moved back out into the streets, ditching the hangers-on for the use of Hale's carriage.

They rode north along the shoreline, eating ham sandwiches as they crossed the Chicago River and made for Lincoln Park. They rounded the zoo, promised for another day since the animals were still in their winter quarters. Neither Argus nor Malini could comprehend an afternoon spent watching wild animals. They passed the archbishop's residence and Argus studied the windows and redbrick façades for signs of holy habitation but all he saw was a layman grooming a horse out in the carriage house. They turned south and on North State Street stopped outside the Holy Name Cathedral, the archbishop's parish church. Argus went in alone, through the massive bronze doors, and knelt in prayer before the granite altar. He asked for forgiveness of his sins and for a new life to begin. It was his first time in a Catholic church and he was impressed by its seriousness—so much stone and stained glass, the Stations of the Cross raised up above the bare wooden pews. The Ambo of the Evangelists served as lectern, cast in bronze, the saints depicted in symbolic form, Matthew the angel, Mark the lion, Luke the ox, John the eagle. In the vestibule there was a framed photograph of Archbishop Feehan, a profile of such benevolence that he found himself sunk again in prayer.

They crossed back over the grimy river, its jaws opening out into the lake, congested with scows and Mackinac lumber barges making test runs and repairs in the clear weather. There was a plan to convert the boats of Chicago into a navy fleet, in the event of foreign foe coming from over the waters. The reporter was telling them all about it. Malini fell asleep as they came back into the tumult of South State Street, the carriage haltered by the stop-and-go, the window-shoppers spilling off the sidewalk, the delivery wagons flouting the rules. Argus waved to a band of Salvationists ringing bells and blowing horns for redemption on the street corner.

Argus did not wake his sister until they pulled up in front of the museum. Like the rest of the public buildings he'd seen that day, the outside was solid and imposing, chiseled from grave-stone. They were welcomed by Mr. Gray, their employer, and Mr. Field, the man who owned the department store where they had obtained their clothes that morning. Miss Cummings looked a little wary when she greeted Mr. Field. Malini stepped from the carriage slowly, still a little groggy from her nap. Argus felt embarrassed that she had slept for part of the tour but Miss Cummings didn't seem to mind. She put an arm around his sister and led the way up the broad stairs. He hung back, taking the stairs slowly so he could eavesdrop on the conversation between the two important men behind him. The reporter scribbled madly in his notebook alongside.

". . . as I say, Marshall, the tour was Miss Cummings's idea. Public institutions, after all, are available to everyone, and we felt it was our duty to show the natives some of the city's finest. Their clothes came from your store just this morning. Can't have them sporting loincloths until warm weather is here for certain."

Mr. Field spoke evenly and without emotion. "I understood that you wanted to take a tour yourself. I've asked one of the curators to guide us."

"Indeed I do wish to take a tour. Along with my charges. What should we see first?"

"I'm not much involved with the day-to-day."

"Surely," Hale said, letting the reporter catch up, "you know your way around. You'll have to come up to my own museum when it's finished. The entire lobby will be used for the summer just for that purpose."

Mr. Field put his hands behind his back and looked at Mr. Gray. "Do you suppose that will sell you more insurance?"

"I certainly hope so. Oh, look, the tour is leaving without us. Let's move along."

As with the other venues, the siblings were led around. Miss

Cummings's colleagues did not seem happy to see her as the party moved through the halls and wings, the deer and bird dioramas, the skeletons of untold heathens, the urns and jewels and chain mail of vanished peoples. The curator waffled on. Malini trudged along, hungry and bored. Argus tried to stay interested but it wasn't until they reached the weaponry of the Pacific Islands that he was drawn in. There behind the glass, labeled with small pieces of typed-up cardboard, were more weapons from Poumeta, just like the ones in Hale Gray's office. The clubs, spears, arrows, and slingstones had belonged to his ancestors, to his great-grandfathers, from a time when village boys didn't go off to the sugar fields or mission houses. The artistry could be read in the woven beckets for throwing spears, the inlays of whale ivory, the child's club, feathered with egret, that his great-grandfather, still a boy, might have used to strike dead bodies to incite bravery, as was the custom back then. Argus could not place the emotion that coursed through him. It resisted naming but, like *chiaroscuro*, combined light and dark, regret and revelation all at once. His dead grandfathers lay in cabinets—both in the museum and in the skyscraper. They were molded into handles, captured in the obsidian flakes that came to a finial point. These items did not belong to the white men but had they saved them from oblivion? He couldn't know what was true. What he did know was that the stories he'd heard as a child of a less complicated time, of generations spent in long hours of storytelling, fashioning the same handicrafts for days, weeks, those were all true, just as his father had told him while reprimanding his boyhood carelessness. A dropped clay jar offended the ancestors because of their artistry and care, a tradition faltering then and now lost forever. Poumeta no longer held villages of his own people. It struck him for the first time since the day he'd left its beach with his sister in the rowboat. He'd come to the other side of the world, into another hemisphere, to see firsthand what his father had told him when he was six years old—that their traditions were waning and would eventually be lost for all time.

Hale Gray stood in front of the glass display case. "I have something similar to these weapons," he said, throwing his voice back toward Marshall Field.

Argus said nothing. The reporter and Malini stood looking out the window at a lone sailboat on the gold-threaded lake.

Finally, Hale Gray said, "Well, we're grateful for the tour, Marshall. We'd best be off."

They moved toward the main rotunda.

"There's one more thing I'd like you to see," said Marshall Field.

"What's that?"

"Something we have on loan from London for a few months."

"Ah," said Hale, pivoting, his mouth held open.

Marshall Field said, "Miss Cummings, would you ask Dr. Dorsey if we might borrow the Bennelong document for a moment?"

Adelaide went to find her boss, certain she would be fired by Monday afternoon. She returned wearing a pair of white gloves and holding a manila envelope.

Hale could see that it was a letter of some kind, a transcript in old cursive.

Marshall said, "To commemorate the visit of the natives to Chicago. Seems they are part of a long line of imports. Reminds us that there are people attached to these objects, no? Bennelong was an Aboriginal fellow from Australia. Went to England with the governor of New South Wales at the end of the last century. Anyway, the original seems to have disappeared but this is a certified copy on loan. Our historian is quite fascinated. Miss Cummings, would you mind reading it aloud?"

This was her punishment. She blushed before she'd even read the date of *Aug'st 29, 1796.*

Marshall said, "It was written, no doubt, from dictation, when the Aborigine returned to his native country. Proceed, Miss Cummings, if you will."

Adelaide read the words aloud, trying not to look at Argus Niu, who was standing very still.

Sir,

I am very well. I hope you are very well. I live at the governor's. I have every day dinner there. I have not my wife; another black man took her away. We have had murry doings; he speared me in the back, but I better now; his name is Carroway. All my friends alive and well. Not me go to England no more. I am at home now.

I hope Mrs Phillips is very well. You nurse me madam when I sick. You very good madam; thank you madam, and hope you remember me madam, not forget. I know you very well madam. Madam I want stockings, thank you madam. Sir, you give my duty to Ld Sydney. Thank you very good my Lord; hope you well all family very well. Sir.

Bannelong.

32.

Dear Archbishop Feehan,

I am writing to you from the top of the world. I have come from the islands of Melanesia to Chicago where I hope to someday become a seminarian. Today I was given a tour of the city and saw your magnificent residence. There was a man brushing a horse in the stable but I did not see Your Excellency. No matter. I have seen Your Eminence in my mind many times. Today I write to you to inquire if you have positions of employment at your bishopric. I have many experiences as a mission attendant. I was the houseboy for the Reverend Mister Underwood of the Presbyterian Church of Melanesia for six years. My employer passed away recently which was sad but I would not be here if it wasn't for his transit. In the mannerisms of cooking, cleaning, ironing clothes, and gardening celery and artichokes I am accomplished beyond my own compare. My soda-scones and chicken egg omelets are famous in all of the Bismarck Archipelago. I am also good at puzzles, analogies, riddles, and reading the scriptures aloud by candlelight. I have a fondness for reading but never shirk my responsibilities for the written word. It would be my honor to serve you in some capability. I know about roses and tulips and penance. Although I have worked for the Presbyterians I have always admired the Catholics. In matters of austerity and temperance your *flock is unparalleled. There is no job beneath me if I could impinge upon your prudence and kindness. Please write back care of the First Equitable Insurance Company, where I am employed presently and until the end of the American summer. My name is Argus Trotwood.*

VII

THE ROOFTOP

33.

The rooftop exhibition opening was two weeks away, scheduled for International Workers' Day, May 1. That day was also, Hale knew, a commemoration of the Haymarket affair. He wanted to divert attention away from any celebrations the bomb-throwing anarchists might have planned, to stem the swelling parades and marches with a statement of his own. It was also annual moving day, when the streets filled with tenement wagons and toppling wheelbarrows, a tawdry procession of mattresses, shovels, tin pots, old shoes. Would the war with Spain over Cuba—less than a week old—dampen any of that? Would people stay at home? Hale doubted it. The city needed distraction. And so, to widen the draw of the event, he'd decided to include a captive balloon ride, tethered to the base of the clock tower, a children's wading pool with imitation coral reef that fronted the thatch-roofed hut, a concession stand selling ice cream and coconut milk served in the half shell. A photographer would be on hand to capture Mr. Haroldson or Tompkins lazing in a hammock, barefoot, toes dusted with sand barged all the way in from Mackinac Island. Junior wading in the lagoon, or maybe paddling a small canoe, play-fishing with a bamboo pole, waving to the big-grinned savages. Hale could see it all very clearly. The missus spotting her neighborhood from the viewing platform, ice cream cone mid-lick, there it is, George, our house, from all the way up here. But George is napping. The commission men move among the crowd, avuncular in sunhats and bow ties, handing out policy brochures, selectively, as if there were a shortfall of paper. Keep them hungry, curious, that was Elisha's mandate. George wakes replenished, ready to sign on the dotted line, the parsed sequence of dashes and spaces that demarcates his new life. A period of inoculation begins. He sleeps better, drinks less. And over time this has a statistical effect on Chicago, all those policyholders breathing easy. Crime rates diminish. A decrease in divorce. A lengthening of handshake duration. A surge in population as George, indemnified and formidable, descends through the floors in the hydraulic elevator, the policy's goldenrod copy in one hand and his wife's elbow in the other.

The lobby museum was almost complete, the opening imminent, the artifacts dusted, arranged, numbered. The chiefly canoe hung from the ceiling on long metal ties, an effect that brought in a maritime bent, reminded people that the First Equitable had sponsored an actual voyage to procure all this for their pleasure. Jethro's cabinet of curiosities, the *wunder-something-or-other*— perhaps it would be a hit with the children—was shrouded by drop cloths, obscuring any hint of its progress. Hale saw his son passing through the lobby at all hours, carrying one strange object after another into the converted cigar shop. He was afraid to see what was on the other side of the shrouded front window. As curator, Jethro had been largely ignored by the workmen. They placed the items into the display cases based on a list provided by Owen Graves. There was very little harm Jethro could manage at this point. If the cigar shop turned out to be a foppish lair then Hale would simply shutter it.

The preparations, then, were in order. The natives had been spending their time learning English and touring the city, all of it photographed for publicity. Their hut was ready and soon they would make the move from their offices to the rooftop. It was a running joke at the company that the two savages had snagged corner offices without selling a single policy.

What kept Hale awake at night were reports of further deterioration in the plate glass, the engineers insisting that the building was inching farther afield as the clay bed thawed from a long winter. The foundation, the concrete raft, these were sliding toward the lake by the second, if you believed the structural engineers. Less than six total inches to date was the pronouncement but they recommended drilling, anchoring, boring steel rods and cables into the hardpan. Hale told them he would make a decision after the summer unless they could convince him of immediate peril. Meanwhile, First Manhattan Life & Casualty was adding stories to their building, set to eclipse the rank of highest occupied floor before the year was out. He lay in bed before dawn, listening to birds maraud the seed feeders in Marshall Field's backyard, thinking of ways to build up. On some level he regretted the clock tower because it inhibited the building's further ascent. If the foundation could be squared up, then they could add another five floors, surely, perhaps ten. But what small and narrow floors they would have to be, to leave the clock tower intact. Then he saw a vision of a second tower rising from the rooftop, shadowing the clock face, a stack of private rooms and suites, his own office at the apex. Hale Gray anchored above the grimy world. He was dreaming, he knew. The shrieking birds slipped beyond annoyance and he saw himself in a dirigible, a zeppelin floating above the Loop and the lake. The great hull was gilded with the leonine company seal. He woke to recall Napoleon using hot air balloons during the Battle of Waterloo, advancing above the British with fire and silk.

34.

The teeth of a mermaid captured in the Aegean Sea, the horn of a unicorn, the feathers of a phoenix, the claws of a salamander, two iron nails from Noah's Ark—all had been among the King of Bohemia's collectibles. Jethro knew Rudolf II had been taken advantage of, hoodwinked by charlatans and peddlers of fraudulent antiquities, knew the unicorn's tusk was probably, in fact, the tooth of a narwhal. The monarch had been vulnerable in his quest to know the mind of God. Who could blame him? That time—the latter half of the sixteenth century—was seething with mysticism and superstition. People believed ostriches ate iron, moles were eyeless, swans sang before they died, chameleons lived on air, elephants had no knees. What a dark epoch, alchemical in its knowledge, science relegated to ingots, salves, unguents, balsams . . . Rudolf had been mesmerized and blinded by the monstrous and the rare, the aberrations of the divine, filling his cabinet of curiosities with apocrypha. Remember, Jethro cautioned himself, that out of this same period also came Gessner's *History of Animals,* the classificatory basis for modern zoology. Innovation rising up the river of ignorance like a tidal bore.

He sat in the waiting room of Dr. Jallup's office deep in reverie. He hated to leave the *wunderkammer* and had taken to sleeping some nights there, surrounded by his specimens and books. The collection was taking shape and he'd struck upon a theme— *variety and structure in the miniature.* He wanted to show the layman how patterns were sewn into the very fabric of Nature: the crosswise parliament of fibers in a certain kind of leaf, the weft of quilled feathers in a bird's undercarriage, the spiraled pigment in a seashell that doubled as camouflage. He would exhibit entire specimens but highlight their minutiae (dynasties of filament and marrow), position magnifying glasses in front of teeth, tentacles, talons. The nurse called his name and from her tone he wondered how long she'd been repeating *Jethro Gray* into the crowded waiting room. Jethro got up from his seat a little too fluidly and the waiting infirm—rheumy, agued, consumptive—watched him with suspicion, waiting for another act of celerity that would condemn him as a faker. It was his mind, he told them under his breath, but that was also a part of the body. What ornamentation did the brain hold in its fissures? It was a ghastly thing to look at, the liver-colored purse of human deception. There was a fish—the remora—that swam beneath ships and attached itself to the hull. Sea captains of all stripes believed that if enough of them barnacled to a ship's bottom they had the power to retard steerageway. This was exactly how Jethro's mind felt in the drag of the festering finger and the poisonous act he had committed. A sucker's maw had attached itself to his consciousness.

The doctor's examination room was its own *wunderkammer*, a cabinet of strange objects and smells. The sickly odor of calamine, a ferric quickening in the nose, followed by pipe tobacco. How could a room smell brown? But so it did. Surgical tools and dental pliers on metal trays—Jallup was not above pulling a rotten molar—and the *materia medica* propped on its own bookstand, splayed as if for recitation. Was that russet stain actually a blood smear on its celluloid page? Jethro tightened the fencing glove on his left hand and shook hands with his right. The doctor was bald, slumped, unsexed, little more than a ponderous head, colorless eyes that skimmed along the surface of the world from behind long-range spectacles. There was small talk, mainly of Hale, followed by a series of *humph*s and *ah*s and *that so*'s.

"Hot was it, out there in the South Sea? I imagine it was, yes."

"I'm not sleeping."

"Let's take a look at the finger."

Jethro had not mentioned his finger. His father had been on to the doctor. He should have found his own physician.

Jallup eased the fencing glove off and whistled involuntarily. He clicked his teeth, filled with clinical contempt.

Jethro said, "I wonder if you can help me—"

"How long has it been like this?"

"Months."

"Painful?" The doctor looked over the wire rims of his spectacles.

"Depends on the day. When I can't sleep I feel it throb."

"Yes. I imagine you do."

"Is there something you can prescribe for my wakefulness?"

"Snakebite you say? In the islands? Nasty. The poison has done damage. That much is clear."

"Oh, no. The snakes are not poisonous there—on the island where it happened."

"Tell that to your riddled finger." Jallup reached for his pipe and filled the bowl. He took a pull of smoke into his mouth and gestured to the finger with the amberoid stem. "Way I see it, you're lucky to still have that finger. Why the rot hasn't spread into the hand entire is quite a thing. Regardless, we need to be prudent. Don't want you to end up looking like an Appalachian coal miner. I'm going to give you some ointments and powders. And keep the glove off from now on. The skin needs to heal in the plain light of day."

"Is that all that's to be done? Are there no other therapies? My mind, you see—"

"Mr. Gray, your parents have been coming to me since before you were born. I delivered you, as it happens, on account of the midwife taken ill. I've had your father on stomach bitters for decades to good result. Point is, I'm not up on the latest this or that. No need to be. Read the papers and it's Eucaine or some such. Some Swiss doctor just removed a human stomach and last week some mangler in Muncie, Indiana, Svengalized a boy's big toe off, frostbite, using nothing but hypnosis to put him out and under. What a lot of noise and bunk! We'll watch the finger closely. But there is no miracle cure for this kind of thing. Avoid touching your eyes with it. The finger."

Several moments of pipe-drawing.

Jethro stared at the finger as if it were a particularly colorful slug. He felt the parasitic remora hard at work, a sharksucker on his brain, enervating his presence of mind. He wanted to say to the old physician, a man he saw now was largely incompetent and outdated, whose walls were filled with department store calendars instead of diplomas, *Sir, a fish is eating my brain from the inside out*. Instead, he said, "And for sleeping better? Is there nothing to be done?"

The doctor stood and fetched a few jars from a shelf. "First, here are the powders and ointments for the finger. Powder in the morning, ointment at night. Then take some of this before bed. It's brand-new. A cough syrup for children but I've been giving it to my anxious wife to great effect."

Jethro took the small bottle and held it up into the hemisphere of pipe smoke above their heads — *Bayer Heroin Tonic and Suppressant*.

"One spoonful before bed," said Doctor Jallup. "Pay the nurse on the way out."

Jethro collected his medications and did as he was told.

It was warming outside — the elms and maples were suddenly a startling green. It had happened in the last hour, he was sure of it: spring. Outside a spaghetti joint he threw the finger powder and ointment into a garbage pail. Let nature take her course. He took a long swig from the bottle of Bayer tonic and kept walking. By the time he reached the commotion of the lobby, he could sense abandon creeping in, a melancholy anthem flowing through his limbs and thoughts. He ducked beneath the drop cloths and went into the *wunderkammer*. Nestled between a fern case and a rookery of taxidermied birds, he slept extravagantly.

35.

The house was on the Near North Side, anchored in a kind of no-man's-land but within walking distance of the Lincoln Park Zoo. It was close enough to hear the lions at night, but far enough from the lake-view mansions on Astor and east enough of Clark to be affordable. Wedged between the residential and the commercial, in a district of breweries and clapboard churches, it was a fixer to be sure—carpenter Gothic on hard times. It hadn't been painted in twenty years, by the looks of it, the arched windows and the board-and-batten siding weathered pale. Owen liked the steep gabled roofline and the high windows, the fact that this was a religious style rendered by American house carpenters, immigrants with awls and jigsaws. It was part barn, part chapel, the way it flashed a big expanse of timber wall at the street but drew the eye up with broad, high windows. From the attic there was a sliver of lake crowning through the trees and room enough to swing a cat. This might be the new home for his collection, though the objects would have to be pared down. The rest of the interior was spacious and mostly intact: bright airy rooms, two parlors, a candidate for a nursery. The big backyard, half an acre, held an overgrown orchard, rows of arthritic trees that Owen guessed were either barren or bore wild, inedible stone fruit in late summer. There was a workshop and stable, a stone garden bench engraved with the letters E.J.Z. The house had been vacant for some years, inherited by an absent nephew, fallowed during the years of financial panic.

Owen wrote a check of deposit and came back with Adelaide

the next day. He gave her a tour and they ended up in the back plot, beneath the gnarled fruit trees, looking back toward the house. From this aspect, he had to admit, it didn't look promising—the eaves sagged and there was a rent of jagged space smashed into the round attic window.

"It needs some work but I can do it myself," Owen said.

"Who's E.J.Z.?" she asked, avoiding his eyes.

She seemed distracted and it annoyed him. She hadn't said one word during the tour, not even when he said the sunny room could be a nursery.

He said, "The dead owner, I imagine. Maybe his mistress. What do you think of the house?"

"You love it, don't you?"

"I think it has potential," he said, trying to sound impartial. He couldn't say why he loved the house so much.

She said, "There's a lot of work to do on it. Should we keep looking?"

He waited for something to curb his mood. It was the beginning of marital discord. For a few seconds he felt it ringing all through him. It was the groom's job to secure housing before the wedding; everyone knew that. Had she been studying the lists of marriage licenses in the paper all this time just to deny him his rightful place?

Then she said, "I'm no longer at the museum."

"Did they fire you?"

"They were considering it. Somebody made a formal, anonymous complaint to the board after the episode with Hale Gray. Said I'd compromised the museum's reputation. I couldn't stand the thought of defending myself before those old sods so I quit. I handed George Dorsey my letter of resignation this afternoon."

He let her anger peter out. She ran her hands down her skirts.

He said, "Without telling me first?"

She flushed, saw where he was headed. "Everything happened so quickly."

"All the same, when I arrived back weren't you complaining that I hadn't confided in you about the full particulars of the voyage?"

She looked up at the warped gables. "Yes, I suppose I was."

"What will you do?"

"Devote more time to charity."

They sat on the stone bench. After a while, he said, "I still don't know what you've inherited. It's probably impolite to ask."

She did not look at him but said, "I don't know the exact figure yet. It will come in stages. That's what the probate attorney tells me." She waited, then added: "It will be our money soon and there's no use pretending otherwise."

His voice broke off then came back: "A rough estimate?"

She swallowed; it would be the first time she said the amount aloud. "Two hundred thousand dollars." Hoping to soften its brashness, she added, "Roughly."

He couldn't speak. He tried to gauge what could be done with such an amount. It was not monumental wealth, not the wealth of department store magnates and steel barons, but it was a sum big enough to make him feel embarrassed on behalf of the tired house listing above them, its little attempts at high Gothic rectitude, the glimmers of pretension where a carpenter maybe got carried away with his scroll saw. Pediments of wood, buff in their seasoned condition, strung along the fascia like ornate icicles.

She said, "It's a lot, isn't it?" Any other man would be happy, she thought, but Owen Graves will carry a grudge against anything easy or given. He probably blamed her for the inheritance. Another absurd ritual of the well-heeled. But she knew something good could be done with wealth. She thought about Dorothea in *Middlemarch* then felt embarrassed for the thought. "I'm not about to start wearing fur coats, if that's what worries you."

He wanted to say something to brush it off and then consider it in private, but nothing came. The silence went on so long that anything would have sounded forced and disingenuous. Finally, he said, "So this house is not good enough for us?" He was staring at her diamond ring, wondering if it had, in fact, been stolen.

"I never said that."

"Wouldn't get the Margaret seal of approval, is that it? Might entail her daughter sleeping—"

"Please stop. I know where this leads."

He went quiet again.

She said, "I could care less about what kind of house we live in. No. That's a lie. I want something comfortable and beautiful. Whoever said we shouldn't surround ourselves with beauty was a philistine. I'm not ashamed to want nice things. It won't make me an aristocrat if we have money in the bank."

"Well," he said, his voice indignant suddenly, "I want to buy this house with my own money. A mortgage, payment by payment, year by year. Interest. The whole arrangement."

"That's absurd. Most of a mortgage is interest. Why would we do that if we have the means to buy it outright?"

"I never said it was rational but that's the way I feel about things." He sounded petulant, even to himself. "I need to know whether you see any potential in this house at all."

She drew her eyes along the roofline then cast them directly at him. "What I see is a man wanting to rescue a charming old house from demolition. It must have been a beautiful house in its day. After the Civil War and the fire—somebody built it to be their pride and joy. But take a look at it now. It can barely stand on its own feet."

"That's an exaggeration. Most of the walls are intact. The roof needs some work, granted."

"It's not much of an exaggeration," she said.

They sat longer on the stone bench, neither of them conceding anything.

After some time, he said, "What if I buy it as an investment? I fix it up in time for the wedding, but if you still hate it then we can sell it, hopefully for a profit. Then you and your mother can find us some redbrick monstrosity on a fashionable block and I'll go along willingly. I'll concede everything if I can't make you fall in love with this house." He leaned closer. "Look at the way she'll catch morning sun off the lake and the way the windows are set overlooking the garden. What about all those rooms with good aspect? The maple skirting boards and honey-colored floors. The high ceilings."

She could hear it in his voice—actual tenderness for the ramshackle house. Her mother would not be pleased but that was true on most fronts. Without meaning to, Adelaide had complicated their union, her father's largesse a liability in their imminent marriage because her husband, soon-to-be, had grown up proud and poor, and now owed a debt to his past. His proposal didn't make much sense; it was more a statement of pride or protest than anything else. She would give in because she didn't have much hope of stopping him, and because she knew the man she wanted to marry was somehow attached to that stubborn plan. The son of a wrecker wanted to build something back up, to save a piece of tumbledown history from the scrapheap.

Released to his vision, Owen finalized the bank loan—issued partly, and to his chagrin, on the prospect of Adelaide's new financial standing. The banker knew of the Cummings family, and while the inheritance was not formally mentioned in the documents, it seemed to be a subtext at the signing. Keys in pocket, Owen worked every day at the house, sleeping on the bare floor in the empty rooms, auditioning them. He made the structural repairs first, gutting walls, replacing roof beams and floorboards, inserting copper pipes into the serpentine network that ran under the pier-and-beam. Next he painted, sanded, varnished, wallpapered. When the job seemed as if it would go on forever he decided to finish out a single room. A room wedged between the dining room and the parlor. It would be his peace offering to Adelaide—built-in shelves from lumberyard spruce, floor to ceiling. He asked Margaret where the dead husband's books were being kept. Apparently Adelaide had told her very little of the house project, because she was cheery and amenable, wanted to be in on the surprise. Owen told her she could see the house when it was all done, but in the meantime he needed to patch things up with her daughter. Margaret tapped the side of her nose, winked as if the first gesture were cryptic, and sat down to write him a letter of consent for the storage warehouse manager.

A few days before Hale Gray's opening, Owen had all thousand volumes pressed onto the shelves, arranged by author and in alphabetical order, the library smelling of wax and sawn wood. He brought Adelaide in the morning, when the light was best, and led her blindfolded into the room. When the room revealed itself—a crypt of sunshine and coralline book spines—she put her hand over her chest as if startled. "It's beautiful," she said, "so very beautiful." She walked around the perimeter of the library, tracing a finger along the edge of the shelves. She opened pages, read text and marginalia, felt her father's mind at work. Then she stopped before a shelf, shaking her head. "Gerald would never have made Dickens a neighbor to Dostoyevsky. The Russians always lived on a separate shelf."

Owen smiled. "*Gerald* and *Margaret*. So proper."

"I know."

"*Owen* and *Adelaide*."

Turning, she said, "Not such a terrible ring to it."

He kissed her cheek as she began exiling the Russians to their own shelf.

36.

The opening day crowds were thin, despite the sunny weather—less than a hundred sightseers and not one policy signed before noon. Hale Gray, rocking on his heels, watched the streets from the rooftop—caravans of headlong immigrants, Cuban and American flags aflutter, patriotic fervor even as they moved from one cramped flat to another one farther west or south. Signs that read: *Down with Spain!* There wasn't a single May Day worker parade in sight, making the meager turnout even more baffling. No anarchists, just babushkas and tias carrying infants on their backs. Hale turned to see a green-faced lad going aloft in the tethered balloon ride—a little Napoleon about to lose his lunch. Perhaps he'd miscalculated and overplayed his hand. Did their own policy even cover death events or permanent maiming in airborne vehicles? The bored salesmen drank chilled coconut milk and watched the siblings mimic island life. Up on the spit of sand, the loinclothed brother stacked wood for a small fire while the sister, dressed in a grass skirt and cotton blouse, prepared a dozen yams. With the fire warden's permission, they were going to cook their lunch in the hearth. The coral for the oven had come from Mexico, just like the coconuts and the bamboo. The two-foot-deep lagoon looked a little brackish so Hale asked an underling to add some more indigo dye.

He took the elevator down to the lobby and Benny Boy, as usual, knew when to keep quiet. A sixth sense for other people's woes—Hale had half a mind to give him a clerking job. After the summer, perhaps he would. Meantime, keep the darkened shafts flowing, Benny Boy, bring up the suburban uninsured by the carload. He patted him on the back, tipped him a quarter as the doors slid wide. Less than twenty people milled in the lobby, smudging their hands along the display cases, glancing casually up at the suspended canoe. They moved in single file, couples and families of four, the husbands in front, bellying up the line of tomahawks, hands clasped judiciously, as if slowed by knowledge or recognition, then composure plundered as the mandatory joke was offered, grinned back, something about scalping the misbehaving eldest or getting even with an offensive brother-in-law. This was Hale's proof against trying to culture the masses. Stand them mute in a concert hall, agape in front of marble sculptures, it didn't matter which. He could have put lumps of coal in the display cases for all they cared. They were here for the ice cream and the view, already sidling for the elevators, ignoring the Cabinet of Curiosities entirely. Maybe Dad had visions of some native cleavage up above. So be it. As long as a few of them—say 10 percent—signed on the parsed line, felt some pang for self-protection.

He crossed to Jethro's storefront. What had been a respectable cigar shop—brass fixtures, humidors, a carved wooden Indian—was now a darkened grove of specimens and curios. For a fleeting moment Hale hoped there was a mob of awestruck tourists tucked away in there, but instead he found Jethro running the small projector from a stool while a single terrified child looked on. Jumbled images rushed in, the island world in miniature, flecked onto a white bedsheet: bell jars of salt water, the sucking armature of a starfish, the eye of a snake at close reveal, the ether of a cloud, the beak of a honeyeater, the woody grain of a ship's mast. His son's mind unspooled frame by frame, while all around, arranged on cigar shelves and workbenches, were corollaries to the filmstrip: obscure animal parts bulging behind optical lenses, dissected plants, beetles and bees pinned in formation. More than anything, it was the look on his son's face that disturbed him. Jethro watched the images play out, rapt, oblivious to his single audience member. The boy's father came to the door of the darkened lair just then, stared up at the bedsheet long enough to see the protruding genitals of a tropical drake, muttered *Jesus Christ,* and took the unblinking child out into the lobby by the scruff of the neck. The paltry crowd is a blessing, Hale thought to himself as he backed out of the store. He went to find a watchman so the storefront could be boarded up before dinnertime.

By the time the last, near-empty elevator went down at ten o'clock, Argus and Malini were exhausted. They'd been on display for twelve hours, acting in the dumb show of island life. Argus had thrown fishnets into the shallow lagoon, whittled pieces of sandalwood, flinted a fire, eaten more yams and coconuts than he ever thought possible. Malini had kneeled by the coral oven for hours, looped twine with shell beads until her eyes blurred. They went into the makeshift hut without speaking, retiring to their separate quarters. Argus read one of his new books by candlelight, traced a finger over a Civil War map, while Malini lay down on her woven mat in a quiet fury. Everything that had gone wrong in her life, she was suddenly sure, could be traced back to her brother's decision to go off and become a mission houseboy. And then to his decision to return. There was no one back home she could even imagine telling this story to. It was beyond telling. They paid us money to pretend to fish and eat yams while clayskins watched and ate frozen cow's milk. They made us live in a rickety hut perched high above the town with a balloon tied above our heads. She heard the attendant folding up the balloon silk and stowing it in the clock tower. Daylong he'd been barking *Bird's-eye View, Savages and City, Fifty Cents!* It repeated in her mind as she closed her eyes and hoped for sleep.

That hope was interrupted when she heard a commotion out on the rooftop. Sometime after midnight she yawned in the doorway of the hut and saw Jethro with his collecting creel and a folding stool. Argus stood beside her. The folding stool kept collapsing and Jethro seemed incapable of setting it right. He finally left it collapsed and slumped down near the edge of the observation platform. Malini returned to her mat, her insides churning. No matter how she tried she couldn't erase his image from her mind—tall, spectral, sobbing with self-pity and remorse. She sometimes woke to believe that he was breathing somewhere in the room. She heard Argus go out in his slippers. Now that night had fallen, her brother had exchanged his loincloth for fleece pajamas and tartan slippers. She covered her head with a pillow—an extravagance, like cake, she could not imagine ever living without.

Argus stepped onto the platform and Jethro smiled good naturedly, keeping his gloved hand in his lap.

"Please, sit with me," said Jethro. He motioned with his good hand.

Argus did so. The wind rose from the north. They sat quietly for a stint. The stippled expanse of the lake reminded Argus of night fishing, of wading into tidal pools and looking below into a faintly glimmering world of polished stones. He watched barges and scows bob, a hundred crowns of yellow and white.

"How is your sister?" Jethro asked.

"Very well, thank you. We remain grateful for your assistance on the ship. For protecting her."

Jethro did not look at him.

"What are you doing out here, if I may ask you?"

"Ah," Jethro said, gesturing across the void with his chin, "seems there is a nest of roosting falcons over there. On the northern lip of the top ledge. I've been coming up here with my binoculars the past few nights. The parents, the haggards, are teaching the fledglings to fly. Takes about a week. They're called eyas. Singular. Eyasses plural."

"Who is called this?"

"The young birds."

Argus drew up his knees, squinted down at the building

opposite. A hundred feet across the stony, gaslit valley was an eighteen-story office building, a few of its windowpanes illuminated from within. Human shadows in lamplight, above desktops, accountants or underwriters no doubt because the whole street, Argus had been told, was involved in finance, from bargaining on wheat at one end to betting against God up the canyon walls. On the top ledge he could make out birdlike shapes hopping about in the light of a window. Jethro handed him the binoculars and he brought the falcons into view—did they think it was daylight because of the lamps? They were shambling about on the ledge, the eyasses, three of them, prodded along by one parent while the other swooped overhead. Jethro fetched the tourist field glasses from the table at the other end of the observation platform and came back.

"Would you like these back?" Argus asked.

"Now we both have a pair."

They squinted, mouths open, watching the fledglings wobble near the edge.

Jethro said, "I want to see who'll take flight first."

A bird at the front of the line of siblings lifted a leg, flapped its wings, squawked. The circling parent alighted on a flagpole, shrieked, waited. This continued for some time—a sort of call and response—before the fledgling flapped once, squawked again, and made a flailing descent to a window ledge three floors below. Jethro smiled, applauded, leaned forward.

"How will he get back to his family?" Argus asked in a whisper.

"The female will bring him a snack down there if he gets stuck. Maybe a whole mouse!"

Neither of the remaining eyasses looked set to aviate. The wind continued to blow off the lake and Argus felt his ears growing cold. He got up to leave, handing back the binoculars.

Jethro said, "Is everything all right?"

"Yes. I'm tired. Eating yams all day made me sleepy."

Jethro made no reply and Argus wondered whether he'd heard the joke.

The heir looked down at the newly initiated falcon. "My father has closed the *wunderkammer*. Boarded it up. Only I can be in there now and I have to clean it out for the new cigar shop tenant. I suppose there is no Cabinet of Curiosities without the curious. People believe what they see and I had great hopes for the miniature to reveal layers of Nature. If only they could all sit up here with us. Watch a falcon take its first flight. What effect would that have? I see now that taking birds as trophies was a crime, perhaps against God. A sin, really. I feel horribly ashamed of some of the things I did on that voyage. I see myself during that time like a tiny ship in a bottle. Somehow part of me was set apart, as if my soul stood inside the glass the entire time, breathing different air." He waved a hand in front of his face, as if to dismiss the idea.

Between the wind and the elliptical speech, Argus had trouble following Jethro's train of thought. He said, "Some weeks ago I sent a letter to the archbishop asking for employment. Do you think he will write back?"

Again, Jethro didn't seem to hear.

Finally, Jethro turned, saying, "Present tense. Does this give you any trouble in English? When I learned German and French the tenses vexed me a great deal. And false friends. The what? The false cognates. Evildoers! Maybe we would all be better off if we just stayed at home."

"Good night, Mr. Gray." Argus stepped off the observation platform and headed for the hut. From the tiny verandah he turned to see Jethro leaning back against one of the railings, a leg swinging freely, back and forth, over the side. Despite the dizzying height, from this angle it seemed like a natural thing to do — the carefree gesture of a boy fishing beside a swift river.

The day after the opening a big crowd manifested in the streets, but not for the First Equitable. A throng gathered in front of the Tribune Building, beneath its bulletin boards, eager to learn more of the American Navy's victory over the Spanish fleet just off Manila. Longtime residents said they hadn't seen such a mob since the end of the Civil War. Hale responded by running a full-page advertisement in the *Tribune,* declaring that life insurance was a brand of patriotism.

> At the prospect of his own death, every man must decide in what condition to leave his family. Saddle them with debt and obligation, and you help to tamp down the American economy, not to mention the wellspring of your sons' ambitions. Carry a prudent policy and the dividends will resound across the generations, leaving our nation richer by decree.

That last word was supposed to be *degree* but Hale liked the way the *Tribune*'s typographical error gave an air of assent by Providence. Below the short essay was a sketch of the many amusements to be found in the First Equitable. The grace note of the ad, Hale thought, was the tear-off coupon for the cafeteria lunch special—the *Commodore Dewey Sandwich* with potato salad and a complimentary pickle spear.

37.

No amount of advertising could bring in the crowds. The siblings mounted their tableaux of island life before groups of four and six while the lobby stood empty, save for a handful of tourists and a bustle of clerks heading out to lunch. Hale was genuinely baffled. The building's inauguration had drawn multitudes, thousands, but perhaps that had been due to its status as world's tallest building. He had added another jewel to the city's crown. But now First Manhattan Life & Casualty was rising by the day, thirty-one, thirty-two, the pipes and windows and elevators already run into the upper floors, the mounting steel like the vertebrae of a dinosaur in Hale's troubled mind. Was the city bored by spectacle after the Columbian Exposition? Had the fair ruined her appetite for the exotic and foreign? Was the city shunning the First Equitable now that her title was about to be eclipsed? Were they ashamed of her?

Life did not come undone in stages; it came undone all at once. Hale felt the veracity of this thought as he looked at brochures for Swiss sanitariums, the next stop in Jethro's itinerary. After the summer was spent, his son would be taking a trip to Europe with his mother and her sister. It was either that or let the lad end up yammering his life away at Dunning Asylum. There had been madness in the Gray family some generations back, Hale recalled— somebody who'd let a penchant for obscure omens mushroom into full-blown lunacy. Life was grim. It was not for the faint of heart or mind, not for sleeping children, as his father used to say. In the span of a month, he'd lost a son and heir, and none of the vice presidents seemed up to snuff. Then the financial statements began arriving in the pneumatic tubes, little warships bearing bad news like ensigns. Despite a buoying economy, underwriting was down and the balance sheet was thinning. Then came estimates for replacing the faulty windows and squaring up the foundation—an astronomical figure on both counts. It was time for action. He would begin by reducing the rank and file. Better to be prudent than be caught off guard. He hollered for Miss Ballentine to bring him some ice and take dictation. She trundled into the room, smelling of iodine and peppermints, without the ice pail or dictation pad, staring at him glumly from the doorway, and in her dim-wittedness, her doe-like stupor, in her creed of desk-drawer sandwiches and tinned peaches, in her perennial tardiness and general lack of comportment, Hale saw his first retrenchment. Once the memo had been drafted, indicating that each business division was to cull 10 percent of its staff, Hale would send Lulu packing, handkerchief in hand. His own hands would be tied, of course. *These are difficult times.* He knew all the rejoinders to the teary protests. How could you tell a person that they were being let go because they were a lumpy dresser, walked too slowly, ate peanut butter before meetings? (She was guilty on all three counts.) She fetched her dictation pad, breathing loudly, and came back. Her face seemed transformed, even stricken, it seemed to Hale, as if she knew what was about to happen.

On Pentecost Sunday Argus thought he saw the Archbishop of Chicago standing before the rooftop lagoon, a man in a dark suit and somber hat. In the dazzling light, it was hard to see his features, but Argus recognized him from the portrait in Holy Name Cathedral—the Irishman's kindly eyes, the gray hair that touched his collar, the high-bridged nose. Had he come to respond to the letter in person? The hat obscured part of his face with shadow. It was absurd to think it was him, especially on a holy feast day, but there was something ecumenical in the man's posture and bearing, the pale, soft hands, the pious regard.

Argus went about his business, flinting a fire from coconut husks. If nothing else, he wanted to appear hardworking. Adelaide and Owen had come to lend moral support amid the sparse crowds, more for the siblings than for the building, and, like the other sightseers, felt coy being there, as if arriving at a slighted party. Owen had been working on the new house sixteen hours a day and had flakes of bottle-green paint under his fingernails. The wedding was only a few weeks away and Argus thought they looked very happy together. He wanted to go and talk with Miss Cummings about books and shake Owen's hand, but instead he had to stack yams into the hot oven. His fingertips were scorched from days of stocking the hearth. He hadn't had a conversation of substance in weeks. The desiccating winds and the glare of the sun made him thirsty all day long and he was forbidden from wearing a hat.

Hunched over the hearth, he watched the man in the somber hat enjoy some chilled coconut milk. Argus could tell he was a priest of the people, just from the way he chatted freely with those around him. Perhaps he took in the city after Mass on Sundays, walked among his flock. And today, fifty days after Jesus had been offered on the cross, each year and eternal, was surely an occasion for fellowship. Argus recalled that the Whitsundays and Pentecost Island had been dear to his very own Reverend Mister, being namesakes for the descent of the Holy Spirit on the apostles, Whitsun being Old English for White Sunday. The islands were named for this exact feast by the Quaker explorer Cook, Argus remembered, who'd gathered coral atolls and volcanic shores for the British crown like so many loose stones. What an auspicious plan if—beyond all hope—his new master had chosen this day to begin Argus's period of service. It was a sham to think so. Vanity at its worst, that a gentleman of such religious rank would seek him out. Looking at the elegant man, Argus remembered the Pentecostal sermons of the Reverend Underwood, the way he recounted St. Peter's famous sermon within his own each year, a lacquered box of jewels, the reverend would say, within his own tattered trunk of Glaswegian brimstone. He could laugh at himself, the reverend, remained humbled by the task of converting wild souls from the bamboo pulpit, of handing out cigarettes from the back verandah after each service.

On their lunch hour, a trio of clerks came larking up from Underwriting, bored and listless. They played cards at a picnic table and surreptitiously peered up the skirts of a young woman being helped into the captive balloon basket. They made bets on whether her underwear was black, gray, or white, loud enough to earn the contempt of several bystanders. A policy salesman guffawed and the girl in the balloon became mortified as she ascended above them. The clerks waved and bowed to her, the victor holding a dollar bill in his hand, saying *white is right*. Argus looked out into the small gathering, sun-dazed, hoping that Owen would correct the situation. But he and Miss Cummings were taking a turn on the observation platform—everyone wanted to see with the binoculars the newly aviating falcons. Then the clerks turned their attention to Malini, leering at her as she bent to her shell work. One of them called, "What's for supper, wifey?" and another said, "How 'bout a stroll on Halsted after quittin time?" Before Argus knew it he was standing on the edge of the sandy spit, a yam in hand, telling them to be quiet. What he actually said was: "Would you mind stopping that?"

Which was met with quizzical tilts of the head, then murmurs, in the crowd of twenty.

"Looks like darkie knows some English," said one of the clerks.

Argus fell back and exchanged a look with his sister.

In Poumetan she said, *They smell like pigshit.* The clerks knew the sound of derision in any tongue and one of them plucked back with, *Maybe they're not brother and sis after all, in which case we might see a savage baby up here one of these days. I'd pay good money to watch her suckle a baby born in captivity!* Argus had no idea how to respond to this but the trio looked satisfied with the fallout of the comment and turned for the elevators. A gong announced the end of the first lunch shift but it dispersed even the nonemployees. The onlookers moved away, including the candidate for archbishop. Argus was painfully aware of his naked chest, of the sun in his eyes, of the humiliation scouring his insides. He reached for a piece of broken yam, about the size of an apple core, and when he thought no one was watching, hurled it after the clerks, pelting one in the middle of the back. A turmeric-colored smear appeared on the back of a jacket. They turned in unison, grim-faced, and Argus saw that he'd found the correct target. He put his hands on his hips and the pelted clerk charged the lagoon, swinging his jacket in the air, trying to get one shoe off at a time, blaspheming, fists balled, wading in with a splash. He stalled out about halfway across and fell face-first into the shallow, indigo water. An outbreak of laughter and *Oh dears* got Owen and Adelaide's attention and they crossed from the platform. The clerk was up again, wild with rage, swinging, trying to get purchase and make the sandy bank. Fifty feet above, the girl in the balloon applauded for his misfortune. Argus took Malini by the arm and retreated to the bamboo hut. Within seconds, one of the guards was stomping into the water. He grabbed the clerk by the collar, trawling him back to pant and swear among the excited spectators. It was the first thing of note to happen all day. The clerk was taken away to cool off.

Argus saw the archbishop turn away and head for the elevators. Had His Excellency been witness to a clerk's petulant display of anger and then to a mission houseboy's cheap, vegetable revenge? The bishop would never have such a servant in his house, let alone an aspiring seminarian. There would be consequences for the tossed yam but standing on the leaning bamboo porch Argus felt prepared to meet whatever came. The voyage and the job were simply the means to a divine end, and if he'd dashed his one chance of serving the bishop then he would find another Eminence. With the binoculars, he'd counted over a hundred church steeples in the city below. But then the man turned while waiting for the elevator and Argus saw a smile on his face. He was grinning to himself, evidently amused by the whole episode. He willed the man to turn back, closed his eyes, prayed. The elevator bell rang and Benny Boy held open the doors. Argus wanted to shout *wait!* His future was about to descend in an elevator. His throat was scorched and he couldn't swallow. The sun caught in the thread of the man's fine suit, his back turning again in a corona of daylight. Argus knew it was the Holy Ghost burning like pitch in his throat. From the top step of the hut, he recalled the words from the second chapter of the Book of Acts; it was all there, every passage, ingrained from years of sermonic repetition, the reverend orating around the mission house while Argus and the cat, Mr. Nibbles, provided him with an audience. Sitting Argus in the front pew every Sunday, had the Reverend Mister prophesied this exact day?

Argus drew breath and aimed his voice for the elevators: "When the Day of Pentecost had fully come, they were all with one accord in one place . . ." It was a preacher's full-rafter voice.

The man stepped closer to the elevator, though Benny Boy directed his scrutiny into the new commotion.

Argus came forward. "And suddenly there came a sound from heaven . . . as of a rushing mighty wind, and it filled the whole house where they were sitting . . ."

He raised his hands in the air, palms out, and stood at the water's edge. "Then there appeared to them divided tongues, as of fire, and one sat upon each of them. And they were all filled with the Holy Spirit and began to speak with other tongues, as the Spirit gave them utterance . . ."

The man stepped back from the elevator, compelled by the look on Benny Boy's face and the small crowd closing in on the lagoon.

Argus could hear Malini from behind him, in the hut, telling him that he had ruined everything but that she was anyway ready to go home. He could see the startled look on Owen's face, his own future suddenly in doubt, and the wry smile on Adelaide's.

He skipped ahead in the sermon, to the dramatic part where the apostle Peter cited the prophet Joel: "In the last days, God says, I will pour out my Spirit on all people. Your sons and daughters will prophesy. Your young men will see visions, your old men will dream dreams. Even on my servants, both men and women, I will pour out my Spirit in those days, and they will prophesy."

The entire rooftop looked on with rapt amazement. Argus now had the man's full attention. He looked directly at His Eminence. "I will show wonders in the heaven above and signs on the earth below, blood and fire and billows of smoke. The sun will be turned to darkness and the moon to blood before the coming of the great and glorious day of the Lord. And everyone who calls on the name of the Lord will be saved . . ."

It being Sunday, Argus's sermon roused the churchgoing spirit in many of the sightseers. They were lapsed most of them, Irish Catholics and Protestants on the lam, but the vision of a native boy waxing holy was strange all right, hallowed and out of place in the noonday sun. A few closed their eyes in prayer while others laid out coins as if he were a blind curbstone preacher, one of the State Street oracles humming and lurching outside a department store. Just as the Holy Ghost had descended on the apostles and the believers that seventh Sunday after Easter, converting their native languages to God's own tongue, a brotherhood of understanding, so too, they saw, the native boy had undergone his own conversion, invoking the sermon in a language he did not himself speak. God had given him the gift of English.

Softer now, filled with his own strange power, Argus said: "Repent and be baptized, every one of you, in the name of Jesus Christ for the forgiveness of your sins. And you will receive the gift of the Holy Spirit. The promise is for you and your children and for all who are far off—for all whom the Lord our God will call."

An elderly woman knelt before the lagoon, hands raised, apparently awaiting her baptism.

Argus clasped his hands in prayer. "Save yourselves from this corrupt generation . . ."

A hush fell on the crowd and the archbishop removed his hat. Whether it was in devotion or not, Argus couldn't say, but in the hard light he saw that the man was an imposter. His nose and forehead were all wrong. The shame and vanity, coupled with the sun and a burning thirst, made Argus feel suddenly weak. He staggered back, fell to one knee in the sand.

To the believers on the other side of the small lagoon this was further proof that the savage boy was a vessel lain to waste, a receptacle of God's enduring promise. They left the building, awed and moved, and proceeded to tell everyone they encountered about what they had witnessed. By the next morning half the city knew what had happened. And the other half found out when a reporter at the *Chicago Tribune,* the same reporter who'd had his story of the natives' big day out banished to the back page, was sent to investigate. Monday's edition carried a front-page article, right beside an update on the war against Spain. The headline read, CHICAGO'S PROPHET OF THE SKYLINE. By that afternoon, the First Equitable's lobby and elevators were full of zealots, patriots, the devout, the curious, the bored, and, to Hale's delight, legions of the uninsured. Instead of closing down the whole spectacle—which had been his cost-cutting plan for the new week—he extended the hours and changed the cafeteria lunch special from the *Commodore Dewey Sandwich* to the *Savage Sibling Sandwich,* complete with a free side of fried yams.

38.

The arthritic and gallstoned came to the rooftop, hoping for a blessing, to be bathed in the indigo waters as if they flowed from Lourdes. Argus, now dressed in a suit and derby hat, recited one of five sermons he knew by rote, sang Presbyterian hymns, prayed aloud. People gave him money and the insurance company let him keep it. When no baptisms were offered—Argus knew he was unsanctioned to perform such a task—the infirm and the dashed sometimes took out a life insurance policy. More often, though, they drank coconut milk from the shell, took in the view, forgot their troubles for fifteen minutes. Malini, like her brother, wore Western clothes, but refused to go back and sleep in the corner office where only sheets of newspaper kept her from staring down into the void. From the hut on the rooftop she could see the distant horizon but none of the chasm that made her weak-kneed. With a night watchman posted, she continued to sleep on her grass mat and woke to see the sun rising over the city's private ocean each morning.

At the first lunchtime gong, they took their midday meal in the cafeteria, at a designated table. A rotation of clerks and secretaries brought them their namesake sandwich or the daily special. Underwriting was up at the First Equitable and many of the employees suspected it was because of the native preacher. He may have saved their skins. To show their appreciation they proffered cake, soup, sandwiches. They came up to the roof on their breaks. A cafeteria worker, Alice Binns, a devout West Indian girl by way of Brooklyn, took a liking to Argus and on several occasions brought him up a piece of cake so he could replenish himself between sermons. Argus could tell by the way she looked at him that she had felt the Holy Spirit move inside her chest. It was personal with Alice Binns.

The rooftop became not only a mecca for tourists and the infirm but also a place for insurance workers to unwind. Actuaries played handball in their shirtsleeves. Girls from the typing pool skipped rope and read racy novels in the sunshine. Salesmen ran bets on the exploits of the falcons and even competed with commission men and brokers on opposing rooftops. Whenever a pigeon was plucked from its roost by a raptor an echo of huzzahs ran back and forth across the gorge of La Salle Street.

Hale witnessed all this and let it unfold. New policies were being added, that was true, but he couldn't help feeling that he'd been duped, that Owen Graves had brought him a pair of half-bloods, the brother a messianic troublemaker. He closed the lobby museum—it remained of marginal interest to the sightseers—and waited for Jethro to clear out his curios so that he could have the repairmen get the cigar store ready for its new tenant. Jethro continued his nocturnal bird watch and sometimes fell asleep with binoculars in hand, slumped against the railing, just feet away from the abyss.

39.

Episcopalians are a stiff mob, Owen thought, standing at the front of the church on his wedding day, the tailored suit plumb against his shoulders. The Cummings tribe and the Boston onslaught sat on both sides of the aisle. Owen's turnout spanned a single pew—two of Porter's old pals from the wrecking days and their desiccated little wives. The retired housewreckers had lingered as long as possible on the church steps, racing form guides in back pockets, missing four half-fingers between them, lighting each smoke with the previous until they were dragged inside, stiff and lank-legged in their suits, pulling tie knots off Adam's apples. Margaret Cummings sat resplendent in her parade float of a hat, beaming up at her imminent son-in-law. Argus and Malini sat up the back, under the choir balcony, and Owen gave them a nod. *At least they aren't wearing loincloths* was the matriarch's quip for her guests; it demonstrated clearly that their presence had been her daughter's impetuous idea.

An uncle on the dead father's side began walking Adelaide down the aisle as the organ moaned a wobbly anthem from the varicose fingers of a very old lady in roseprint. Owen's bride smiled, coming toward him under a veil, ethereal and lovely, but with a look of chagrin as the organ faltered and fell flat. Margaret bustled to her feet, shot a death-stare at the raised organ bench. The congregation stood, mouthing well-wishes and tearing up. Adelaide arrived, still smiling, and Owen swallowed at her veil-scrimmed beauty. A Boston cousin stood by with the rings and a prep school friend of Adelaide's served as bridesmaid. The priest gave the welcome, various relatives read lessons from the Old Testament and the epistles, then came the Declaration of Consent. Objections were begged of the church pews but none came. Owen half expected someone to stand up and block the union—an industrialist uncle or society wife—for no other reason than the groom's guests could be numbered on one hand and included an old wrecker who'd fallen asleep, mouth open, head propped on the back of the pew. A sharp elbow from his wife brought him *humph*ing back to consciousness. With each item passing, the readings and the sacraments, Owen felt himself being marched toward his lucky—but complicated—fate.

. . . until we are parted by death. This is my solemn vow.

Her right hand was in his.

Those whom God has joined together let no man put asunder.

They were going gladly into battle.

The people said *Amen*—none louder than the old demolitionists, both of them suddenly bright-eyed, raising their voices as if a dynamite fuse had been lit.

The newlyweds walked out into the summery June air, under the newly fledged cottonwoods and horse chestnut, into a cloud of cheering and tossed rice.

The wreckers and their wives weren't coming to the reception at the Palmer House. The Loop and all its hoopla wasn't for them anymore, they said, shaking Owen's hand.

"Porter Graves's kid in a wedding suit. Makes me feel a hundred," said one of them.

"Thank you for coming," said Owen.

"She's worth it," said the other wrecker, of Adelaide, then gave his own wife a nudge.

Owen watched them walk down the street, toward the streetcar. They disappeared around the corner, the last thread to that time suddenly vanished.

Margaret practically had a floor named after her at the Palmer House by this point and the hotel spared nothing in lavishing the

ballroom with fine silver and crystal, silk bunting, flower arrangements as tall as a child. A chandelier drizzled its light on an ice
sculpture of a swan. There came a marathon of speeches, toasts,
stringed quartets, champagne, arias, lobster. The new couple had
to slice through a skyscraper of wedding cake and portion it out
before being released into the night.

Owen had the ribbon-braided carriage take them to the newly
renovated house and they crossed the river, lamps burning, passing on to the North Side with a few hoary cheers from barge
pilots and fishermen. Owen made Adelaide close her eyes when
they came within half a block. The house, once clobbered by rot
and weathered paint, once sagging along the roofline, reared up
now, windows lit, the oyster and ruby trim getting a second gloss
from the streetlamps. Owen led her up the stone walkway as she
bunched the train of her dress in one hand. "Will you always have
me close my eyes before anything good happens? What if I don't
like it?"

He told her to be quiet and squared up her shoulders. She
opened her eyes onto the swooping verandah, the balustrades
painted fresh and twined with flowering vines, the porch swing
suspended from two chains, the big front door, varnished and
inset with panels of rose glass.

"Aren't you going to say anything?" he said.

She shook her head; she was afraid she wouldn't do it justice.
He sighed, took her hand, led her up the front steps. From under
the doormat he retrieved the key, opened the door, and stepped
aside so his bride could enter.

Adelaide said, "You're going to carry me across the threshold
because if I trip on this ridiculous dress then it might bring bad
luck on the marriage."

"Did Margaret tell you that?"

"Yes, as a matter of fact, and on that score her superstition is
right. She says it dates back to the Romans."

Owen scooped her under the legs, turned her sideways,

entered the house. He said, "My only suggestion is to imagine the house with furniture. A bed, that's the only thing I've managed to provide at this present moment."

"My mother has a barn full of decrepit heirloom furniture that she's threatening to send by rail. We need to buy furniture before she sends it."

Owen set her gently down and put his hands in his pockets.

"And we have books in the library," she said. "What more do we need besides a bed and books?"

He kissed her gently, nervous.

She said, "I may not say anything until I've seen it all. Don't be offended."

"Of course. And remember our deal. If you don't like it then we sell it off or rent it out and move elsewhere. I was going to give you a tour but I think I'll let you wander. I'll wait out on the porch swing. Otherwise I'll be watching your face for twitches and sighs."

She gave him a little wave and headed off, taking in the downstairs first. The hardwood floors had been sanded and refinished to a waxy sheen, the mantel replaced in the parlor with inlaid mosaics around the grate. The daguerreotype of Owen's mother, her hair long and braided, hung above the fireplace. The wainscoting and picture rails were new and in the hallway dropped a light fixture of wrought iron and frosted glass. She passed through the library and dining room to stand in the kitchen. He'd made pantry shelves from Michigan pine and the cabinets were lined with new maple. The hinges, the handles, and the doorknobs were all of a vintage finish, a kind of workmanship she hadn't seen since her grandparents' house. She would need to go on a rug-buying spree—the empty house was cavernous and prone to echo. A little out of breath, she went upstairs and into the nursery. He'd lied. There was more than just a bed somewhere in the main bedroom—he'd made a crib with iron and spruce, a crescent moon sawn into the little headboard. She walked down the hallway and began to notice odd fixtures and mountings—carved lintels and pediments, brass door handles that looked to be from old banks, stately and oversized, a Gothic window that was surely from a razed church. In the main bedroom, as she looked on the hand-chiseled bed, hewn from rosewood and teak, it came to her that Owen had revitalized the house from his store of rescued objects. The decades of accumulated fixtures and boards, the ornamental and strange trophies of demolished banks, warehouses, salons, and theaters, were now distributed throughout the rooms. Had he hauled wagonloads of salvaged wood and bricks and brassware from the scrapyard across the river? The overall effect was unmistakably beautiful, as if someone had contemplated the smallest detail—the kind of handle one should touch when opening a door to a bedroom (brass, magisterial and stately); the kind of window one should look through to the garden (Venetian); the kind of tiles one should set foot on when rising from a bath (tessellations from an old bathhouse). She noticed the skylight above the bed and couldn't contain herself any longer. She raced down the staircase and out onto the verandah, collapsing in his lap on the swing.

"I take it you like it," he said.

She kissed him on the mouth.

They went inside and he locked the solid front door—revived from a South Side inn, its brass fixtures something from a medieval keep. Owen told her to go on up and began extinguishing the lights—his new neighbor had been kind enough to keep an eye on all those burning lamps while the nuptials were going on, just so he could have the house ablaze when she first saw it. Married, he thought, dimming the living room. He laughed to himself when he saw the Malekula effigy, standing sentry beside the fireplace, a few feet beneath his mother's portrait. How could she have missed it? He had made them a house of such burnished detail that she would have no choice but to let him keep the monster where it was, in all its spiderwebbed and human-haired grotesqueness. Maybe he'd hide it when guests came over. Technically pilfered from the coffers of Hale Gray, the effigy was Owen's now and it would get pride of place. It was his grim reminder, he thought, climbing the darkened stairs, a candle in hand, his shadow spilled on the wall. It stood for all that waited beyond the brink. All that could arrive without invitation. He reached the top landing and turned into the hallway. In the bedroom she was already in her negligee, lying with her hands behind her head, looking up through the skylight. He'd made them a stateroom, no less well-appointed than the one on the burning ship. He closed the door, undressed, lay beside her under the bedlam of stars.

With Margaret safely back in Boston, they killed off days in bed. They made love in every room, picnicked on chocolate and cherries in the gnarled orchard. She read him overblown poetry and deliberated about furniture while he reclined in the bathtub, blowing bubbles of protest. They came upon each other in the hallway and for minutes at a time pretended to be strangers, asking about the other's biography before undressing. Owen thought it was obscene, this degree of contentment. The morning sun flashed off the lake, filling the empty rooms, and for hours they sat behind the Gothic church windows, amid the courtroom fixtures and theater doors, watching the day burn itself up.

Eventually, Adelaide dug her heels in, plucked up some resolve, and began to make garden beds in the back. She planted flowers and herbs. They ventured into the city—dazed and slow, as if leaving quarantine—to pick out furniture. With each new arrival, each chair, table, and rug, the house began to fill out, the echoes retreating to a spot above the stairs. On warm nights they slept outside on the verandah, to the puzzlement of their neighbors. They listened to the lake, its murmurous lappings buoyed above the tree crowns, the bellow of an occasional barge rising above the braying of the lions at the zoo.

They learned each other's annoying domestic habits by the end of the first week: Owen crumbed and cluttered up the kitchen counter and Adelaide never blew out a lamp. She said nothing about the effigy and knew this was the sweetest kind of revenge; her martyred, quiet disdain for this hideous intruder. They fought ardently and briefly, forged truces within the hour. They took walks at night, holding hands, around the neighborhood, into the brewery district that smelled of hops and yeast. They happened upon the Presbyterian Theological Seminary, just a few blocks from the house, where they would come back during daylight to make enquiries on Argus's behalf.

Some afternoons they walked over to the zoo, where the foxes had shed their winter coats and yipped at the perimeter of their enclosure, where rival circus lions—who'd been fallowed at the zoo all through the cold months—roared at each other through blacked-out fences. They became regulars at the zoo, before the noon rush, and were given a discount on admission. They were shown into a back room where, in a dry goods box, five black wolf whelps twitched and slept. Owen hadn't seen that particular smile of Adelaide's face in a long time. Unguarded, an open embrace to everything alive. He wanted to grab her hand and run her back through the streets to their little wooden fortress. She said she wanted a dog and then, weeks later, just as the orchard began blooming, just as knobby stone fruit bulbed in the upper branches, peaches and apricots, she told him she was pregnant. They told no one at first, not even Margaret, and the discussion of furniture became a discussion of first and middle names, boys on the left, girls on the right, the candidates penciled on a kitchen wall that would be painted fresh when the Graves kid finally arrived.

Then one night she asked the question that had been idling beneath the surface ever since his return—"Will you go to sea again?"

They lay in the hand-chiseled bed, the skylight blotted with cloud. Owen had extinguished the lamps and the room was nothing but silhouettes and half-light. "I wondered when we would have this conversation."

"We have plans to make. Nine months will go by quickly."

He breathed. They heard the wind blowing through the orchard.

He said, "In the islands I had good luck. Hale was delighted with the artifacts and his payment reflected that."

"Good." Her voice sounded brittle, even to her.

"But looking back on the trip I can't help feeling like it was just that—luck. I worked hard and knew what to look for, but it's becoming more difficult to find good artifacts. The natives want money and guns these days and they had me beat a lot of the time. Argus was a lifesaver on that front. The collecting era, the days of trading tobacco for some savage war mask, might just be over. It may have been over a long time ago." Until he spoke these words, cast his suspicions above their heads, he hadn't realized just how true this was. For weeks it had left him feeling vacant about his future. There would be no reason to go to sea and anyway it would be criminal to leave a pregnant wife or, later, a new baby and mother. As he'd worked to restore the old house, fitted doors and windows from teardowns, he'd been considering his prospects. The premise of more voyages, of trading stints, had been part of his mental landscape for years, since those days of reading travelogues in the library, so that giving it up felt like defeat. Then something had cleared and he found himself unable to conceive of being gone six months at a time. Whether it was the finality of marriage or, now, a child on the way, he couldn't say, but it struck him that he would have to be his own person on land. For the foreseeable future there would be no more sabbaticals, no more jaunts at sea in which to grasp his life in profile. He was up along the treacherous coast of daily happiness, had surrendered to it some time ago and was just now letting himself know it.

"What will you do?" she asked.

He could hear the relief in her voice.

He sat up and leaned against the headboard. "I have an idea for a business venture."

"Should I be nervous?"

"You'll be pleased to know that it doesn't involve travel."

She sat up as well. "I am pleased. Go on, tell me."

"I don't want to jinx it."

"Out with it."

"I can't tell you how much I enjoyed working on this old house. I'm thinking of taking the trading money and starting a construction company. We'd specialize in restoration and refurbishment. I still know a lot of men in the trades. Who knows, maybe someday it'll be called *Graves and Son Construction and Restoration*. That would put a smile on my dad's grim face. His little demolitionist nailing things together instead of busting them apart. What do you think?"

She heard the note of tenderness in his words, the same tone he'd used to describe the proposition of breathing new life into the weather-beaten house. The transformation of objects was one of the things that gripped his attention. A childhood of loss, of tearing things down, had somehow merged with a life of searches. The right object, the house with hidden promise, the vacant lot with noble aspirations. She had been reading too much Emerson and Henry James of late, her father's handwritten insights skewing her own reading, but she felt that it made perfect sense. Owen Graves wanted to bear things up to their rightful place. She leaned close to kiss him in the dark.

Summer got a proper foothold by late July and the rooftop continued to draw crowds. Argus delivered his sermons and hymns, wood-backed and pious in his celluloid collar. He tilted his shoulders, projected from behind a bamboo pulpit on the spit of sand. He spoke of redemption and damnation, the twin faces of the gilded coin. The lapsed and the devout alike found something to admire; even the nonbelievers couldn't help marveling at his showmanship. *Rooftop revival meetings* was the phrase in the press. He took his meals with Alice Binns and they talked about God's grandeur while watching processions of clouds bulk over the lake. Argus did not know if this was marriageable love but suspected he would know when the time came. Malini slept in the hut each night and took English classes twice a week in the second-floor library. Hale sent a photographer to capture her sitting at one of the desks, her hand raised in the air. She recited verbs and nouns and greetings lying on the grass mat while Argus, two stories below, knelt and murmured his prayers beside his bed. They waited for job offers but none came. Argus visited the Presbyterian Theological Seminary near the Graves house and the head clergyman encouraged him to apply for admission. He would have to take exams to verify his education level and perhaps enroll for college extension classes, both of which made him nervous. What if the Reverend Mister had neglected entire aspects of his education? Did he know enough mathematics? Would that be a requirement? What he mostly knew was scripture, history, and literature, specifically writers named Dickens, Kipling, and Stevenson. He had to trust that God's plan did not waver and every time he saw Jethro in the upper floors at night, wandering around like some dead penitent, he gave praise for all his good fortune.

40.

The day of the First Equitable suicide, Jethro was on the roof-top watching the fledgling falcons. It was late in the evening and through the haze of the Bayer tonic he sensed a sort of communion with the birds and with the ethereal lights on the lake. The visitors had mostly left the native pulpit and the city had resiled itself to smoky slumber. The El rattled far below and he thought of an anchor chain mooring a ship in place. *I have found bottom and am tethered,* he thought or said to himself. His finger, the throbbing briefly subsided, felt heavy in the open air. He saw one of the fledglings make a sortie to a lower ledge—a clumsy burst of wings followed by a scattered landing. It pleased him to think of the young birds striking out on their own. Would they find another rooftop on which to roost or would they go further afield? He wanted them to fly away from the city, to retreat to some stand of untainted woods where Nature could reclaim them as her own.

A pale man, dressed in a suit, a double Windsor snug around his neck, appeared from the alcove. The only note of discord that Jethro detected was in the man's shoes—the laces were untied and they were spattered with vomit. He remembered the ordeal of going aloft on the ship, of retching from the crosstrees while the brimming ocean spun far below.

Coming forward, the man said, "Didn't think the night watchman would ever leave."

Jethro smiled but said nothing. The man had a meticulous manner about him, but also a heaviness, something gruesome and wholly private. He came to the observation platform and stared out at the city and the lake. He swallowed hard. Jethro imagined the stranger was surprised by what he saw, by the city's roughened beauty, the little diamonds of light winking up through the soot.

"Up with the clouds," said Jethro.

"Three hundred feet," said the man. He peered over the edge of the railing. "God Almighty, my tongue feels like leather in my mouth."

Jethro held up his pair of binoculars. "You can see them better with these."

The man stared down into the pit of La Salle.

Jethro said, "The fledglings have their wings and should be off soon. Any day. Worked their way up from dragonflies and soon it will be pigeons for the taking. Can you see them over there?"

The man ignored him. "The coppers are posted at all the favorite haunts—High Bridge in Lincoln Park, the south side of the Rush Street Bridge, and now patrolling the skyscraper roofs. Is this still a free country?"

Jethro could see that he was shivering badly, his hands white-knuckled against the railing. "Would you like my jacket?"

"To jump in?"

"You look cold." Jethro got to his feet. Poor fellow was freezing to death.

"Stay over there!"

"Very well. I'm right here."

The man looked down again. "This makes sense to me . . . It's my birthday."

Softly, Jethro said, "Happy birthday, then."

A rush of wind. Jethro saw that the man was going to jump and he would be left watching. The fellow wasn't shivering from cold; he was racked with nervous fear. He noticed the suicide wasn't wearing a belt, that he'd forgotten it, and this turned

Jethro's mind to the act of knowing, to the notion of how one really knew anything at all. Slowly, absently, he said, "I would be jumping with you if I weren't such a coward."

"You can jump from that end. Leave me be." The man shoved off his jacket and yanked his tie free and put them both on the platform. "I can't breathe up here!"

The clock struck ten and they stared at each other.

"You're going to jump, I know. It's fine. I'm not going to stop you."

The suicide rubbed his eyes and hawked a line of spit over the side. They watched the thread of saliva lengthen, silver-spun, into the void.

Jethro said, "Have you done terrible things?"

The man winced. His face was burning up.

Jethro took a step forward. "Do you see that hut over there?"

The man began humming to himself.

"There is a native girl in there. Very beautiful. Skin the color of caramel. In the islands, I had my way with her. Took it, you understand? I'm telling you this so you'll know. I would take it back but now there is no way to make amends. So it's fine if you jump but take that with you. Will you please take that confession with you?"

The suicide said, "You take one more step in this direction and I will bring you with me."

Jethro turned his palms up, as if warding off a stray. But the suicide was within reach.

The man raised one leg and then the other, rested the seat of his pants against the railing. Here it was. Jethro saw the man's vomit-splotched shoes on the stone ledge, the frayed laces above the chasm. There were pedestrians walking jauntily along La Salle, down there in the summer evening, their hats passing far below like acorns on a stream. The man blinked and took a folded piece of paper from his pocket. As he held it out, Jethro felt something thickening in his throat, tasting the man's oblivion. He heard a cable car grind into a turn as he unfolded the note and read the words:

> My name is Theophile Lewcynski and I have chosen to leave this world at my own hand. Some persons prosper but most suffer and I cannot find a way back. It was five years ago that they were killed in cold blood and when I came to this country. I am the one at fault, not this land. Anna, Jakob, Lucja, Roman. Please, God, let me see them once through the gates of hell. I am sorry to those who read these words.

The man stood on the narrow ledge, his eyes clenched shut. Jethro extended his good hand to him but then Theophile stepped above La Salle, without flourish, as if alighting from a train onto a platform. Jethro saw him rake his way down, a diver in the phosphorous depths. The image repeated in his mind, the white shirt ripped apart at the buttons, winged up, fluttering. A report of pedestrian screaming shot up the building façade and for a few seconds Jethro contemplated jumping himself. But then he felt strangely moved by what he'd witnessed, as if he'd known the truth of another mind in its final seconds. One of the falcons, a haggard, darted after a pigeon from the upper ledge across the way. Midair, it folded its wings, stooped, and brought the stunned bird back to the waiting raptors.

Jethro felt oddly invigorated in the days that followed the suicide and for several nights he slept soundly in his old bedroom on Prairie Avenue. He wanted to believe that his confession to the suicide had absolved him in some measure, but then his finger pulled him awake. He took up a magnifying glass from his desktop and reached for a birding scalpel. Carefully, he made a small slice in the purpled, fleshy tip, to ease the pressure. A stream of yellowed blood pulsed out and the smell was immense. The poison was in his mind but it bled from his finger. He took a long sip of Bayer tonic and returned to bed, wrapping a corner of his bedsheet around the finger as a bandage.

In the coming days, the finger began a whole new process of infection, which he described in one of his field journals—*suppuration is irregular and viscid, puts one in mind of geological processes, the siphoning of magma from hidden chambers beneath the earth* . . . He hid away in his room, refusing to come out for meals, until finally one of the maids reported the bloody bedsheet to Mrs. Gray. Within the hour the Grays were in Dr. Jallup's waiting room, Hale consoling his sobbing wife and her sisters, Jethro in the surgery suite, etherized, going under while the doctor hummed Brahms as if from a distant, atonal shore. Jallup removed the finger below the first knuckle. Lucky to keep that hand, the doctor said when the patient came to. Jethro felt a florid telegram of pain travel up his arm as he looked down at his bandaged hand. The white-cottoned nub was spackled with tiny islands of blood. It was clearly and definitively gone—a finger-shaped void. "I want to take it with me," he said after a time. The doctor let out an asthmatic sigh and placed the jar on the table. Jethro watched the finger turn slightly on its axis and said, "Just like a sea horse in its own bottled ocean."

41.

It was early August but translucent flurries of snow or ice appeared to be blowing off the upper ledges of the First Equitable building. From down on State Street, lunching brokers and secretaries thought their eyes were playing tricks on them. A crizzled veneer of glass had begun peeling off the defective windows in the full heat. The shimmering continued for days, billows and eddies of glassy grit, as fine as sand. Hale assembled his panel of experts, threatened to sue the window manufacturer if they didn't replace the glass at their own immediate expense. One of his engineers suggested the building foundation had moved another inch and this had made the situation worse. "Something between a liquid and a solid, glass is, so picture it stretched on these shifting curtain walls like some kind of hardened frosting. And now the cake is being cut, gentlemen."

That same week an arctic storm swept through the city, the mercury and the barometer taking a plunge, followed by a late-summer heat wave. All that flux and pressure, coupled with months of foundation shift, caused the faulty windows to finally buckle and crack. Hale, the first one in the building besides Benny Boy, heard the bracing sound from his office. Not all at once, but a serial progression, floor to floor over several hours, like a set of murderous footsteps crunching over packed snow. Hale went to one of the windows in his office and saw that a hairline fracture had riven the pane in two. It divided the world outside in half, crosswise, split the gathering day between two mottled hemispheres. He placed his hand to the pane and was horrified to find that it had a slight give. He rushed out into the hallway and went to inspect the other floors. Benny Boy came with him, calm under pressure, the two of them walking the floors to inventory the havoc. They traced their fingers over the fissures—*like frozen lightning,* Benny suggested during his one lapse in decorum. And then they watched as a piece of glass, about the size of a lemon wedge, fell free and glinted down into the pit of La Salle Street. Hale gently opened the window, stared below, and saw that no one had been hurt.

As soon as the building maintenance crew arrived for the day, Hale gave the order to remove the faulty windows at once. They would have to use the utmost care and team up with the window-washers. Twenty men went out into the floors with rubber mallets and muslin sacks and all morning the sound of breaking glass rode above the chittering of the typing pool. The window-washers attached themselves to the stone ledges to ensure no glass fell into the street. Sudden updrafts and intakes of air blew policies in all directions, as if the building itself were inhaling a colossal breath. They placed rectangles of plywood over the unglazed windows, cutting a floor's daylight in half. Clerks and secretaries joked and complained in the sudden dusk and turned on their worklamps.

A wheat broker was the only injury, his head gouged open from a shard of glass no bigger than a bottle cap. It fell with such force that it dropped him where he stood. One second he was expounding to his colleagues, evangelizing on the morning's trades, and the next he was prostrate, bleeding at the curbstone. They thought he'd been shot. For fifteen minutes La Salle Street turned to bedlam, the traffic blocked by a swelling tirade of onlookers. An ambulance arrived and took the broker away. Hale looked out his window to see hundreds of faces upturned, accusatory fingers raised in the air. He ordered Benny Boy to cease all elevator operations to the upper floors.

Then, just before noon, the city descended on the building. The mayor had been scrutinizing the building ever since its recent suicide and had heard about today's injury. An army of inspectors raided every floor. They took glass samples, tapped at the window frames with rubber mallets, checked for health and fire code violations. They sent structural engineers into the basement and drilled holes into the substructure. While a final report on the integrity of the building would not be ready for some time, they found that the concession stands on the rooftop were not in compliance with city ordinances, that the balloon ride was unlicensed and unsafe, and that the natives had not been properly documented or vaccinated upon their arrival in the city. Health Department nurses arrived with syringes and inoculated Argus and Malini against smallpox. It took three of them to subdue Malini, who swore at them in two languages. The mayor wrote a personal letter to Hale Gray and itemized the transgressions, pending the final report. Hale responded by closing the exhibition and writing a letter of apology to the mayor. He consulted his lawyer and offered a settlement to the injured wheat broker.

42.

With the rooftop closed and cordoned off, Argus and Malini were out of work and they returned to their converted corner offices. Hale said they could stay until the end of the summer. He would arrange passage back to Melanesia or they could find alternative employment here in the city. Argus read the help-wanted ads in the newspaper and studied for his seminary entrance exams. His limbs ached from the smallpox immunization and he missed the singing and murmuring crowds. Alice Binns came up to see him each noon and they sometimes left the building for lunch. Argus was known by now in the lunchrooms of the adjacent blocks and Alice enjoyed his celebrity, the discounted sandwiches and free desserts from proprietors. The prospect of Argus leaving the country was never discussed, because they both knew that he was hardworking and, if push came to shove, could get a job washing dishes until a seminary took him in. Argus believed that someone of distinction had seen his sermonizing and it would only be a matter of time before an offer came in the mail. He took the elevator down to the mailroom each day, hoping for a letter. If not the archbishop then a parish priest or rector, even a godly layman in need of a butler would tide him over.

Malini often heard Argus moving about in his room late at night. Unable to sleep, she went in one August night to find him sitting cross-legged on the floor. In Poumetan she said, "Why don't you use the little table?"

"Desk," said Argus, in English. "I can spread everything out on the floor. How are your lessons coming? No one will hire you without proper English."

Malini said, "Very well, thank you." A moment later, she added, "Will you marry Alice Binns as a wife?"

Argus smiled, looked down at his open textbook. "She's pretty, don't you think?"

"Far too pretty for you." Switching to Poumetan she said, "You need an old hag with gigantic, sagging bosoms. Or a widow with lots of dogtooth money."

"Alice has never missed a Sunday church service."

"Bully for Alice."

"Where did you learn *bully*?"

"At the night classes. Idiomatic impression."

"Expression."

"Yes."

"We need to find you a husband."

"I will never marry again. I have no use for men. If someone gives me a job as a nanny I will have my own bedroom and ride a bicycle like Adelaide Cummings. She says she will teach me how."

"Her name is Adelaide Graves now."

"Why?"

"Because white people take the groom's name after marriage."

Malini looked around the room. It was strewn with books and papers. She said, "What are you studying?"

"History and mathematics. Are you bored?"

Malini nodded.

"If you are still awake in an hour we can play cards again."

"You always win."

"It is God's will."

She threw him a weary look and closed his door. She went back to her room, where one of the big windows was now blacked out by plywood, and the others were still pasted over with newsprint. Slumping onto her mat, she returned to her knitting, something Adelaide had taught her. It kept her mind busy and she was making a little blanket for the baby. Without being told, she had known as soon as Adelaide came up with the yarn and needles; it was in her face, her eyes bright enough to light up a room. Malini couldn't contain herself and guessed the new bride was carrying a child. Adelaide teared up behind an enormous smile and wrapped her in a hug. "We've told no one yet. It's a secret for a while longer." Malini nodded and that night began on the blanket. She imagined Adelaide as her sister and giving her the Poumetan preparations for motherhood—braiding her hair with flowers, massaging her stomach with hibiscus oil, showing her the secret swimming hole where only pregnant women could bathe. There were no secret places in Chicago; pregnant women wandered the city, unchaperoned, hair imprisoned under ugly hats.

Around midnight she woke to footfalls outside her door. She realized that Argus had never come for the card game and she called out to her brother. There was no answer. She'd dozed off with the knitting needles still in her hands, the beginnings of the blanket no bigger than a hand towel. She got up to use the bathroom but when she opened the door she nearly stumbled on a glass jar at her feet. She bent down groggily to pick it up. The finger floated in a slow spin, the thinnest remains of blood tinting the liquid inside. In the wavering of the lamp behind her, she lifted the jar to eye level, the white finger bulging slightly through a meniscus of water and glass and lamplight. She dropped the jar but did not scream until the glass shattered at her feet and the finger rolled once before coming to rest on the floorboards.

Argus came running and stared down at it. For a moment he didn't know what it was, then he made out the bitten nail bed; in the lamplight it appeared translucent and faintly blue. He held his sister as she sobbed. Then, after a moment, they heard the fire door close at the stairwell.

"He has cursed me," she said in Poumetan, "taken up in my dreams."

Argus tried to be logical about it, patted her back. He knew it was Jethro's finger but couldn't imagine why he would give it to Malini. The heir had gone crazy, that much was certain, and the finger had been a source of ridicule on the ship—seamen's wagers placed on when it would fall off—but now, here it was, six inches from his left foot. Argus fathomed the situation aloud for his sister's benefit: "White men don't curse people. He protected you on the ship, remember? Maybe he thinks the finger is an offering because he misunderstands the customs, doesn't realize that finger bones are trophies of war to be put in the longhouse. Yes, that's it." He could feel her shaking. "A madman. I've seen him up on the roof watching those birds at night as if they were angels. Pay no notice."

Malini pulled back from the embrace, her face rife with something. "You followed Mr. Graves onto Tikalia because you love white men more than you love your own blood sister. You pray to their God instead of calling to your dead uncles. It's your fault this has happened—" She broke off, turned away.

"What are you saying to me?"

She was rigid, overcome. "He poisoned me on the boat and put me to sleep."

A complicated silence unraveled between them.

Argus opened his mouth, then closed it again. The look on Malini's face made the breath go out of him. Quietly, already knowing, he said: "What is it he did to you?"

There were three Poumetan words for rape—one for the act of a relative, one for the act of a stranger, and one for the act of a warring tribesman during a raid. She used the latter term, the word *rakshik* rasping dry in her throat.

Argus couldn't say anything to her while she smoldered with the memory of it.

Without looking at him, she said, "You must make amends in our father's name. It is a brother's duty . . ."

He looked down at his hands and then at her bare feet. "Sister—"

She shook her head, hearing the timidity in his voice.

BRIGHT AND DISTANT SHORES 447

Steadily now, he said, "I cannot murder a man. He is our employer's son . . ."

She folded her arms and brought her burning gaze up from the floor. "When our parents died I told my Kuk kinsmen that you were dead also. They have a word for brotherless just like childless and barren. My mother-in-law said I was unwanted by anyone. Flung out. I was useless to them." She looked him dead in the face. "You have never been a brother to me."

It hung in the air between them for a full minute. Then she retreated to her room and he heard her sobbing on the other side of the door.

Argus picked the finger up in his handkerchief and took it to his room. He set the appendage on his desk and lay on his bed. Lately he had taken to sleeping on the mattress and he suddenly wondered what remained of his Poumetan self. His father and uncles had been bound by the rules of retribution. Action against wrongdoers was swift and severe in the islands. When a man died of sickness it was assumed that black sorcery was at play. The elders sat on the beach, looking for omens in the flight of a flying fox or the drift of oven smoke, and then a payback runner would be off into the bushes, wielding a tomahawk against an accused enemy of the village. It seemed thoroughly unchristian to him now, this endless cycle of violence and payback, but then he thought of the Old Testament, of his own actions against the shipwrecked Englishmen. *Genesis 4:23–24 . . . for I have slain a man to my wounding, and a young man to my hurt. If Cain shall be avenged sevenfold, truly Lamech seventy and sevenfold . . .* The reverend had believed in this brand of justice but it was always mixed with the beatitudes of the New Testament; the merciful God emphasized over the wrathful one in each of his sermons. Wars could be holy, Argus had learned, could be waged in God's name. Blood could be shed for a noble cause. He might will himself into a fury and strike out. He had incited the Kuk clansmen toward their revenge against the hoary Englishmen but he'd led the way with poisonous leaves rather than a pistol or a sword. He could project religious fervor into the rooftop crowds but he seemed unable to petition wrath from within himself. He stared up at the ceiling, aware of the finger on the desk, and tried to imagine his sister's defilement beneath the waves. Nothing came. The scene fell away behind cold abstraction and he hated himself for it. But then something mounted in him and he went to the stairwell.

Jethro had long known about the spare keys in the secretary's desk and used them to let himself into his father's office. He poured himself a drink and sat behind the hulking cherrywood desk. The high-backed leather chair made him feel stately. He could imagine issuing edicts and decrees from a chair such as this. Several of the windows were boarded up. The clock boomed from up above, grave and paternal. Life continued with its little oscillations. The young falcons were hunting on their own, had left the nest a few days earlier. The building was like any other organism—maintaining, creating, declining, all of it happening at once. He felt lightened without the finger, unburdened by its psychic weight. Civil War amputees spoke of phantom limbs but he had no such sensation—the gap itself was empty, senseless as a vacuum. It was a void, a formless reminder of those blanched days at sea. The mulled thoughts had stopped since the finger's removal and now he'd made an offering to the woman he'd wronged. He was shaking off the remora's grip. The balance would be restored. Europe in the fall would be a time of rejuvenation. He would write poetry beside Keats's grave and continue his study of Pythagoras. He crossed to the display case and unlocked a partition with a small key on the ring. A cascade of velvet was lined with obsidian knives and cutting stones. He moved down the compartments, opening the glass doors and handling the contents. Staring at the crude knives, he realized that even the most primitive of men performed surgery—extracted teeth, removed spear tips. Science, however brutish, flourished everywhere. How many autopsies had been performed by the light of bamboo torches? Even the barbarous are curious, he thought.

He heard a sound and turned to see the brother coming toward him through the open doorway. The boy was stiff-backed and righteous; Jethro knew that the primitive had stirred the crowds with his penitential fury. "You've come," Jethro said. No use dallying, he thought.

Argus said nothing.

Jethro put an obsidian knife back onto its bed of velvet. "Would you like a drink? No ice, I'm afraid. The weather's sweltering. Though probably not for you." He made for the liquor cabinet, leaving the display case open. He poured two glasses of single malt and held one out to Argus. When he didn't take it, Jethro set it on the edge of the cherrywood desk. He watched as the native crossed to the display case and began studying the artifacts. It was weapons mostly, the kind of martial handiwork his father liked to collect. The native held up a blunt club studded with mollusks, a bone dagger, a stone hatchet. He did it casually, like a polo player selecting a mallet in a clubhouse, but then he said somberly, "These weapons are from my island." He turned a wooden haft—two serrations of shark teeth attached—in the lamplight. "They were used by my grandfathers and dead kinsmen in times of war."

Unsettled, Jethro said, "Please sit and have a drink. We will work everything out between us." When this failed to sway the native, Jethro drained his glass and dropped into the leather chair, braced for whatever would come next. The wind pounded at the night-backed windows and rattled the sheets of plywood. Jethro gave in to his nervous desire for chatter and said, "I consider myself between religions at present. On a grand tour of belief. Pythagoras had his own commandments, did you know that? Precepts to live by."

Argus turned slightly from the display case. "Only God's commandments can be lived."

Jethro was up, pouring himself another drink. "These are rather amusing, though. Little puzzles to hold in the mind." Yes, this was the right tactic. The tribal prophet was fond of philosophizing, he remembered, so he could be lulled and placated with conundrums. Like stroking the belly of a fish before you plucked it from its watery domain. "For example . . . feed not the animals that have crooked claws. Abstain from beans. Eat not fish whose tails are black. Never eat the gurnet." He slumped once more into the chair, his glass poised in front. "And my favorite: speak not in the face of the sun." He looked up at the smoky portrait of his great-grandfather reposing in an English manor; the face was inscrutable, unyielding. Was the Gray bloodline, Jethro found himself wondering, about to be cut short? The native held a weapon in each hand.

Quietly, Argus said, "My sister expects revenge."

Jethro nodded, blinked, though he thought the pronouncement sounded a little wooden and rehearsed. He would offer money, of course, as compensation, but also use of his family's connections in obtaining employment for the pair of them. He swallowed a burning quench of whiskey and thought—*Nature herself is not always moral . . . entire species are propagated by ravishment. Take certain species of duck, for example*. He imagined for one terrible moment the bone knife cutting into his skin, the sharpened femur of a centuries-dead warrior slicing him open. With the finger gone, he no longer felt the need for such bloody redemption. And his confession to the suicide, to a man at the threshold of death, had also lightened his mind. Breathily, he said, "Yes, I expect she does."

Argus saw his own reflection in the glass-fronted cabinet—his dolorous face above the celluloid collar. With each step in the stairwell he had tried to descend into a rage, to loosen the grip of everything measured, watchful, and Christian. Now, standing there with his grandfathers' weapons in hand, he felt more sadness than anger—for his barren sister and her ordeal, for the man watching him who was clearly out of his mind, for the Poumetan clans who had crossed over into oblivion. There was also, running below that mournfulness, a feeling of utter desolation, as if he'd been emptied out where he stood. His sister, his island, his own boyhood self, they had all been defiled, each in their way. The heir, his sister's rapist, floated in the reflection of the glass, then he saw his own stricken face once more. He was stranded in thought, rowing between islands in his mind. Finally, he said, "I wish to take these back." He hadn't considered much beyond these words and they hung in the room for a long time. The club and hatchet were in one hand; the dagger and shark-tooth haft were in the other. Argus began for the doorway, having no idea what he would do on the other side.

Jethro sat up in the big leather chair. "I'm afraid I cannot allow that. Those are my father's and were acquired fairly through trade."

Argus stopped and turned to look directly at Jethro. The windows behind the desk shook with the wind and were bloated with nighttime. "My sister wants your blood spilled and it would be right punishment, but I cannot bring myself to do it. Perhaps I am a coward . . . but if you try to stop me, sir, I will bring bloodshed upon you." These words had the tone of an invocation and there was something biblical in their quiet menace. Argus heard them as if from another room. He had no idea what he hoped to accomplish— they would come after him, repossess the weapons, toss him and Malini out into the street, perhaps put him in jail. But he wanted the certainty of the objects, the possession of that distant time. The heir stood, buttoned his coat, and walked toward him.

It came to Jethro, as he crossed to the display case, that he'd been outmaneuvered. He'd been preparing to barter for his life, but here the savage was asking for something he didn't have the right to give away. He stopped a few feet away and slowly placed a conciliatory hand on the native's wrist, just inches from the hatchet and club. They both stared down at his pale right hand, all the fingers intact, the knuckles whitening. There was no resistance, then a jolt as the boy tried to pull his arm free. Neither of them said anything. It occurred to Jethro that neither of them wanted sloppy combat, that even though he could poleaxe a man in the boxing ring, under the auspices of Queensberry rules, he had no use for a

common scuffle. He tightened his grip but again the native resisted.
For what seemed an eternity their arms yanked back and forth, the
tomahawk whirring, the native emitting little grunts—ridiculously,
it seemed to Jethro, they were like two men on either end of a
crosscut saw, trying to fell a tree. Then a burst of bright pain shot
up his right arm and he winced as he looked down at his arm—it
was flayed open, the shark-tooth haft augered into the flesh above
his cufflinked wrist. They both watched the welling of blood as
Argus pulled the haft free. With that terrible extraction, Jethro felt
opened to the air itself, as if the brimming world had rushed into
the dozen incisions. He dropped to his knees with his mouth open.

Argus watched Jethro kneeling on the floor. There was no
trembling in the hand that held the haft and the dagger and there
was still no anger. He had simply brought his arm down. The
action had seemed entirely separate from him, as if he'd watched
a gate swing into place from a high window. His shirtsleeve was
spattered with blood. He set the weapons down, reached inside
the display case, and yanked free a swath of velvet. Kneeling
beside the heir, he wrapped it snug around the wound, applying
the same pressure he'd learned during his first-aid classes with the
mission schoolteacher, keeping the arm raised, the fingertips pink
and warm. Argus stood again and gathered up the weapons. The
heir looked up at him wordlessly, blinking and cross-legged on
the floor now, as if he were waiting patiently for something else
to happen. Argus went out into the elevator lobby, the weapons
under one arm. It was only when he was in the darkened stairwell
that he understood fully what he'd done, saw himself out in the
streets under the cover of night, the savage in the celluloid collar,
moving down Michigan Avenue with a tomahawk and a shark-
tooth club in his hands. He let out a gasp and it echoed down the
cavernous stairwell, into the precipice that ran the length of the
building. Then, steadying himself, he took up the thread of prayer,
already pleading for forgiveness as he began the long descent.

VIII

❧

CENTURY'S END

43.

Ada Rose Graves, named for Owen's mother. Her first winter and the storms came off the lake a few days before Christmas 1899. Owen did everything he could to keep the house warm but with all those windows she vented heat and he was enslaved to the woodpile. But he liked this bracing contact with the elements—swinging the axe through the cold, cleaving a cord of firewood every other day it seemed like. A northerly gust felled one of the knobby orchard trees in the fall and the house had smelt like apple wood ever since. Their first Christmas as a family and Margaret would arrive on Christmas Eve with her digestives and tonics. She'd lend the occasion a sense of personal sacrifice, the way they imprisoned her in a Pullman sleeper since Boston, all of it endured so she could hold her granddaughter in the flesh. Owen had half a mind to leave the web-faced effigy right beside the fireplace to keep Margaret on her best behavior. He raised the axe, let it fall, putting his arms and back into it at the last moment to drive the split. The wood let out a breathy punch, a sneeze of sawdust. He stacked the wood into the waiting barrow after each cut, even though he knew this to be inefficient. Porter Graves did it this way because he was impatient for a neat pile and didn't like splintered logs lying at his feet. We carry dead men in our hands, Owen thought, lining up another log on its end.

He came upon the house with his barrow of wood and a sadness roused through him. In the lighted window he could see Adelaide and the baby in the rocker. Swaddled in her favorite blanket, Ada Rose was eight months old. It was time for her afternoon nap. The child had to be rocked to sleep every day at three or she would run them ragged all night. Malini stood by his wife with a cup of tea. She was a godsend, like family. More than a nanny, she added to the rhythm of the house. From her green-painted room at the top of the stairs, next to the nursery, she descended each morning cheerful and hungry. She was a terrible cook and they did their best to keep her out of the kitchen. They fed her pancakes until her eyes rolled back in her head and then she would take up the baby for part of the day while Adelaide attended charity board meetings and organized benefits. Malini could be seen carrying Ada around in the plush blanket she took a year to knit, so big that the swaddled creature had the privileged air of a pasha being conveyed between palace rooms. When Ada crawled down the hallway, toward the stairs, Malini was always ready and waiting. She had a sixth sense for the baby's intrepid curiosity and would think nothing of reading aloud the same picture book five times in a row, each recital prompted by the baby's slurred utterance that meant *again*.

What plunged Owen into a few moments of melancholy, standing outside the window to his house under a bruised afternoon sky, was not only the tenderness of the scene—mother rocking child, devoted and adopted aunty standing nearby—but the thought of the vanished brother. He might have been a seminarian by now, deep into his pious studies. Owen had already spent months searching for Argus and vowed to continue until he was found. He'd ventured out into the tenements and docks with a *Tribune* photograph in hand, chased black men down the street on the thinnest premise—a similar build, a certain straightness of posture. None of it had come to anything. In the Back of the Yards he'd gone traipsing through the clamor and squalor, calling out the brother's name. Near the stockyards he'd watched the faces emerging from the slaughterhouses at dusk, the Poles and Slavs almost violent with the day's jokes, anything to rid them of the bloody toil, but the few black faces held nothing like the boy's

high cheekbones and implacable eyes. Owen levied the same per-
sistence toward finding the brother that he'd used in the Pacific—
Argus was an elusive object waiting to be found.

He briefly convinced himself that Argus had hopped a series
of barges and freighters through the Great Lakes, stowed away
down the St. Lawrence, leveled out in New York and was living incognito, with gypsies, in the Bowery. Maybe he'd grown
a beard to throw the police off. At least it wasn't murder they
had him for; he would hang for that. Or maybe he'd gone west,
stolen away in a train's mail compartment and struck out for the
islands again from San Francisco. For all Owen knew, he was
back in Melanesia giving Mass from a bamboo pulpit at this very
moment. It was hollow comfort. Wherever he'd ended up, Argus
would not be living in peace. He was on the run or in hiding. A
praying fugitive.

Malini wouldn't talk about her brother's attack on Jethro or
what had transpired the last time she'd seen him. It was in the
past, she said, and she had no use for it. But Owen saw the grief
she carried for her brother. He sometimes found her in the attic
looking out at the lake, sobbing quietly into a handkerchief.
Maybe he was dead. That was another cruel possibility. He'd run
out into the city without money or connections, recognizable to
lunchroom waiters and rooftop sightseers. It would not have been
easy to find his way. Owen stacked the wood by the back door
and wheeled the barrow out to the shed. The workshop served as
the office for his construction business. He'd kept the scrapyard
for storage but now it held more building supplies and restoration
hardware than artifacts.

He could imagine going to sea again but it seemed a very distant prospect. With wife and child and days spent unearthing the
promise of old houses, the heat had gone out of the idea. Some
Friday nights, the workday completed and all the tools locked up
at the scrapyard, he went with his men to one of the saloons in
Little Cheyenne. Amid the din and inebriate jostling, he would

fall back on his old habit of reticence in the face of wild good cheer. He stayed several beers behind the carpenters and masons, chimed in only when he had a particularly lacerating quip, and was always the first to leave. But these hours spent in rowdy communion with his men gave him a sense of possibility, that other lives run parallel to his own, to one so staid and predictable. But there was never a moment when he wished for anything different. He would trundle home, gently drunk, and find that the whole house had gone to bed. He would sit in the parlor with a drink, grateful and speculative, alternating his gaze between his mother's daguerreotyped face of smoky pearl and the grimacing effigy. Two different ways of honoring the dead, he would think. One suspended the departed as a million drops of mercury, capturing likeness as a memento of the past, while the other reminded the living that the dead had never really left, that they were too curious and meddlesome to turn away.

44.

Just weeks before the wireless system was due to be tested, the upper floors were still stripped bare, the curtain walls removed. Canadian winds keened against the steel frame in the late December bluster. Birds nested in the pockets of dead space between floors and the construction workers had to flush them out with broom handles each day. The new windows on the floors below were rollered to perfection, so translucent that the girls in the typing pool sometimes forgot they were in an office. They sat high above the lake, swimming in ether, typing out a policyholder's fate, the dividends of sudden decline.

The renovations of the upper floors were behind schedule. After the final report had been delivered by the city panel, Hale decided to exceed its recommendations and mandates. He wanted to woo Chicago back like a jilted lover. Not only did he replace the windows and square up the foundation, but he embarked on a completely new design for the top two floors. The foundation would not support the addition of more floors—conceding the title of highest commercial perch to First Manhattan Life & Casualty—but he had a new architect re-envisage the offices for senior executives. A public company required a forward-looking image, a sense of strategic mission. The executive offices would wrap around a central area where the entire city was platted out like a giant chessboard. Each neighborhood would be rendered in miniature, by the block, some of it painted and some of it modeled from wood. Landmarks and historic churches would receive to-scale renditions. It would be like the view from the roof, only more manageable. It would be a battlescape, a campaign field. The lake, an expanse of blue paint, would run to the east of the tracts and in this way remind his senior executives of their own limits. It would also remind them that the First Equitable still offered maritime coverage with a good margin. On this giant grid of the city they would track the sale and renewal of policies, using colored squares to denote activity. Hale could come down from his own office and, at a glance, know the state of affairs—the greening upswing in the Near North, the middling blue of the Near West, the red, unprotected barrens in the Far South.

As for his own suite, he had ordered the removal of the display cases, all of it going into storage, and requested the construction of a private apartment. There were nights when he could not face going home to the house on Prairie Avenue. Jethro's private nurses did their best to keep him out of harm's way but the heir moved from one crazed scheme to another. One day last week he'd tried to excavate the backyard, telling Hale at dinner that there was a Potawatomi burial mound beneath the hedgerows. His right arm was near useless after the attack so the thought of Jethro plying a shovel and trowel made it even harder for Hale to bear. Eventually they would have to find a rest home for Jethro, but for now Hale's wife wouldn't hear of it. She was rearing a child again, a precocious boy with an eye for bird feathers and honeybees.

The rooftop, of course, would be a recreation area for employees and, pending the results of the upcoming tests, an outpost for wireless Marconi telegraphy. Hale hoped to have the first Marconi station in the city, sending out bulletins and orders across the voids above La Salle, even farther, perhaps, traversing countless rooftops and the jungle of electrical wires. Hale envisioned the radio signals as a natural complement to the beacon at the pinnacle of the clock tower. That perennial light beckoned to the flock and he hoped the radio signals would find their way into the symbolic mind of the city. In the small hours, wakeful in bed, he imagined the yellow beam of light pulsing with radio waves—signals of distress, weather warnings, orders to sell wheat or buy pork, pithy farewells to lovers, the city's entire halting anthem.

That was, if they ever finished the renovations. The unions and combines had their teeth in and he was lucky to get a full day's work without some complaint about bathroom facilities or meal breaks. And recently he'd asked them to work in shifts around the clock. The construction workers responded by pissing off the side of the building in protest. They tracked mud into his lobby. Used to be that night construction was a natural part of things, that all winter long the derricks and hammers went at it. Now construction workers earned more than insurance clerks and were twice as demanding. Benny Boy, recently promoted to underwriting clerk, earned less than a fledgling carpenter. It seemed wrong, like a misplaced allegiance, but Hale would pay only what the market demanded. He could feel the new century in the offing and it reeked of self-regard.

On New Year's Eve, despite the ongoing construction, the small event went ahead. Just before midnight the Marconi wireless system underwent its final tests. There were two messages to be sent from the rooftop of the First Equitable—one to the Tribune Building and another to a steamer bearing two miles north on Lake Michigan. Professor Tabits, from the University of Chicago, had set up his transmission apparatus above the clock tower. A zinc ball topped the flagstaff and an insulated wire connected it to the top floor. Amid the bared steel and renovations, the professor had placed a makeshift telegraphy station. He sat behind the little wooden desk holding the induction coil and battery, exposed on all sides, and prepared to tap out the same Morse signals to both destinations, sending dashes and dots out into frozen space. A zinc ball and receiving apparatus waited on the steamer and at the top of the Tribune Building. They would send their own messages as well. The waiting crowd was small—a few patriots with tiny flags, a manager from the Western Union Telegraph Company, a reporter from the *Tribune*, foremen and telegraphers from a few railroad companies. Hale had outfitted them with logoed mittens and scarves and they waited amid the exposed steel as the professor tended his apparatus. Hale hoped to win their regard if he could send the first wireless message of 1900. He turned to them on his heels, braced against a headwind, told them it should be any moment now.

They heard the clock tower gearing up and then it opened its baritone chords all at once, announcing midnight and the new century. Some champagne was poured, though it threatened to freeze the flutes. The visitors drank a hurried toast to prosperity but were fast losing their patience. There was a lot of foot-shuffling and wringing of hands going on. The Western Union manager had frost in his beard. Hale tapped the professor on the shoulder for an update but the telegraphy expert raised a hand to fend him off. Hale, stalling, sermonized on the new age.

May we be the chosen generation, friends. Let us send wireless messages around the globe and bring down the horizon. I'm a firm believer in science and wish to offer this experiment as a promise to be its ally. When these floors are finished there will be a dedicated telegraphy station, right where we stand, next to my office. We will send and receive the lifeblood of commerce. Information. The beating heart of the enterprise. Just as the pneumatic tubes in my building carry the flow of paper, this wireless device will carry waves of—

The wooden speech was cut off by Professor Tabits bundling forward in his fur hat. He whispered in Hale's ear and the spectators leaned in. The company president smiled benevolently and told them the ship and the Tribune Building had both received their messages. A timid round of applause. Hale said, "Another message is coming back from the steamer right at this moment." They circled the professor's little wooden desk as he jotted down the Morse code. The dashes and dots inevitably reminded Hale Gray of the signature line at the bottom of a life insurance contract:

-.-. .- -. -.-- --- ..- .... . .- .-. -- .

.. ... .- -. -.-- -... --- -.. -.-. - .... . .- . .

The Western Union manager, his frozen beard like an arc-tic explorer's, asked, "What does it say?" on behalf of the timid crowd. He couldn't see the code because of the professor's fur hat.

Tabits said something but between the driving wind and booming clock his words were lost. He said it again, louder, but it may as well have been a foreign language. Finally, he wrote out the message on a piece of paper and held it up.

Can you hear me? Is anybody there?

They all stared at it for a moment, nodding, feigning gravity but wanting to get out of the cold. The clock continued tolling, resounding like a rebuke from the old dead century.

45.

Both Davids had been in exile and Argus was no different. The icefields of Wolf Lake hemmed in life's possibilities. After ten days of cold the ice had hardened enough for the horses to pull the snow-scrapers across the frozen lake. Argus worked with the others to marshal the snow into long windrows, revealing the ice below, a glaucous eye, he thought, looking straight up at heaven. They began to lay off the field, gouging furrows three inches deep, a grid of lines twenty-two inches apart. Then the deeper blade was plowed along behind the horses and the gangs came out with handsaws and hooks. Argus piloted a raft along one of the canals because after two seasons cutting and a summer caretaking he was considered an old hand. He used a pike pole to deftly maneuver the raft into position for loading. A muffled gang began stacking it with the cubed, frozen lake, their breath smoking with cold. They called Argus *Romeo Mowgli* and told him he ought to move to Venice and become a gondolier. *You'd make a killing,* one of them called across the ice. As far as they were concerned, he was from Borneo or some unlikely place and knew about twenty words of English total. They loved to watch him pole a raft, wend along the slushy streamway, toward the elevator incline and the icehouse. He was nimble and uncanny on the ice. Years back, the bunk-house legend went, there had been an Esquimau escaped from the fair who wintered here and cut for a season. That native couldn't pike-pole to save his life. They called out bawdy encouragements as Argus piked his way along the canal, his gondola laden with ice. He raised a mitten in response.

Argus watched the icecakes trundle and glint onto the incline; the endless chain with its crossbars was a slipstream that he carried into his dreams each night. Before each block of ice was loaded it was passed over a vent of steam, scalding the underside clean so that slush didn't form and slow the conveyance. The cakes mounted their way toward the towering icehouse and another gang waited inside with icehooks, sluicing and angling the harvest into tiers. By the end of the season the house would be stacked full, half a foot of sawdust on top, the doors clapped into place. Argus and a few others would remain throughout the year, fixing fences and cutting weeds, hauling dead beavers from the lake. They would load the delivery wagons in the early light of summer. Argus would think, as he did last summer, of the ice making its journey into Chicago, to the breweries and lunchrooms, of the way it would be chipped for drinks, dropped into soda and whiskey, touching the lips of people he once knew and loved. The bricks of ice ascended, the chain clacking in its groove. The conveyance needed greasing and he went to tell the foreman in his practiced broken English.

In the evenings, when steam breathed out of the newly cut lake, Argus sat in the messroom with the others. He listened to them complain about supper and the beds they slept in, about unfaithful wives and girls abandoned in pregnancy, and he remembered the ribald seamen on board the ship. Men living in groups, separate from women and polite society, brought out the godless swagger, he knew, but he liked them just the same. They were fair-minded and treated him well. His position among them allowed him to live slightly apart. They thought nothing of his nightly habit of retreating to the bunkroom before anyone else. In secret, he read the Bible by a kerosene lantern and put the great book under his pillow before they came to bed. His penance, in addition to the burning cold, was silence. He didn't sing or preach and his conversations were limited to transactions about food, weather, and ice. This future was furrowed for him long ago, he thought, but by his own hand. God was merely watching and waiting for his next move.

He could feel something going out of him in these endless white days. Prospects and plans used to quiver at the edge of every thought; now he thought about fences to be repaired when spring came, of the way an entire year's harvest could be ruined with one night of unseasonable warmth. Like the icemen themselves, he had feverish hopes for dismal weather, even though it crushed him. The freezing jaws of winter were his closest ally, his livelihood, his camouflage. He felt the cold and his somber mood as defeat, a deflation in his chest and stomach. He thought about the kanaka boys in the sugar plantations of Queensland and the stories of them dying from homesickness. Actual death from longing. They would stop eating, work listlessly in the fields all day, speak to no one, then quietly slip away one night. Death of the soul, he thought. What good are we without a candle burning behind the glass? He wondered if it would come to this. He missed the islands and thought of them every time he looked at the tribal weapons locked in the trunk under his bed. But the Pacific came to him as a series of abstractions rather than volcanic atolls and reefs—the smell of salt in the aura of rain, the sound of surf reefing on coral, the languorous hum of the forest at night, the unbroken, warbling line of the horizon. These were bound up with his own sense of discovering God. When he looked out at the muted woods that rimmed the lake he knew that there was endless land and townships beyond, farther afield, that there were churches full of parishioners on their knees, repenting, an entire continent peopled and taken up. More than the two Davids, he thought about Peter in exile. Fleeing Jerusalem after imprisonment, Peter, the Reverend Mister had insisted, ministered in Babylon to Jews and colonists alike. It was here that he wrote his first epistles. He spoke of a holy nation and a peculiar people, praised the chosen generation. Argus leafed through the Bible to Peter's first epistle and bathed it in lamplight ... *though now for a season,*

if need be, ye are in heaviness through manifold temptations . . .
The ice gangs, sinners like himself, were caroling outside in the
frozen dark, coming toward the bunkhouse in a dirge of drunken
accents. He thought about his sister and wondered if she had forgiven him, whether she had gone back to the islands. He knew
from the newspaper that Jethro Gray was alive and for this he was
thankful. He thought about the trial of faith and read — *be sober,
and hope for the grace that is to be brought unto you . . .* Holding the pigskinned scriptures up to the lamplight, he wondered,
finally, what God thought of him and when his self-imposed penance and exile would be over. He had ruined his chances for a life
in America and now he craved the islands. He wanted to redis-
cover his place there, to forge an alliance with a mission and use
his citizenship in two worlds to God's advantage. If Alice Binns
still loved him he would ask for her hand in marriage and they
would begin a life of service in Melanesia. These thoughts buoyed
him through the dark days and cold nights. He glanced at the simple note he had written months ago and tucked inside the Bible —
Tikalia is no place for horses — a cryptic message that would be
carried by one of the icemen some hot day on a company wagon,
trundling into the Near North Side, toward the resurrected house
with the big church windows. Owen Graves would come for him,
Argus knew, just as the lake would thaw in the spring. Argus
tucked the note back inside the Book of Genesis and placed
the Bible under his pillow. Outside, the men clambered up the
wooden porch and someone missed a step in the dark.

ACKNOWLEDGMENTS

Of the many books, archives, and resources consulted for this novel, I would like to acknowledge several in particular. My desire to devise a seagoing story was inspired by Charles Johnson's wonderful novel *Middle Passage* and Barry Unsworth's beautiful and harrowing *Sacred Hunger*. In terms of research, the project was aided enormously by the collection of the Chicago History Museum and the digital archive of the *Chicago Tribune*. I consulted many texts about Melanesia, nineteenth-century sailing, natural science, and the history of architecture and demolition, but there were a number of crucial works—*Rubble: Unearthing the History of Demolition* by Jeff Byles, *The Rise of the Skyscraper* by Carl W. Condit, *Chicago 1890: The Skyscraper and the Modern City* by Joanna Merwood-Salisbury, *The Melanesians: People of the South Pacific* by Albert B. Lewis, *Growing Up in New Guinea: A Comparative Study of Primitive Education* by Margaret Mead, *The Way of a Ship: A Square-Rigger Voyage in the Last Days of Sail* by Derek Lundy, *We, the Tikopia* by Raymond Firth, the pamphlets published by the Smithsonian Institution under the heading *Instructions to Collectors of Historical and Anthropological Specimens*, and *A Handbook of the Melanesian Mission*, made available by the Anglican Church under Project Canterbury. I'm thankful to Jonas Collins for answering my emailed nautical questions whenever he came upon the Internet while sailing a thirty-five-foot Pearson Alberg sloop solo around the world.

Thanks to Wendy Weil, Gaby Naher, Sarah Branham, and Jane Palfreyman for their encouragement and discernment.

Special thanks to my wife, Emily, for her patience and love, and to my daughters, Mikaila and Gemma, for their book hunger and loving support.